I0742206

First hardback edition: April 2019
Second hardback edition: June 2019
Third hardback edition: April 2021
Fourth hardback edition: July 2022
Fifth hardback edition: December 2022
Sixth hardback edition: February 2024

Cover text by Brock Mays
Cover illustrations by Jessica Nielsen (Instagram: @yessidraws)
Map by Brock Mays

ISBN: 978-1-7338165-0-2
Website: bit.ly/theascensionsaga
Instagram: @BrockMaysAuthor

SHAY

TABLE OF CONTENTS

EMBERS

BOOK ONE OF THE ASCENSION SAGA

BROCK MAYS

CHAPTER ONE
BURNING MEMORIES

Cold. Darkness.

And then it was all replaced by blinding light and flame. Indescribable pain tore through the man's charred body as his fingers dug into the earth; his muscles spasmed as he tried to pull himself forward, but the agony threatened to claim him. He collapsed onto winter's frozen ground, smoke blanketing his fallen form as dancing hues of angry red and orange illuminated the world, and the forest burned. Even the silvery specks of light in the night's sky were blotted out by the rising plume of curling smoke.

His heart thundered in his chest, fear gripping him just as the frost clung to his burned limbs. He cried out in misery as his skin screamed in pain as if hundreds of insects were swarming over him. One question clawed at the back of his fragmented mind.

Who was he?

His body ached, and he wondered why the blackness of death had not yet claimed him. None of his thoughts made any sense. His reality was beginning to stitch itself back together, but he couldn't summon a single thought of any loved ones that would mourn him if the blazing wildfire killed him.

Why not?

Isn't that what was supposed to happen just before you died?

No memories at all trickled to the forefront of his mind.

Not even his own name.

Through the spaces in his blackened, ruined clothing, he saw that his flesh had faded from the dark crisp it had been mere moments ago to a pale pink, but it prickled with the pain of a thousand needles.

Without warning, an armored hand clutched his shoulder and hoisted him upward. The soldier struck him in the jaw, spraying crimson over the white snow that had not yet been licked up by the ravenous tongues of flame. The confused, burned man groaned and wiped his mouth on the back of his sleeve.

"Why?"

"Because my little girl can't sleep at night, and do you know why that is? Because of people like you." His attacker climbed back upon his war horse and urged the beast to crush the man's skull with its hooves, missing by only a few inches.

The man rolled to the side just in time, confusion and darkness pressing in on all sides. He wiped the blood from his throbbing forehead as the enemy on the horse pulled on the reins to force his steed to crush him again.

He raised his arm to shield himself from the beast's powerful hooves, but the blow never came. He heard the twang of a bowstring, and the man above him cried out in agony before falling from the saddle. His horse bolted into the forest that hadn't yet gone up in flame.

Once again, the man racked his mind for the one question that truly mattered. Who was he? What was going on? As he began to panic, he glanced down at his arm, which only minutes before had been blackened and burned. All signs of the burns had somehow faded apart from one jagged scar on the back of his arm running from the back of his knuckles to his elbow. Upon closer inspection, he gasped, realizing that it formed a macabre string of bloody letters.

ALEKSANDER

Was that his name? If not, it would have to do for now.

With great caution, Aleksander approached his attacker, who was now lying in the frozen dirt with an arrow protruding from his side.

It didn't look fatal, but perhaps it would slow the soldier down enough for him to escape. He took advantage of his foe's misfortune and thrust the toe of his boot into the wound before stumbling away.

Armored fingers wrapped around his ankle and yanked him hard to the ground. He landed another kick at the man's face, resulting in a clang from a metal faceplate beneath his hood.

"Who are you?" Aleksander exclaimed, crawling backward. "I don't know what you want, please—"

Before his assailant could answer, a second arrow thudded into the ground between them. He took advantage of this momentary distraction and fled; perhaps someone was on his side, even if he couldn't remember who it was—or, for that matter, who *he* was. The cold bit his lungs as he followed the horse's tracks into the dense woods. Perhaps he could locate the beast and use it to find his way to safety.

"Wait!" a voice echoed, but he did not heed the command.

Aleksander's confusion and instinct for survival took precedence over trust, even if the stranger had saved his life. He glanced over his shoulder to see four more soldiers on horseback racing toward him, all dressed in the same cloak and armor as their fallen comrade.

"Stop!" the voice called again, ringing through the otherwise silent, burning woods. "Seriously, trying to help here!"

One of the soldiers broke away from the others to follow the voice. Perhaps he had an ally after all.

He bit his lip and limped into a thicket covered in a thin layer of ice and snow before crawling into a space just big enough for him to hide. He closed his eyes, searching for any scrap of information he could salvage from his ruined mind.

Still nothing.

As his lungs begged for air, he heard the twang of a bowstring and then the metallic clang of an arrow glancing off armor. Just then, a cold drop of water splashed against his cheek, and he shifted in his hiding place, cursing the soggy ground.

His new ally let out a cry of pain, and Aleksander vowed to come to his aid in whatever way he could; the stranger had risked his own life to protect him, and he couldn't just leave him to die. Pulling a long, sharp, and sturdy enough branch from the thicket, he ventured from his hiding spot.

Aleksander emerged just in time to see the jet-black horse and armored rider gallop past. He snuck out behind their enemy as it circled the stranger, and he whacked the horse hard in the rump with the stick. The beast whinnied and jolted forward, much to its rider's chagrin.

Aleksander's ally launched another arrow into the soldier's shoulder blade then darted into the woods for cover, gesturing for Aleksander to follow.

"Hurry, in here!" the stranger said in a low voice, and the two snaked their way through a dense grove of dead trees too small for any horse to follow. As another soldier made himself known, Aleksander acted on instinct, thrusting his palm forward; a jet of flame burst forth, setting the armored warrior's winter cloak ablaze.

"And away we go!" the other man exclaimed, grabbing Aleksander's forearm to pull him along.

"Who are you?" Aleksander asked as he dodged a branch that his ally had pushed out of the way.

"Shanthah Kalen, scout of the royal guard—you know, the Kraluv Mek?" the man replied as they hurried through the woods. "And I'd venture to say that yours is Aleksander?"

"I think so." Aleksander glanced down at his arm as they snuck through the forest. The scar shaped like his name—if that *was* his name—wasn't healing like his burns had. "To be honest, I—"

"You think? Well, that's a problem for both of us," Shanthah said. "There aren't many reasons a man should ever forget his own name, and none of them are good."

"If I don't even know my own name, how do you know if you can trust me?" Aleksander asked, miming a stabbing motion with the sharp branch. "Why'd you save me?"

"Because you're not a Talohiran slaver," Shanthah said.

"Those were slavers?"

"And you'd be awfully ungrateful to betray me now. I just saved your life, and I wouldn't fancy a knife in my ribs while I'm sleeping, just to be clear. Besides, you have no reason to make me not trust you."

"Don't get me wrong, I'm definitely thankful for the help. What were you doing here, anyway?" Aleksander asked. "I'm sure it wasn't by chance."

"I was sent to the village you just escaped from," said Shanthah. Aleksander couldn't remember any village, but he kept silent on the matter.

"Sent to do what?"

"Uh, well, to salvage what was left," Shanthah said.

"Salvage? Gold, or something? Are you—"

"Bad choice of words. I wasn't sent to salvage valuables, no. I was sent to salvage *people*. I hoped to save anyone that survived or escaped the slavers, but you must be the only one."

"Not very good at your job then, eh?" asked Aleksander. Shanthah pushed another branch out of the way, which swung back and hit Aleksander right in the forehead.

"That was on purpose," Aleksander said.

"While that does sound like something I'd do, we need to hurry. Come on."

Aleksander stepped over a gnarled root and followed him down a rocky trail through the woods. The man seemed to know just where he was going, and their enemies were nowhere to be seen. Safe, for now.

"Well, thank you for 'salvaging' me," Aleksander said in a sincere tone. "Who sent you?"

"Like I said, I'm a scout from the royal guard. So, you know, super important. We've been fighting the slavers, but they're getting—oh, what's the word? They're getting bold. They're venturing farther and farther into Thanatanos."

"I have to be honest with you," Aleksander said, stopping for a moment. "It's not just my name that I can't remember. I don't know what to do."

"Let's see if we can help, then. If anyone asks, say you're from Cineca—it's a tiny farming town no one cares about on our side of the border. You were delivering a shipment of grain and were ambushed by the slavers, okay?" Shanthah said.

"And if whoever is listening chooses to attack instead?" Aleksander asked as they continued through the woods. He realized the question seemed foolish as soon as he asked it.

Cineca. The name of the town sparked jagged, broken memories that faded as soon as they appeared. He said nothing of it.

"Then I'll let you do the fighting. I talk, you fight."

"Then what are those weapons for?"

"Okay, fine, let me do the fighting too," Shanthah replied with a wink. "I'm used to it by now, and I'll be doing it until Valistaran's backside is off of that blasted throne."

"Valistaran Talohir," Aleksander said. The name brought more unfamiliar memories to his mind. Blurry faces. Voices.

"Hey, good job," Shanthah said with a laugh. "Looks like your memory is coming back. Before long, you'll be telling me stories of the horrible holidays spent with your overbearing great aunt, and I won't listen to a word of it, and—"

"Are we going to talk about what just happened?"

"That you set one of Valistaran's men on fire? That'll get you locked away faster than anything," Shanthah answered. "That's why we need to get you farther away from the border, yeah?"

"You shot two of them!" Aleksander retorted, ignoring Shanthah's comment. "I think they'd want us both!"

"Yes, but at least I didn't use powers. Everyone knows that's outlawed here and in Talohira." He stopped walking for a moment and added, "Okay, everyone who hasn't lost their memory. Listen, just don't show everyone that you can throw fire, alright? You'll either get drafted into King Romiton's army or taken by King Valistaran's slavers."

Aleksander replied, "I didn't even know I could do that. It just happened."

"I don't care. Don't do it. You don't seem like a novice. Beginners at fire-throwing can barely make heat, and you started a forest fire, Aleks. Can I call you Aleks? Before your identity crisis, I'd wager you were someone pretty important—so I'd suggest you start remembering."

"Can many people do what I can? Or do they stay hidden?"

"Some bloodlines have powers, some don't. It isn't something you can learn—it's something you're born with. Really only the military is legally allowed to use them though."

"And are you magic?" Aleksander asked. As they passed by a gnarled old tree, he glanced over his shoulder. With a knowing smile, he put a single finger to his lips as if to tell Aleksander to keep a secret.

Shanthah chuckled. "And no, it isn't magic. It's science."

They spoke no more on the matter.

He stopped with such abruptness that Aleksander bumped into him. Aleksander began to speak, but Shanthah shushed him. It was not playful banter, for they had both heard something huge moving in the charred forest. They crouched behind the gnarled tree and remained still as something smashed its way through the blackened trees.

Something was there. Close. They could hear its deep breaths and heavy footfalls, and the world went silent as if everything in the woods were hiding from whatever it was. He nocked an arrow and drew the bowstring. He aimed the weapon in the direction of whatever was coming. Nothing happened.

A squirrel disturbed the undergrowth a few yards behind them, startling Shanthah so that he stumbled backward, sending his arrow flying. He swore under his breath and nocked a second arrow.

A massive, grunting beast splintered the trees as it crashed through the dense wood; a deafening bellow shattered the stillness of the night air, and Shanthah's arrow slipped from its string but missed its mark.

The monster emerged into view; its vicious horns protruded from an oxlike head, but the creature stood on two thick legs and brandished a huge axe that could split a tree—or a man—in half.

Shanthah aimed straight at the monster's forehead and let go of the string. The monster raised its heavy weapon to deflect the arrow and let out another bellow. Terrified birds scrambled from their perches, and the two men stumbled backward to avoid a swipe of the axe.

"What is that thing?" Aleksander shouted. He brandished the sharp stick, but he knew it would be useless against the monster.

"That *thing* can understand you," Shanthah replied. "You're not alone, are you, Mr. Minotaur?"

"Of course not," the beast replied with a snort. "But I am here to prevent your escape, not kill you." Shanthah's eyes darted toward Aleksander, as if to tell him to follow his lead.

"I thank you, then, mighty minotaur, for your mercy," Shanthah replied, his inflection betraying a hint of sarcasm in the words. Five men emerged from the dense woods, crossbows raised and loaded. Several more pushed their way through the thicket behind Shanthah and Aleksander as well.

"Under the laws of Talohira, we claim you as our prisoners," said one of the soldiers. Aleksander's heart thundered in his chest. Were they the slavers Shanthah had mentioned?

"Prisoners, slaves, what's the difference, right?" Shanthah asked. "You soldiers and the slavers are all the same."

His eyes darted to each of their new enemies as he judged whether or not he stood a chance in a fight. The minotaur snorted and slammed his axe against the ground to intimidate the prisoners as a woman who looked to be the leader of the Talohirans stepped forward. He decided to drop his bow.

Armored gauntlets removed a sleek helmet, and shoulder-length black hair tumbled down. Aleksander was taken aback, but Shanthah remained unfazed. The woman's gaze held a certain ferocity that accompanied her beauty; her cold eyes held darkness in them as if they had beheld truly horrible things.

"My name is Lavinia, governor of Timishuara, and one of the Mistresses of Dusk to Queen Codruta. You will answer to me as we make our way back to the labor camps outside of Bukaral. There, you shall decide your own fate."

"Meaning what?" Shanthah asked. "And what's a Mistress of Dusk doing rounding up slaves? A bit beneath your station, eh?"

"Your obedience will be rewarded, but defiance will not be," Lavinia answered, ignoring him. She snapped her fingers, a signal for her troops to bind them and move on.

"How many times have you used that speech?" Shanthah called as she walked away.

A soft chuckle escaped her throat before she answered.

"You have no idea."

CHAPTER TWO

THE NIGHT WITCHES

Shanthah and Aleksander said nothing more as they were forced into a packed prison cart pulled by several horses. Shanthah pulled his legs to his chest and drifted off to sleep, and Aleksander decided to try to do the same. They were prisoners, but safe, after all.

Aleksander wondered how long that would remain true.

He lost count of how many times he dozed off only to be wrenched from sleep during the journey, but at long last, he awoke with such a jolt that he could not fall back into sleep's sweet embrace. The prison cart's wheel had collided with a large boulder, causing the vehicle to buck up and crash down.

The other prisoners stirred and groaned as they tried to find more bearable positions, a seemingly impossible feat. Aleksander could hear his captors in the cart's front compartment speaking in a strange language; it was harsh and beautiful at the same time, much like winter itself.

He rubbed his eyes and realized he had no idea how long he had been tied up next to Shanthah and the ten other prisoners, but it felt like an eternity. They had only eaten a few scant meals of stale bread and fetid water and had only been allowed to stretch their legs or relieve themselves in the woods twice. He turned to see Shanthah awake, his face stern and eyes fixed on him.

"How long have we—" Aleksander started to say.

"Two days now," Shanthah answered before Aleksander could finish. "That's how long we've been traveling. Right, beautiful?"

"Unfortunately," came Lavinia's cynical voice through the bars between the cart's two compartments.

"Just wait. She'll warm up to me, and then she'll let us go because we're in love. It'll be a funny story to share at the wedding," Shanthah said loud enough for Lavinia to hear. He turned his head back to Aleksander as Lavinia let out a scoff. When he spoke again, he did so in a hushed whisper. "Have you remembered anything?"

"I remember the men on the horses, the fire, the minotaur, and then being thrown into this cart," Aleksander answered.

"You know what I'm asking."

"Sorry. I still don't remember anything before that."

"Pity," Shanthah said.

"For you or for me? I don't even remember my own name. My own personality. What do I find funny? Do I have anyone I care about? Believe me, it's as frustrating for me as it is for you," he said in a venomous whisper.

Shanthah winked at his new ally. "No worries. We'll get out of this."

The terrain was becoming rockier and rougher, adding to the tense atmosphere inside the cart. Through the bars, Aleksander could make out the faint outline of low foothills and the base a mountain range in the distance.

"What is the first thing that comes to your mind when I ask if you remember anything?" Shanthah asked.

"Food," said Aleksander.

"My kind of guy! At least you haven't forgotten food," Shanthah answered. He turned his attention once again to Lavinia in the front of the cart. "How much longer until we get to Bukaral?"

"Prisoners don't generally talk this much," she responded.

"I do," Shanthah said.

Lavinia let out a long sigh. "We're not taking you into the city. We're to escort you to the slave camp southeast of Bukaral where you will be sorted into work districts upon arrival."

"Mistress, the king doesn't like us using the phrase, 'slave camp.' Maybe you should say—" Lavinia smacked the driver on the back of the head, cutting off the end of his sentence.

The sound of a crow cawing in the distance caught Aleksander's attention. Shanthah pulled himself as close as he could to the bars and pressed his face between them, squishing his cheeks together.

"You didn't answer my question," he said. His words were a bit muffled due to his squished cheeks. Lavinia didn't even bother to look at him.

"What question?" she asked with more than a hint of annoyance evident in her tone.

"When are we getting there? I'm anxious to get working!" Shanthah answered as another crow call sounded outside the carriage. This time, Aleksander cocked his head to listen, for it almost sounded like a human voice.

"Soon," Lavinia's driver said. "Keep your tongue away from Mistress Lavinia. She doesn't enjoy banter with—"

There was a sudden crash against the side of the armored cart, and it was knocked onto two wheels, teetering for a moment before crashing down, the slaves inside screaming and crying as they were tossed about.

Lavinia groaned as two leathery wings erupted from beneath her cloak; she shot up and out of the cart into the night sky. Her driver was slumped against the wall, a deep gash across the side of his head dripping blood down into his face.

"She's a Night Witch!" one of the slaves exclaimed, and then everyone screamed again as something tore the back hatch of the vehicle away and tossed it into the darkness.

Two of the prisoners at the back scrambled for the new exit and were yanked from the cart, pulling those chained to them along. Their screams filled the night and were followed by the sound of chains snapping and bones breaking.

"Stay back!" Aleksander exclaimed to the rest of the slaves. He watched as Lavinia soared past, thrusting a long black spear into someone before flying upward once more.

"You might want to get some fire ready, Aleks," Shanthah ordered. "Everyone else, do as he says. Get back!"

"But you said not to let them know I have powers," said Aleksander, but Shanthah shook his head back and forth.

"I think they already know."

The remaining prisoners, chained together in two groups of four, huddled at the back of the cart. The cry of an angry bull drowned out the rest of the clamor and then a sickening crunch signaled the fall of an axe. And then, silence. No one moved or dared give breath until Lavinia appeared at the back of the overturned cart, shouting orders in the Sangoran language.

With a painstaking grunt from the minotaur outside, the cart rose up and slammed back down, right side up. Aleksander tried to calm the other prisoners, and Shanthah peered outside to see several broken corpses lying behind the cart.

"What hit us?" asked one of the prisoners.

Lavinia clambered into the driver's seat and ordered two of the men who had been riding alongside to surrender their steeds.

They attached the horses to the cart and climbed into the back of the carriage with the prisoners. Lavinia whipped the horses hard, and they lurched forward with an angry, collective whinny. The minotaur thundered just behind them with his axe raised high over his horned head. No one, not even Shanthah, dared speak.

Aleksander tried to shield the other prisoners from the carnage behind the minotaur. He could now see the mangled corpses of a group of men, but the shadows hid most of the scene.

"What could have hit us?" Aleksander asked.

"Maybe someone with powers. A Telekinetik, maybe?"

The cart lurched as Lavinia spurred the horses on through the winding pass. No one spoke for a long while until someone repeated, "Night Witches."

Aleksander looked at Shanthah in confusion yet again.

"Don't let them hear you call them that," Shanthah whispered. "They're Sangorans. You know, from the country of Sangora." He glanced at Aleksander to see if he remembered, but he shook his head. "Still nothing? Valistaran took their leader as his queen as some kind of alliance between their countries."

"People say they suck blood and steal babies. Nasty creatures," said one of the prisoners.

Shanthah looked at her with an odd expression. "I don't think that's true, but—"

"They have wings! Wings!" exclaimed another prisoner.

They glanced through the bars and over Lavinia's shoulder to see the lights of a sprawling city growing nearer. Aleksander began to speak again, but one of the guards silenced everyone in the cart.

They pulled through the gates of the great stone wall surrounding the city sometime later without meeting any more resistance.

"I thought we weren't going into Bukaral," Shanthah said loud enough for Lavinia to hear.

"Plans changed. People died," Lavinia answered and spurred the horses on again. A couple of guards had to leap out of the way of the oncoming cart and the stampeding minotaur behind it. The horses led them through the streets of the city of Bukaral as Talohiran citizens emerged from their hiding places to witness what disturbed the night's silence. The cart stopped with a sudden lurch, and the minotaur lumbered past.

"Get out," Lavinia ordered, slapping her hand on the side of the ruined vehicle. The eight remaining prisoners as well as their guards obeyed the order and climbed down. The soldiers helped the prisoners descend, but one auburn-haired woman slapped the guard hard across the face and hopped down without his help. The guard was so taken aback that he said nothing, but the others readied their weapons.

Lavinia didn't seem to care, so nothing happened. The slaves and guards alike stretched their aching limbs, a welcome relief.

"Follow Mistress Lavinia," the minotaur boomed.

"Thank you, Gad. I'll take it from here," Lavinia said.

The captives complied, trailing behind their Sangoran captor. She led them down a path toward a second set of gates where a company of soldiers stood ready.

"Wait here," Lavinia ordered.

The minotaur barred the way so they could not follow even if they wished to do so. Lavinia lifted her wings and shot into the sky, landing nearby on the cobblestone street near the soldiers. They saluted upon her approach, awaiting orders. The torchlight reflected off her black armor, giving it an ethereal glow.

"Mistress Lavinia," they heard a soldier with a rugged beard say. "This is truly an honor."

"No, it isn't," Lavinia answered, dispatching any semblance of courtesy. "These prisoners are to be taken to the slave camp."

"I thought you were in charge of escorting new slaves there?" The captain of the soldiers scoffed. "What went wrong? Did some prisoners outsmart a Night Witch? A Mistress of Dusk too, no less!"

The other soldiers who had been laughing amongst themselves fell dead silent.

The captain's eyes widened as regret for what he had just said washed over him. Lavinia seemed to stare into his soul for a moment before thrusting twin blades affixed to the tips of her wings through the captain's ribs.

She withdrew her wings and let the man fall to the ground. A collective gasp escaped the prisoners and soldiers alike, but no one rushed to his aid as he groaned and rolled in pain on the cobblestones.

"Anyone who uses that slur will be treated the same as your captain. Who's next in command?" Lavinia asked. "It's been a long couple of days, and I am in no mood for any of your nonsense. I warned you what I'd do, didn't I? And I always keep my promises."

The soldier with a rugged beard stepped forward.

"Lieutenant Darthon, mistress," the man said.

"Captain, now," Lavinia said. She pointed to another soldier and said, "Get this idiot on the ground to a healer. I need the rest of you to escort us to the slave camp in case of another attack. And shave that damn beard—you look horrible."

"Yes, mistress." Captain Darthon offered a stiff salute.

"Be careful. One of them is a Dragonsoul, and another, a Telekinetik. They could become a problem," Lavinia said. "If they do, you know what to do."

She gave a signal, and Gad the Minotaur escorted the prisoners toward the gate, flanked by Captain Darthon, his men, and the remaining guards from the carriage.

Dread gnawed at Aleksander's stomach as Lavinia walked away. And then, the prisoners and their captors set forth toward the looming, unknown horrors of the Talohiran slave camp.

.

CHAPTER THREE

THE QUEEN AND HER KING

A light breeze played with the thin curtains, allowing the shining moonlight to stream through the window and illuminate High King Valistaran Talohir's face. He strode toward the balcony overlooking Bukaral, his cape flowing like a dark serpent trailing behind a silent master.

He withdrew the curtains and opened the glass door behind, bathing the entire room in the silvery twilight. He emerged into the crisp night air onto the garden patio and glanced at the moon, waiting.

Why was she *always* late?

The night air gnawed on his bare face; tiny ice crystals floated by as if dancing for their king. In the summer, the night was pleasant and humid, but these days the moisture froze into beautiful icy flakes.

Despite the cold, the king was always enraptured with the winter view of his capital city from this particular vantage point. The frozen season somehow made the stately city even more beautiful, blanketing the red rooftops of old town Bukaral with white.

"You're late," Valistaran's voice echoed through the night. "You should not keep your king waiting."

A hooded figure cloaked in a low-cut robe of crimson and silver stepped onto the balcony and tucked a pair of black, leathery wings below her cloak. She stepped forward and removed her hood with a smile before kissing the king's lips deeply.

"So serious, my king. I warned you when you married me that I do what I want, when I want." The reply was as playful yet cold as the night. "Your position has robbed you of your patience, I think."

"And I fear yours has robbed you of purpose." Valistaran answered. "My queen, I have been troubled."

"As a king should be. If you weren't, I would think you negligent of the kingdom," Queen Codruta Talohir said as reassurance. "What is it, love?"

She smiled again, but Valistaran did not, instead leaning upon the stone terrace of the balcony. He watched the illuminated flakes of snow dance around the golden torchlight for a moment before speaking again.

"We've been fighting this war the same way for far too long," Valistaran said. "Too much death."

"Is this not a conversation you would rather have with your generals? Or perhaps with my council?" Codruta asked. "You know I'm not one for militaries and tactics."

"No, but you are my greatest tool," Valistaran said.

"Just what a lady likes to hear."

Valistaran chuckled. "Sorry. I wasn't finished. It was not by chance that you became one of the Mistresses of Dusk in your own country and queen in mine. You possess certain skills and connections that no one else can offer."

"Certain skills indeed," Codruta said with an air of seduction, tracing a line down the king's chest with her forefinger. Valistaran laughed again and continued.

"Both sides of this war have been focusing on simply reducing the number of enemies they face. Killing. Destroying. Conquering cities. Blood for blood. This is not how I believe a war is won. It just brews future conflict and revenge in an endless cycle," Valistaran said, and Codruta cocked her head to the side, her curiosity piqued. "This war will be won from the bottom up."

"What do you mean?" Codruta asked.

"Imagine the kingdom of Thanatanos as that window," Valistaran said, gesturing to a massive stained-glass window on a neighboring tower. Codruta nodded. "Do you see those cracks and chips in the glass?"

He motioned to some places on the window where weather and war had taken their toll. Codruta nodded again. "If we were to target those places, it would be easier to crack and the whole thing would come crashing down. We could remake it how we wanted. It's just the same with our enemy. We exploit cracks in their societies rather than raise our swords."

"So, you are not going to kill King Romiton?" Codruta asked.

"Perhaps in the end I still will," Valistaran answered. "But if we kill him, his son Xanthurias becomes king. We kill Xanthurias and Prince Verahim replaces him. Do you see? His court beyond his family is all indoctrinated with the same ideology, the same blind worship of a dead god—killing him shouldn't be my priority. It can't be. And I trust you understand why."

"But perhaps they should believe that it is. Let them think that you are leading a grand campaign on Laniras itself."

"Exactly. But the real victory shall take place without bloodshed or destroying their people," Valistaran said, nodding.

"How will we find these cracks?" Codruta asked.

"I have become bored in my tower. It's been too long since I ventured out on one of my adventures. I'll bring others along as well, of course. I want to hide amongst them and earn their trust—it's all been arranged. I'll put others in charge of the military campaign until I return."

"And I expect that I will have my fun as well," Codruta said with an unnerving smile. Her words resonated with the authority of a queen's order more than a mere inquisition.

"That you shall, my queen. Come now; let us sleep. Things are already prepared. We will depart tomorrow."

She led him by the hand into his bedchamber, and he closed the tall glass-paned door, leaving the balcony bathed in eerie, silver moonlight.

CHAPTER FOUR
INTO THE SLAVE CAMP

Chained at the wrists and ankles with the other six prisoners, Aleksander and Shanthah marched along the icy path into the slave camp. Lavinia and Gad the Minotaur led the group, escorted by Captain Darthon and his men. Now that he was visible in the daylight, Aleksander noted several fresh wounds across the beast's torso.

They approached the makeshift gates which seemed to be thrown together using pieces of old furniture and homes that had been ripped apart to create a perimeter around the camp.

The bulwarks themselves were not high, but they were covered in vicious, thorny vines that looked impossible to clear. Furthermore, guards were stationed on tower platforms around the entire area, crossbows at the ready.

A deep ditch lined with spears also surrounded the temporary compound. Aleksander peered down into the pit to behold a macabre scene; carrion crows feasted upon decomposing bodies of those whose escape attempts had ended in a gruesome death.

At the center of the cruel encampment stood an unfinished, yet dignified stone building. Small groups of tents around campfires surrounded the building in concentric circles all the way to the walls. A little boy peeked his dirt smeared face out from inside one of the tents, his eyes wide before disappearing back inside at the sight of Lavinia, Gad, and the soldiers.

The new slaves halted near the unfinished building, and Lavinia turned to face them. Several other groups of soldiers stood ready, their own prisoners chained to an overturned monolith upon which the slaves were permitted, or rather, forced to sit.

"Chain yourselves with the others. No funny remarks." She pressed a finger into Shanthah's sternum, and he raised his hands in mock surrender. "Misbehavior will not bode well for you here. You will soon be sorted into different working districts that have sustained losses."

"Losses?" asked Shanthah.

Lavinia scoffed in response and shook her head then snapped her fingers as an order for her men to remove the chains binding the prisoners' limbs together. They raised their spears to ensure the group's compliance with Lavinia's order, and the reluctant slaves clasped their shackles to rings on the collapsed pillar. With a click, they sealed themselves to the heavy stone, preventing any escape.

Lavinia stepped away to greet a potbellied, cruel looking man with a whip.

"Does she seem annoyed to be talking to him?" Shanthah asked in a low voice. Aleksander nodded.

"Wouldn't you be? Look at that guy," he said.

A slaver struck them both lightly with the butt of his spear to make them stop talking as Lavinia returned to the group. The pot-bellied slaver lumbered after her and cracked his whip lined with sharp spines.

"To your feet," Lavinia ordered. "I'm turning you over to Belokej, who will take you from here."

All but one of the prisoners clambered off the pillar, but one feeble, old man was weak from the long journey and collapsed to his knees. He struggled to get to his feet, and Aleksander grasped his shoulders to help him up. The slaver's whip struck his arm with such force that he yelped and dropped the man.

"Pathetic," the slaver said under his breath before striking Aleksander and the old man with a lash from his whip. He raised his arm to deliver another blow, but Lavinia intervened, spreading her long black wings to create a barrier. The old slave got to his feet wheezing and clutching his wounds. Aleksander let out a slow breath.

"Each slave is valuable to the king, Belokej. You know he dislikes it when you kill them," Lavinia said. "Now, carry on with the sorting."

Belokej the slaver pushed his way around Lavinia's leathery wing and opened one eye wide, looking Aleksander up and down.

"He's strong," he said, pushing hard on Aleksander's chest. Aleksander fell backward onto the stone, tripping over his chains. "But clumsy."

He continued, examining Shanthah without a word then gave an indistinguishable snort of either approval or disdain. He moved on to the next prisoner, a young man, clutching his chin before yanking it upward. Black hair fell across his face as the slaver smacked him across the cheek with a gloved hand. As the young slave recovered, he adjusted his tunic to reveal a long scar running down his neck and down his chest beneath his shirt; Belokej caught sight of the wound and sneered.

"That scar. Does it stop you from doing anything useful?" Belokej asked. "If so, it'd be best to toss you out now."

"It's healed. It's only a bad memory now," the prisoner answered. Belokej gave no warning as he cracked his whip across the man's torso. The whip tore through fabric and flesh, knocking the young man to his knees, a line of blood running parallel to the existing scar. He staggered to regain his balance, breathing heavily.

"Yer gonn' see that this place has a way of making you relive bad memories," Belokej said, continuing his inspection. "You, woman." The next slave, the petite woman with auburn hair and a fiery resolve in her eyes looked toward him with an exasperated sigh. "How can such a small a woman like you do work?"

"I can do anything the others can," she answered. Belokej raised his whip, and as it came down, her fingers wrapped around it. Tears filled her eyes as the slaver pulled it away, cutting her palm in the process. "But it doesn't mean I will."

"You have spirit. I will break it—and you—before you die here," Belokej said, dragging the whip behind him like some deranged child's toy. "You four, and the old man. You'll be assigned to building district sixty-eight workin' on the new senate building for the new administrative district. The rest of you'll go to the mines where you will extract 'nough stone for 'em to do work each day. Let's see… Yes, you'll be in mining district two-eighty-one." He wound up his whip and attached it once more to his belt. Without another word, he lumbered away.

"An unpleasant reminder of what not to become," Lavinia said. Aleksander glanced up in surprise. "What, do you think your masters are so evil that even we cannot recognize cruelty? You will come to see that this world is not as black and white as you may believe it is back in Thanatanos."

She motioned for the guards to escort the two groups to their respective districts. The soldiers led Aleksander, Shanthah, and the other three to a small circle of five tents around a campfire on the north side of the unfinished Senate Hall.

"Get to know your fellow prisoners," one of the guards said. "Elafris the Fallen himself knows you'll need company in here."

The soldiers left them there to await the next day's coming assignments.

"New people?" a booming voice called from a tent. The owner of the voice showed himself, a large, barrel-chested man. "Come on out!"

A woman with flowing black hair and crystal blue eyes that glittered in the torchlight emerged from her tent first. She stared into Aleksander's eyes for a long moment with an expectant expression. He smiled politely back at her but said nothing, and she let out a deep sigh before averting her gaze. Four other men emerged from the other dwellings of weathered canvas.

"I'd say I'm happy to meet you, but I truly wish you didn't have to be here," she said. She offered a mirthless grin and brushed her hair the color of ravens' feathers, from her eyes. She glanced at Aleksander again. "My name is Mara."

"Hello. I'm Patrik," the elderly man said, hobbling toward them. He offered his hand in greeting to the large man and the woman first, and two of the slaves helped him to the ground.

"Looks like you met Belokej," Mara said, eying his blood-soaked arms. "He's the worst of any of them here. If I could choose for him or Valistaran himself to die, I'd choose him every day for a million years." She seemed lost in thought for a moment before exclaiming, "Introductions!"

"Well, I'm Drahomir," said the man with the scarred chest. "I come from Laniras."

"Laniras, eh? Josman Faros," said the large man in introduction. "Looks like we've got another capital boy here with us. That was my home too until my wife decided the big city life wasn't for us and moved us north to a small town you've probably never heard of."

"Oh, yeah? Where at?" asked Drahomir, shaking Josman's outstretched hand.

"It's called Melnik. You know it?"

"Ah, yeah. That's where the best milk and cheese in the kingdom comes from, of course I know of Melnik," Drahomir replied with a nod.

"If you like our cheese, you're good people, Drahomir! The slavers don't venture as far as Laniras, so you must have been outside when they got you, eh? You like our cheese too?"

Aleksander laughed. "Love it."

He and Shanthah shared a knowing glance before they each introduced themselves to the rest of the group. Mara pushed past the men and approached the auburn-haired woman.

"I'm not going to lie, I'm most excited to meet you," Mara said as she clutched the other young woman's arm. "We've never had another woman in our district. Finally! Someone to even out the smell of all these boys—sorry, *men*," she said in a half mocking tone."

"Hanna Samsa," the feisty auburn-haired woman replied with a laugh. "I'm from Vudapas."

"Ah, I was born in Vudapas! Then I lived in Nitra for a while, of course, but been livin' in a village called Siofak right near the border, which it was only a matter of time before I ended up here," Patrik said. "We wouldn't give up the children in our town, and, well…"

"We?" Mara asked, cocking her head.

"Aye, my wife—well, she didn't make it."

Mara placed an understanding hand on his elbow and then turned to Aleksander.

"And you?" she asked.

Shanthah gave a nod as if giving him permission to proceed.

"I'm Aleksander," he said. "I'm from—"

"Yes?" Mara asked.

"Cineca," he said.

"Cineca," Mara repeated, and Aleksander nodded.

"Mara and I—she's my sister, by the way. We're the Bartuneks," said a boy no older than eighteen. "Before they took us on that giant slave ship—"

Aleksander and Shanthah shared a quick glance.

"Pol, they don't need to hear our story. Not today. They've all got their own. This is Apolinarius, but we just call him Pol," Mara said, clapping him on the back. "And these two are Borek and Kamil. They're big, strong, and handsome, aren't you?"

The man named Borek, a stocky man with a long black beard laughed and nodded. Kamil was shorter with dark skin and kind, piercing eyes. Although he was handsome, he didn't fit Mara's 'big and strong' description, but he smiled at the compliment.

"Kamil is from the country of Kurash. One of the few here they let live. He doesn't talk much since Valistaran had his tongue cut out for disrespecting the queen. He was exiled from his home, too," Mara explained. "He's had a hard life, but we love him. We generally understand him well enough, and Borek can sign with him when we don't."

"It's good to meet you all," Mara said. "Let's hope we get to know each other for a long time outside of this damn place."

"You've got a fire-thrower and a member of the royal guard here now. We'll get you out in no time." Shanthah offered a wink and a theatrical bow to the group.

"Ah, good. Another escape artist. It can't be done," Josman said. "Believe me, we've tried."

"But you're from the royal guard! That means they'll come to save you—and us!" Patrik said, his eyes wide in awe. He lowered himself to the ground in an attempt to bow back.

"No, stop," Shanthah said, feigning discomfort as he tried to hide a slight grin. He pulled Patrik's frail frame to his feet. "But honestly, they don't know I'm here, so we can't count on them, but I promise help however I can—if escape is still on your mind, that is."

"Our escape plans are what got you assigned to our district. You had to replace some good people—friends of ours—that Belokej killed," Borek said. Kamil offered a sad nod.

"Enough for now. We need to get our rest. They'll wake us up in a few hours and we'll start the whole process over again," Mara said. With a big smile, she turned to Hanna. "And *you*. I am so glad to have another woman around. *Please* take the empty mat in my tent."

"It isn't empty!" Pol exclaimed. "You're kicking me out?"

"It is now, and yes," said Mara in a matter-of-fact voice.

"Finally. I'm getting my own tent," said Pol.

"Not so fast. You're with Patrik now. Ten beds. Ten of us." Josman said as he pulled Drahomir over. "And you're going to tell me about everything going on in Laniras, tent-mate."

Drahomir gave a nervous thumbs up.

"That leaves you two," Pol said, pointing at Aleksander and Shanthah. "Hope you don't snore. Good night, everyone!"

The others all retired to their respective tents as Patrik reassured Pol that he wouldn't snore, and Josman threw a sack of dirt over the fire to extinguish it. Aleksander turned toward his own shelter, but Mara pulled him away.

"Can I have a second?" she asked.

"Sure—I, uh—right now?" Aleksander stammered. Mara nodded and gestured for him to follow. They walked a short distance from their tents, and she let out a deep breath.

"You're not from Cineca."

It wasn't a question. Her distrust was nearly palpable.

With a nervous chuckle, he said, "Why would you say that?"

"Pol and I *are* from Cineca, apart from the obvious."

"What's obvious?" Aleksander asked. Before she could respond, he added, "Okay. Honestly, I woke up in a burning forest before they took me here. The only thing I could remember was my name and the fact I could make fire from my hands before they threw me in here."

He showed her the scar on the back of his arm.

"Hm. Well, *Aleksander,* just promise me you'll be careful," she said. "Please."

"I—yeah, of course," Aleksander said, taken aback. Then, with a smile, "It's good to meet you, Mara Bartunek."

She hesitated for a long moment. "I'm glad you're here."

She led him back to the tents. Sleep came to those exhausted enough to earn it, but for the others, a night full of worry for the morning was all that awaited them.

CHAPTER FIVE
SLAVE DISTRICT SIXTY-EIGHT

The pale glow of dawn had not yet peeked over the horizon when the alarm sounded. Soldiers at each of the guard towers blasted one piercing note through the entire compound, removing any hope of continued sleep. Aleksander and Shanthah emerged from their district sixty-eight tent to see the others already awake, preparing themselves to start the day's work. Before they could greet them, however, a soldier approached the camp to assign their district's daily tasks.

"District sixty-eight's duty today is the same as it's been—no changes. You will continue to set and mortar brick on the north wall. Check in with the guards there once you arrive," the soldier explained before marching off to the next campsite with more orders.

"Well, let's get to it," Josman said under his breath, cracking the knuckles of both his meaty fists.

He led the ragtag group of slaves until they joined the flow of other beleaguered workers packed shoulder to shoulder on the narrow path. The hopelessness in the air was thick, and the entire camp reeked of sweat, decay, and often, death.

They made it to the northern wall which was covered in high scaffolding and pulley systems used to lift heavy bricks into place. Aleksander wondered how many slaves had fallen from those heights by accident or otherwise.

"Patrik, today I'm going to put you, Hanna, and Pol in charge of spreading mortar between bricks. Pol, please show them how it's done," Josman said. "The rest of us will haul stone."

"Isn't there a soldier in charge of us?" Aleksander asked.

"No. I'm our district captain. I assign our work for the day after receiving assignments. I think it's a way to encourage us to work, by making us feel 'important' and letting us govern ourselves. As long as each district finishes all the work, they are allotted each day, we have nothing to fear. They are actually pretty lax on us once we finish. *If* we finish, that is. That means the harder we work, the sooner we are done," Josman answered.

He scooped three trowels out of a bucket and handed them to Pol, Hanna, and Patrik. Pol led the other two up a ladder to prepare bricks for setting.

"What the rest of us will be doing all day is hauling the big stone brick from the drop off point to here, and then the second half will use the pulley systems to raise them to their spots. It's mindless work. Stay sane." Josman said. He sighed and explained, "Sometimes we build with smaller bricks, but the architect wanted the massive ones here, or whatever."

He ordered Aleksander, Mara, Kamil, and Drahomir to haul brick while he, Borek, and Shanthah would lift them into place. A night crew had left several large stone slabs at the base of the wall for the morning crew to set on the wall instead of finishing their work, and Josman mentioned his hope that they hadn't been punished. The group broke away for their separate assignments, feeling exhausted even before the day began.

"I'll show Aleksander how to do this. You two go ahead," Mara said. Kamil nodded, and he left with Drahomir. "These bricks take two people to move. They give us rollers to move them, and one person moves the roller in the back to the front while the other pushes. It's not too hard. Even a little guy like you could do it." She winked at Aleksander.

"Little?" Aleksander asked with a laugh. Mara winked, and they approached a partitioned area guarded by a troop of soldiers. A second troop stood at the back side of the area and opened a gate for carts hauling stone.

"This is one of the most guarded areas in the encampment. Workers from Bukaral bring the stone from the slave mines for us to use," Mara said.

"Other slaves?" Aleksander asked.

"No, just people from the city. They tell them we all have a plague and that's why we aren't allowed in the staging area until they leave. It's also why the general population doesn't help us escape. We're seen as expendable because we're going to 'die' anyway."

They entered a short line waiting for their turn to retrieve a brick. While she waited, Mara folded her arms and scanned the wall for any sign of an escape route, just as she did every day. She whispered to Aleksander to keep their spot as she stepped out of line; she made sure no guards were watching, and she pushed through the thorny vines behind a giant broken stone, revealing a little girl no more than six years old hiding within the wall.

"Hey," Mara said, kneeling next to her. The little girl tried to make herself as little as possible and shut her eyes, as if Mara had not already spotted her. "I'm not gonna hurt you."

Aleksander watched from afar as Mara sat in the dirt next to the young girl behind the brick and held out her hand. A head of blonde hair tangled within the dirt, vines, and brambles peeked out of the hole. She looked up at Mara with big green eyes and hesitated for a moment before pushing herself out of her hiding place. Mara held out her arms and the little girl came forward.

"What's your name, beautiful?"

"Diana," answered the timid girl.

"What are you doing in the thorns? You're going to get all cut up," Mara said in a sweet tone.

"Hiding."

"From the scary men? I'd like to hide too. Do you think there's room for me in there?" Mara asked. Diana shook her head from side to side in an exaggerated 'no.'

"I'm too big, huh?" Mara asked.

"Big people don't get scared," said Diana.

This touched Mara's heart, and she grabbed the bottom of her own long tunic and tore off a piece of the ragged, discolored fabric. She glanced over to Aleksander who gestured that it still wasn't their turn to retrieve a brick and that she had time. She turned back to Diana and pulled her close.

"Can I get these out of your hair?" she asked. Diana nodded. Mara plucked each of the brambles from the little girl's golden locks and dropped them to the dirt. She gathered a handful of her blonde hair and twisted it into a simple braid. She then tied the strip of fabric into her hair, making a crude bow. The little girl's eyes lit up, and she clapped her hands on her cheeks.

"I look so pretty!" she exclaimed, hugging Mara around the neck. "Thank you, thank you!"

"Tell you what, you go hide again, but you can't be sad in there okay? Happy girls are the prettiest." Mara said, pausing for a moment before adding, "but brave girls are the happiest." Diana nodded and kissed Mara on the cheek.

"Will I see you again?" Diana asked. "I hide here every day, except when they make us go on the wall. Then I can't hide."

"Of course. We have to stick together in here. I promise I won't tell anyone you're here," Mara said, tying her own dark hair back. Diana gave a toothy grin and tucked herself back into the hiding place. With the dirt on her face, she was almost unnoticeable amidst the thorns.

Mara hurried out of Diana's spot and met Aleksander back at the entrance to the brick drop off point. She hoped that no guards had seen her speaking with Diana, and if they did, that they would not punish the little girl.

"Sorry, we can get our stone now," Mara said as she pushed past Aleksander. "I noticed her the other day, and…"

"That was adorable," Aleksander said with a smile.

"It's easier to survive in here when you have connections," Mara said, trying to maintain a hard exterior.

"Connections? Come on. That was not about *connections*." Aleksander scoffed as they started to push their brick out of the gate. Mara placed the back roller at the front, and they continued onward. "You just wanted to see a little girl smile. Admit it, you're just a nice person."

Mara smiled but shook her head. "You don't know me."

"How long have you been in here?" Aleksander asked. Mara sighed and kicked a small rock out of the way of their block.

"That's a tough question. Here? Two, maybe three years? Maybe more," Mara answered. "I don't really know. Not as long as Josman, and he claims he's been here four years. Longer than the others though."

"Why did you say the word 'here' like that?" asked Aleksander. Mara stopped and leaned on their block, hiding her eyes, and Aleksander pretended not to see the tear roll down her cheek. She took a deep breath.

"I don't think I know you well enough to talk about that."

"I'm sorry, I didn't mean—" Aleksander.

"No, it's fine. Let's just say I'm no stranger to this life. I was a slave before this camp was set up, and we'll leave it at that," said Mara. "Not a first-date type of topic, Aleksander."

"Oh, is that what this is?" Aleksander asked with a chuckle. "I apologize for not bringing you somewhere nicer."

She chuckled and moved the roller. "You're forgiven."

"Tel me about Lavinia," Aleksander said to change the topic.

"You're not one for small talk, I see. Why can't we just talk about the weather or how much we hate the camp, or one of the usual topics? Lavinia. Well, she's a Night Witch. I assume you've noticed that?" Aleksander nodded, and Mara continued. "She's one of the Mistresses of Dusk."

"The what?" Aleksander asked.

"She's a high-ranking Sangoran under the queen. She's on her ruling council, I think. They get their title because the 'dusk comes before the night' or whatever garbage they spew. I guess it shows that they're more important than the rest of their kind."

"She doesn't seem enthusiastic about her job. Would she help us escape?" Aleksander asked.

Mara laughed and shook her head as she pushed her long, dark hair from her eyes. Aleksander couldn't help but appreciate how beautiful Mara was, even covered in the sweat and grime of life in a slave camp.

Her face was carved with the haunted beauty of one who had endured and survived more than he could ever imagine. But it was more than beauty—strength. Bravery. A fierce intelligence and the will to survive against all odds. She was a warrior.

She answered Aleksander's question after a few moments of thought. "Eh, I don't know. Lavinia isn't a traitor. Working with the slave camps and construction is beneath her. It's pretty common knowledge she's assigned here as a punishment, but we don't know why. She's actually got more humanity than some people here. Humanity, Sangority, whatever."

She looked toward a group of slavers as she said this.

"You mean Belokej."

Mara winced as he said the name.

"Belokej, the other slavers. He's the worst of them, but they're all disgusting and perverted. I'd love to see King Romiton's people come in and kill every single one of them," said Mara. "To be honest, I'd do it myself if I could."

"Why don't they? Kidnapping citizens of another country has got to have ramifications," said Aleksander. Mara gave an apathetic shrug.

"They would have done it by now if they were going to," she said. The end of another short conversation.

They reached the wall and Shanthah greeted them with a warm smile. "Ah, my friends! Brought me a gift, have you?"

Mara chuckled and helped him strap the brick into the leather pouch on the end of the pulley system. Josman and Borek heaved on a massive rope, lifting the square boulder into the air. Aleksander gathered the rollers and followed Mara back to the partitioned drop off area.

"And this is what we do every day, all day?"

"Mhmm."

"So, what are the chances you would like to join me tonight in making an escape plan?" he asked.

"Ooh, our second date? I'll have to find something nice to wear." She winked. "Of course, I'd like to get out of here. But you have to know something first."

"What's that?" Aleksander asked.

"Belokej hires people from Bukaral to pose as slaves in here and find people trying to escape. They're usually excited about getting out of here and bold in attempts—and then they get everyone else killed or captured." Mara said. "It's a game for Belokej. He brags about how many people he's gotten killed."

"And you think I'm one of those?" Aleksander asked, pushing their second block forward. He felt a bit guilty at suggesting escape if she did.

As they continued on, the sun began to cast its warmth over the camp, bathing the valley in gold.

"I'm cautious. We've had spies in our district before. I don't want to accuse you of anything, but the story of losing your entire memory before you were captured is a little suspicious."

"I can't make you believe me," Aleksander said, "and for all I know, I *could* be from Talohira. I don't know who I am other than this name. I could be a spy without even knowing it."

"You know, normal people don't just carve their name into their arm," Mara said. "You knew something important before you lost your memory."

She seemed to want to tell him something but refrained.

"Shanthah seems to think the same way," Aleksander answered as they once again reached others, who hoisted the brick onto the wall.

Mara sighed and looked high into the heavens, watching a flock of birds who had returned from their southern winter escape. She examined the senate building as it grew brick by brick, constructed by the sweat and blood of thousands of slaves.

The hours dragged on, and the sun arced over the sky before nestling under the western horizon. Soon, the steady flow of new bricks began to wane until they heaved the final stone onto the wall and set it with mortar.

In time, the guards atop the towers encircling the camp blew their horns to signal the shift change. The signal released the exhausted slaves in district sixty-eight from their duties, and they returned to their campsite. Drained from hoisting bricks all day, Josman crashed on his cot without a word; Shanthah and Borek soon followed his example.

"There's something I need to do," Mara said as the others settled on the ground around the dead campfire. With Kamil's assistance, Hanna attempted to start a new fire to warm her shivering body.

"Alright, take care of yourself, girl," Hanna said. "Dinner will be ready for you later if we don't freeze or if I don't eat it all."

Mara smiled in thanks before wandering away, heading south. Aleksander looked over his shoulder after her; she was already relatively far away, but he would catch up.

He knelt next to the cold ashes and held out his hands. His palms began to tingle and then a thin jet of flame sparked life into the center of their camp. Soon, a warm glow illuminated the group's cold faces.

"Oh, praise you," Hanna said.

"Be right back!" he exclaimed. As the others gathered around the fire, Aleksander hurried after Mara.

"Mind if I join you?" he asked as he caught up to her.

"I thought you'd be tired and want to rest after your first day," Mara said, not stopping for him. She smiled and said, "You aren't tired of me yet?"

"I am. Tired, I mean—not of you. Oh, dear. But it's important to me that you trust me," Aleksander said. "Because, you know, while we were working, I got the feeling you don't."

"Because I basically told you that I didn't?" Mara asked, flashing a dark smile as she continued walking. Aleksander matched her quick stride.

"Well, yeah, that's exactly why. Where are you heading anyway?"

"That doesn't make me think you're not a spy for Valistaran," Mara answered. "If you really want me to trust you, go back to camp. Help the others unwind. Cook them dinner."

"Alright," Aleksander said. "I'm sorry."

"No, I'm the one who should apologize," Mara said, grabbing Aleksander's arm. "I've been rude. It's just been a long day—a long week—I'm tired. I really did enjoy working with you today." She gave another attempt at a smile and squeezed his shoulder. "I'll see you tonight, okay? We'll build up to trust."

Aleksander nodded and walked away.

Mara continued on, counting the number of tents as she went. Aleksander watched her go, choosing to trust his new work companion. Soon, he hoped he'd be able to call her a friend.

CHAPTER SIX
THE TUNNEL

After counting the campsites to make sure she was in the right place, Mara crawled into one of the tents at the base of the scaffolding. She closed the flap of the shelter and moved the dusty cot aside. She brushed the dirt away to reveal a hidden trap door, onto which she gave three slow knocks followed by a fourth quicker one. This was the secret sign that she was to be trusted.

Someone on the other side of the door withdrew a bolt and unlocked the door. For a moment she wondered where the man inside was able to locate a door for his hideout, but she then realized he had procured stranger things. She pulled it upward and a familiar face smiled up at her.

"Hello, Mara!" came a low voice from within the hidden chamber. Mara climbed a ladder into the secret room and shut the door behind her. "What can I do for you today? Do you need something? Tools, medicine, hygiene supplies? Or are you here about tonight's escape attempt? Planning's done, right?"

"Yeah, yeah. It's all squared away. We just got some new people in my district today, which throws the plan off a little."

"You're here early. I thought you'd want to rest."

Mara turned from the ladder and shook her head. She glanced over a pile of odd supplies and goods.

"No, Rehor. I'm looking for some supplies. I want to make something before we go."

"What do you need? A weapon? A tool?" Rehor answered.

"Neither. I don't suppose you have a needle or thread in here?" Mara asked. Rehor rummaged through the stacks of things and drew out a small fabric pouch.

"I do, as it turns out. How much do you need?" Rehor replied. Mara thought for a moment, wiggling her finger in the air as she thought. After a moment she held out her hands as a rough measurement.

"And I'll need some fabric. Maybe some fluffy cotton too if you have some," Mara said.

"I have some rough fabric from spare clothes, but good, soft cotton—that's hard to come by, miss Mara. Could I offer you some straw? I got it from some old pillows. It's soft enough when it's covered," Rehor said.

"Yes, that will do," Mara said. "What do I owe you?"

"Mara, my friend, if we make it out of here tomorrow morning, I will have no need of this shop. You owe me nothing. Even if we didn't escape, I wouldn't ask anything of you," Rehor answered. "I want you to survive. That's how you can repay me. Survive and do good in this world once we escape. Help people."

Mara smiled again and nodded. "Rehor, about the new people in my district—I'm really worried."

"You think one is a spy because they arrived the day of our escape attempt," Rehor said. Mara nodded.

For the entire time she had been enslaved, her friend had always felt like a father. He had supported her with advice and, more often than Mara would admit, a shoulder to cry on. Rehor handed her the straw, needle, and a small bundle of fabric. She turned to leave, putting one foot and one hand on the ladder.

"You don't smile with your eyes anymore, my friend. Not like you used to," he said in a soft tone.

Mara rested her forehead against one of the rungs of the ladder, and she felt her heart begin to race. She felt dizzy, and her hands began to tremble; all at once the world seemed to close in upon her and breathing seemed impossible.

"I can't do this," she said, holding onto the ladder with both hands. She pressed her face between her hands, hiding the tears from Rehor, even though she knew she didn't need to. She felt the old man's gentle hand on her shoulder, and she flinched, not knowing why. She turned to meet his gaze and tapped her hand against her chest three times in rapid succession as if to tell him that her heart wanted to leap out of her chest.

"Breathe, my friend—breathe. Just like I taught you."

Mara wrapped her arms around the portly man and took one long breath. And then another. Another. She closed her eyes and focused on the world around her, thinking about the things she could hear, smell, and feel. Her breath. The smell of the earth, and her own sweat from a long day's work. The warmth of

Rehor's hug. It was a simple technique Rehor taught her several months ago, but it helped to calm her troubled mind. Rehor stood with her in silence until she let go of the hug.

"You're doing great, kid," said Rehor. Mara said nothing but smiled through teary eyes and climbed out of the trap door.

She took her time returning to camp, and when she did, she found Hanna sitting alone next to a dying fire. Her new friend smiled and handed her a bowl of lukewarm porridge. The rest of the group had already retired to sleep.

"Hey, Mar—can I call you that? I waited up to make sure you got something to eat and to make sure the boys didn't eat your share."

"Thank you, Hanna." Mara's voice was almost inaudible. Mara brought the bowl to her lips and began to slurp up its contents. Hanna smiled again and sat next to her, placing her hand on Mara's knee and handed her a crude wooden spoon.

"How are you, beautiful?" Hanna asked.

"Come with us," Mara blurted out. Hanna stared back at her in confusion. She waited for an explanation until Mara continued in a low whisper. "We're leaving tonight. Patrik's too old and will slow us down. I think the others might be spies for Valistaran."

"But you trust me?" Hanna asked. "I could be a spy, you know. I'd be a good spy."

"You snore, you know," Mara said. "If you were a spy, you wouldn't have fallen asleep so quickly."

"Well, maybe that's what makes me such a good spy," Hanna answered with a wink. "You don't *think* I'm a spy."

Mara shook her head. She set down the bowl and glanced toward Josman's tent.

"I'm serious. We're going soon. Pol will give the signal when he thinks Patrik is asleep," Mara said. Hanna returned the comment with a disapproving look. "I know. I wish we could bring everyone. We don't have time. We've planned everything so carefully and if anything goes wrong—I'm risking everything by telling you about it, but Hanna, please…"

She trailed off as Josman emerged from his tent, leaving a sleeping Drahomir behind. He glanced at Hanna as Mara nodded toward her, and Josman agreed to this wordless addition to the plan with a thumbs up, knowing exactly what she meant.

Mara poked her head into her tent, deposited the materials she obtained from Rehor beneath her sleeping mat, and withdrew a small silver dagger. She hid it in her belt and emerged from the tent.

"Woah, where did you get that?" asked Hanna in a hiss.

Mara waved her off.

"Hanna's coming," said Mara to Kamil, Borek, and Pol, who stood waiting. They rubbed black coal dust from the dead fire onto their skin, and none of them objected to Mara's request. Mara and Hanna did the same, smothering their faces in the dark dust in order to better blend in with the darkness.

Like black shadows, they sprinted along, careful to avoid torchlight and guards. When they reached his camp, Rehor coughed, a signal that the coast was clear, and the group hurried into his tent. Each member of the group lowered themselves into the trapdoor under his sleeping mat to enter the cramped chamber below. Rehor pulled the trapdoor shut and proceeded to the far side of the chamber. He shifted a heap of various goods he had collected to reveal a small tunnel.

"Everything is set," Rehor said in a low whisper. "The tunnel will take you past the wall. It's taken two years, but we've done it! Hurry, another group is soon to arrive. Remember, stick to the shadows, and follow the thorn wall until you make it to the river. There, you will be able to swim away. From there, you are on your own."

"Thank you, my friend," Mara said, kissing the man on the cheek. She was the first to enter the tunnel, followed by Hanna. Josman motioned for Pol to enter next and made sure Borek and Kamil got in before he crawled inside too.

The tunnel was dank and freezing, and the group could not see anything in front or behind them in the total blackness. The only sounds that filled the claustrophobic tunnel were the scraping of knees against dirt and the group's breathing.

As Mara pulled herself forward, she felt that her heart was beating as loud as thunder from nerves and the hope of freedom that the others would be able to hear it. After a few minutes of blind crawling, they came to a dead end. The tunnel tapered upwards here and there was enough room to kneel.

Mara placed her hands on the wall, feeling for the exit. Days ago, Rehor had explained to her that there was a slab of wood covered with dirt to cover the exit of their secret tunnel. She knocked on the wall and found the hollow sound of wood.

"Josman, help me," Mara said, pushing against the makeshift door. Josman pushed his burly shoulder into the wood until it bulged, began to bend, and then splintered outward. Light streamed into the tunnel as Kamil and Borek rushed forward on hands and knees to help pry away broken pieces of wood.

Mara peered out of the tunnel as she emerged from the cliff face over a steep slope. She ventured out and strained her neck to see further, making out the river in the distance.

"Rehor said to follow the wall," Borek said, motioning to Mara's left. She nodded and did so. She pulled herself up the rocky crag onto a small path barely big enough for one person.

"After you," Hanna said, looking into the deep ravine below.

From within the tunnel came the sound of more escapees crawling to freedom. Mara led the group down the side of the cliff parallel to the thorn covered wall above.

She was careful with her footing so that she wouldn't take a tumble to her death. She lost her balance a few times, but she pressed on. Soon, she made it down the decline onto stable ground. She looked back to see the rest of her group halfway down the slope with Borek and Kamil at the fore. Hanna was still cautious of the height, letting the others go first.

Mara turned the corner around the cliff to see a hill covered in loose gravel that threatened to make them lose footing. She dropped to her bottom and scooted down the hill, starting a slow flow of tiny pebbles down the slope with her. She stumbled and fell forward, scraping her palms, knees, and forearms with the sharp rocks. She tumbled down the hill and smacked hard into the bottom of the rocky cliff face. With a groan, she glanced behind her to make sure the others were safe.

Borek and Kamil soon made it to the bottom with more grace than she had exhibited. Josman came next, holding Hanna's hand to guide her down. Pol was the last to arrive but had no problems, and he even looked like he enjoyed sliding down the hill.

"The second group is on the cliff. They'll be down soon. We need to hurry so that too many of us don't get caught up here. A third group should already be in the tunnel, I think," he said.

Mara nodded and motioned toward the river in the distance. They broke into a run toward their freedom.

"Oh no," Josman said as their surroundings became clearer in the darkness. As they neared the river, they beheld a deep ditch separating them from the river, and a second wall higher than the first on the opposite bank of the river. Mara smacked herself in the forehead with the palm of her hand. She paced back along the deep fissure, trying to find a way down.

"They locked us in. They knew we'd escape, eventually."

She kicked a small rock into the fissure.

"We can find a way across," Borek said. "We have to."

With a shaky hand, Kamil motioned at the fissure as if to say that it was too far across.

"We can climb down," Pol said. Mara shook her head.

"There are probably spears on the bottom like the ditch around the northern wall and gates," Mara said. "We'll have to find another way." She ran along the edge of the ditch and the rest of the group followed. The second group approached the fissure, and their groans of disappointment filled the night air.

"How did we not see this?" Pol asked.

"I guess they must have used the cliffs and terrain to hide it from us," Josman answered. "Don't worry. We will find a way."

They followed the fissure to the very end where it met up with the cliff once more. Mara swore under her breath and looked down. She couldn't even make out the bottom of the pit.

"Go back. Tell the other group to get back to the camp. There's no way we can make it over there without more planning," Mara said. Josman nodded and explained the situation to the second group just as the third group discovered the fissure.

"This is not good," Borek said. "With so many of us, there isn't time to get everyone back before they see us."

A sudden shout rang out from above, filling the hearts of all with a sudden panic. Mara pushed the group to go back as a Sangoran began circling above them.

"A Night Witch. They saw us." Borek said, shuddering with fear. "Oh, Thanatan help us…"

"Not just any Night Witch," Josman answered, pointing to the sky. The Sangoran soaring above them was crackling with white energy. "One that has lightning powers of some kind."

The Sangoran shouted and sent a bolt of white-hot lightning straight into the group. A member of the second group cried in agony and collapsed, his chest a smoking pit of burned flesh.

"Go!" Mara screamed.

All three groups stampeded back up the gravel slope, but it was too steep, and their footing too loose. Another bolt of lightning struck the man right next to Mara, who collapsed without a word and rolled down the hill. His body tripped some of the scrambling slaves, who then tumbled to the bottom.

The Night Witch landed at the top of the slope and sent two more bolts of electricity into the nearest slaves, sending a spray of blood over the group. Mara counted each of her friends; everyone in her company was still alive for now.

"We have been aware of your tunnel for weeks now," their assailant said, her voice echoing in the night. "I have a special punishment for you. Up!" She zapped another slave, who cried out in pain, but survived. He collapsed, gasping for breath.

With great difficulty and electrical shocks from their captor, the entire group of escapees made their way up the gravel slope and back across the narrow cliff face.

When they made it back to the tunnel, the Night Witch gestured for them to crawl back through. Mara, Josman, and Pol made it into the tunnel first. The complete darkness inside the tunnel overwhelmed them once again as they made their way toward the camp. Behind them, a sudden scream filled the air followed by the sounds of a scuffle, but they kept moving.

Outside the tunnel, one of the slaves had surprised the Night Witch by thrusting a sharpened bit of rock into her ribs from behind. She retaliated by blasting him in the stomach with lightning and then kicked his body from the cliff. She whirled around just as three more tackled her to the ground.

She cried for her fellow soldiers, but none came.

"Go!" cried Borek as they held their enemy to the ground.

Many of the slaves leaped from the mountain and rolled down the slope toward freedom, but the rest stayed to fight or return to the camp. Hanna entered the tunnel, followed by three male slaves. Borek kicked the Night Witch in the jaw with a sickening crunch, spraying blood into the dirt.

The broken-jawed Sangoran threw her wings into the air, knocking Borek and the three other slaves to the earth. She brought the blade-tipped wings down into one escapee's chest, killing him instantly then ripped them out and whirled around, blasting Borek in the arm with electricity from her palm.

One of the other slaves bashed her over the head with a large rock, knocking her to the earth again. Borek grasped the blade at the end of her wing and ripped it off, resulting in a shriek from the Sangoran woman's broken jaw.

"Go!" Borek exclaimed as the third group started to enter the tunnel. He was sure that his own district was all safe, and he smiled. Four more slaves joined the fray, kicking and punching the Night Witch's battered form. A bolt of lightning tore through the back of one of the slaves, knocking him down the gravel hill. Borek swung the wing-blade, severing a vital muscle to control her opposite wing.

The Night Witch managed to get to her feet but screamed in pain as she tried to take flight. She raised her mangled wing as high as she could and drove the weapon upon its tip deep into Borek's stomach.

"Go!" Borek shouted as the last of the group entered the tunnel. Borek slumped to his knees with the blade still embedded in his torso. He grimaced, and he glimpsed around at the rest of the brave slaves slain around him.

He vowed to avenge them.

The Night Witch stumbled to her feet, limping to the wall to keep her balance. Six of her attackers were still living, but their energy was fading fast.

"Get in," she wheezed.

Five of the slaves did as they were told, believing that their fate would be worse if they disobeyed. As soon as they crawled inside, she blasted the earth above the exit, destroying the way out. The end of the tunnel collapsed, filling the entire tunnel with screams and dust. She turned to Borek who lay bleeding against the cliff face.

"As for you," the Night Witch said, coughing up blood. "You cost me my wing."

"Then I guess you won't survive the fall," Borek said, leaping to his feet, smashing his shoulder against the bewildered Night Witch's chest. He caught her by the front of the shirt, pulling her off the edge with him.

Together they plunged into darkness.

CHAPTER SEVEN
THE DECEIT OF HAVEL

Weary from his ride, High King Valistaran Talohir dismounted and led his horse toward a crumbling and weathered well just off the wooded path. He lowered the broken bucket into the depths of the earth and slowly drew it back into the light. He found it fortunate that the water at the bottom was not frozen.

He dropped the pail to the ground, and the water sloshed about with bits of ice and dirt. It wasn't clean water, but he led his skinny steed to drink. The old horse happily plunged its face into the cool water and drank until the bucket was empty. It nudged Valistaran with its forehead for more. He smiled at the beast and once again lowered the bucket to repeat the process.

His own personal war horse, or any borrowed from the military's stables, would have no problem carrying him to his destination. However, he had requested a malnourished and sickly animal that would not be recognized as a sturdy and groomed military animal belonging to Talohira.

Once his horse drank its fill, Valistaran led it onward, his men following close behind. He had only chosen to bring four guards and Queen Codruta along should his plan turn to disaster. However, he did not believe himself to be in any danger of being captured. Neither did he expect anyone in the countryside of Thanatanos to be able to identify his face, but his pride had been his downfall in the past. He made meticulous plans and was prepared for any compromising situation.

Still, his heart leapt in excitement. In his youth, he'd gone on many adventures across the world, scheming with his friends searching for treasure or other mysteries, and despite the power he'd amassed in the past decades, he did miss those days of exploration and intrigue. This was something akin to that, he told himself.

"We are within an hour's ride of the first town, my lord," one of his men said.

"Good. Clear a space in the woods to set up camp. Don't let any campfires get high enough that the smoke is visible from the town," Valistaran answered. "I will go on ahead."

His men nodded and saluted their king as he stretched out his arms; they assisted him in removing his crown, dark armor, and regal cape as Codruta rummaged through her horse's saddlebags and withdrew a worn tunic and a threadbare cloak.

He entered a small tent set up by one of his men and changed into his disguise. He then grasped a handful of dirt and crushed it in his palms, making his hands grimy for added effect before emerging from the tent. He appeared very different indeed from the king that stood in his place moments before.

"Codruta, my queen. I have your first task," he said. Although he now resembled a peasant, he still bore the air of a king.

"Yes, my love?" Codruta asked.

"I need you to intercept a small party of Thannish soldiers," Valistaran said. "Kill them and bring me their armor intact. If all goes to plan, I will need it for my next disguise. I will come to this place every two days after nightfall to meet you—or sooner if I discover anything of use." He turned to Codruta and said with a smile, "I shall see you soon, my queen. I love you."

Codruta smiled and wrapped her arms around her husband. She looked up to say something, but one of the soldiers interrupted.

"How long should we plan on staying here?" he asked.

"Long enough," said the king, a look of annoyance on his face. He kissed Codruta on the forehead and said, "I need time to plant seeds of mistrust in this village. Weeks, perhaps. I will have Captain Mallen do the same in the next town. Hopefully, we can start enough problems in the kingdom before they catch on to us. I now take my leave, until we meet again."

His queen waved, and his men saluted him as he turned away, heading for the unsuspecting village.

The sun hung low in the sky as the disguised king reached the town. He clutched at his ragged hood with one hand to keep it from blowing off his head in the winter breeze as he led his frail horse with the other. He ambled through the streets and came across a quaint market in the center of town with several stalls set up. Vendors ambled about selling their wares as the townsfolk went about their daily routines.

The king's feeble horse lowered its head to nibble at a pathetic patch of thistle. He urged it on, and it shook its head into a fence without warning and kicked him hard in the leg. He shouted a profanity as his beast ran off through the marketplace. He struggled to stand, pain blinding him. A couple of Thannish villagers hurried to his aid and helped him up. His leg pulsed where the hoof struck it, and he wondered if it was broken.

"Are you alright, sir?" a woman in a tattered dress asked. The man pulled Valistaran's arm over his shoulder and helped him hobble along.

"I'm alive," Valistaran said, "but I hope my horse doesn't run off too far."

"He's gone into the market. Looks like he's already being taken care of," the man supporting him said. He was correct. Two men in the market had restrained the wild horse and guided it back to Valistaran.

"What's your name, mister?" the woman asked. "I don't think I've seen you around town before."

"My name is Havel," Valistaran lied, a common name in Thanatanos he'd chosen as his identity. "Originally, I'm from Born, but the price of living in the big city was too much. You know how it is. I was planning on finding somewhere to live in Feren, not far from here. I was on my way through, and, well—you know the rest."

He glared in the skinny horse's direction.

"Well, welcome to Cineca. I'm Killian and this is my wife, Daniela. Let's get you inside and patched up," the man said, leading Valistaran to a small shack not far from the market. Daniela opened the door for the two men, and they helped Valistaran onto a poorly stuffed sofa in the center of the room.

"Let's see what we've got here," Daniela said. "Oh, I hope it's not broken. Nope, but that horse popped your knee clean out. Dislocated it right good."

The improper speech irritated Valistaran, but he pretended not to mind. She continued to examine his knee, prodding it and poking at the swollen joint.

"I don't suppose there are any cottages in Cineca for sale?" Valistaran asked. "It seems a nice enough place."

"Well, just across the street, an old neighbor died, and it's gone empty for weeks now. I'm sure no one would mind if you moved in. It'd help us, anyway, once your leg goes and heals," Daniela said with a smile.

"Help you? What do you mean?" Valistaran asked.

"Well, Havel, there've been kidnappings in Cineca. There aren't enough hands to do the farming lately. I know, I know, don't let me scare you off. It really is a peaceful place. We don't have any crime and—"

"What Daniela is saying is—slavers from Talohira have been crossing the border pretty often these days, and they've been taking our people away. We heard they're making them work on something or other near the capital, but it's only rumors," Killian said. "They even took our own children a few years ago."

He covered his eyes with his hand and turned away. His wife patted his shoulder and kissed him on the cheek.

Jumping at the chance to hear gossip that he might be able to use against Thanatanos, Valistaran spoke up. "They took your children?! And King Romiton? What has he done to help?"

"Nothin'," answered Daniela. "We're all getting real mad at the kingdom. They look out for Laniras right well, it being the capital and all, and Nitra and bigger towns are doing fine, but they don't have much care for the border towns. Taxes. Not doing anything about slavers. It's all too much."

"Yes, I think they just use us as the soldiers on the front of the battle who get killed first," Killian said. "They expect us to keep supplying grain from our fields to help feed the soldiers in the sieges and battles in the war, but they aren't doing anything when our men keep getting' snatched away. Just like the government to steal from its people, eh?"

"There has to be something we can do," Valistaran said. He hadn't expected to gain this type of information so soon. "Have you tried fighting back?"

"None of us is fighters, sir. A few of us served in the army years and years ago, but we're no match for Talohiran soldiers, everyone who can really fight was killed by the slavers anyhow," Killian said with a frown. He shook his head and put a kettle over a small fire in the corner. "Tea?"

"Yes, please. That would be nice," Valistaran answered. "I was in the Thannish army for a while, until I was discharged for—well, it's embarrassing."

"Oh, Havel, you can tell us. We aren't going to judge you! We don't think much of the army anyway," Daniela said.

"Well, I was sneaking out at night to meet a girl I loved. They caught me and threw her in prison for encouraging me, and then I was discharged. They didn't put me in prison, but I've been homeless ever since," Valistaran lied, playing to their sympathies in an attempt to lessen their ideas of King Romiton's government.

"Oh! Why, isn't that horrible?" Daniela said, shaking her head. She folded her arms and walked over to the fire to serve the tea. Her husband sat near Valistaran and coughed without covering his mouth. Valistaran cringed.

"And what about your girl?" Killian asked.

"The slavers took her too," Valistaran replied with a sad expression. "My point is that I can help train fighters, once my leg is healed." Daniela handed him a cup of tea, and he thanked her with a gracious nod. She went back to examining his leg, and he asked, "Do you have weapons?"

"The town's got farmin' tools, simple spears and a few swords and hatchets," Killian said. "I've got my old scythe. Maybe enough for a small militia to defend against the slavers. Now that we've got you, maybe we stand more than a chance."

"I'd be willing to help." He was cut off as Daniela pushed hard on his knee. He screamed in pain as she readjusted it; he leaped to his feet, spilling his tea on the floor and collapsing back onto the sofa.

"Sorry dear. Don't mind the tea. I'll get you more," Daniela said, unfazed. Valistaran massaged his injury and nodded.

"I have to thank you for your hospitality. I owe you a great deal. I do not have much money, but perhaps I can thank you somehow," Valistaran said.

"Oh, no," Killian said. "You can repay us by training the town boys to fight against Valistrin's men."

Valistaran cringed again at the mispronunciation of his own name. "If it wouldn't be too much trouble, could you show me to the house I could stay in? I'd like to look into purchasing it."

"Are you right fit to walk?" Killian asked.

Valistaran tested his knee.

"I should be fine."

Killian grabbed a crutch from the closet and handed it to Valistaran. The king accepted the tool and used it to walk out the door behind Killian. They made their way across the street, and Killian opened the unlocked door; the two walked into the dusty home to see that decay and neglect had overtaken the room. Although disgusting, it would be enough for his purposes. Valistaran limped across the tiny room and dropped into a wooden and wicker chair. He flicked a cockroach off the table which collided with the wall and scurried away.

"Thank you, friend, if I can call you that," Valistaran said. Killian tipped his hat and turned to leave the room.

"Of course, you can. What will you do now?" the man asked.

"I'll rest a little while and get settled. Perhaps I will visit the market. I would like to visit the town armory as well to see if I can try to arm the new militia. Before that, I'll scout out the woods behind the village to plan strategy and how we can defend from the slavers," Valistaran said.

"Busy man. We don't do that much in three weeks!" Killian said with a smile before leaving the room. When he was sure Killian was gone, Valistaran rose from the chair and left the house. He untied his unruly horse, which had been tied near his new hut by one of the villagers. He limped in the direction of the market but instead continued on through the forest.

With a painstaking grunt, he mounted the horse and urged it on in the direction of Codruta's camp. It was dark by the time his horse plodded into the ring of tents where his soldiers stood at attention. They greeted him with a collective salute. The camp was in such a state that it was apparent that they did not expect his return so soon.

"I already have important news," Valistaran said. His men snapped to attention. "I have secured a dwelling in Cineca. I met two villagers there who informed me that they mistrust King Romiton because of his taxes, his neglect of the border towns, and that slavers from Talohira have been taking their citizens."

"They're right, the new administrative sector outside Bukaral isn't going to build itself," Codruta said. "Let's let them think that's the only reason for the labor camps."

She winked and then motioned with her head in the direction of a dead man clad in Thannish armor propped against a rock.

"I see you've brought me a gift," Valistaran said. He examined the corpse from afar. The armor seemed intact and would serve his purposes. "I was hoping it'd be empty, however. As I was saying, they are unhappy that Romiton has not sent help to defend their village against us. They told me that the border towns all feel the same way."

He turned to his men and said, "Captain Mallen, I need you to infiltrate another nearby village. Head to Feren. It's not far from here to the southwest. Tell them that fighting broke out and there were deaths in Cineca because Thannish soldiers were enforcing these policies. If the sentiment there is the same, they won't take long to convince to join our cause."

"My lord, what good will a couple of unarmed border villages do against the capital of Laniras?" Captain Mallen replied.

"These towns supply most of the grain for Romiton's armies. If we can get them to cut off the grain supply, it will do two things: first, it will hurt Romiton's forces in Talohira. Second, it will cause Thanatanos to press harder on the villages for supplies. That's the important part. Eventually, I'd very much like to cause a civil war in Thanatanos."

"Yes, my lord," Captain Mallen said.

"Codruta, I need you to deliver this man's armor to my hut in Cineca. Do not be seen." He scribbled the location of the shack on a piece of parchment and handed it to his queen.

"Over the next few days, I will put the next part of my plan into play. I will earn the trust of these people and I will turn them against their king."

CHAPTER EIGHT
THE WHIPPING POSTS

The group of slaves, their escape attempt foiled, stood chained to a line of whipping posts. In all, twenty-one of them had survived, including Mara, Hanna, Josman, Kamil, and Pol. Josman looked at Mara and mouthed Borek's name as if to ask if she had seen him. She shrugged her shoulders and pressed her forehead against the whipping post in despair. Rehor had also been captured and stood next to his fellow slaves.

Belokej the Slaver chuckled to himself as he paced along the row of runaways, trying to decide who would be his first victim. He approached Hanna who glared back at him with fiery indignation. He raised his whip and struck her back three times. He laughed with each bloody stroke that soaked through her tunic.

Tears filled Hanna's eyes, but she refused to cry out, denying Belokej any more satisfaction.

"Stop this!" Josman shouted.

"My first treat of the day," the slaver said, setting his sights on Josman next.

He tore the back of Josman's shirt clean off and slashed the barbed whip against his back, relishing in the fact that he could cause such a strong man such blinding pain with no fear of retaliation.

He cocked his head in confusion, for the strikes of his weapon had barely broken the man's skin. Josman followed Hanna's example, refusing to cry out in pain, which granted him another couple lashes to his calves, causing him to collapse.

"Stand up, slave," Belokej ordered, circling the whipping post to gaze into his victim's eyes. Josman stood, and Belokej brought his fist around into his jaw, knocking him backward; he would have fallen to the ground, but his chains prevented it. Several Talohiran soldiers came forward to prevent him from murdering the slave, but he shook his finger to send them away.

"As punishment, I will leave you all here for two days with no food," the slaver said. "Whoever survives is free to return to work." He walked down the line and delivered two nonchalant lashes against Pol's back, resulting in a scream and a groan.

The slaver stopped behind Mara, who stared straight forward with hatred etched on her face. He grabbed the back of Mara's tunic, a disgusting smile crossing his face.

"One of my favorites," Belokej said.

"You coward!" shouted Rehor, and Belokej let go of Mara's collar. She widened her eyes and shook her head at Rehor, as if trying to make him stay silent.

"It's okay," she mouthed. Belokej walked over to Rehor and tore off his ragged coat before dropping it to the cold ground.

"Ah, you care for her?" Belokej asked.

Rehor said nothing and Belokej kicked him in the back of the leg, knocking him down. He brought his whip up and back down, leaving six crimson stripes in all. Rehor did not rise. Mara shut her eyes as a tear rolled down her face, positive that Belokej was going to kill him.

Belokej grabbed Mara's collar and ripped her tunic down to her shoulder blades before delivering seven strikes to her as well. She collapsed from the pain, and she heard the man raise the whip once more, but the strike didn't come. She glanced over her shoulder to see Aleksander gripping the slaver's arm as a group of guards rushed toward him.

"That's enough!" Aleksander shouted, his brow furrowed.

"Guards! Chain this swine next to the rest of them!"

As the guards hurried to follow Belokej's order, he raised his whip to strike Aleksander only to feel a burst of hot flame against his ribs followed by a fist to the chin and a second to the mouth.

Belokej struck the earth hard with a pathetic groan as Aleksander picked up the fallen whip. He stepped on his back, grasped the back of Belokej's robe, and tore it away. The two guards stopped, smirking behind their helms.

Belokej spat at Aleksander who struck the slaver three times with his own whip. All the captives and even some of the guards erupted into cheers as Aleksander raised the whip in victory.

The rest of the soldiers swarmed the platform as Aleksander whipped Belokej one more time before he was overtaken. He raised his hands in defeat as the slaver moaned and got to his feet, bleeding from the corner of his mouth. He spat a tooth into the dirt and grabbed Aleksander's shoulder.

"Send him to The Cage," Belokej said. "Five minutes should suffice." One of the guards nodded and grabbed Aleksander's arm. They led him off the stage as the head slaver limped away, holding his arm.

"Why is he limping?" Josman asked.

"Because clearly, Aleksander broke his leg when he punched him in the jaw," Mara answered with a laugh. She pressed her forehead against the post with a sigh, but her smile did not fade.

A feeble and bleeding Rehor glanced up and saw Mara smiling, and joy overwhelmed him despite his wounds.

"You okay, Hanna?" asked Josman. It was her first whipping, and he hoped it'd be her only one. Hanna nodded.

"One of us now, eh?" said Rehor. "Welcome to the family."

"And Mara?" Josman asked.

"I'm okay," Mara said. "We've got someone to thank."

Far from the whipping posts, one of the guards pushed Aleksander up against the rough brick wall of a small building, restraining him as the second soldier knocked on the door. A moment later, Lavinia appeared in the entrance.

"What?"

"My apologies for the interruption, Mistress. Belokej ordered that this one goes to The Cage," the guard replied.

"Very well. Bring him in," Lavinia said.

She motioned for them to leave with a flick of her hand. The guards saluted the Mistress of Dusk and marched away. Aleksander entered the small room, and when Lavinia indicated for him to do so, he sat in the only other chair in the room.

"Ah, you. It didn't take long for you to get in trouble. What'd you do?" Lavinia asked.

"I stepped in at a whipping," Aleksander answered. "And then I, uh, whipped Belokej."

Lavinia howled with laughter, slamming her palm on the table. A jar of ink splashed to the ground, but she took no notice. Or perhaps, she didn't care. Grinning from ear to ear, she grasped Aleksander's shoulder.

"You know, if I wasn't bound to keep you here, I'd say that would be enough to win you your freedom," the Mistress of Dusk said. "I hate that man with all that I am. I won't send you to The Cage."

"Where is The Cage?"

"Complicated. Stay here with me for five minutes and I'll tell the others that you met your punishment."

"You're helping me?" Aleksander asked, bewildered.

"No, I'm just not punishing you. I don't care about what Belokej wants. The murderous pervert is having a fit like a child because he didn't get his way," Lavinia said. She poured a drink of something foul and dark and handed it to Aleksander. He declined, and Lavinia chuckled. "It isn't poison if that's what you're worried about. It's the finest Opikorla in all of Sangora— finest meaning it prevents sobriety the best. Listen. I'm bored. For standing up to that monster, I want to offer you something."

"What?" Aleksander asked.

"I *can* help get you out of here, despite my orders to keep you," Lavinia said. "All you need to do is help me out with one small favor. Given recent events, I think you'll enjoy my offer."

"And the others?" Aleksander asked. Lavinia pressed her fingertips together and sighed.

"They're not part of my bargain, no," the Sangoran replied. "Why do they matter to you? I hear you have no knowledge of your past, but you care for those you have just met?"

"That's exactly why. They're all I know," Aleksander answered. Lavinia sat back, leaning her wooden chair back on two legs. She placed a short, polished dagger on the table in front of Aleksander. It wobbled for a moment before coming to rest.

"Nevertheless, I will put forth my offer. Kill Belokej. Bonus points if you bring me his heart."

"What?" Aleksander asked with a grimace.

"Joking," Lavinia said. "Unless, you know… Anyway, I will turn a blind eye to your friends should they attempt to escape again." Lavinia said. She met Aleksander's gaze then looked toward the dagger. Aleksander dragged the knife along the surface of the table without breaking eye contact.

"I'll think about it," Aleksander said, stashing the weapon in his tunic. Lavinia smiled.

"The goddesses know I have."

She stood, walked around the table, and opened the door for her prisoner. They shook hands in silent agreement, and he was guided back to his district by two armed soldiers.

Mara, still tied to the whipping posts, spotted him approaching first. She cleared her throat to get Hanna's attention and gestured at their new friend with her head. Hanna gave a lazy nod in acknowledgment, her energy all but spent.

"What happened in there?" Mara asked. "What did they do?"

"Did they remove any body parts?" Shanthah added. "Oh, yeah. I'm here too. They tied me up for your crimes. Thanks."

Aleksander laughed and raised his arms to show they were both still attached. A guard shackled Aleksander's hands together and hoisted a rope to raise and lock them to the post.

"Relax. They didn't send me to The Cage. They didn't torture me at all," Aleksander answered in a low voice, making sure that only Mara and Shanthah could hear. Mara raised an eyebrow. "Lavinia gave me a proposition. It might just save all our lives."

"A Night Witch made a deal with a slave?" Mara asked.

"She doesn't seem to like our slaver. I think she has some kind of grudge against him," Aleksander said. "She told me that if I kill Belokej, she will get me out of here."

"What about us?" Shanthah asked.

"She said she'll turn a blind eye to another escape attempt," Aleksander answered. Mara glanced at Shanthah, who shifted to try to find some semblance of comfort.

"It could be a trap," Mara said. "The punishment for killing one of the guards or slavers is—"

"The Cage?" Aleksander asked. Mara nodded. "What is it, anyway?"

"No one knows, but everyone who has been thrown in there comes out crazy, and I mean completely insane. No one has ever been in there longer than a few minutes, but they are never the same when they come out," Mara answered.

"She gave me a dagger too," Aleksander said. "Do you think we can trust her?"

"No," Mara replied.

"She seems to hate this camp as much as we do, to be honest," Shanthah said. "Maybe we should find out why she hates Belokej so much."

"Good idea. That might show us if she's being truthful or not," Mara answered. A guard noticed the trio deep in conversation and marched toward them.

"Prisoners are not to communicate with each other," the soldier said, eying the three slaves. He slammed his spear against the ground as a threat and strode back to his post near the thorn covered wall. They fell silent, and the only sound, save the construction of the senate building nearby, was the faint patter of freezing rain. Shanthah sighed as it began to soak everyone tied to the whipping post from head to toe.

The rainwater mixed with grime and blood on their exposed backs and limbs. Groans filled the air as it stung their wounds, adding even more pain to the uncomfortable situation.

"So, how'd they get you, Shanthah?" Aleksander asked. "Apart from knowing us, that is? You didn't have any part in this."

"Did I not?" Shanthah asked. "When I realized that everyone was gone except you, me, Patrik, and Drahomir, I figured out what everyone else was trying to do, and so I headed in the direction as the soldiers, which I assumed were going to head you all off. I tried to buy some time for whatever escape plan they'd concocted to work—even though no one bothered to tell me about it—but the soldiers overpowered me."

"So, where are Drahomir and Patrik?" Hanna asked. Shanthah shrugged his shoulders.

"When they found out our district was involved, they sent Patrik away to the mines and I haven't seen Drahomir since I was brought here, obviously. I hope they're alright, but—well, they might be in the same amount of trouble for failing to turn the rest of you in." He paused before changing the subject by saying. "Two days sure is a long time to be stuck here."

"The company is pretty good, though," said Hanna.

Aleksander nodded and tried to get as comfortable as possible against his post.

Shanthah began to hum a merry Thannish folk tune, encouraging the others to join in. They grumbled at first, but at last, they all began to sing along, keeping their spirits up. Shanthah and Hanna sang the loudest in exaggerated tones as if they were each other's personal audiences.

Aleksander smiled as he listened to Mara's sweet voice in particular, although she sang quieter than the others. He shut his eyes and simply listened, feeling that angelic voice melt away his fear and anxiety, and for whatever reason, he found a newfound hope burning in his chest.

The sun began to set several hours later, signaling the end of their first day. One of the fatigued slaves had already yielded to exhaustion but was hanging by his hands against the post unable to collapse. The group had long since given up on conversation and song to conserve what energy they had left.

Shanthah had discovered a way to hang backward suspended by his chains and was somehow able to sleep in that position.

Aleksander glanced over at Mara, who was glaring with eyes full of malice in the direction of Belokej and his fellow slavers. Aleksander whistled to get her attention, and she turned her livid countenance toward him.

"Kill Belokej?" he mouthed, careful not to make any sound. To wake any of the other sleeping slaves would bring them back to their torment. Mara's eyes widened, followed by a vigorous nod of her head.

"Yes please!" she mouthed.

Aleksander made a stabbing action with what little motion he could muster, and Mara let out one weak but joyous laugh. She imitated Belokej's lumbering walk and then dying, her tongue sticking out of the corner of her mouth.

Aleksander grinned and suppressed a laugh of his own. He turned his face to the heavens, where the stars twinkled like tiny lights against the black curtain of night.

"Can I tell you something?" he whispered. She nodded. "You have a beautiful voice, even if you didn't think we could hear it."

"Thank you. You have no idea what that means to me."

He wondered why that was, but they said nothing more about it. About an hour or so later, he looked over to see her in the midst of falling asleep with a smile on her face for the first time since he had known her.

CHAPTER NINE
A NEW HOPE FOR FREEDOM

Aleksander woke up some time later to a vicious pain in his back with Belokej and the rest of his slavers looming behind him.

"You're brave when we can't fight back," Aleksander shouted. Another stinging stripe followed. He winced and dug his fingernails into the wooden post. He didn't know how much more he could take.

"Then fortunately for you, I've arranged a little show for the rest of the slaves," Belokej answered. A group of soldiers started to unlock each of the prisoners from their posts. "You get off a day early if you can survive a fight with me and my men."

Aleksander glanced toward Mara, who nodded. They both understood the wordless conversation meant that this might be their chance to kill their tormentor. Perhaps Lavinia had even arranged for this to happen.

"And those who are too weak to fight?" Aleksander asked.

"I don't care. Let them rot," Belokej grunted. At that moment, Aleksander realized just how much the man resembled a wild boar. "So, who will be our entertainment?"

Aleksander, Mara, Shanthah, Josman, and three others raised their hands. Hanna, Kamil, Pol, and Rehor had all collapsed against the whipping posts out of exhaustion. They stood no chance to succeed in the arena and would have to survive their own battle against the whipping posts.

Belokej reeked of alcohol as he walked by, laughing to himself. He and his minions released the group of volunteers and led them toward the center of the unfinished senate building.

"We need to get water to the others somehow," Mara said in a whisper to Aleksander and Shanthah. Shanthah nodded, looking at Hanna with particular concern.

"One obstacle at a time, Miss Bartunek," Aleksander said.

Belokej led them through the opulent front doors and down a long, straight hallway. They came to the senate chamber in which tiered stone benches lined each wall in the room.

The domed ceiling was not yet complete, letting the gloomy morning light and chill into the chamber. Before the tiers of benches was a flat space for speakers to stand, and Aleksander assumed this area would serve as their arena. Humans and Sangorans alike sat waiting in the unfinished benches, chatting amongst themselves. A few other slaves sat interspersed with their foes, ready to watch the fight.

Belokej ordered his men to remove the chains between each of the slaves' shackles. They did so and lined them up on the far side of the room. Belokej cracked his whip in the air and several soldiers entered from a gate between the sections of benches.

"Any surviving slaves are free to rejoin their districts and avoid any current punishments," a Talohiran soldier announced.

His voice echoed, amplified by the chamber's acoustics. As the sound of Belokej's whip marked the beginning of the fight, Aleksander caught Lavinia's eye at the far side of the chamber.

This had to be her plan to get Belokej killed all along.

Aleksander, Mara, Shanthah, Josman, and the three other male slaves stood their ground as ten soldiers advanced. Belokej stood at the end of the chamber, watching the madness begin.

Aleksander dodged a spear thrust from one of the soldiers and hopped around his foe on quick feet. The spear whirled around, and he twisted once more out of the way. The soldier grinned and brandished his weapon like a hunter stalking its prey. As he lunged once more, Aleksander delivered a quick jab to the man's jaw and a second punch to the sternum, forcing him back.

Meanwhile, Mara took the full lash of a whip straight to the chest, knocking the breath from her lungs; she collapsed to her knees, and the slaver jumped upon her, but she retaliated by jabbing her fist into his throat. He wheezed and fell backward as she leaped upon him then wrenched the whip from his hand and snapped it across his face, leaving a trail of crimson.

She pressed her knee into his chest and raised the whip again. Just as she was about to strike, another soldier slammed the butt of his spear against her shoulder, knocking her forward. Her foe scrambled to push her off, but she brought a swift elbow to his eye with a crunch. The second soldier grabbed her by the collar and pulled her backward.

With a nimble sidestep, Shanthah dodged a slaver's knife and sprinted to Mara's aid. He reached the fallen whip and slashed it across her attacker's arm, causing him to drop his spear. Mara and the slaver tackled one another for the chance to claim it.

One of the other prisoners screamed in pain as the slaver he was dueling thrust a long knife into his side. The prisoner dropped to the ground and punched the man in the knee. The slaver toppled to the ground and Josman ran forward, kicking him in the head.

"Everyone get together!" he shouted, elbowing one of the soldiers in the face before receiving a lashing on each arm from two other slavers. He stumbled as they struck him again in unison. He let out a bellow and grasped each of the whips, twisting them around his wrists to pull the soldiers closer. With great difficulty, he yanked on the whips, knocking the two slavers' heads together.

Each of the surviving slaves grouped together, and Mara cried out as she parried the blow of a sword with the shaft of a stolen spear. Shanthah whipped the man in the back, giving Mara time to drive the spear through the soldier's stomach.

"Good one, Mara!" Shanthah exclaimed.

He twisted around to avoid being stabbed by another soldier and struck his foe across the neck with the whip. The slaver dropped his sword and Shanthah scooped it up, slicing out the man's ankles before landing the killing blow to his back. Two other soldiers overtook him, smacking him on the back with the shafts of their spears. He collapsed and dropped both weapons.

More slavers flooded through the gates, brandishing their weapons and shouting obscenities. Aleksander snaked through the fray, jumping over the corpse of the man Mara had stabbed.

Nearby, Mara missed her mark as she hurled her spear at a soldier guarding Belokej, but it gave Aleksander enough time to dart past before Josman shouldered the slaver to the ground.

"Get to Belokej!" Mara shouted as Josman parried a blow from a spear with a salvaged sword. Mara hurried after Aleksander through the fray and scooped up her fallen spear. They ran headlong at Belokej, who lashed his whip in the air as a challenge. Lavinia's dagger remained Aleksander's secret.

"Come on!" Belokej taunted.

His whip struck Aleksander between the neck and shoulder, and he stumbled and set his heel to the earth to steady himself. He recovered and leaped toward the slaver, who drew a blade from his hip and lashed out in a wild motion. Aleksander threw himself to the ground to dodge the strike, rolled, and pulled the dagger Lavinia had given him from his tunic.

Belokej whipped him hard in the hand, making him drop the blade. Mara wrapped her arms around the man's neck and began to choke the life out of him, but he slammed her against the wall behind her, and she released him.

The slaver kicked the dagger away and swung his blade over his head, grazing Aleksander's side. Blood soaked his tunic, and he grimaced, but knew he'd have to worry about it later.

Mara scooped the dagger from the dirt and threw it to Aleksander, who brought it around in an unsuccessful attempt to stab Belokej, but the slaver parried with the flat of his own sword. Mara tried to tackle Belokej again, and the slaver's sword flashed in the dim light as the weapon sprayed blood from her shoulder.

As more guards came to their leader's aid, Aleksander thrust the blade into Belokej's thigh. He pulled the crimson blade from the man's flesh and lashed out for his neck. Before he could land the blow, two guards grabbed him and pulled him back, making him drop the dagger.

Belokej raised his sword one more time to slice Aleksander's throat but screamed as Mara plunged Lavinia's dagger into his back. Once. Twice. Three times.

She twisted the blade, and he stumbled against the wall. More guards grabbed Mara and dragged her away as she roared with laughter.

Belokej collapsed in agony, but no more of his companions came to his aid. Aleksander caught a glimpse of Lavinia smiling from her seat at the head of the chamber as a soldier smacked him over the head, knocking him unconscious.

"Enough!" Belokej coughed. "Enough!"

The fighting did not stop. No one heeded his words as he crawled toward the exit, blood soaking through his clothing.

Lavinia stood and raised her wings high over her head. Everyone stopped fighting; without a word, she was able to end the battle when Belokej could not.

The surviving slaves regrouped at the far side of the chamber, and the soldiers and slavers exited the arena. In all, more soldiers lay dead in the makeshift arena than slaves. The three other slaves had perished, Aleksander was unconscious, and the others apart from Josman were all injured, but alive.

Lavinia entered the arena and grabbed Belokej by his unkempt, greasy hair and dragged him along, ignoring his piggish squeals of pain. As she left, she turned back to the slaves.

"The show is over. Go back to your districts," she said, looking somehow both pleased and disappointed.

"On your feet," Lavinia ordered, tucking her hair behind her ear. Belokej stood, and Lavinia pushed him against the wall of the exit tunnel. She wrenched the whip from his hand and pressed her thumb into his neck.

"What are you doing?" Belokej asked, wheezing, as his men shepherded the slaves away.

"What I should've done a long time ago to a coward who deserves it. You know exactly why. Do not forget this day."

"Killing me won't bring her back, you know!"

"You shut your disgusting, illiterate mouth unless I give you permission to speak. Is that clear?" Lavinia shouted the question and gave him five quick lashes, aiming for the wounds Mara had inflicted earlier. He collapsed backward, and she kicked him in the jaw, knocking one of his last remaining teeth into the dirt.

"Anything you'd like to say?" she asked.

He shook his head without looking up, and she dropped the whip onto his face then stepped over his limp, cowering form before exiting the chamber.

CHAPTER TEN
CRACKS IN THE WINDOW

The sound of hooves thundered through the village of Cineca just before the break of dawn. Villagers emerged from their homes to see soldiers clad in the regalia of the Thannish military. One held their banner aloft as if to answer any question of authority.

"What are you doing here?" asked Killian, the first man to approach the soldiers as a crowd gathered.

"We bring proclamation from his royal majesty, King Romiton Romus of Thanatanos, son of Jaromir, son of Rastislav, son of Vladislaus, son of Ottokar, son of Neklan, son of Nezamysl, first king of Thanatanos. By his order, the farming villages are to add a further twenty-five percent of their yield to fund the sieges in Talohira," said the soldier at the head of the party. "Your contributions will guarantee we at the front line are able to maintain your freedom—"

"Twenty-five percent?" cried one of the villagers. "We can't give any more than we do!"

"We'll be giving more than half of our harvest! There won't be enough for us to survive!" shouted someone else.

"All those who oppose the decree or cannot pay will be drafted to serve in the war in order to contribute where they can," continued the soldier. "We must all do our duty."

"Like hell!" cried Killian as he scooped a stone from the dirt. He tossed it over his head and missed his target but struck the flag of Thanatanos. This caused an outcry from the soldiers, who dismounted their horses and drew their blades.

The other villagers started throwing rocks as well, pelting the warriors as they advanced. Killian grabbed a sharp pitchfork from outside his house and charged the soldiers; his fellow countrymen followed close behind with rocks, sticks, or any farming equipment they could find close by.

"We do not want violence!" cried the soldier holding the banner as he was struck in the face by a heavy rock. "We are here to help!"

He fell from his horse holding his broken nose as the villagers swarmed him. The lead soldier swept his sword across the back of one of the countrymen, causing him to howl in pain. The rest scattered, and the soldier helped his fellow soldier to his feet.

"The king will hear about this, and the consequences will not end in Cineca. All men in the countryside will be taken to join the sieges!"

"Yeah? Then who the hell will do your precious farming?" cried Killian. "Get out of Cineca!"

He ran forward and thrust his pitchfork into the man's stomach. The soldier collapsed, blood soaking his leather armor. The others raced to his side, and the warrior holding the banner dropped the flag to the earth, drew his blade, and ran Killian through. Killian gasped and caught a glimpse of Valistaran's face beneath a helm crested with the colors of Thanatanos.

"Havel?" Killian whispered as he slumped to the ground.

His dying accusation faded away with the man's final breath, a single word that would have revealed Valistaran's treachery. Beneath his disguise, the king let out a breath and pulled the blade from the man's chest. He didn't like having to resort to this, but it did help his cause a great deal.

"May this man's fate be a lesson to you!" cried Valistaran as he helped the wounded soldier onto his horse. "We shall return tomorrow with further word from the king!"

With that, the disguised Talohiran soldiers departed, a cloud of dust trailing behind their horses. The villagers tried to help Killian, but there was no hope for the dead.

"He's gone," said one of his neighbors. "Someone— someone go tell Daniela. I..."

He trailed off as he cradled his friend's head in his lap. The townsfolk cursed Thanatanos and King Romiton, not knowing who was actually behind the vile deed.

The villagers held an impromptu funeral for Killian that night. It was without eloquence or flair, instead filled with immense sorrow. Some town musicians paid their respects, and the townsfolk listened with bowed heads.

Valistaran, under the guise of Havel, was in attendance and spoke of the hospitality of both Killian and his wife, Daniela. Daniela then also spoke with plain humility about her husband's life and her love for him and their missing children. He was laid to rest, and the village returned to their dwellings to await the morning.

A faint twinge of guilt gnawed at Valistaran's heart, but he recognized the fact that it might be the only way to end the war and prevent even more death. Perhaps, he thought, he'd have a statue of Killian brought one day to adorn the center of town to commemorate his role in ending the war. A memorial of which they would never know the true meaning.

When dawn arrived, a troop of soldiers approached the village on foot, and Valistaran grinned, for his plan was unfolding just as he had planned. He learned hours prior to the funeral that a real entourage of soldiers was coming to visit Cineca to bring word of the sieges and condolences for those that had lost loved ones to the slavers in Talohira. However, Valistaran had used his disguise and brought his own men to impersonate them a day early.

"They're back!" cried a sobbing Daniela, hoisting her husband's pitchfork over her head. The village was ready this time. Almost every citizen of the town was ready with sharpened farming instruments, knives, and the bravest of which wielded the dull swords, spears, and shields from the ramshackle town armory.

Valistaran led the charge, and before the soldiers could react, the townsfolk knocked two of them from their steeds and surrounded the other three. The soldiers called for the villagers to stop, but the defenders of the town did not heed their words or believe their claims of peace.

As the violence escalated, the Than soldiers had no choice but to draw their swords against the villagers, and four more citizens of Cineca fell to Valistaran's plan. In the end, the group of soldiers retreated, and a boisterous cheer escaped the crowd.

"We've done it!" cried Daniela, her heart filled with joy knowing she had done something to avenge her husband.

"More will come," said Valistaran as he slid the rusty sword into his belt. "Please, get the wounded to safety!"

"Havel, what will we do?" asked a villager brandishing a fallen soldier's sword.

"We can't fight them forever. This fight isn't won," said Valistaran. "We are stuck between two kingdoms at war. We cannot go to Laniras, but Talohira—"

"Sangora will take us!" cried Daniela. "A group of Night Witch soldiers—they came to our village a year ago. They said that we could join 'em if we'd like. They'd give us anything we need, long as we support them instead of Thanatanos."

"Well, what say you?" asked Valistaran. "I am no leader of your town, but in the short time I have been here I have felt a great love for this people. I will fight for you."

"Talohira!" cried another. "We could go to Talohira!"

Valistaran held his sword aloft.

"We cannot let Talohira bring us to their labor camps, but Elafris the Fallen knows that we cannot go to Thanatanos. I shall go to Sangora and Talohira for the rest of you. I will tell them what has transpired here, and I believe that they will defend us from Thanatanos. What do you say?"

There was a cry of approval from the crowd, and Valistaran nodded before saying, "Then it is decided. I shall go on your behalf. But what of the other villages? We can't beat this injustice with one town alone. While I am gone, you must warn the other villages. Spread this news."

"We'll do it, Havel!" said one villager.

"We can set out right now!" cried another.

In the hustle and excitement of the moment, the villagers departed to warn their countrymen of the new threat. Daniela remained behind.

"Thank you, Havel," she said. "I know Killian would have gone with you to Talohira to the courts of the king himself. The two of you would've done great things there to protect us."

"I will go in his stead, Daniela," he said, holding her hands between his. "Your husband's name will be sung in glory when this blasted war is over."

"Thank you again," she said.

"I will make this right," said Valistaran with a smile. And with that, he left Daniela and the village behind with no intention of returning. The cracks that would bring down the window that was Thanatanos had begun to spread.

CHAPTER ELEVEN
MARA'S MONSTER

A week's time passed since the ruse to kill Belokej had failed. During that time, several slaves had perished from hunger and fatigue while chained to the whipping posts, but the guards set the rest free, allowing them to return to their districts. Their final punishment was to collapse the escape tunnel from Rehor's tent, eliminating any chance of using it to gain freedom. Morale plummeted across the camp, and the slavers exploited the despair to torment their prisoners.

Mara sat next to the fire, sewing together the scraps of material Rehor had given her. She was the only one still awake, exhausted from the day's work but too anxious to fall asleep. She grimaced as she pricked her finger on the needle, and a dot of red blood welled up where she had pricked herself. She stuck it in her mouth to ease the pain as someone approached from behind, but she did not look up from her work. She did not care.

"I think I know the answer to this, but why did you need these materials, if you thought you would be out of here by now?" Rehor asked as he sat down next to her.

"If you know the answer, why do you ask?" Mara answered, continuing her sewing project. "I knew we weren't going to get out of here. I needed something to take my mind off our failure when we got caught."

"*When?* Oh, Mara. Have faith that what we're going through is not forever," her friend said. "Just think, a year from now, this slave camp will be a distant memory."

The corners of Mara's mouth moved in a feeble, yet feigned smile. Rehor patted her on the shoulder and glanced at the scraps of fragments in Mara's hands. They were beginning to take the rough shape of some kind of animal.

"How can you stay so positive?" Mara asked, choking back tears. "I feel like I'm drowning."

"Because of something a dear friend of mine once told me," Rehor replied. "She reminded me when I thought I was going to freeze to death this winter that spring will soon come. I've thought about that a lot, Mara. Spring always comes. Remember that, and you will be able to get through anything."

"Who was that?" Mara asked, starting to sew again.

Rehor laughed and stretched his tired legs toward the fire.

"Oh, just a young woman I know named Mara Bartunek. You might know her. The hope of new spring always comes back into our lives after the cold and darkness have taken it away. Hope is only dead when those that stoke its fires are too. Never forget that."

He kissed Mara on the top of the head and ruffled her inky black hair before getting to his feet. He turned to walk away.

"I think that girl is dead," Mara answered. Rehor chuckled again and stroked his scraggly beard.

"Dead? No. She's making a stuffed animal for someone who is scared. That girl is still alive, even if you can't see her. We all see her within you. Good night, my friend. Sleep well."

As Rehor walked off, Mara looked down at the crude imitation of a creature she was sewing and smiled softly to herself. She stuffed the empty animal with some straw and began to sew it up. She pulled a small chunk of coal from near the fire and drew a silly face on the creature's head. She stowed her creation in her tent without waking Hanna and headed back outside to sit alone in the solitude of night.

The next morning, Aleksander awoke to the sound of a soothing lullaby sung by someone outside. The sweet tune was somehow familiar, and the words seemed to spark something within him. Fleeting images of a broken family from his forgotten past faded from his mind like a dream upon waking up. And then, *that voice*.

"Whatever it takes, I'll hold your heart with mine…"

He emerged from his tent to find Mara cuddled against the bench near the dead fire. She was humming the lullaby to herself, her eyes pink as if she had been crying for quite some time.

"You slept out here last night?" he asked, sitting on the log next to her head, careful to keep his distance.

"I didn't sleep much, but yeah, I guess so," Mara answered. "I am so exhausted, Aleksander."

Too drained to listen to the mistrust gnawing at her mind, she scooted closer to Aleksander, letting her head fall onto his lap. Aleksander ran his fingers through her hair, assuming for some reason it would soothe her. He began to sing, continuing the lullaby where she had left off.

"…And from your side never will I depart… Even when my heart breaks, my dove… There with you, yes, there I'll be…"

She grabbed his hand and held it tight, not willing to let it go. He wondered why he knew the song but said nothing. They sat together hand in hand in the calm silence before the others awoke. Aleksander glanced down to see Mara silently sobbing onto his knee, but he said nothing of it.

Sometime later, Josman emerged from his tent, dragging a half asleep Drahomir with him.

"Ready for the new day?" he asked. Mara bolted up as they approached and shook Aleksander awake.

"Of course, never slept better in my life," Mara said.

"Glad to hear it even if I don't believe it. You'll need that strength to get through today," Josman replied, clanging the wooden spoon against the metal cooking pot hanging above the fire. The rest of the slaves groaned as they woke up.

"We're getting an early start today," Josman said as the others emerged from their tents. "I know it's rough, but the slavers have agreed to let us have the rest of the night off if we complete the tower's brickwork on the north wall. Can you imagine?"

"Almost like a vacation," Mara said. "I've got to change—I'll be right out. Don't eat my mush, Shanthah!"

Shanthah threw his hands up as the others started breakfast. She ducked into her tent and sat on her sleeping mat, head in her hands. She let out a long breath and undressed down to her underclothes before pulling on a set of work clothes that *weren't* covered in blood and pulled out her raggedy monster creation. As she did so, she saw a small scrap of parchment on her pillow.

Mara is a wonderful person. and we are lucky to know her. :)

—Aleksander

Her eyes welled up with tears, and a smile crossed her face, unable to look away from the note for a long moment. Her pockets both had large holes, so she stowed the parchment in her shirt and hurried back outside. There, she found her friends speaking with a stranger she'd never seen before.

"This is Antan," Hanna said with an exasperated expression and handed some porridge to Mara. "He's new. Isn't that *great?*"

"Can't wait to meet you, Antan," Mara said.

"Spy," Hanna muttered when she was sure he couldn't hear.

"They're not even trying to be sneaky," Mara muttered. "I'll be right back. I'll meet you guys back at the worksite."

She waited for a moment to say something to Aleksander, but he was deep in conversation with Antan and Shanthah, so she walked away from the group, taking her bowl with her. Her little brother Pol ran after her. Ignoring his questions asking where she was going, she strode as fast as she could to the thorn wall where she hoped she hoped to find the little girl Diana hiding there. She shook the brambles and vines, and soon Diana's grimy face appeared from the darkness.

"Hello beautiful! I have something for you," Mara said. Diana's eyes widened, and her smile brightened up her grimy face. "But you have to close your eyes!"

Diana did as she was told and held out her hands. She squirmed with excitement as Mara placed the stuffed creature in the little girl's hands. Diana opened her eyes and hugged Mara, burying her little face in her older friend's chest.

"Thank you, I love it!" Diana exclaimed, hugging the monster. "Thank you, thank you!"

"Diana, let me explain who your new friend is," Mara said, smiling. "This is your worry monster. You tell him what you're worried about, and he will gobble up all your worries and fears. He won't let anything bad happen to you."

Diana smiled and clutched the worry monster against her neck in a tight embrace. Mara hugged her little friend and sent her back into the crack in the wall to hide from the soldiers. She led Pol away, asking him to say nothing of the encounter as they joined their group on the way to the senate building.

When Mara and Pol made it to the worksite, Hanna greeted her with an exasperated sigh.

"He claims they sent him here from the mines."

"Belokej obviously sent him here to keep watch on us after the fight. We can't trust him," Drahomir hissed. Kamil nodded in agreement. "He's not the only one. Aleksander didn't use his powers at the fight, which was our main advantage."

Mara glared at Drahomir. "If you trust me, trust him."

"Yeah, but you don't think it's strange—"

"No. Drop it," Mara said. Kamil gave a thumbs up in agreement and started smearing the thick mortar where they would set the final bricks.

"Fine, whatever. Well, do you think Lavinia keep her word not to stop us even if we didn't finish Belokej off?"

"We have no other plans," Mara said. "So, it's irrelevant."

"Kamil has one," Hanna said.

"Yeah, but his plan is too complicated. We need them to bring us out on their own. I've seen them haul dead slaves out on a cart from the brick drop off. Couldn't we hide in there?"

"They check that cart. They'd know we were alive," Mara said. "But maybe. We can look into it if we can't think of anything else. Thanks for the idea."

Kamil raised his hand, and Mara turned her attention to him. He tapped the side of his head and smiled with a nod. He led Mara to the other side of the tower and then up the scaffolding. They climbed up to a hidden pully system and complex mechanism he'd constructed out of salvaged wood, rope, and various metal pieces atop the senate building.

"I don't understand," Mara said, cocking her head. Kamil pantomimed a catapult with his arm, and her eyes went wide.

"This might be an even crazier plan than Drahomir's. Is it finished?"

Kamil nodded.

"Then if we give you time to get it ready, could we try to escape today?" Mara asked, laying a hand on his shoulder, and he nodded once again. "Do you need anything?"

He then spread his arms wide, pantomiming a huge rock. He pointed to Josman and the others below.

"Okay, I'll tell them you need a big rock." Kamil shook his head and raised two fingers. "Two big rocks. This better work, you crazy genius."

She lowered herself down to the others by standing on the pulley platform and letting the rope go. She jumped off as it reached the ground, and she motioned for Josman to follow her.

When no one else was watching, he followed her toward the boulder staging area, explaining Kamil's request as they went.

Together, they searched for the two biggest boulders they could find and rolled them toward the tower. Using the pulley system, they raised the two boulders up to Kamil.

"What are you two doing?" Antan, the new worker asked from behind a pillar. "That's not the size of brick we're using."

"We needed to finish another part of the wall from yesterday," Hanna lied. "We needed a bigger piece."

"Then why didn't they tell us that information?" Antan asked. "You're doing something to sabotage the building, aren't you? I need to tell—"

Aleksander smashed Antan over the head with a wooden plank, and the man collapsed to the ground.

"I hope no one saw that, but I think we can all pretty safely say he was a spy," Aleksander said.

Mara and Josman just nodded.

"Yeah," was all she said.

"He's a very bad actor," Josman added.

Josman and Aleksander dragged Antan's unconscious body behind an unfinished wall and threw a dusty tarp over him.

"If you still don't trust me, you don't have to tell me what you're planning, just know that I'm here to make sure they don't find out," Aleksander said to Mara as Josman began hoisting the massive pieces of stone up to Kamil with Shanthah's help.

"We're not the ones you need to convince, kid," Josman said, huffing as he operated the pulley. Shanthah nodded.

"Oh?" Aleksander asked. Mara took his hand and led him a few yards away out of earshot of the others.

"Drahomir still doesn't trust you, which is stupid, because he's just as new as you. Neither did Borek. Hanna didn't, but she came around after the fight," Mara explained.

"And you?" Aleksander asked.

"I have more reason than the others to trust you," Mara said.

"I thought you had more reason *not* to."

Mara shook her head. "Not now. Listen, we can talk tomorrow, and I'll explain everything."

"I can wait," Aleksander said. Mara squeezed his hand.

At the top of the tower, Kamil tied a final knot, putting the finishing touches on his creation. He groaned as he used a pulley system of ropes to hoist a boulder onto the top of an archway.

He then attached a second empty net tied to the wooden beam atop the construct and beamed at his contraption.

"Kamil, you are a genius," Hanna said as she reached the top of the tower. She shook her head in amazement as she examined Kamil's handiwork. "Seriously good job, if I understand what you've made. If not, cool… thing."

She began to walk around the construct, but Kamil grabbed her arm and waved his other hand in a frantic circle. An apologetic look crossed the Kurashian's face, and she looked down to see dozens of notes scribbled in the dirt in Kamil's native tongue, Kurashic. Alongside the notes were dozens of diagrams and mathematical equations, which Hanna could not decipher.

"Oh, sorry!" Hanna exclaimed, and he gave her a gesture to know that all was well.

They continued working throughout the day until the last brick was set and mortared into the wall. Kamil and Drahomir remained behind to cover and disguise the creation until they were ready to use it, but the others made their way down to meet the rest of the group.

"Well, we're done for today," Hanna said, winking at Josman. The rest of the group set out, minus Antan, Drahomir, and Kamil. As they walked, Hanna and Mara explained the full plan in hushed whispers to the others. A soldier stopped the group in their tracks, his palm raised toward them.

"Where do you think you lot are off to?" he asked.

"We were told by Captain Darthon's men that if we completed the bricks on the tower, we could have some extra leisure time tonight," Josman explained.

"Unlikely. But if so, I'll examine your work," the soldier said.

Each member of the group hesitated, knowing that they would be punished if they found Kamil's device. The soldier led the group back toward the north wall of the senate building and began his ascent up a spiral staircase, avoiding the use of scaffolding, which was fit only for the slaves.

"If he sees what Kamil made, we're dead," Mara whispered to Josman, who nodded in agreement. The soldier continued upward, followed by Josman, Mara, and Hanna. They followed the guard across the wall and up a ladder leading up to the tower.

"Drahomir! Now!" Josman exclaimed.

Drahomir glanced down the ladder and saw the soldier approaching. He kicked the top rungs so that it fell backward, and it smashed against the opposite wall while Josman shouldered the bottom to make the soldier fall. The spur-of-the-moment plan worked, and the guard plummeted downward, screaming as he fell. The clang of his armor hitting stone echoed through the air. Josman breathed a sigh of relief and hoped no one heard the commotion. He looked at the guard's face and recognized him as one of the cruel slavers from the fight.

"Let's throw him in a hole!" Hanna said enthusiastically.

"Or even better, we can take this opportunity to find out what's in The Cage," Mara answered. "Take his armor."

Josman raised both eyebrows in curiosity and unbuckled the soldier's armor to remove it while Mara explained her plan.

"Drahomir! Get down here," Hanna called. Drahomir made his way down, and Josman and Shanthah climbed up to help Kamil with his creation. "Want to be useful?"

"I mean, yeah."

"Good. I think this armor will fit you best," said Hanna. Drahomir glanced at the unconscious guard. "Put this on."

"What are we going to do with *him?* Why am I doing this? What am I doing?" Drahomir asked. "Give me details, ladies."

"You're going to pretend to be a soldier. Take him to The Cage. I don't know, say he assaulted you or something," Mara said. "We need to find out what's in there."

"Why, exactly?" asked Drahomir. "Make Shanthah do it."

"Stop asking questions and do what we say," said Hanna with a chuckle. Drahomir shrugged in defeat as the two women helped him strap the armor on. "We think it might be able to help us somehow, and if Kamil's tool doesn't work, well…"

"You know, I could get used to two pretty girls helping me with my armor. I feel like a knight," Drahomir said. Mara deliberately pulled a strap too tight, restricting his breathing. He coughed and both Mara and Hanna laughed.

"When you get back, tell us everything you find out. We'll have finalized the escape plan by then," Hanna said. "Good luck, our brave knight."

Drahomir rolled his eyes at the sarcastic comment but smiled all the same. "Bye, princess."

"You know we're just giving you a hard time," said Mara.

Drahomir winked, and Mara and Hanna both saluted him in the guard uniform.

"You going to help me carry this thing?" Drahomir asked. He hoisted the man's upper body as Mara and Hanna each took a leg then made their way southward to the small hut at the far side of the encampment known only as The Cage.

"Okay," Mara said. "Don't die?"

"Don't die? That's all I get?"

Mara and Hanna hurried back to the others.

Fear filled Drahomir's racing mind as he wondered what he would find inside. He took a deep breath and knocked three times on the wooden door of the hut containing The Cage. Someone opened the door, but no light escaped the room. Whoever was inside was sitting in total blackness. His heart thundered in his chest, but he stepped inside, dragging the guard with him. The door slammed shut behind him.

The sweet fragrance of burning incense drifted into his nostrils; the complete darkness, utter silence, and the underlying scent of decay seemed to warp his very reality. He jumped as a soft, almost inaudible whisper filled the room like mist wafting around him. Whether out of fear or some strange magic, he could not move or speak, and a feeling of unease washed over him. He fumbled in the dark for the handle but to no avail.

"Hello?" he asked at last, drawing the soldier's stolen blade. There was no answer. "I was told to bring this prisoner to The Cage for assaulting a slaver—on me, that is."

"You are a liar, Drahomir." The speaker emphasized each syllable of his name before her voice faded away like smoke. "Tell me the truth."

"I am," Drahomir responded, once again frantically searching for the handle of the door. His heart pounded in his chest as the Night Witch stirred in the shadows. "You're a Mindspeaker, aren't you?" No response. He hated Mindspeakers. "Well, I need to get back to—"

The Sangoran cut off his words as she grabbed his arm and clasped a cuff of cold metal on his forearm. He wrenched it open, but a sharp spine within the object pierced his arm, causing him to stumble to the ground and hit his head hard against the wall.

Drahomir groaned and ripped the cuff from his arm then lashed out with his stolen blade, striking flesh.

He could not explain it, but the brief moment that the needle had pricked him felt like hours that stretched into days. When he broke free of the feeling, he frantically slammed his shoulder against the door to escape. He stumbled into the daylight, dizzy and confused, before kicking the door shut to prevent the Sangoran inside from following.

A sudden, splitting headache tore through his skull, and his vision began to spin. Voices that were not his own screamed in his mind, and he collapsed behind the hut as he tried to flee.

The cuff's inner spine had ripped a chunk of his flesh away when he removed it, and blood was trailing down his forearm. He stowed the cuff in the small pouch he used to carry building supplies, and then he lost consciousness.

CHAPTER TWELVE
QUEEN OF THE SLAVES

Three months of grueling work, malnourishment, and both physical and mental torture since the failed escape attempt had devastated morale and crushed all hope of freedom for Slave District Sixty-Eight.

Until now.

They had gained certain advantages, namely the stolen soldier's uniform, the cuff Drahomir had stolen, and Kamil's device constructed upon the unfinished tower, but an increased military presence in the camp had stalled their next attempt.

The crew, except for Hanna, sat around their campfire in silence after a particularly torturous day, but due to their suspicions that Antan was a spy for the slavers, they dared not speak of anything of substance.

No one even felt they could mention the harshness of Hanna's unjust punishment, although they all thought of it. She'd insulted a guard and then was taken away. They all suspected that Antan had been the one to turn her in. She hadn't said anything upon her return, but she was sopping wet and without a coat. Mara was now lying with her in their tent to get her body temperature back up.

Pol excused himself from the dinner circle without another word, and Aleksander took his empty bowl, setting it with his own. Sleep quickly claimed the boy's exhausted body and mind. In short, morale was as low as it had ever been.

At long last, Josman got to his feet and clapped Antan on the back. "You know, buddy, I haven't gotten to know you very well. How about we take a walk?"

Antan looked around and saw the spiteful eyes of all the other members of District Sixty-Eight boring into him, and he shrugged, clapped his hands on his thighs, and stood up.

"You know what, that'd be nice. I'd like to stretch my aching legs," he said, flashing a smile to the others. "I'll see you all later."

Josman led him away, and the group let out a collective sigh of relief. Antan looked over his shoulder, and Mara met his gaze with a vindictive glare, refusing to break eye contact until the man turned away.

"Thanatan bless Josman," Drahomir said. "I can't take that guy anymore! Can you believe that fake smile?"

Aleksander nodded. "Do you think he's even trying to hide the fact that he's a spy? He has some nerve, especially after—"

"Agreed," Shanthah said, cutting Aleksander's words off. "I hope Josman kills him for what he did to Hanna."

He let out a deep breath through his mouth to calm himself, but it didn't help. Nothing would until he knew Hanna was safe and was going to live.

He excused himself and ducked into Mara and Hanna's tent. A moment later, Mara emerged and took his seat without a word.

Antan had claimed that he'd been taken to be whipped several days ago but returned in a suspiciously good mood. The next day, Drahomir had been dragged away, interrogated, and beaten. The day after that was when Hanna had been taken. Drahomir shrugged it off, knowing Hanna had it much worse.

Mara's heart ached as she dwelled on thoughts of the horrible torture her friends were being forced to endure. She did not have to wonder what had happened to Hanna—she too had been subjected to all the torture their captors could imagine, and her heart was breaking for her friend.

"If Josman doesn't kill Antan, Belokej, and the rest of them, I'll do it myself," she said, trembling. She shook her head as a tear rolled down her cheek. "I swear it."

"I think we'll be right there with you. We've got to get out of here. I think it's time we use Kamil's trebuchet," Aleksander said.

"What if we get caught?" Drahomir asked. "I don't think it's a good time, and I don't want to end up like Borek or Patrik."

"Is it *ever* a good time?" Aleksander asked. Kamil nodded in agreement. "Antan's gone. What are we waiting for?"

"You know what? I do agree," Drahomir said as he finished bandaging a wound. "No time like the present, right? If we get caught, what more can they do to us?"

"If we do, I'll take the blame," said Aleksander. "About time I get my share of the suffering, don't you think?"

"We can't let you do that, and you know it," Mara said. "Maybe we shouldn't do it tonight, but if Antan is gone, maybe at least we can plan or—"

She stopped talking as Hanna emerged from the tent wrapped in both Mara and Shanthah's coats, as well as her scratchy blanket. Her auburn hair was wild, but dry, at least. She sat next to the fire, warming her hands. Mara hadn't let her earlier, knowing the dangers of warming up too quickly.

As if they had been waiting for Hanna to emerge, six sneering slavers approached their small camp. They whispered between one another snickering and pointing.

Mara approached with hatred and fury in her eyes.

"Well? Want to start something? You saw what we did to your boss!" Mara shouted. "Who wants to be next?"

"You're prettier than your friend," said the slaver with a chuckle as he grabbed Mara's wrist. "Come on, you're next."

Regret filled his eyes as Mara grasped the man's hair and pulled his head down with a crack, kneeing him in the face. He writhed on the ground holding his broken nose.

Aleksander, Shanthah, Kamil, and Drahomir scrambled to their feet to help, but before they could intervene, Mara grabbed the second guard's forearm, twisted his wrist in an unnatural direction, and then punched him twice in the throat.

The others joined the fray as onlookers cheered.

"Who wants some?!" Shanthah exclaimed and was instantly knocked to the ground with a blow to the chest. Aleksander's flame illuminated the night as he charred the neck of Shanthah's attacker, who dropped his dagger.

Mara wrestled the man for his fallen weapon; she drew her knee close then and kicked him hard in the chin. He cried out in pain and yanked her ankle backward as she reached for the knife.

Her fingers just grazed the hilt, and she swore under her breath as he dragged her away. She managed to flip onto her back just as the hulking man brought his foot down into her sternum, forcing the air from her lungs. He gasped as Mara thrust the knife into his leg then a moment later, drove it into his stomach.

"That's for Hanna!" she shouted.

He stumbled backward, and she drew in painstaking breaths with fiery rage emanating from her crystal blue eyes. Without another moment's hesitation, she swiped the blade across his neck and kicked him to the ground. He held his throat, gurgling with blood, as Mara buried the blade in his heart up to the hilt.

"And *that* is for *me*."

She rose, victorious and covered in blood over his limp body.

The other members of District Sixty-Eight had managed to subdue their assailants without killing them, having suffered only minor wounds. Hanna cheered and wrapped Mara in a hug.

"She just killed a slaver!" someone in the neighboring slave district called. In a matter of moments, the three other districts around them began to rise up against their masters as well.

Aleksander watched Mara with a smile as she stood like a queen among the slaves as they followed her example, fighting for everything they had left and everything they hoped to regain.

"I think it's time," Aleksander said, turning to Kamil, who looked toward his makeshift trebuchet. "You ready, buddy?"

Kamil nodded and took a deep breath just as Josman came running back to their campsite without Antan. Horns sounded all around the slave camp, and armed soldiers rushed in.

"Not sure what you did, but it's working! Get going! We'll hold them off!" Josman ordered. Aleksander and Kamil hesitated, and Josman pointed at the senate building. "Go!"

Aleksander and Kamil raced toward Kamil's creation as more districts joined the riot, clashing with their captors. To their good fortune, the soldiers' focus was on the commotion, so they ignored the two men as they sprinted toward the unfinished senate building.

Aleksander helped Kamil scramble up onto a high platform beneath the main pulley system. Kamil signed to Aleksander to send him up, and he obliged, hoisting the thick ropes to lift Kamil up past the scaffolding to the top of the building. His breathing was heavy, but he anchored the pulley and hoped Kamil knew what he was doing.

An crossbow bolt struck the wall behind him, and he crouched behind a column of an arch. He could hear a couple of guards shouting at him to show himself. He didn't have much time; they'd be on him—and Kamil—in moments.

Aleksander knew he was Kamil's only defense, so he took a deep breath, let it out through his mouth, and then emerged from his hiding spot with a fireball in each palm. As he hurled flame at the soldiers, a boulder soared through the sky. The soldiers watched in awe, and Aleksander kicked one from the platform and then cast a ball of flame into the other's face.

High above Aleksander, Kamil readied the second chunk of brick, using a set of rollers to maneuver it into place. He hoisted a rope that dropped a large boulder from the top of an arch, causing the wooden arm of his construct to swing around, hurtling the second chunk of stone through the air.

He prayed to the many gods of Kurash that his calculations were correct and cheered as the brick crashed against the wall of the slave camp; a large portion of the barrier exploded in a shower of bramble, stone, and splintered wood.

Slaves from all over the camp raced toward the new opening and the hope of freedom. Those still on a work shift stopped their labor and joined the flow of the others, and the rest of the guards pursued them. Kamil smiled at the beautiful sight before he readied the final block.

He adjusted the weapon to face east, reset the arm, and tied up the final boulder. With his heart thundering in his chest, he tugged the rope, sending the last missile flying. He scrambled down the scaffolding and smashed the mechanism of the pulley so it lowered the lift with him aboard.

The boulder decimated the eastern gate, and Kamil cheered once again with a wide smile. The riot had pulled most of the soldiers from the heavily guarded area, leaving it vulnerable.

Kamil tried to climb down the scaffolding toward Aleksander, but a rush of guards below blocked his escape.

Aleksander looked up at his friend in horror, knowing he was about to be overwhelmed.

"*GO!*" An unfamiliar voice spoke directly to Aleksander's mind as he watched Kamil gesturing for him to flee. The mute Kurashian flashed a thumbs up as if to indicate he would be okay. Aleksander took a deep breath and reluctantly obeyed.

"Aleks! Over here!" Aleksander heard Mara's voice ring over the madness, and he raced toward her, his heart filled with guilt.

"Kamil couldn't get down from the tower!" Aleksander shouted. "Where are the others?"

"Damn it! We can't find Pol or Drahomir either!" she replied. "I had to come back for you, but we have no more time to wait!"

Tears streamed down her face as she scanned the riot one last time trying to locate her brother and their friends. She stalled for as long as she could then they ran for their lives.

Josman, Shanthah, and Hanna waved them over as they arrived at the eastern gate. Mara grabbed Aleksander's shoulder before they followed their friends through the breach.

"Listen—you have no idea how happy I am that you were telling the truth and are on our side. There's so much you need to know. I know who you are, Aleksander. Who you *really* are."

She grabbed his hands and looked down at his lips for a brief moment before meeting his gaze. His heart fluttered, and he cursed himself as his next words slipped from his mouth.

"I hate that I'm saying this, but let's get out of here first."

"No time now, I know," she replied, and they ran to the gate.

"Kamil didn't make it down—have you seen Pol or Drahomir?" Aleksander asked, although he already knew the answer. Josman shook his head with a sad expression, and every member of the crew knew they had to move on.

Several soldiers stood in their path, but Aleksander kept them at bay with bursts of flame. He knew he couldn't keep them away forever; he was tiring, and his arms felt as if they were going to explode from the heat of his fire.

Dozens of other slaves raced through the eastern gate, but a group of Sangorans and heavily armed human Talohiran soldiers stood in the way of their freedom. Aleksander stumbled, completely exhausted from overusing his powers. Mara draped his arm over her shoulders to help him along.

"Come on, Aleks! You've got this!"

The group of slaves that had made it to the gate hesitated, surrounded by their foes. Several slavers with bows nocked arrows, pointing them into the crowd.

"The western breach is closed," said a man with a sniveling, nasally voice to his compatriots. Mara stood on her toes to see over the crowd and swore loudly as Belokej waddled up next to his fellow guards. "And you, slaves! Everyone dies, unless whoever is in charge of this shows himself. That person confesses, or you all die! So, what'll it be, you useless lot?"

No one moved for what felt like an eternity until Mara stepped forward. The wind played with her dark hair, and she stood still, staring at her foes with courageous resolve.

"I am to blame," she said.

Hanna hurried out of the crowd after her, followed by Aleksander, Josman, and Shanthah.

"I didn't think anyone would actually show 'emselves!" Belokej shouted. "What a wonderful surprise!"

Standing behind Mara, Hanna closed her eyes to focus, and a small stone floated from the ground before settling in her palm. She cried out and launched the stone like an arrow straight through the nearest guard's throat in a spray of crimson.

The archers let loose their arrows into the crowd but were lost in the stampede that ensued; the slaves trampled their former masters, and the soldiers and slavers that remained followed Belokej's command to protect him from the onslaught.

"That was amazing, Hann!" Shanthah shouted. "So gross, but amazing!"

At last, the crowd of slaves broke through the ruined gates with great cheers only to meet a small company of Sangoran soldiers wielding crossbows, spears, and swords.

A collective despair washed over the group of slaves; they had escaped the camp's walls, but even their larger numbers would not be enough to overwhelm their foes this time.

Mara stepped forward, completely unarmed, closing the distance between the slaves and the soldiers.

"Well?" she asked after a few moments of silence.

Lavinia emerged from the midst of the soldiers with a smile. She met Mara where she stood between the two groups.

"Well, what?" the Mistress of Dusk asked.

"You know exactly what we want."

"I do. And who are you now, the queen of the slaves?"

"So, what if I am?" Mara asked.

Lavinia said nothing for a few seconds. "Is he dead?"

"Who?" Mara asked. Lavinia chuckled.

"You know exactly who I mean."

"No," Mara admitted.

"I'm sure you know of the deal I made with Aleksander?" Lavinia replied. "Kill Belokej, get a free ticket out of here."

"I'll tell you what—let us go, and I'll gladly kill that monster with my bare hands," Mara said. "I'm a bit busy right now, though, so I'll have to come back after they're all free."

Lavinia smiled.

"I like you, Queen of the Slaves," Lavinia said. "You're free to go. I'll be in touch."

Mara recoiled in shock. "What? Why?"

"Valistaran had my sister, Natalia, captive to keep me in line. Let's just say that the leverage these monsters once had over me is no longer an issue," Lavinia said. "You are free, as are we."

She called for her troops to return to the camp. The company moved on, confused, but obedient to her order. The mass of slaves cheered in celebration, but the former members of Slave District Sixty-Eight did not, for three of their friends had been lost somewhere in the fray.

With that thought heavy on each of their hearts, Aleksander, Hanna, Shanthah, and Josman encircled Mara and piled onto one another in a massive group hug. Slave District Sixty-Eight was no more, but its former members, even those that were missing, were now bonded as close as family. They embraced one another amidst tears of joy and grief. When they let go, Mara led her companions and the rest of the slaves away from the camp.

Freedom belonged to them.

CHAPTER THIRTEEN
WHATEVER IT TAKES

In the two days since their escape, thirteen of the runaway slaves had succumbed to the elements, starvation, or infection. The rest were not far behind. Many believed that it was Lavinia's twisted way of killing them without having to do it herself, but Mara did not believe that to be the case.

The sound of horses and carts making their way over the hills filled the air, and panic spread through the group.

"Everyone, quiet!" Shanthah said, jogging in the direction of the commotion. "Into the forest, but not too far—and stay low!"

As Aleksander helped an older slave hide amongst the trees, Shanthah turned and winked in his direction before turning invisible. Aleksander had to stop himself from crying out in surprise as he watched Shanthah's footprints trail through the mud.

"Did you guys know he could do that?" Josman whispered.

"I did," Hanna whispered back with a wide smile. "He tried to keep his powers secret in the camp, but he did a lot of good with them and didn't even take credit."

Aleksander smiled as he lay face to face with Mara in the undergrowth. The trees of the forest were sparse enough that the escapees were visible, so they obeyed Shanthah's command and pressed themselves as low as possible in the shrubbery.

The thunderous crashing of wheels and hooves on stone grew louder, and no one dared breathe, fearing that their captors would somehow hear them.

The carriages were close enough now that they could make out the angry voices echoing through the woods. Someone called out that they found one of the shallow graves filled with those that had died, and another proclaimed that he had found footprints leading into the woods.

Mara watched Aleksander close his eyes, as if doing so would banish the slavers. She let a slow breath before doing the same. She felt his hand brush hers, and a jolt of surprise filled her, and her chest swelled with unexpected joy. She found his fingers and they interlaced with the spaces between her own.

Screams and the sound of metal clashing against metal replaced the voices of the soldiers and slavers. Mara's eyes shot open, and she instinctively withdrew her hand from Aleksander's.

The commotion ended, but nothing happened for several minutes. At last, A collective sigh of relief filled the woods as Shanthah returned.

"It's safe to come out now, everybody," he said.

The runaways all got to their feet, speaking in worried tones and hugging one another. Hanna leapt to her feet and wrapped Shanthah in a tight hug.

"What was it?" she asked. "Slavers?"

"Yes, but not many," Shanthah said. "A scouting party. They're not a problem anymore, but it looks like they broke off to look for our group specifically. A company of Talohiran soldiers recaptured the rest of the escapees, so I think we're the only ones who made it out."

"Did Lavinia go back on her word?" Aleksander asked.

Shanthah shook his head. "They were not Lavinia's people. The king's men. The main group is heading toward Bukaral. Probably to the empire prisons."

"That means they're still alive, and *that* means there's still a chance to save everyone that got left behind," Josman said.

"If you think we're going to be able to infiltrate Bukaral Prison, you're mad," Mara said, gesturing to the group of slaves. "This is all we have to work with."

"Well, not *all* we have to work with," Shanthah replied with a grin. "Everyone, I'd like you to meet a friend of mine from the Court of Thanatan. It's okay—you're safe!"

Aleksander, Hanna, Josman, and Mara emerged from the woods first, and Shanthah coaxed the rest of the timid escapees from their hiding places. They spoke in hushed voices, their words excited and hopeful as they referenced guardian angels, miracles, and the Court of Thanatan.

A man wielding a circular, golden shield and a long spear with a pointed blade stood next to Shanthah. He set the weapon in the earth, placed his shield on his back, and removed his plumed helmet to show that he meant no harm.

"I am General Hokkod, and as Shanthah correctly said, I am from the Court of Thanatan. He wasn't correct in saying that you were safe, however. Far from it," the warrior said. "Come."

He placed his helmet back upon his head and turned away.

"It's okay. You can trust him," Shanthah said.

It took a few minutes, but each of the runaways ventured out of the sparse woods and followed Hokkod up the nearest hill where a grizzly scene of dead slavers and crashed carts greeted them. A second group of slaves Hokkod had freed moments earlier sat traumatized and shaking behind an overturned cart.

"I was only able to stop three slave carts from escaping, but the rest got away," Hokkod said with a sigh. He opened the back doors of one of the vehicles and motioned inside. "Please, would the elderly, sick, or injured please climb aboard? Everyone else will have to walk, I'm afraid."

As he readied the horses to pull the cart, Aleksander wondered if he had set the others free, as no animals were attached to the other ruined vehicles. Shanthah helped Hanna into the cart, and she squeezed his hand gently as she collapsed, exhausted, onto one of the benches.

"Where are we going?" Mara asked. "We can't possibly be walking all the way back to Thanatanos."

"The Court of Thanatan has a safehouse nearby where I monitored the situation in the slave camps," Hokkod said.

"The Court knew we were there and did nothing about it?" Josman exclaimed. The rest of the slaves cried out as well.

"Believe me, I agree. I've been trying to get authorization for our order to help, but it wasn't granted," Hokkod answered. "But perhaps we will be able to rescue those of your friends and family that weren't as lucky as you."

"There's nothing *lucky* about what we've been through," Mara replied. Hokkod nodded in apology but said nothing.

With the weaker slaves safely aboard, they set out. They traveled for an hour into the woods until the cart stopped near a massive oak tree. Hokkod climbed off the vehicle and pulled back a fake bush, uncovering a nondescript wooden panel built into the base of the tree. He knocked three times, and the panel withdrew, revealing a tunnel lined with torches.

"How are you doing, friend?" Hokkod asked Shanthah.

"Oh, fine," Shanthah replied. "Did you think I was dead?"

"We all did. Your segment of the Royal Guard all is."

Shanthah nodded, his expression sad. "I know."

"But of course, I'm sure the story of your escape is as theatrical and dramatic as should be expected of you," Hokkod said with a chuckle. "Are you able to help plan a rescue mission?"

"Absolutely," Shanthah said. "Although I think we could all use a good meal first."

"Coming right up," Hokkod replied with a nod.

As they spoke, Aleksander and Josman helped everyone from the back of the cart. They each took a moment to stretch their aching limbs, and then Hokkod led them all into the tunnel.

It branched off into various chambers, but Hokkod led them straight until they came to a large amphitheater lined with cots instead of chairs. Several men and women began to distribute warm bowls of stew and a chunk of bread to each of the newcomers, many of which broke down crying at the sight of real food, and graciously accepted it. The healers at a makeshift medical station began tending to the wounded.

"Please, everyone—eat as much as you'd like. There is plenty of food for everyone," Hokkod said, gesturing to a massive cauldron filled with the hearty stew. The feeling of joy and hope in the room was almost palpable.

He paused by the door, and Shanthah hurried over to his former crew, holding a bowl of stew in each hand and a chunk of bread between his teeth. He dropped it into one of the bowls so that he could speak and greeted his friends with a smile.

"Hokkod invited me as a scout of the royal guard to help coordinate getting everyone home and to save those being taken to Bukaral," Shanthah said, glancing over his shoulder to see Hokkod waiting by the door. "We're going to try to save everyone, but we have another important mission that I'll tell you about later. One a bit more related to my old job."

He paused for a moment and Aleksander raised his eyebrows. "You want to tell me now, don't you?"

"Obviously, yes. Okay, apparently, the crown prince, Xanthurias Romus was captured after a diplomatic mission into Doftaan. So, we're also planning how to save him and a few other members of the Court of Thanatan!"

Mara's eyes shot up at the mention of the prince's name.

"That's great—I'm glad you get to be of use," Aleksander said. "Hopefully we can help too."

"It seems like something I'd brag about, but no—I mean, what I was trying to say is don't leave or get repatriated or whatever until I get back, okay?" he said, glancing at Hanna in particular, who offered a happy smile and a thumbs up.

"We'll be here, sleeping and eating," Aleksander said. Shanthah chuckled and jogged back to Hokkod.

"You know, I'm relatively content right now," Hanna said as she, Aleksander, Josman, and Mara sat together slurping their stew. "Relatively meaning, well, the fact that I'm dreading pretty much everything to come after this moment."

Mara laughed. "Then enjoy this one. I know I sure am. Food and friends—what more could a girl ask for?"

She bumped Hanna's shoulder with her own.

She motioned over her shoulder in Shanthah's direction, and a thin smile stretched across Hanna's lips. Hanna gave a quick nod in response and brought a spoonful of stew to her mouth before her smile gave away her thoughts.

"What was that?" Josman asked.

"Absolutely nothing." Mara laughed and winked at Hanna, who stuffed a lump of bread in her mouth as she began to laugh.

"Josman, I wanted to ask—what happened to Antan? You took him away just before the riot started. Thanks for that, by the way. He was really bringing us all down," Aleksander said.

Josman laughed darkly into his stew.

"Josman Faros, what on earth did you do to that weaselly little snitch?" Hanna asked. Mara pushed her empty bowl away and lay on her stomach next to Aleksander, resting her chin on her hands.

"Ah, him. Well, I guess you could say I lost him," Josman replied, fluffing his pillow.

"Where?" Mara asked.

"In a hole, where he belongs," Josman said with a shrug.

"That's *exactly* what I wanted for him! Thank you!" Hanna exclaimed, hugging Josman from the side.

Their laughter echoed through the chamber as Josman lay down on his cot and shut his eyes, a wide smile still on his face.

"He deserved that, and you deserve a good night's sleep," Aleksander said, still chuckling. "Good night, big guy."

He let out a great snore, much to Aleksander and Mara's amusement. They looked to Hanna, who had also drifted off moments before. Mara turned onto her side, supporting her head with her hand.

"So… Where will *you* go?" Mara asked.

Aleksander knew the question wasn't idle chatter to fill the silence, and he let out a deep sigh.

"I think you might know the answer to that question better than I do." He sat cross-legged on the floor next to Mara's cot so that their faces were level with one another.

"Yes and no," Mara said, drifting off. She averted his gaze.

"You said you know who I am—where I'm from," Aleksander said. "Is now a good time—can I know my name?"

"No. I wish it were, Aleks." It was her turn to sigh, and she massaged the bridge of her nose. "How do I put this? It isn't a story I'd like to rush—and one I'd like to share with a bit more privacy. Besides that, something else came up. A question I need answered first. It's impossible to explain right now."

"Okay. I won't push. Can you at least tell me where I'm from so that I know where to go next?"

"I owe you that much," Mara said with a nod. "You're from Laniras, but I don't know if you'll go back there. That's why I said yes and no. I'm sorry—I know that's frustrating. After we find Pol—if we find him, I mean—"

"When we find him," Aleksander interrupted.

"Yes. When we find him," Mara said with a sad smile. "When we find Pol, I'm going to head back home to Cineca." She hesitated before continuing. "I want you to come with me."

"I think—I think I would like that very much," Aleksander stammered. "Is it nice there?"

Mara smiled, remaining silent as she gazed into Aleksander's eyes. "It's the best. I know you'd like it. I wanted to run away from there for so long, but after everything that's happened, I want to go back more than anything. We have—well, had—little concerts in the center square almost every night, you know."

"That sounds great," Aleksander said, and Mara nodded.

"It is." She moved next to Aleksander on his cot.

"I have to ask. When you held my hand earlier, was that—"

Before Aleksander knew what was happening, Mara leaned forward and pressed her ruby lips against his. At that moment, nothing else in the world mattered. He placed his hand on her cheek, and she smiled back at him, letting out one little laugh, her forehead pressed against his.

"I know this is a strange request," Mara said. "I feel silly asking, but—well, will you sing to me? The song. You know—"

"I know," Aleksander said, glancing at the others. Everyone was already asleep. "One of the few things I actually remember."

She rested her head on his pillow, and he lay next to her. He brushed his fingers on the bare skin of her arm, and his voice was shaky as he began to sing.

> *Whatever it takes, my love*
> *I'll hold your heart with mine*
> *And from your side never will I depart*
> *Even when my heart breaks, my dove*
> *There with you, yes, there I'll be.*

Mara's eyelids began to droop, and Aleksander felt her grip on his hand relax. He stopped singing for a moment to check if she had fallen asleep.

"That song is from my village," she muttered, her voice soft and happy for the first time in ages. "My mama's song…"

> *Whatever it takes*
> *My dear sweetheart*
> *For both our sakes*
> *far from death's black dart*
> *There with me, yes, you'll be*
> *Whatever it takes.*

From her breathing, he could tell she was at last asleep. He kissed the top of her head of dark hair and smiled.

"We'll save the others, Mara—whatever it takes."

CHAPTER FOURTEEN

BLOOD FOR BLOOD

Mara flinched at the sound of the breakfast bell ringing out throughout the entire underground facility, and she turned the shower knob, stopping the flow of warm water raining down on her. Her heart thundered in her chest even though she knew she was safe. It had been three days, and the sound of the bell still set her on edge, for it was far too similar to the ones used in the slave camp. Despite that, standing in the shower was the most human she'd felt in years, and she couldn't stop thinking about how grateful she was for running water—*warm* running water.

She retrieved a scratchy towel and quickly dried off and dressed, leaving her hair damp and messy so that she wouldn't miss the important meeting, but more importantly, that she wouldn't miss breakfast.

She approached her friends just as Hanna awoke with an exaggerated stretch and saying, "Good morning, everyone!"

"Good morning, beautiful!" Mara said, wrapping an arm around Hanna. "Ready for our collective nightmare to be over? I can't believe we're actually going home soon!"

She sat next to Aleksander on his cot, and a soldier immediately handed her a fork and a bowl full of eggs and bread, which she accepted with a gracious smile. The others were also already happily eating their own breakfast. Aleksander slid a crispy strip of meat into Mara's bowl.

"They ran out before you got back, so I wanted to make sure you got some," he said. A smile lit up her face, but before she could thank him, Hokkod approached a podium at the head of the amphitheater, his voice amplified by the shape of the room.

"While you eat, we need to discuss the day's plan. Before that, however, I would like you to meet the three other members of the Court of Thanatan that will accompany you on your respective journeys."

Surprised whispers filled the room as three other figures filed into the chamber and joined Hokkod near the podium. The first was clad in similar armor as Hokkod, but his two companions were a massive minotaur and another man clad in a full suit of armor at two feet taller than the other men. An axe was strapped to the Minotaur's side, and he carried a curious obelisk with a large gem set in its face on his back.

"Let me introduce Lieutenant General Itrus," he said, pointing to the towering warrior, "and, of course, his lieutenants, Bovin the Minotaur and Manitrius Ondrus."

"Itrus is a spirit warrior," Shanthah muttered as Hokkod continued speaking. "There are a few of them left—basically, they're warriors who have died or been injured and had their spirits somehow fused to those giant suits of armor. Thought you might be confused. Oh, and Aleksander, don't worry about Bovin. He's not like that one that ambushed us. He's a big softy."

Aleksander chuckled, and the others nodded in understanding. Shanthah gave a thumbs up, and they turned their attention back to Itrus and Hokkod.

"Sangoran insurgents ambushed and captured Prince Xanthurias Romus and General Valakor on their way back from a diplomatic session to negotiate the end of Talohira's Siege of Vudapas. We do not believe they were under direct orders from state actors to do so, however. We have received intelligence that they will be moved from Doftaan's prison into Bukaral sometime today. Lieutenant General Itrus will lead a small force into Bukaral to intercept the transfer, while Bovin and Manitrius will accompany those who wish to return to Thanatanos on their journey. Likewise, I will be leading the mission into Doftaan to save the slaves taken from the camp. General?"

"Thank you, Lieutenant Hokkod," Itrus said. His voice bore an ethereal quality, but what was most strange to the others was that it lacked any kind of echo. "My men will accompany me, but I have been informed that several of you that have escaped possess abilities. Magic, some call it. We invite any with military training to accompany us. Please, step forward."

"Hokkod gave me permission to replace the dead members of my company in the Royal Guard," Shanthah said quickly. "I was going to ask you later, but now's a good of time as any."

The former members of Slave District Sixty-Eight looked to one another and nodded, as if having a telepathic conversation. The four friends stood, as well as two others nearby. Shanthah raised his fist as if he had secured a great victory.

"I had hoped for more, but I thank each of you," Lieutenant General Itrus said. "Please, come forward."

The six volunteers set down their finished bowls of porridge, except for Shanthah, who continued to eat as they walked.

"That will be all," Hokkod said, and the rest of the slaves went back to their breakfast. He turned to the volunteers. "Please, be aware: this is not a diplomatic mission. These are military operations, and the chance of death or injury is high," Hokkod said. "Please exercise sound judgment before agreeing to come along. If you would, please inform me of your abilities."

Josman stepped forward. "Corporal Josman Faros. I served under Captain Horvath in the Thannish armed forces."

"Very well, Corporal Faros," Itrus said, sizing Josman up. He gestured to the other side of the podium. Josman the Lieutenant General. The visor of the warrior's helm seemed to lead into darkness, save for two glowing, cyan eyes.

"Shanthah Kalen of the royal guard—please join Corporal Faros and Lieutenant General Itrus. We are well aware of your ability of invisibility and your qualifications. And the rest of you?" Hokkod asked, turning to Aleksander, Mara, Hanna, and the other two volunteers.

"Private Petar Goncharov and my brother, Private Sandor."

"Any powers?" Hokkod asked.

"Not that we know of," answered Sandor.

"Very well. With me, then," Hokkod said. He looked to the others, and Hanna glanced at Mara, who offered an encouraging nod. Hanna reached out for Shanthah's finished bowl of porridge, and it floated out of his hands. Those watching let out a collective gasp as she caught it before setting it on the floor.

"Ah, a Telekinetik," said Hokkod. "Very good. Perhaps your skills will be most useful to save our prince and general."

He gestured for Hanna to join Shanthah and Josman behind Itrus. Aleksander lit a ball of flame in his palm before extinguishing it, and Hokkod gestured in the direction of the Goncharov brothers.

"And you?" Hokkod asked.

"No powers. No military experience," Mara said.

"Then you're going home," Hokkod replied.

"Like hell. My brother is in there somewhere, and if I have to, I'll take your spear and I'll walk in there myself," Mara replied. Shanthah pulled Hokkod aside and whispered something to him.

"And if that threat isn't enough, you did tell me I could recruit my new squad members," Shanthah said. "And powers or not, this woman could walk into Bukaral, punch King Valistaran right in the throat, and walk out unscathed. I've seen her do things like that before, man. You want her here."

"So be it," Hokkod said. "With me, then, but please, don't let your brother's freedom cost you your life."

"Well, I won't let *my* freedom cost him *his* life either."

The minotaur unstrapped the stone pillar from his back and set it up before the others. He placed his massive, hairy hand on the gem, and it thrummed to life, emanating a dim green glow.

"Thank you, Bovin," Itrus said. "Now, if you and Lieutenant Manitrius will accompany the rest of the refugees outside, we have arranged enough carts to carry them all home."

Bovin and Manitrius led them away, and Mara grasped Aleksander's hand and gave it a nervous squeeze.

"This Teleportation Pillar, or Telepillar, will send us where we need to go. First, I will send one group to intercept the slave carts heading to Doftaan, and then I will recalibrate the machine to send the rest of us into Bukaral," Itrus explained. "Those heading to Bukaral will take the pillar with them and will need to complete their mission in enough time to help the others get home. The signal to reunite will be a ray of blue light."

Mara's heart pounded in her chest. She hadn't considered the specifics of the mission, and her thoughts turned dark.

"Please, place your hands on the pillar," Itrus ordered.

Aleksander, Mara, Petar, Sandor, as well as a handful of the Court of Thanatan's soldiers did as they were commanded. Hokkod took a deep breath, and then he slammed his fist on the green gem. There was a flash of green light and flame, and Mara and Hanna shared a smile before the first group vanished.

"And now, the same for us," Itrus said. He, Hanna, Shanthah, Josman, and some soldiers took their turn to touch the pillar of stone and metal.

Itrus activated the machine, and green flame engulfed them. Hanna felt her body dematerialize in a sudden burst of light energy before stitching itself back together, but she could not scream. She reappeared with no air left in her lungs, and she took a few deep breaths before regaining herself.

She glanced around, finding herself within an abandoned home furnished with only a rickety table and several chairs. The windows were covered with dusty wooden planks, and the door was barred with a heavy steel beam.

"Where are we?" Hanna asked. "Should we talk about this before we run in?"

"We don't have time," Itrus said. "We're near Bukaral's prison. Shanthah, use your powers to scout ahead. Hurry back here when you see them approaching. They will have a military escort, but not as heavy of one as they had traveling between Doftaan and Bukaral, which is fortunate for us."

"Might as well get some rest before Shanthah gets back," Josman said as he pulled up two chairs—one for himself and another for Hanna.

"I'll be back soon," Shanthah said. He and Hanna shared a brief hug before he vanished. Itrus unbarred the doorway, and the door seemingly opened and closed itself as an invisible Shanthah departed. Hanna sat down next to Josman while Itrus and the few soldiers that had accompanied them readied their weapons, handing a sword to each of them.

"Does something feel off about all this?" Hanna asked, just loud enough for Josman to hear. She unsheathed the blade then rested it on her lap. Josman leaned his chair back on two legs, resting his head against the wall with a heavy sigh.

"You mean that they're only sending one spirit warrior, a couple soldiers, and a ragtag team of exhausted slaves to save two of the most important people in Thanatanos and infiltrate Doftaan? Yeah. I just didn't want to say it."

"Think they'll be alright?" Hanna asked. Josman shrugged.

"I don't know if any of us will be," he said. "Sometimes stories just don't have happy endings—not to say that ours won't, as much as I hope it does."

Hanna nodded. "Yeah. I know what you mean."

The group sat in silence for nearly an hour until there was a sharp rap on the door. Two of the soldiers let Shanthah inside, and he stumbled into the room, his breath heavy.

"They're coming!" he exclaimed. "Itrus was right. They've got Sangoran and human forces guarding them, but not many."

"Stay with the pillar," Itrus ordered, and one of his soldiers nodded, while Shanthah and the others followed him out.

Hanna and Josman shared an apprehensive glance before they followed Shanthah, Itrus, and the other soldiers from the chamber. They made their way up a path and then crouched behind a low wall and patch of trees lining the street.

The whistle of a merry tune broke the silence, and Shanthah peered over the wall. "It's a little girl."

The girl whistled three times like a bird before continuing her original tune. Itrus popped up and unsheathed his twin blades as he eyed the child standing in the middle of the road whistling.

"What are you doing?" Hanna hissed.

Itrus crouched, readying himself to leap over the wall, but as he did so, Hanna cried out, slamming the warrior to the ground with her telekinetic ability. He struck the earth with a resounding clang, and he raised his head as if peering into Hanna's soul with eyes glowing with blue fire.

"What have you done?" he asked as the girl ran away.

"You were going to kill a *child?*" Hanna exclaimed.

"A child signaling that she had found us!" Itrus shouted in response. "We lost our cover, and with it, our only advantage!"

He leapt over the fence, and his soldiers followed close behind. Shanthah turned toward Hanna, who threw up her hands in frustration, tears in her eyes.

"I know," Shanthah said, touching her shoulder. "I know."

Itrus shielded his soldiers with his own body as a shower of arrows rained down, bouncing off his thick armor.

"Take down those oxen! Kill them!" Itrus ordered, gesturing at the animals pulling the cart. Shanthah and Hanna hurried toward the beasts while Josman and the other soldiers engaged the Talohiran soldiers, and the clash of blades filled the night air.

The oxen bellowed as their harness fell away, loosed by Shanthah's unseen hands. Hanna then pulled on it with her mind, and the animals ran free down the streets of Bukaral away from the sudden battle. Hanna smiled, knowing that Shanthah had freed them rather than kill them.

She cried out as a massive minotaur charged at her, and then Shanthah shouted in pain as knocked him to the ground. He covered his head to avoid being trampled, and the creature nearly tripped over him as it rushed toward Hanna.

"Hanna, go!" Shanthah shouted.

Hanna turned and ran as the beast thundered toward her. It raised its massive axe, intent on splitting her in two, just as she summoned a sharp stone to her hand with her mind then sent it flying. The minotaur roared in pain as the rock buried itself in his wrist. He stumbled backward and dropped his axe. The beast struck the ground, and the heavy shaft of the weapon crashed down on his own forehead, momentarily dazing him.

Hanna helped Shanthah to his feet, and they dove under the cart. They watched Itrus's metallic boots go by and then heard the minotaur's bellow.

"Come on!" Shanthah exclaimed. "The prince!"

Hanna nodded, and they crawled out from their hiding place. As Josman and his allies dueled the Talohiran soldiers, six Sangoran women holding spears swooped down from the sky.

Hanna scooped up a handful of stones from the road and hurled them with her mind, peppering their foes across their exposed flesh. Shanthah brandished his blade high above his head, slicing through one of their ankles as she flew by. He turned invisible as he drew them away, leaving Hanna alone with the prisoner cart.

She let out a deep breath and summoned a large rock from the ground. She thrust it forward with all the strength her mind could muster, smashing the lock from the cart's doors.

Just as Hanna met the gaze of Crown Prince Xanthurias, the minotaur gored Itrus through the chest, pinning him against the side of the vehicle and knocking it onto two wheels. Although he was a Spirit Warrior, and his body was artificial, he screamed, nonetheless. Blue flame and sparks crackled around the wound.

The minotaur pushed the cart over, and Prince Xanthurias and a second spirit warrior Hanna assumed was General Valakor crashed down. A groan filled the air.

Hanna screamed as the minotaur struck Itrus in the side with his axe, sending him flying. He struck the road as Hanna scrambled to the cart's opening to find Prince Xanthurias bleeding from a wound on his forehead.

"Oh no, oh no, oh no," Hanna said, looking around for a way to free them from their chains. General Valakor was bound from head to foot with heavy fabric bands in addition to the chains that kept him attached to the cart.

"The keys!" Xanthurias exclaimed, gesturing past Hanna with his head. "They're on the—"

Hanna and the prince screamed as the minotaur slammed Itrus against the cart, rolling it twice until it landed upside down.

The beast raised its axe, and Hanna covered her face with her arms, knowing it would never be enough to stop the blow. At least she wouldn't have to watch it come.

A bellow rang through her ears, and she glanced up to see the minotaur stumble backward, a deep gash in its right leg. Shanthah reappeared and stumbled toward Hanna.

"Go!" he shouted. "I've got this!"

Hanna cried out and sent another rock flying faster than any arrow, imbedding it in the beast's chest. It roared and fell backward with a crash over the fence lining the road. With shaking hands, Hanna handed Shanthah the keys.

"Or you do," Shanthah said. "Thanks!"

"Please, see to the prince's safety first," General Valakor said.

"Yes please!" Xanthurias exclaimed. Shanthah nodded, unlocking each of Valakor's chains as Hanna sliced the fabric bands binding him.

The minotaur got to its feet, blood soaking its leg and chest. It thundered toward them just as Valakor leapt from the cart.

The massive Spirit Warrior grabbed the beast by the horns and flipped him backward over his head to the ground.

Valakor grabbed the minotaur's fallen axe, stepped forward, and planted it in the beast's sternum. The minotaur let out a final breath and did not stir. Valakor wrenched the bloodied blade from its chest, and Shanthah cheered.

"Hey, old friend," Shanthah said, helping Prince Xanthurias from the cart.

"Truly good to see you," the prince said with a grin.

"Guys?" Hanna called, pointing toward the city. Shanthah turned to see a group of ten Sangorans flying toward their position. Josman returned from the fight and crouched next to Shanthah.

"I'm the only one left," he said, his face smeared with blood.

Shanthah clapped him on the shoulder and pulled him into a tight embrace. "I'm glad you're okay, buddy."

"We've got to get out of here," Hanna said.

"I'll hold them off. Return to the pillar!" Itrus's voice came from the other side of the cart. He limped toward them, cyan sparks and ethereal flame flowed from each of his many wounds as if his spirit were leaving his metallic body.

"No, you must go," Valakor ordered, hefting the minotaur's axe. "Get the prince and General Itrus to safety. Now!"

Itrus nodded and obeyed the order, limping toward the shack housing the Telepillar. As he, Prince Xanthurias, Hanna, Josman, and Shanthah made their way to safety, a wall of dark fire erupted between them and their destination.

"Oh no," Xanthurias whispered. "He's here."

"Who?!" Hanna exclaimed.

"King Valistaran and his queen!" Xanthurias shouted.

Hanna glanced over her shoulder to see a man in dark armor standing beside a Sangoran woman in elegant, crimson robes. Lightning crackled around her hands and wings while the world burned with black flame around her husband.

"Run!" Valakor shouted, shielding his allies with his body against Valistaran's river of flaming darkness. Nearby, the Sangoran queen blasted Itrus's arm clean off with a bolt of lightning.

"Kill her!" Itrus shouted.

He slumped to his knees, and before the others could react, Queen Codruta sent a second bolt through his head. His armor crashed to the ground, cyan smoke trailing into the wind. She readied another barrage of light, and Hanna held her hands aloft, stopping Queen Codruta's barrage by holding her limbs in place.

Hanna groaned under the strain of her powers, but Shanthah took the opportunity to thrust his blade through the queen's stomach. She collapsed, and Shanthah abandoned his blade.

King Valistaran's cry filled the night as an explosion of dark flame sent Valakor, Shanthah, and Hanna flying. Hanna helped Shanthah to his feet as Josman burst through the door.

The others ran into the room to see that their companion had already configured the Teleportation Pillar for their escape. With his armor glowing white hot from the fight, Valakor slammed his fist against the pillar. Before they vanished, the last thing Hanna saw was a sobbing king cradling his dead wife.

CHAPTER FIFTEEN
THE INFILTRATION OF DOFTAAN

Unaware of what had transpired in the blood-soaked streets of Bukaral, Aleksander and Mara clambered over the rocky terrain at the base of Doftaan's high walls. They were accompanied by five of General Hokkod's soldiers and two other freed slaves, the brothers by the name of Petar and Sandor that had volunteered to help save the others.

The group had been forced to abandon their old plan after the caravan of slaves had moved straight through Bukaral and driven onward for Doftaan, the capital city of Sangora just across the plain from the Talohiran capital.

"I can safely say we aren't going to be able to climb over, so what's the plan?" Aleksander asked. "Too bad the others still have the Telepillar, or this would be a lot easier. You sure you only have the one?"

Hokkod ignored the comment and was silent for longer than Mara preferred.

"Any ideas, fearless leader?" she prompted.

They could see the caravan of slave carts accompanied by dozens of soldiers crossing the plain between Bukaral and Doftaan. Their only advantage was that the pillar had helped them beat the slaves and their masters to their destination.

"Ideas, but no plans," Hokkod replied. "We don't have the numbers for a full-on assault on the caravan before it reaches the city."

"We at least need a way to break into the city," said Petar.

"And we'll need a map—how else will we find the way?" said his brother, Sandor.

"Climb over, tunnel under, or break through?" Aleksander asked. "None seem very likely to work but take your pick."

The others began arguing over the most viable way into Doftaan, and Mara folded her arms in silence before letting out a sigh. She shook her head.

"Typical men. You're missing the most obvious solution," she said, gesturing to the wall. "There is a huge gate—a literal doorway into the city *right there.*"

"What, do you think we're just going to knock on the gates of Doftaan and walk right in?" Hokkod asked with a hearty laugh. "One does not simply—"

"Watch me," Mara said.

And that's what they did as Mara left the cover of the rocky outcrop and strode toward the gates.

"She's going to get herself killed," Sandor said.

"Or she's going to make us look like a bunch of idiots," Aleksander said. "Come on."

They snuck along the base of the wall after her as she rapped her fist three times against a small wooden door at the base of the gates. The rest of the group couldn't hear what she said, but the way opened just enough for them to walk through unimpeded.

Mara glanced over her shoulder, gestured to the others, and walked through. Aleksander led the way after her with an amused smile on his face.

"By the gods, she did it," Hokkod said, scratching his head.

The rest of the group made their way through the gate, and it closed behind them. Mara sat smiling on a bench near the road.

"So, how'd my plan work?" she asked with a snide smile. Hokkod grunted something under his breath.

"What did you tell them so that they let you pass?" Hokkod asked. "What lies did you have to tell them?"

"Nothing. I just told them I wanted to come in." She handed Aleksander a sheet of parchment as he approached.

"What's this?" he asked as he unfolded it.

"It's a map, what does it look like?" Mara replied. "While I was waiting for you, I picked one up at the Doftaani tourism center. A very nice woman named Daria gave me one for free because I *asked* for one."

"Bested again," Hokkod said.

"It looks like we're in the Paudbramah neighborhood. If we take the road east across the river, we'll cross into Dubovparkh, and then the next neighborhood over is where the prison is," Mara explained.

"There are multiple prisons on this map," Petar said, pointing to a second prison to the east. "How do you know which one they're heading for?"

Mara shrugged. "It's closer."

Aleksander followed along on the map and located where the Southern Prison was marked in a neighborhood called Kaljacjana.

"How do you even pronounce that?" Aleksander asked, taking the map. "Kal-uh-jan-suh?"

"Kal-yuh-tsyah-nuh," Mara said. She laughed and asked, "Seriously, do they teach you *anything* in the schools in Laniras?"

"I wouldn't know," Aleksander responded with a chuckle. "Alright. Let's get going. And we'll need a *real* plan. We can walk into the city, but I doubt we can do the same into a prison."

Mara gazed up at the buildings around them in awe, for she had never seen such a beautiful city. She marveled at the towering spires and shining, onion-shaped domes that dotted the city. Laniras was made for humans, and humans didn't like to climb stairs. But this place was made for people who could *fly*, so therefore, the towers could stand as high and as proud as they wanted. She craved to see more.

The others, except for Aleksander, did not seem to care. Hokkod seemed paranoid and apprehensive, and the others all seemed terrified.

"Come on, act normal," she said. "It's just a city. These are just people here living their daily lives. Not all of them are spies for Valist—"

Hokkod shushed her with wide eyes.

"You don't know that." He glared down at Mara, but she simply shrugged, leading the way across the bridge into Dubovparkh.

Old Sangoran women with colorful, flowered headscarves dragged rickety carts full of vegetables, and children chased one another in the street playing a game involving a large ball and rhymes they didn't understand. She smiled as the older children took flight, carrying the ball high into the air.

She appreciated the beauty of the people and smiled at the charming architecture made of black and red stone; endearing little stores and markets lined the long boulevard through Dubovparkh while colorful multistory homes were stacked high above them, clearly only accessible to those that could fly.

They moved on. The men all argued in hushed tones about the best way to infiltrate the prison tower as they crossed into the Kaljacjana neighborhood. This part of town was much more run down, the homes much shabbier and dilapidated than those nearer to the gate. No children played in the streets, but several patrols of winged soldiers stood at the base of the prison tower.

"Figure out how we're going to get in?" Mara asked, whistling at the impressive height of the prison. "Too bad we can't fly…"

The others nodded, for there didn't seem to be any doors accessible from the ground.

"Hokkod thinks we should kill some soldiers and impersonate them," Petar said. "Sandor agrees, but I don't think it'd work."

Aleksander nodded, agreeing with Petar.

"Why not?" Sandor argued. "It's simple. We—"

"Once again you're missing a very obvious, and very important point," Mara said. "Anyone in the class want to make a guess of what that is?"

Aleksander raised his hand.

"All the soldiers guarding the tower are women," he said. Mara pointed at Aleksander with a wink.

"All the soldiers are women," she repeated. "And they *probably* know each other."

"You know, why is that?" Sandor asked.

"Everyone knows the women kill their husbands after they mate," Petar said. "I would know, a guy I worked with married one and moved here, and I never saw him again."

"I don't think that's true at all," Mara said with a scowl.

"Oh, he did, believe you me. It was disgusting. Can you imagine marrying one of those things?" Petar said. "They killed all the men. That's the rumor I heard, at least. Think about it."

"And if that was true, where are all those Sangoran children we saw coming from?" Mara asked. Petar and Sandor both shrugged. "They're not monsters, and I don't think they're disgusting at all. I think they're actually beautiful. Don't you wish you could fly?"

"They beat you in the slave camp. I see the scars. How can you think Night Witches are *beautiful?*" Petar asked.

"I don't think I know you well enough for you to judge me like that—or to let you judge them," Mara said. "Don't judge an entire nation based on the cruelty of a few. Anyway, I'm uncomfortable with this conversation. Let's move on."

Hokkod seemed lost in thought, nodding at her words.

"Yes. They're expecting the caravan, so if Mara and Private Luciana impersonate Sangoran soldiers, the rest of us can pretend to be slaves," said Hokkod.

The brothers both scoffed.

Hokkod turned to them. "Privates, do you have any other suggestions?"

They both shook their heads.

Mara gripped Private Luciana's elbow. She was the only other woman in the company and would therefore play the other Sangoran guard. The other soldiers began removing their armor.

"There's only one issue," Aleksander said. "Maybe I'm stating the obvious, but maybe I'm missing something."

"Wings?" Mara asked.

"Yeah, wings," Aleksander replied.

"Leave that to me," Mara said.

"I'll want this back when we're free," Hokkod handed Mara his golden shield and silver spear. He placed his helmet on her head and helped her fasten the chin strap. He shifted from one foot to the other, clearly uncomfortable without his weapons.

"It's a bit roomy, but thank you," Mara said. "I'll treat them with respect."

The warrior nodded in thanks. He untied his cloak and wrapped it around Mara's shoulders. He drew a knife from his belt and sliced the bottom of the fabric so that it didn't drag on the ground.

"There. Most Sangorans hide their wings beneath a cloak anyway, so I hope they won't question the fact that neither of you have wings," Hokkod said. "Who knows, maybe there are humans here too…"

"Then can I pretend to be a guard instead?" Sandor asked.

"No, the role is taken," Mara shot back.

"Well, what are we waiting for?" Aleksander asked. "Ready to be slaves again? We already look and smell the part, so it shouldn't be too hard."

"We just got out of this mess," Sandor muttered. The others, including his brother, ignored him, and they moved on, leaving the male soldiers' weapons along with any Thannish insignias buried beneath a bush.

They moved onward, approaching a low gated wall covered in metal spikes similar to the prickly brambles in the slave camp. One of the enemy soldiers guarding the tower called something to them in Sangoran.

"First group of escaped slaves," Mara said in Thannish. "The wheel on our cart broke, so we brought them ahead on foot."

The guard nodded and signaled for the others to open the gates. Mara took a deep breath and led her allies through the barricade. Several other Sangoran soldiers stepped forward as they approached.

"Hi, uh—here to drop off these slaves. Can you bring us up?" Mara asked, glancing up at the prison.

"That's why we're here. Are they all human?" one of the soldiers asked, gesturing to Hokkod's four female soldiers.

"Oh, yes. I'm Sangoran, of course," Mara replied. The guard seemed suspicious, as if she knew there were no wings beneath Mara's cloak. "Sangoran human, of course."

"I assumed as much," she said. "Humans, always trying to make sure we know they're not like us."

Mara let out a slow sigh and shifted nervously.

"My apologies. If you could fly us up, that'd be much appreciated," Mara said. The Thannish speaking guard let out a sigh.

"Or you could just use the lift," she said, unlocking a door that led inside to a large platform.

"Right," Mara said.

They all loaded onto the lift, and a moment later, the mechanisms sprang to life, and they began to ascend the tower.

When they reached the floor where the guard had sent them, another soldier stopped them as they stepped through the door of the landing and said something in quick Sangoran.

"Ja nerruthu Sangorškan rruthan," said Mara. *I don't speak Sangoran.*

"Ah, Talohirans, then. I thought as much. First prisoners of the day, I see?" the woman said. "Follow me, please."

Mara thought she heard the woman mutter something about slavers under her breath.

The group obeyed, and they followed the guard up several flights of a spiral staircase until they reached a bridge connecting two halves of the prison tower.

A storm was rolling in, and the tips of the towers were now shrouded in a dense fog, which they could see from each window. The guard led them to the other side of the bridge to an open doorway. As they walked, Mara marveled at the dozens of bridges above and below her and wondered how they had been constructed.

"Wait here. Feel free to restrain the prisoners to this wall if you think it necessary. Mistress Lavinia will be here soon, and I'll need you to check in with her, as she'll need help to coordinate moving the rest of the prisoners."

"Lavinia? Here? When?" Mara asked.

"A few minutes, I think," the guard responded. "The second wave of prisoners will be up shortly. I'll be back. Thanks for relieving me, I've needed to relieve *myself* for quite a while."

She paused as if waiting for a laugh, which Mara faked. The guard hurried out the door, and it slammed shut behind her.

"Lavinia is coming *here*?" Aleksander whispered.

"We need to slip away," she said, biting her lip.

"Split up. I do hate the 'impersonating guards' plan that seems to keep coming up, but it may be our only hope so we aren't actually thrown in prison," Hokkod said and gestured for Sandor and Peter to follow.

They left without another word to search for appropriate disguises. Hokkod's soldiers went the opposite way, leaving Mara and Aleksander to search the third corridor.

"This is insane," Mara said. "It's never going to work."

"It's worked this far, and you're clearly a genius," Aleksander said. "We'll get out of here."

"We find Pol and the others, and we get out. Okay?"

"I know. I hate to say this, but I don't think it's possible to save everyone," Aleksander said. "Maybe if Hokkod gets the rest of the Court of Thanatan here, or something. What is that, anyway? Some kind of—"

"Do you think this was too easy, Aleks? To get in here?"

"Honestly, I don't think they care about who comes in, just who comes out," Aleksander replied. Mara gripped Hokkod's spear and shut her eyes.

"I don't know if we'll make it out of here," she said. "I appreciate the optimism, but—do you want to talk now? We have a little time, and—"

Aleksander knew she was referring to the talk about his true identity, but he shook his head.

"No. It'll give me something to look forward to when we get out of this," Aleksander said in a reassuring tone. "Because we *are* getting out."

"Thank you." Mara smiled and took his hands in her own.

"I'm glad you're here with me," she said. "You're going to love Cineca. There's this beautiful hidden lake that I'll take you to, and there's a few families that will give you a place to live until you can find our own place, and—"

She covered her mouth with her hands.

"Our own place?" Aleksander asked.

"I misspoke—your own place. Yours. Your own."

"I mean, unless you want to," Aleksander said. "I've enjoyed 'living' with you and the others for the past few months, and I don't know anything different." He offered a reassuring smile.

"I just can't wait for you to see it," Mara said with a sigh. "There's this certain time just before nightfall where the sun makes the surface of the lake look like it's on fire."

"I can't wait," Aleksander said. Then, with a laugh, "By the way, you look very intimidating in Hokkod's armor."

"In Hokkod's armor that clearly doesn't fit, you mean?"

At that moment, the others returned with an assorted pile of dirty guard uniforms.

"Found a laundry room. These clothes stink, but so do we, so they'll do," Petar said.

The men began undressing, dropping their dirty clothes into a large heap. Mara and Private Luciana each retrieved one of the uniforms and went around the corner of the corridor to change away from the men. When they returned, the pile of old clothes was smoldering in the corner.

"What in the name of Thanatan?" she asked.

"Well, we had to dispose of them, right?" Aleksander answered with a sheepish grin. Mara shrugged, nodded, and tossed her old, tattered clothes onto the heap. Sandor brushed the ashes into an old cupboard just as the door opened, and a crowd of slaves was herded into the corridor.

Mara grabbed Aleksander's arm; he gasped in excitement and clutched Mara's hand as he caught a glimpse of Pol and Drahomir entering the tower. Pol met Mara's gaze for a brief moment before being whisked away.

They had made it to Doftaan's Kaljacjana prison, but Mara couldn't help but wonder how many of them would make it back out.

CHAPTER SIXTEEN
A KNIFE UPON THE TOWER

A shiver of guilt crawled down Mara's spine, for although she was in the prison to save her fellow slaves, they all thought her to be one of the cruel slavers. She bit her cheek to prevent herself from speaking as the prisoners yelled profanities at her.

"How are we going to do this?" Aleksander asked.

"I don't know, but I do know that they went this way," Mara replied. As they followed the flow of slaves, she marveled once again at the beautiful construction of the black stone tower. She shook the thought away. Why was that important now?

Soon they reached the wide double doors of the tower, and along with the other slaves, they were guided like cattle inside the building. Mara felt a whip strike her shoulder, and she turned with hatred burning in her eyes.

"Watch your aim," she shouted, spitting in his direction. "Try that again, and you won't like what I do with that whip."

The slaver raised his hands in an apologetic gesture and continued to push the slaves inside.

"I'm glad you're on my side but remind me not to make you angry in the future," Aleksander muttered into her ear.

"Maybe I'm just acting," she answered with a wink.

"No—I don't think so," said Aleksander.

He shared Mara's hatred for the slavers' whips, and he knew the strike had pulled back to the slave camp under Belokej's power. The reaction had been legitimate and more than justified.

A spiral staircase snaked up the center of the building surrounded by a veritable sea of cages, and slavers and soldiers directed the slaves into dozens of jail cells on every floor of the tower. They were not built for comfort, but to fit as many prisoners inside as possible. Some weren't even tall enough for their inhabitants to stand straight up, and others were so cramped that prisoners had died, their corpses still standing pressed against the others. A shiver traveled down Mara's spine, and grief filled her heart, but she fought back tears.

"Is this just where they store their food?" she heard Sandor ask. "I'm sure they don't eat humans—right?"

She pretended she hadn't heard. She wanted to believe in the good in Sangorans, but seeing the conditions in the tower was too much for her to bear. The group continued upward with the to higher floors in the tower as the cells on each floor were filled.

Mara felt another sickening knot in her gut as she recognized many of the people she had labored with mere days before. She knew that if she found Diana or Rehor in this hellish prison, she would not be able to control her sobs, but at the same time, she hoped that she *would* spot their faces.

"How are we getting out of this?" Sandor asked. His brother looked too terrified to speak. "This is suicide."

Aleksander agreed with Sandor, saying, "Even if we do free the slaves, what then?"

Soon every cage was stuffed over capacity with prisoners, and the band of slavers and their Sangoran comrades congregated in an office at the top of the tower. Aleksander sighed in relief seeing that the Sangoran woman that seemed to be in charge of this tower was not Lavinia. Fortunately, Belokej too was absent from the group. Where was Lavinia, then?

Aleksander watched Hokkod counting their foes with his eyes, making a silent tally of how many enemies they would need to face. Aleksander did the same, counting ten slavers, five of Valistaran's soldiers, and ten Sangoran guards, with dozens or even hundreds more on the lower levels. Their band of eight warriors was very much outmatched and outnumbered.

The lead Night Witch gathered keys from each of the slavers and strung them onto her necklace chain before glancing out the lone window in the room as if waiting for someone to appear. She placed the chain around her neck, and the keys disappeared beneath her tunic.

"You there, go inform Mistress Lavinia that this tower can't receive any more slaves," the leader said, pointing at one of the slavers, who nodded and left the chamber via the staircase below before closing the wooden hatch behind him. "I need half of you to guard the lower floors of the tower, and the rest will go outside to deal with any slaves who don't fit in the east tower."

Mara saw one of the remaining Night Witches lick her lips, and she cursed Sandor for putting the thought in her mind that the guard was salivating over the thought of fresh blood. She thought of Pol. What if they wanted to drink her little brother's blood? Was that rumor even true? Even if it wasn't, the thought made her dry heave and almost vomit, but Aleksander grabbed her hand, and she took a deep breath to regain her composure. Most of the Sangorans exited, followed by two of the guards. The oncoming fight was now starting to be in their favor.

Pol and Drahomir had made it into the tower, but she hadn't spotted Kamil or Rehor. If they didn't make it into either tower, they would die at the hands of their captors if they weren't dead already. She gripped Hokkod's spear and waited.

"What are you still doing here?" asked the lead Sangoran.

Hokkod must have had the same idea as Mara, for as soon as they were out of earshot, he grabbed the spear from Mara and drove it through the soldier's chest. She let out an ear-piercing scream and fell to her knees. Each member of the rescue party engaged the confused guards, and within a second, they were all locked in combat.

As the leader drew her final breaths, she hurled a bolt of lightning from her palm, striking the shield on Mara's back. The blast knocked her against the wall, and she tumbled to the floor. One of the slavers scrambled for the closed door covering the exit ladder, but Petar smacked him over the head with his spear. As Petar turned, one of the slavers stabbed him in the side with a jagged dagger that ripped his flesh as it withdrew. He cried out for his brother as Hokkod dispatched their enemy with a swift stab.

"Mara!" Hokkod cried. "Pull the lever inside my shield, and everyone else—get down!"

She did as instructed, locating a small lever within the shield she hadn't noticed before. She pulled it down, and to her great surprise, a shockwave of cyan energy erupted from the shield, knocking everyone still standing to the ground and shattering the windows in a spray of glass.

The blast gave the rescuers enough of an advantage that the battle was soon over with only Petar sustaining a life-threatening injury. Mara grimaced at the sight of the wound, and she and Sandor knelt next to Petar, who appeared to be in shock.

"You can have this back," Mara said. "I don't trust myself with it!"

"They must have heard that downstairs. We need to be quick," Hokkod said, taking the shield back from Mara.

"What about him?" asked Mara. She gestured to Petar's injury as Hokkod looked down the trap door. "We can't leave him here, Hokkod. We can't leave anyone behind. That's the entire idea of why we're here in the first place!"

"I understand, and I will help Petar. Find your friends. As soon as we can, we need to get to the top of the tower where I will signal the others to extract us. If we get separated, meet at the top of the tower," Hokkod said. He yanked the keys from the dead Night Witch's neck and handed them to Aleksander, who took them and led the way down the ladder. "And remember, you two, we cannot save everyone. Now go!"

The only Night Witch guarding the next level turned just in time to feel Aleksander's spear collide with her side with a sickening crunch. She was not dead, but her broken ribs would prevent her from pursuing them.

Mara and Aleksander started their search for the rest of their companions, unlocking every cage on the floor. The thankful slaves rushed out and followed the rest of the group to the next level, ready to fight or flee.

"I don't care what Hokkod says. We might as well have an army behind us," Aleksander answered as he unlocked another cell, ignoring Hokkod's order. "We all have the right to be free."

Mara's heart rushed with gratitude for his words.

They continued down the tower, once again engaging the Sangoran soldiers on the next landing. Mara cried out as one of the guards struck her with such force that she collapsed against the wall, and then a moment later, the same Sangoran smashed her in the chest with both wings, forcing the air from her lungs. The escaped slaves came to her rescue, pulling the woman off Mara before pummeling her with their fists.

Several freed slaves fell against their enemies, but the rescue party and the escapees fought with tenacity and a fierce will to survive. As the slaves continued their way down the tower against their Night Witch captors, Mara spotted the familiar face of Drahomir inside one of the cages.

"Drahomir!" she called, taking the key ring from Aleksander. She rushed to his cage and fumbled to find the correct key for the cells on this floor. Her heart thundered in her chest, desperate to save her friend.

"It's okay, Drah, we've got you!" she said with a feigned smile. "We're going to get out of here!"

"Aleksander? Mara!" Drahomir exclaimed. "What the hell are you doing here? Get out of this place!"

"We're here to save you," Aleksander said. Drahomir reached through the bars and grabbed Aleksander's wrist.

"It can't be done, get yourselves out," he said, pushing something cold into Aleksander's hand. "Take it! Take it away from me! I don't want it!"

"What is this?" Aleksander asked, examining what Drahomir had given him. It was a metal cuff with intricate, unreadable writing sprawling on its surface. On other side, an inward facing spine jutted out of the otherwise smooth surface.

"Remember when I went into The Cage? I stole that from the crazy Sangoran inside. We've tested it in here, and it's how they did it, Aleks! It's how they tortured people in the slave camp!" Drahomir exclaimed. "I'm sorry I never told you."

Aleksander examined the sharp spine on the inside of the cuff, and Drahomir showed a deep scar on his forearm where he had worn it.

"Do *not* let that thing prick your finger," Drahomir warned.

Aleksander nodded and stowed the cuff in his pocket. After testing almost every key, Mara unlocked the door to let the slaves out of their cage. She moved on to unlock the rest of the cells on the floor. Drahomir did not move, but instead continued speaking to Aleksander through the bars.

"If they put it on you, you seem dead to everyone else," Drahomir said. "But there's more—"

Before Drahomir could explain what else the cuff did while worn, Aleksander heard a scream from the floors above. Night Witches must have entered the tower at a higher level and discovered the bloody trail of their slain allies.

"Go!" Aleksander cried, pulling Drahomir from his cage. Drahomir dropped to his knees, hyperventilating. He grasped the bars of his cage and tried to pull himself up, but the agony from standing in his cramped cell made his legs throb with pain.

"Don't let them take me back!" he said. "I only had it on for a couple of seconds, but—"

"We're getting you out of here. We won't let them take you anywhere," Aleksander said, "but you do need to get moving or they're going to kill all of us!"

He pulled Drahomir along and followed the rest of the slaves down the spiral staircase. Mara started unlocking more cages and the sound of Hokkod's shield ringing against stone filled the air from the floor above. Had he struck a wall, or had he fallen?

"Drahomir, where is Pol? We saw you go into the tower together. Where's my little brother?" Mara asked. Drahomir pointed out the window to the other tower.

"They took him across the bridge with the rest of the slaves who didn't fit in this tower," Drahomir said. Mara cursed under her breath.

A pair of Sangoran warriors soared into the room from behind the group; in her fury, Mara thrust her spear through the first's neck. The Sangoran crumpled to the floor as the second tackled Aleksander, carrying him across the room. He ignited a ball of flame against the base of her wing, and the two hit the ground, tumbling over one other.

Mara ran to his aid, kicking their attacker in the back. The Sangoran shrieked, sending Drahomir into another frenzied panic. The Sangoran twisted away from its attackers and leaped through the nearest window, took flight, and was gone.

"How do I get to the bridge to the other tower?" Mara asked, wiping the guard's blood on her tunic. "That Night Witch has gone to get friends, no doubt."

"I can—I can show you," Drahomir said. "I saw it. The entrance is on the next floor down." They followed the sounds of battle and the trail of slain bodies of both slave and captor.

"Did you see Kamil?" Aleksander asked.

Drahomir shook his head as he guided them to a large door on the far side of the tower.

The prisoners had armed themselves with torch sconces, bricks, and blades taken from their fallen foes. As the slaves in front were slain, their allies behind them would take up their weapons and continue fighting.

"We need to go *up!*" Mara shouted at the slaves. "Up! We have a way out for you up there! Drahomir—go with them."

"No," Drahomir replied. "I want to help."

The message quickly spread throughout the crowd, and they turned back upstairs as one mass.

"I hope these keys work in the other tower or we're out of luck." Aleksander tried the door to the bridge, and to his surprise, it was already unlocked.

He pushed it open, and the trio made their way across the bridge. There were no guard railings on either side, which meant any misstep would result in a long fall and a quick death.

"Wait!" someone shouted. Sandor and one of the Thannish soldiers supported Petar, who was now pale and shaking.

"Where are you going?" Sandor asked.

"My brother is in the other tower, and if you're going to stop me, you're going to end up like the rest of the guards in there," Mara said, pointing to the first tower.

"There isn't time. Hokkod sent us to find you. We're leaving," said Sandor.

"The hell we are," said Mara with a look of indignation. "I'm finding my little brother."

"I've got my own brother to save," Sandor shouted, pointing at Petar's wound. "Believe me, I get it!"

"Sandor, it's okay, we can do this," Petar said through the pain. "Hokkod said they're not going to wait, but—"

"Thank you," Mara said. "I can't lose him."

She turned to Aleksander, and they hurried across the bridge.

The group, including Petar, Sandor, and Private Luciana followed close behind. Mara barged through the gates to find a room filled with caged slaves but no sign of violence.

"They must all be focused on the other tower," Mara said.

"Yes, but we need to act fast," Aleksander said. "If we're not back soon, Hokkod *will* leave us."

They examined each cage for any sign of their friends as the slaves in the cages called for help. They pushed on, surrendering to the truth that they could not save them all.

"I have to go back," Petar said. "I'm sorry, I was hoping I'd be able to help. Get back as soon as you can, or we are going to leave you behind. I'll—I'll try to stall Hokkod for you."

Mara nodded in acknowledgment, and Private Luciana escorted Petar back to the other tower. Mara, Aleksander, and Sandor scanned the room as they climbed to the next floor. Mara's heart leapt as Pol's voice broke through all the others.

"Mara! I'm here!" Pol cried from a cell on the far side of the room. Mara rushed to his cage and crammed each of the keys into the lock one after another. The other prisoners on that level called to them as well, and tears cascaded down Mara's cheeks, their pleas tearing her soul apart.

"Pol, thank goodness, are you okay?" she asked as she tried to find the correct key. At last, she found it and released Pol and the rest of the slaves in his cell.

"Where's Kamil?" Aleksander asked.

"And have you seen Rehor?" Mara added.

"I know Kamil was in the group behind me. He's on a lower level. I didn't see Rehor, I'm sorry, Mar," Pol said.

Mara swore again and pulled her brother with her, making their way to the level below. The slaves in Pol's cell followed, but the rest of the unfortunate slaves cried out not to leave them, and regret and guilt gnawed at her heels like voracious beasts.

Two Sangoran guards stood watch in the next room, and the armed members of the group rushed them. One of the guards batted Aleksander away with a swipe of her wing then thrust her bladed wings through Sandor's chest. Drahomir pulled a torch from the wall and clubbed her over the head.

"Sandor!" Mara screamed. "Get him back to Petar!"

He was already gone. As Mara crouched next to his body, an unfamiliar voice filled each of their minds.

"Aleksander! Mara! Pol! Drahomir!"

Aleksander spotted Kamil's face pressed between the prison bars, a wide grin spread across his face.

"Kamil!" Mara shouted, trying to open his cell as the last Sangoran guard in the room slashed at her with a spear, but the slaves in the cell grabbed her wings and pulled them into their cage. She shrieked as they tore her wings apart with their hands, pinning her against the bars. Aleksander took pity on the guard, for it seemed a terrible way to die. He pierced her heart with his blade, and she was still. Mara unlocked Kamil's cell and commenced opening the rest as well.

"Go up two floors and cross the bridge then meet up with the rest of the rescuers," Aleksander said, sending them toward Hokkod, and he hoped, to freedom. The slaves thanked their rescuers but quickly followed his directions. He glanced down at Sandor's bloodied body, and a guilt filled his heart.

"You deserve more of a funeral than this," he said to the dead, brave, volunteer. "I am so sorry..."

"Who was he?" Pol asked.

"A hero. Pol, I need you to go with them. You'll be safe. I need to find Rehor, but we'll be right behind you, ok?" Mara said, holding her brother's arm to assure him.

"Hurry back," Pol said, giving his sister a quick hug, reluctant to leave her behind. As the siblings pulled away, Mara assured him once more that everything would be alright if he followed the soldier.

"I love you, Pol," Mara said.

"Love you too, Mar."

"You'll find Rehor on the floors above us."

The voice filled Mara's mind as Kamil stared into her eyes.

"Kamil, you're a Mindspeaker?!" Mara exclaimed. "Why didn't you ever tell—"

"I didn't know either. Go!" Kamil thought to her.

He clapped her on the shoulder twice, a sign of good luck.

"Thank you, my friend," Mara said.

Kamil accompanied Pol and the rest of the group back up the stairs. When they reached the door to the bridge, he saluted them and took his leave. Mara, Aleksander, and a distraught Drahomir climbed the stairs to the room above.

"Drah, why don't you go with them?" Aleksander asked. "We can find him. Seriously, go."

"No, I'm okay. I can help."

They peeked their heads into the room where two guards sat at a table playing cards while the rest of their fellow soldiers fought and died in the nearby tower.

Aleksander ignited a fireball in each palm and with a cautious step entered the room. The flames cast eerie shadows on the walls, giving color to the black stone of the chamber and hope to the beaten down slaves in the cells. One guard attempted to flee, and the other sat paralyzed by fear in his chair.

"Grab him!" Aleksander cried. Drahomir tackled the man and wrenched the keys from his grip. The slaves pulled him against the bars, and he dropped his blade. Mara tossed it to Drahomir, who pressed it against the guard's neck to keep him down. The other guard dropped his weapon and held his hands up in surrender.

"Rehor!" Mara shouted.

He was either not in the room or did not hear her calls but managed to open the cells on the first try of a key to let the slaves out. Aleksander pushed the soldier into the cage as the prisoners filed out; Drahomir forced his captive inside as well, and Mara locked the gate. Drahomir wandered up the stairs, but Mara held back for a moment, blocking Aleksander's path with her body.

"Aleks, just in case something happens—before we go up there, I just wanted to say thank you."

"For what? I didn't find Pol or the others. It was all of us," Aleksander said. "We've gotta go, Mar."

"No, you helped me find joy in that dark place. Thank you," Mara said. "I had to tell you before—well, I just wanted you to know that you made a difference. I needed you to know."

Aleksander clutched her hand and with a smile said, "I've said it before, and I'll say it again. I'll help you get out of here whatever it takes. We're *so* close."

"Whatever it takes," Mara said with a nod. She hesitated for a moment and pulled him into a deep kiss that seemed to fill his entire soul. When their lips parted, she simply said, "Let's go."

A thousand conflicting thoughts filled Aleksander's mind. The kiss. The escape. Rehor. Surviving. Going back to Cineca with Mara. Kissing Mara again. He knew they had to go.

They made their way up the stairs after Drahomir.

"I already told your companion! No slaves are permitted to leave. You know what's going on in the other tower. Perhaps, if you were—"

Mara cut his words short as she kicked the seated man in the throat. He fell backward in his chair, hitting his head on the brick behind him. He slumped onto the table as his chair slammed back down, its legs splintering. The unconscious guard tumbled to the ground and did not stir.

"Woah, savage," Drahomir muttered, stepping around the fallen guard. "I had him convinced I was a fellow guard—It was working, I think, but, anyway, I think I found a way out. There's another bridge nearby that connects to the other tower. They're not allowing any living slaves over."

"What about dead slaves?" Mara asked.

"What?" Drahomir asked.

"Mara, my friend!" Rehor's voice came from a cage nearby.

His booming laugh melted the worry from her heart. Mara sprinted to him and after a few tries, unlocked the door to his cell. The rest of the slaves emerged from the cell as Rehor embraced Mara.

"You look well," he said. "Which, of course, is more than I can say for myself."

"Come on, we're getting you out of here," Mara said. She tossed the ring of keys into the next cell, and the slaves scrambled over them.

"Please, save the others if you can!" Mara exclaimed.

The sound of approaching footsteps and voices warned them of danger coming from below.

"They're coming up. We can't go down, so we need to cross *now*," she said. Aleksander nodded, and they tested the door. Locked. Aleksander scowled, and both he and Drahomir tried forcing the door, but to no avail.

"Perhaps you'd like to try the key?" Rehor asked, putting a small wrought iron key into the lock.

"Where did you get that?" Aleksander asked.

"From the body of the guard you killed. The simplest solution is usually the best," Rehor said.

He turned the lock and opened the door to the bridge. The guards below had met the slaves, and screams filled the chamber. Aleksander rushed toward the stairs, but Drahomir grabbed him.

"There's no time, Aleksander!" he said, pulling him out the door. "There's nothing you can do for them."

Aleksander relented, and they hurried to the bridge, leaving the door unlocked. Several Sangoran sentries stood watch upon the bridge.

"There is no way we're fighting through this," Aleksander said. "The rendezvous point is on top of that tower. We need to meet Hokkod and the rest of our rescue team there if we want to escape."

"The guards aren't letting any living slaves through," said Drahomir. "Mara and Aleksander, you're still dressed as slavers."

"So?" Mara asked. "I'm not leaving any of you."

"We're nearly dead, how hard could it be to act the part?" Rehor asked. "Drag us across the bridge."

Rehor lay on the ground and feigned death, letting his arms go limp. Aleksander let out a deep breath and dragged him through the door and onto the bridge, and Mara took Drahomir's wrist to do the same.

Mara watched in horror as one of the Night Witches stopped Aleksander and examined Rehor. He covered her mouth in shock as one of the Night Witches dug her clawed thumb into Rehor's shoulder, causing him to cry out in pain. The sentry then grabbed Rehor by the arm and threw him from the bridge. Aleksander retaliated by blasting the soldier with an explosion of flame.

Mara held her hands over her mouth in shock, tears streaming freely down her cheeks. The other Night Witch advanced, shrieking at Aleksander in Sangoran.

"I don't speak Sangoran!" Aleksander exclaimed. "I was instructed to move this slave with some kind of plague so that it didn't spread to the rest of the tower!"

Mara hurried out of her hiding spot, much to Drahomir's protest. The second guard shouted at her too, but Mara brought her fist up into the woman's jaw. The Sangoran woman took flight and shot up into the night.

"She'll be back with friends," Aleksander said.

Mara knelt on the edge of the bridge, staring down at Rehor lying still on the stone walkway below. Tears streamed down her face as Drahomir pulled Aleksander aside.

"The cuff," he said. "It makes someone appear dead. It isn't pleasant, to put it lightly, but you could get Mara out."

"And you?" Aleksander asked.

"I died the day they threw me in that camp," Drahomir said. "Get her out. Go live a happy life, or whatever."

"Mara, we've got to go," Aleksander said, and she stood, wiping a tear from her face. She pushed open the door to the tower to find four more guards inside.

"You've got to be kidding me," said Mara.

"This slave has the plague!" Aleksander exclaimed again, pointing to Drahomir. "Mistress Lavinia instructed us to—"

"Mistress Lavinia, nothing," said one of the soldiers inside. He drew his blade and stood. "We know exactly what you've done and the mess you've caused today."

"We don't want a fight," Aleksander said, lighting a ball of flame in his hand. "Just let us through."

"Tell you what," said the soldier. "Kill the girl, and I'll let you two pass through without another word."

"Or I can kill you all," Mara shouted.

"Mara, it's okay," Aleksander said, pulling the cuff from his pocket. It seemed to open of its own accord as he looked at it in his palm. "I promise."

"What?" Mara asked.

"Everything will be okay. Trust me," Aleksander said.

"You're lying," Mara whispered.

"I love you, Mara."

With that, Aleksander clamped the cuff Drahomir had stolen from The Cage onto Mara's arm. It sealed itself on the other side of her wrist, and he heard a small buzz from inside the cuff. She collapsed, and he caught her in his arms. He held her close as tears rolled down his cheeks.

"I am so sorry," he whispered. "Please, please forgive me…"

"What the hell did you do to her?" the guard asked, nudging her face with his boot before checking for a pulse, which he did not find. "Wow. Well, go ahead."

The Night Witches watched with rapt attention as Aleksander dragged Mara's unconscious body up the stairs and out of sight.

He was breathing hard, his energy and will to continue nearly spent. He had to stop for a moment, his head spinning, as he gazed down at Mara. Her face seemed peaceful, somehow, despite what he had done. She wasn't dead, but he had no idea what was happening to her.

At the top of the stairs, Aleksander and Drahomir came to a door, which wasn't locked but jammed as they tried to force it open. It took them twenty minutes to finally do so.

As they emerged to the top of the tower, the Sangoran soldier that had escaped earlier swooped down without warning and tackled Aleksander off the edge, carrying him out of sight.

"Aleksander!" Drahomir screamed but failed to spot him.

He turned to Mara, who was still lying on the ground with the cuff from The Cage clasped on her wrist.

Drahomir felt a raindrop land on his cheek. Thunder tore through the heavens, and at the same moment lightning illuminated the sky. He unclasped the cuff but left it on her wrist.

"Mara, it's time to go," he whispered.

Mara stirred and awoke with a scream. She scrambled away from Drahomir, dazed and confused. Terror gripped her as she stumbled to her feet but collapsed against the tower's ramparts.

Drahomir steadied her, but she was completely distraught and unresponsive.

"Talk to me, Mara! We're at the rendezvous point!" She did not respond, instead releasing a blood-curdling scream. "Mara, we're here. We're going to be safe as soon as the rest of the team gets here, we are going to be free! We made it here before them! Aleksander and Pol and Rehor—they're all going to meet us here, and you'll be okay. You're safe, oh by the gods, Mara…"

Mara still said nothing but rocked back and forth on the ground. Drahomir walked to the edge of the tower and peered over the side. He could see Aleksander and the Night Witch dueling in a dance of blades and blood on the lower bridge now, the Night Witch's severed wing twitching on the cold ground. Farther down, Rehor was gone. Was he alive, or had the Sangorans moved his body?

He watched through curtains of rain as Aleksander finished the deed, piercing his enemy's heart before pushing her over the bridge. Drahomir then spotted Rehor, and together, the two wounded men limped to the door of the tower. Locked.

"Mara, look! Rehor and Aleksander are both alive! But I've got to get down to them, okay? They're alive but locked out of the tower. We need to get the keys down there to save them. There's no way they'll escape if we don't."

Mara sobbed and shook upon the ground, and Drahomir swore to himself. He peered over the edge, took a deep breath, and dropped the keys down to Aleksander's level, hoping they didn't bounce from the bridge. He shouted to Aleksander and Rehor, but the sound of the downpour muffled his voice.

He cursed under his breath again and turned back to Mara, placing his palm on her shoulder. She recoiled and refused to look at him.

"Mara, I know what's going through your mind. I know the torment you're going through. I know what the cuff does, and it was on there for about twenty minutes. Believe me, I understand," he said. Mara stopped screaming and finally looked up at Drahomir, tears mixing with the rain that streamed down her face.

"Where are we?" Mara asked. "Drahomir, is that—is that you? What are we—"

Drahomir said nothing as he took in the smell of rain on earth and gazed over the city of Doftaan, home of the Night Witches. The city's countless spires seemed to reach into the heavens, taller than any he had ever seen in Thanatanos. Each tower seemed to be hewn from the black mountains to the west, and crimson banners rustled in the light breeze across the city. It was oddly beautiful for the last thing he ever expected to see.

"Doftaan," said Drahomir at long last. His terse reply gave no comfort and little explanation. "We're in Doftaan."

A cloud of Night Witches circled the tower below them like the great storm that beat down from above. He looked down toward Aleksander and Rehor; they were gone. They had either died or escaped, but in either case, they were gone.

He glanced to the north and caught a glimpse of his allies gathering at the base of the tower below where a ray of brilliant blue light marked the site of their salvation—no, *his* salvation.

Droves of slaves flocked toward the shining beacon that pulsated with a brilliant blue light as an army of soldiers descended upon them. Aleksander had said that their rendezvous point was to be atop this tower. Had something gone wrong? Did the rendezvous point change, or had he been mistaken?

The bridges were swarming with soldiers; if anyone was stranded in the towers, they now had no hope of escape. His thoughts turned inward to himself and Mara. They, as it turned out, had no hope of escape either. Not anymore. He watched the Night Witches circling the tower, coming ever nearer with every passing second.

"There's too many of them," Mara said. She was still hyperventilating, but her tears had stopped as if she had no more tears to cry. "Escape will be—"

"Impossible," Drahomir finished the sentence for her then added, "Yes, I know."

The breeze played with Mara's hair as she looked over Sangora.

"Where is—where are…" she trailed off.

"They're safe," Drahomir replied as he began to cry as well.

"Well maybe we could escape if we—" Mara thought out loud as Drahomir took her hand into his own. She glanced up at him in confusion as he drew a knife from his belt.

"No—I told you. Escape is impossible. For us, at least," he said, a twisted look on his face.

"We can make it the same way as the others," Mara said. "We've just got to get down, right?"

"We can only help our friends," Drahomir answered. "The noble thing to do would be to sacrifice our own lives, so that they have time to escape."

"Why die a martyr, when you can live to become a hero?" Mara asked, remembering something Rehor had once told her. "Our blood won't save anyone."

"Maybe yours will. You'll be a hero, Mara."

Mara cried in surprise and pain as Drahomir's blade bit through the flesh on her forearm, spraying crimson upon the prison's spire behind her. She grasped her wrist and collapsed to her hands and knees, shock gripping her very soul. She screamed and punched Drahomir in the leg.

"Drahomir—what the hell?!"

She held her arm to staunch the flow of crimson, but the pain in her arm was nothing to the agony in her soul. She continued to scream amidst sobs of excruciating tears.

"I'm sorry for this," Drahomir said. "I truly am. I know what torment your mind is in—I've worn that cuff, and only for a second. I can't imagine how horrible it is for you."

Drahomir dropped his bloodstained knife next to her as if cleaning his hands of what had been done.

Tears streamed down his face.

"Drahomir—you know blood attracts them!"

Drahomir didn't know if that rumor was true, but he hoped so. Nonetheless, he knew her screams had drawn the Sangoran host away from the escaping slaves.

"I'm doing this to save both of us," Drahomir said. "Believe me, you would thank me."

Her former companion abandoned her to die as bait for their foes; the swarm of Night Witches spiraled around the prison tower as one until they reached the top.

Drahomir watched Hokkod on the ground send another bolt of cyan energy into the sky as a signal for Itrus and the others to teleport in to save them. As the creatures plummeted downward, he threw himself from the tower.

He fell through the cloud of Sangorans, and before he hit the ground, the Telepillar appeared at the base of the tower; in a flash of bluish green light, the entire group at the base of the tower vanished.

Mara's screams haunted Drahomir, even as he faded away.

Alone. A single tear carved a path through the grime on Mara's cheek as the black hurricane of Sangoran warriors engulfed her. She felt a blade pierce her back, and another cut her shoulder.

Her world went dark, and she shut her eyes, resigning herself to death.

CHAPTER SEVENTEEN

THE MISTRESSES OF DUSK

Only an occasional echo broke the cold stillness, and no torchlight banished the darkness. An empty bottle slipped from the king's hand, and it rolled down the cold stone steps before shattering at the bottom. The remainder of the foul liquid soaked into the opulent carpet that led to the two thrones.

One was empty.

The sound awoke Valistaran from his drunken slumber. He was slumped against the back side of his high seat, grasping for the bottle that had escaped his grip; he managed to roll over onto his knees to pull himself upright and used the arm rest to steady himself as he made slow progress away from that dark place, but he collapsed. He traced a line with his finger from his arm rest to the now vacant throne that had, until recently, belonged to Queen Codruta.

The king let out a roar of anger and despair. Loss and hatred. Confusion. He twisted around and hurled a mighty stream of black flame into Codruta's throne. The king's rage manifested in a concussive blast, unbridled due to his alcohol-soaked mind. The explosion shattered the stone and metal of Codruta's empty seat, sending debris and flame across the back of the chamber. Valistaran tumbled backward and down the carpeted steps.

Hearing the calamity inside, two guards rushed into the chamber in order to ensure their king's safety. Valistaran looked up at them from his hands and knees and through his matted black hair screamed at the interruption, raising his right hand into the air. The nearest guard began to run away, but the king unleashed a tongue of flame that threw the man across the chamber.

The other guard did not hesitate to flee without his companion. Valistaran stumbled after him but collapsed, hitting his head on a column. Blackness surrounded him, and an empty silence descended upon the throne room.

When the king awoke, blinding sunlight was streaming through the tall windows of the chamber. He rubbed his aching temples and got to his feet; his head pounded like a stampede of Minotaurs had trampled him. He groaned as he followed the scorch marks and a trail of blood leading out of the throne room.

There was no corpse to accompany the blood, so his victim must have escaped after he lost consciousness. He picked up his fallen sword and slid it into his belt, hoping he hadn't done anything terrible with it the night before.

He saw Codruta's broken throne, and he hung his head.

The two members of his royal guard standing outside his chamber were silent as he strode out of the room. They must have heard tale of what had transpired the night before, for they hesitated for a moment before following their king through the hallways of his fortress.

"My king," said a short, bespectacled man in a nasally voice waiting for Valistaran outside his chamber. He ran his hand through his wispy gray hair to look presentable for his master, who did not seem to care or even notice. Valistaran did not break stride, and the man hurried to keep up.

"Assemble the Mistresses of Dusk," Valistaran ordered. "Signal for them to come at once."

"There are several who are currently preoccupied. What of them? Lavinia has the slave breakout to deal with, and Mistress Delia…" The diminutive man prattled on and was likely to continue for quite some time. Valistaran held up his hand to interrupt.

"Advisor Vadim. Are each of the Mistresses of Dusk in Doftaan, busy or not?" asked the king.

"Yes, my lord," Vadim said in a squirrely voice. "They were gathered to attend the Lunar Festival when Doftaan prison—"

"Good. I need to fill two new positions in my council. If the others do not come, tell them that I will replace *them* as well, and that I will do so before anyone mourns their passing. I have more pressing issues to discuss than a festival or prison break,"

Valistaran interrupted. Advisor Vadim nodded and scurried off to do his master's bidding.

Valistaran crossed the corridor and opened the door into what was once his wife's council chamber. He took the queen's seat facing the inward curve of a half-moon shaped table, flanked by his two guards. He pressed his fingertips together and rested his forehead against them before letting out a deep sigh. His thoughts turned to Queen Codruta as he waited for Vadim to gather her councilors.

He missed her.

Within an hour, three Sangorans clad in a variety of elegant robes entered the room. They stood at attention near the table, awaiting their king's command.

"Sit," he said with a flick of his hand. The members of the council obeyed, taking their respective places around the table. "When you are all here, you will notice that some members of our council are absent."

"My liege, it is not hard to notice when Florenta is absent," said one of the newcomers. The old Sangoran's robes were costlier and more elegant than any of the others in the room and her head seemed to be encrusted in gems, for her opulent headpiece was covered in various shimmering jewels. On each of her fingers were shining rings, many of which bore diamonds and rubies bigger than even Valistaran had ever seen.

"Yes, Mistress Delia, you are quite right. We can wait a moment longer for Mistresses Florenta, but we all know how she likes to take her time." He turned to his other councilors. "Welcome to you both as well, Mistresses Ihrin and Raluca."

He nodded to the other two Sangorans seated at the table. Ihrin sneered, jealousy etched on her face. She disdained the attention given to Delia, and she did not try to hide it. His eyes lingered on Raluca—as Codruta's little sister, she wore the same dark hair and brown skin, although her features were somewhat more elegant than her late sister's. Still, every bit of her—every memory, every mannerism, and every word reminded him of her.

Her gown was elegant, yet simple, and her hair, black as the night's sky, cascaded over her back in large curls. Valistaran looked at her with sad eyes, and she returned his despair.

A few minutes later, both double doors of the chamber burst open, and a corpulent Sangoran, Florenta Karpaska, riding on a seat carried by at least ten other Night Witches entered the room. She was so large that her platform took up nearly the entire space of the doorway. Her servants huffed and struggled as they set her down at her place at the table. Even sitting, she was taller than the other Mistresses of Dusk.

She had what looked like half of a roast pig on a platter near her and in her hand was a glass of wine. She took a bite from one of the pig's legs, chewing loudly even before addressing Valistaran. The rhythm and volume of her chewing was sickening, and bits of meat flew from her mouth.

"I am here, my king!" she announced.

"That you are," Valistaran said. "And now we wait for the last of our remaining council, Mistress Lavinia, who is dealing with the recent prisonbreak. Because of that, I've decided to start without her. Raluca, please fill her in when she arrives, won't you? Even without the breakout, she would be late."

"Of course," Raluca said.

Advisor Vadim entered the chamber and sat at a desk behind Valistaran to take notes on the meeting. Several other high-ranking men and women entered the chamber and sat in the tiered seating on the edges of the room to watch the proceedings, and Florenta's exhausted servants joined them.

"Let's begin, then," Valistaran said. "We are here to discuss the loss of two members of our council. First, the vacancy left after Mistress Nedelcu's passing. You were all at her funeral pyre and the Festival of Blood to honor her memory. Age takes all of us, of course. However, it is with great sorrow that I confirm the rumors regarding the loss of my beloved Queen."

His voice faltered as he said the last few words.

He hesitated for a moment. It would have seemed a moment of weakness, but the rest of the chamber burst into commotion. Valistaran knew that only Raluca felt any genuine sadness regarding the queen's passing, and he sighed. They were all aware that the next queen would be chosen from their number, and although they cried out in apparent despair, Valistaran was aware of their true feelings, and they angered him beyond words.

Valistaran glanced at Raluca, and they shared another moment of understanding; he nodded at her, and she returned the gesture. That was enough.

"Silence," the king ordered. The Sangorans in the stands and around the table hushed, and the room fell to an eerie silence, broken only as one of the double doors opened. Lavinia, clad in dark armor spattered with dried blood and grime, strode into the room, her cape billowing behind her as she collapsed into her seat. Delia sneered at the mess on Lavinia's armor.

"Lady Lavinia," Valistaran said. "How nice of you to arrive."

"You pay me disrespect by using my old title, Lord Valistaran," Lavinia said. "But you may proceed."

Valistaran chuckled and bit his tongue, knowing the Mistress of Dusk was baiting him by giving him, the king, permission to continue. He ignored the disrespect and turned to address the council once again. Raluca turned to Lavinia and whispered into her ear to fill her in on the few details she had missed.

"It is the custom of the council and Sangora itself to bring forward names of those who should be nominated for the honor of being named as Mistress of Dusk. Just as the dusk comes before the night, so too does the opinion of the Mistresses of Dusk before the People of Night."

Lavinia noted that Valistaran used the correct traditional term, refraining from using the term 'Night Witch,' which the people of Sangora regarded as a disgusting slur.

"I therefore call for nominations for elevation to aforementioned rank. I am open to your comments at this time," Valistaran said before adding, "This should come as no surprise. Your tribes and states will have been suggesting names to you since before Nedelcu's death, no doubt. Please only state the name of the person you nominate. No more."

Lavinia knew that the traditional method of choosing nominations came from each state with an absent Mistress of Dusk representative, but after the alliance with Talohira, things in Sangora felt somehow different. Changed. Corrupt. It was now more of a military occupation than an alliance, and Lavinia resented Valistaran's presence on the council, sitting where his wife should be. She hated his wife too, but for other reasons.

Advisor Vadim readied his quill to jot down each of the suggested names. As Florenta opened her mouth, Vadim knocked the bottle of ink onto himself and the table, and he scrambled to salvage what room on the parchment that remained. Valistaran and the rest of the council took no notice.

"I nominate General Anca of the Isle of Krim, Nightmare of Thanatanos," Florenta said through a mouthful of pork.

"A bold choice," said Valistaran. Florenta and General Anca did not agree on many matters and openly mocked one another. He wondered what malice accompanied the nomination.

"And I, Lady Lacramora," said Raluca.

"I second the nomination for Lady Lacramora," said Delia.

Valistaran glanced up at this.

"Do you not have words for yourself? Can you not think of one simple name to suggest?" the king asked.

"I apologize, my king. I—I nominate Lady Draguta, then," Delia stammered. Valistaran did not acknowledge the nomination.

He turned to look at Lavinia, awaiting her answer. Lavinia took a long while in thought before naming her nominee.

"I have a nomination, but will refrain from naming her at this time," said Lavinia.

"This is highly unusual!" cried Florenta, slamming her meaty fist down. "I will not stand for it! A name, Lavinia! A name!"

"If not just to annoy Florenta, I won't give her name at this time, but know that she is a Persangoran in the Wingling home here in Doftaan," Lavinia said.

Silence fell over the room, and even Florenta stopped chewing. She dropped her pig's leg, breaking the silence. Valistaran got to his feet and placed his palms on the half-moon table. Ihrin looked irritated as she was still not yet given a chance to nominate anyone.

"You nominate a *Wingling?*" Valistaran said in a low whisper.

"Well, to be accurate, in a few days she will be a Halfwing, so I apologize. I nominate a Halfwing in the Wingling home," Lavinia said.

"Your disrespect me and test the limits of my patience, Mistress Lavinia," said the king. "Do you want this Wingling to take your place at this table? My buffoon of an advisor would make a better choice!"

At this comment, Vadim scrawled his own name on his parchment then realized what he had done and blotted it out with several lines of ink.

"I mean no disrespect, my lord," Lavinia said. "I have recently become acquainted with my nomination. She is—how should I put this? *Extraordinary.* I am told by the laboratories that her body is compatible with every single test they conducted on her during her sleep. A universal recipient."

"A powerful weapon, then," Valistaran said. "Lavinia, please have our engineers and magicians grant her whatever powers you deem necessary."

"She is not even a real Sangoran!" Florenta shouted. "She was born human and will always be one!"

"Yes, my lord," Lavinia said, bowing her head in Valistaran's direction. "As someone not natively born here, she is also moldable to your will. She is untainted by the politics of our country and the dark history our people have faced. Most of all, I believe she craves vengeance against Thanatanos. You can make her whatever you want to, my king."

Valistaran thought for a moment and then smiled. Lavinia seemed taken aback as Valistaran seemed to agree with her.

"Ihrin, speak," Valistaran said.

"I nominate Adriana of Krim," Ihrin said. She began to speak again but was cut off as Valistaran got to his feet, and the rest of the chamber except Lavinia stood out of respect. Vadim scribbled Adriana's name on his parchment as he stood up, causing him to smear the ink and blot out the name. He scrambled for a new piece of parchment, realizing he should have already done so.

"I will inform you of my decision in the coming months," Valistaran said. "As you are all aware, this will mean there are eight Mistresses of Dusk when your culture demands that there only be seven. Because of this, one of you will be made my queen of both Sangora and Talohira."

With no further words, he strode from the room flanked by his guards, who shut the heavy doors behind them. The entire room erupted into a commotion of discussion.

While the rest of the chamber argued, Lavinia smiled.

CHAPTER EIGHTEEN
THE WINGLING

Blinding light replaced the darkness. Pain racked her body, and the only other sensation she could feel was the intense cold of the stone chamber. Her breath was slow and painful. Forced. Blackness was all around her, and pain was all she knew. Yet, she could remember.

She remembered everything.

Betrayal. She remembered the traitorous blade. The tower. But most of all, she remembered what Aleksander had done to her—what he did hurt her deeper than Drahomir's knife ever could. Had he known what the cuff did? He had to have known. Mara cried out in agony and despair, pulling on the thick chains that bound her arms and legs to the stone table.

"You are awake, good." The female voice echoed through the chamber, speaking Thannish in a heavy Sangoran accent.

"Where am I?" Mara asked.

"You are safe," the woman said. "Everything is alright."

"No—what is this place? Where am I?"

She cried out as sharp needles pierced each of her arms and felt a hand smooth down her hair to soothe her. Her doctor, or perhaps her captor, said nothing but placed a strange mask upon Mara's face. Another needle pierced her arm, and Mara watched her own blood flow from the needle through rubbery tubing that led somewhere out of sight.

"Your body and blood type are compatible," said the doctor, "and that is the reason that you are still alive. Poor thing."

"Compatible for what?" Mara wheezed. The mask somehow made it easier for her to breathe, as if it had some spell placed upon it for her comfort.

The Sangoran did not respond, and as Mara struggled against the needles and chains, she felt herself fading to the blackness. If this was death, she welcomed it yet again. She felt her mind cloud over, and dizzy thoughts made her reach up for an absent Aleksander.

He did not squeeze her hand.

She awoke in a luxurious four poster bed adorned with brass and gold. She looked around in utter confusion; she was nestled in sheets made of the finest silks and fabrics she had ever felt. The contrast between her intense agony moments ago on the stone table to her comfort in this bed was absolute—when had that even happened? Was she dead? Was this the Afterworld? What was going on?

There were no chains restraining her to the bed. She sat up with great effort and propped herself against the headboard. Her entire body ached, but her shoulder blades and eyes seemed to hurt more than the rest of her body, including the myriad bruises and bandaged wounds across her body. The pain in her eyes didn't hinder her vision, though. In fact, for whatever reason, things seemed to be in sharper focus than usual. She could hear the faint chirping of birds outside her open window, and the sun shined into the room through the thin curtains that danced in a gentle spring breeze as if everything were normal.

Mara exerted herself again to climb out of the opulent bed, and she limped toward the window, parting the curtains. She let the golden sun bathe her face for a moment, letting it warm her skin. She stood there basking in the warm sunlight as she examined her bandaged arm. The sun felt hotter against her skin than the spring breeze, and she began to feel uncomfortable.

She looked out the window and beheld a vast city. She rubbed her eyes to adjust to the light and saw several hooded, winged Sangorans walking and flying in the streets below. She must still be in Sangora—Doftaan. She admitted to herself that the city was much more beautiful in the sunlight and when she wasn't in mortal danger. She knew Sangorans were mostly nocturnal, which meant the streets were mostly empty, giving the city a serene calm. She touched her face and winced at how tender her skin was; why was the sun hurting her skin?

The door of her chamber burst open, and a plump Sangoran woman sporting a wide sun hat entered Mara's room. She set down a dish of food on the table next to the bed and hurried over to her.

"Oh, dear, get away from that window!" the plump, winged woman said. She drew the curtains tight over the window, blocking the sun from getting in. Mara looked at her with a perplexed look. "You'll be able to tolerate it later, but the sun will really damage that sensitive Wingling skin! Oh, no, you wouldn't know that. Silly me."

"Wingling? Who are you?" Mara asked. The plump woman laughed and led Mara over to her breakfast. Eggs. Toast. Sausage. Some kind of fruit that she had never seen before.

"I brought you some familiar food for breakfast as well as a Talohiran pomegranate—I think you'll like it. It's very nutritious! I'm Elena, by the way, and I'm in charge of making sure you're happy and full of food," she answered, pushing Mara back onto the bed. Her voice was soft and kind, but she also spoke with the authority of a mother. "Now eat up. You've been sleeping for almost a week, and you must be awfully hungry."

"A week?" Mara asked.

"Would you like to go to the Blood Festival today?"

Mara did not hesitate to tear into the meat on the plate. She had not eaten barely anything more than disgusting, watered-down porridge since being thrown into the slave camp, however long that ago had been.

"I'm sorry—the what?" asked Mara, hoping she had misheard Elena's words.

"The Festival of Blood, darling!" said Elena.

"Night Witches have a festival for something so gross and evil?" asked Mara, scooping some seeds out of the pomegranate with a small spoon, although she had no idea how to properly eat it. She had heard that Sangorans drank blood, but she was worried about bringing it up.

"No, no, we don't use that word here," Elena said. "It's very rude. Please, use the word Sangoran."

"I'm sorry," she whispered. She hadn't realized it was a slur.

"It's quite alright. You'll have quite the adjustment to be sure. And I know that in Thanatanos, blood is seen as something dirty and crude, but here, it's sacred. It flows through our bodies and gives us life. It isn't an evil thing, sweetheart," said Elena, fluffing one of Mara's pillows. The word 'evil' triggered thoughts in Mara's mind about recent events. Her friends' betrayal. Elena's hospitality. Who *was* evil in all of this? Was anyone?

"Why are you being so kind to me?" Mara asked.

"Because I'm people, and so are you. That means we're supposed to be kind to each other," Elena replied. "Now, what else can I get you? Still hungry?" Mara shook her head as she swallowed the last bit of meat on her plate. "My, my—you *were* hungry, weren't you? Well, there are fresh clothes for you in the closet near the mirror, if you're ready to leave your chamber." She picked up the tray and made her way for the exit.

"Wait, Elena." Elena stopped and turned her head.

"Yes, dear?"

"Thank you."

The words choked in her throat, but the plump Sangoran smiled. "Of course, sweetheart. Now, get comfortable, and when I come back, I'll explain everything."

Mara flashed a mirthless grin, and Elena left the room, closing the door behind her. Mara slid back out of bed, walked over to the closet, and opened the door. Inside was an array of beautiful dresses, and hanging next to them were a large sunhat, several shawls, scarves, and what looked like coifs and hoods.

Mara selected a dark black dress and smiled. She had never seen such a beautiful piece of clothing, let alone been able to wear one. She removed her nightgown and let it drop to the floor. She gasped in horror as she caught a glimpse of her naked body in the full-length mirror.

Nearly all of her from head to toe was covered in bruises and bandaged wounds, but strangest of all were two bony protrusions between her shoulder blades. How had she not noticed them before? She put a hand to her mouth at the sight and kicked the backless black dress back into the closet as if to hide the gruesome fact she had discovered.

Instead, she selected a less revealing red dress and laid it on the bed, pulling on some undergarments she had found in a drawer. She pulled the dress on and sighed as she draped a red shawl over her shoulders to hide the ugly protrusions. She pulled the sunhat from its hanger and placed it on her head. Was the assorted headgear to protect against the sun or for fashion?

Mara shut the wardrobe door with a longing glance at the black dress piled on the bottom before she exited the room.

She adjusted her dress and shawl then snuck out the unlocked door. Elena was nowhere to be seen, so she creeped barefoot down the hallway.

The opulence of the rest of the building mirrored that of her own chamber. Chandeliers hung at regular intervals from the ceiling, and there was a soft red rug beneath Mara's bare feet; she wiggled her toes between the fibers, for they were even softer than grass. She ran her fingers over the elegant statues and looked at the beautiful oil paintings and murals of events in Sangoran history. It was the most beautiful place she'd ever seen.

She examined one piece in particular of a king standing victorious over a dead Sangoran in a crown.

Was that supposed to be Valistaran?

She snapped back to reality from her fixation on the useless, intoxicating opulence of the room as the sound of footsteps echoed through the corridor. As silently as possible, she turned the corner away from the newcomer. She shouldn't be here, and she wondered how she would be punished if she was discovered.

She broke into a run to escape and came across a wide staircase leading to the lower levels. She took the steps two or three at a time toward the unguarded front gates.

She tripped near the bottom of the stairs and tumbled to the ground. She winced as she hit the carpeted floor, biting her lip as she did so. At least it was more comfortable than hitting stone. She groaned and ran her tongue over the wound as the metallic taste of blood filled her mouth. A foul realization of what was happening filled her thoughts, but she buried the thought deep within the recesses of her mind. This was all far too much.

"Wait, Mara!" It wasn't Elena, so she ran.

The owner of the footsteps was standing atop the staircase clad in flowing black robes adorned with curling silver that twisted into armored shoulder pads in an elegant combination of beauty and power.

Mara turned away from the Sangoran woman and darted toward the door. She pushed it open and hurried away.

She grimaced as she crossed the street, as her eyes could not adjust to the painful sunlight stinging her skin. She pulled her hat over her face, and she hid herself in the shadows of a nearby building. As she hyperventilated, she glanced over her shoulder and saw the armored Sangoran soar from the doorway with her leathery wings fully outstretched.

Mara hid her face and continued to creep along the shadowy alleyway, following the sounds of a celebration where she hoped to slip into a crowd and disappear. What would they do to her if they caught her? She shut her eyes, her heart nearly exploding in her chest.

Hundreds of Sangorans danced and sang in the marketplace. They were all wearing beautiful crimson scarves and head coverings as they celebrated; the rhythmic music seemed to placate Mara's fear, and she even found herself tapping her foot to the beat of the drums.

The melody calmed her, as music always had. The melodies and ethereal, scarlet ribbons of satin trailed after the dancers, and people smiled and laughed in the streets. Elena had said something about the pain from the sun being temporary, and she wondered how long it would take for her to feel comfortable.

Someone grabbed her wrist, and she screamed. She put her hand over her mouth and saw a man covered from head to toe in tattered gray rags standing beside her. He had no wings, and therefore he was not one of *them*. That meant he was an ally. Or did it? The figure put a single finger up to his covered lips, and Mara nodded in understanding, or something akin to it.

He led her away from the festival and down a shadowy alleyway. With no other option, Mara chose to follow.

He guided her toward a pile of firewood that shifted out of the way as he pulled on one of the logs, revealing a hidden door leading underground. They said nothing, even as they descended into the earth. She wanted to run, but for whatever reason and despite her better judgment, she followed the stranger.

"Where are we going?"

"You are a new Persangoran, are you not?" the man asked through his rags. The light cast eerie shadows onto the wrappings covering his body. "A converted human. A Wingling?"

"I don't know what that is," Mara said. "The Night Wi— sorry, Sangorans—called me that and said something about a transformation and that my body was compatible for—"

"Yes, yes. I know. We are here to save you, and if possible, heal you. My name is Emil. I am taking you to meet the Lord of Walkers, Ronin Jakoni."

"Mara," she answered in a simple introduction.

Mara said nothing after that, accepting the fact that she was not going to understand anything that was happening and wondered what danger she had mistakenly put herself in now. Emil led her to a chamber where he knocked three times. A voice called for him to enter, and they obeyed.

"Lord Jakoni, I bring you a Wingling by the name of Mara," Emil said. He bowed to his master.

"Greetings, Mara," Lord Ronin Jakoni said with a warm smile as he shook her hand. "You have an opportunity to do this world a very great service, if you so choose."

"What are the Walkers?" The question slipped out.

"We are Sangoran men and women—or the slur you probably know our kind by, Night Witches—who have severed our connection with the queen. We are free to act as we wish, unbound by the Queen's Control and her Mistresses of Dusk."

"What do you want me to do?" Mara asked.

"We have a plan that may help us to win our war against the rest of Sangora and Talohira, but we need a Wingling. One with your special gifts," Emil said.

"Gifts?" Mara asked. "I don't have any powers."

"Our foes know our mission, and that is why they keep Persangorani in the lavish palace in which I assume you found yourself."

"Persangorani?"

"Converted humans," Ronin said again. "In the first stage of a Persangoran's transformation, you are a Wingling. We have word whispers that you are imbued with a particular power, and as a Wingling, you are not yet under the Queen's control, so we must act quickly. But your blood type—it is special. Exceedingly rare. If you allow us to analyze it, we could end the entire war," said Lord Ronin Jakoni.

"How do you know that? Why would I trust you?"

"As soon as your wings begin to develop, and you become a Halfwing, your mind will be enslaved by the curse known as the Queen's Control. She can control you with a thought and make you do horrible things," Ronin said. He pulled a short dagger from his belt and placed it in Mara's hand. A sign of trust, perhaps.

Ronin answered the other. "Have you ever wondered why you have seen so few men of our race?"

"Yes. Why?" Mara asked, her curiosity piqued.

"Because of the curse of the former queen," Ronin replied. "A genocide that was covered up. I promise that I will tell you the story, but you can help us prevent a similar tragedy today."

"I—no. I don't like this. I won't be any part of this. What is this control you're talking about?" Mara asked, backing away.

"The queen's will was always corrupt, as was that of her predecessor and those that will come after. We, the Walkers, sever our wings as they develop to prevent the queen's control. We can do the same for you. This has created a divide in our race—we are outcasts. Exiles," Ronin answered. "Some call us terrorists and extremists but those people do not understand."

"So, you are called Walkers because you do not fly. Clever," Mara said. "So, what is my role in this, and what's in it for me?"

"We need your blood," Emil said.

"Alright then, do you have a vial or something? I can cut my hand and you can take as much as you need. Wrap it up, and I'll be on my way. No stranger to pain here!" Mara said, trying to be helpful so that she could escape. Emil glanced at Ronin, who shook his head.

"You misunderstand us. We need all of it. Without your blood, we cannot end the queen's control. We cannot create our cure for Sangora's greatest curse," Emil said.

Mara stepped back with her hands raised.

"Woah, no. You can't have all my blood. I need my blood," she said as she backed into the door. "I can help you get someone else. I can help you capture one of the other Winglings."

"Are you not listening? Not all Winglings have your gifts."

Emil unsheathed a short dagger and grabbed Mara's wrist.

"No!" she cried; her mind shot back to Drahomir's blade, and she felt a disorienting panic overtake her. Ronin brought the knife toward her neck, but a weak bolt of lightning erupted from her palm and struck Ronin in the shoulder, knocking him into the table. Mara looked down at her hands in shock and confusion. Emil leaped toward her, but a second instinctive arc of electricity threw him back, and she darted from the room.

"You've made your choice, but be warned, Mara, that you've also made enemies of us all!" Ronin shouted.

She sprinted down the hallway as fast as she could and heard the sound of a whisper carried on the wind behind her. Ronin materialized from a puff of black smoke in her path and seized her by the neck. Emil appeared in front of her as well.

There was a crash and the trap door above them collapsed. A Sangoran woman dropped into the secret room and pulled Mara from Ronin's grasp. Ronin responded by brandishing his dagger at her, but in one fluid motion, she deflected the blow and brought her elbow up into his face in a spray of blood. She took Mara by the hand and shot into the light.

Together, Mara and the Sangoran soared over Doftaan. Mara caught sight of her face with a gasp.

"Lavinia?!" Mara exclaimed as she recognized her.

"Lucky for you. Are you alright, Mara?" Lavinia asked. "Did they hurt you?"

"No. But they wanted to. What the hell is going on?"

They landed at the steps leading up to the Wingling house, and Mara let out a sigh of relief, glad to be on solid ground again.

"Are you still surprised that I am helping you?"

"Um, yes?" Mara replied.

Lavinia chuckled, checking over her shoulder to make sure they had escaped the Walkers.

"You know I hold no allegiance to Valistaran Talohir. It brings me great pleasure when his plans fail, and I hate the Walkers even more than I hate him. They're trying to destroy everything we value. They're terrorists and thieves bent on our destruction. They're traitors, my friend," Lavinia said, guiding Mara back to the crowded festival.

"How did you know where I was?" Mara asked.

"I watched you escape. I followed you through the Blood Festival, and I saw the Walkers take you. Now that we know where one of their hideouts is, we can destroy it. Thank you, Mara," Lavinia said. They reached the Festival of Blood again, and Lavinia tapped her foot to the beat of the music.

"I'll be honest. I don't know what's happening. I don't know who to trust," Mara said.

"By the way, your friends are safe. At least the three I saw."

"Who?" Mara asked.

"They were in your slave district. The big man, the red-headed girl, and the one that always—" She seemed to be at a loss of words of how to describe him. "The snarky one. They're safe. I allowed them to escape as Valistaran and his queen attacked. Shanthah—yes, that was his name. Shanthah killed Queen Codruta, and if you can keep a secret, Mara—I let him do that too," Lavinia said, a twinkle in her eye.

"Why would you do that?" Mara asked.

"Did you not hear what I just said? Your other friends caused me quite a bit of trouble at the prison towers." Lavinia gestured in their direction, and Mara could see their outline in the far distance.

"I know. I was there too, and I can safely say that they are no longer any friends of mine. They betrayed me—twice, actually. But why don't you just kill King Valistaran? Why don't you—"

"Hmm. A shame. So many questions. Sangoran and Talohiran politics are over your head. I wouldn't expect you to understand any of my motives. Just remember that any of Valistaran's losses are my victories," the Sangoran replied. "I am one of Codruta's Mistresses of Dusk—her ruling council. I was, at least, until she died. My position has made it difficult for me to oppose Valistaran, as we are so tied to the queen and therefore to his influence. I've been a prisoner as much as you. Mara, I want to propose an alliance. One that I think you'll find very beneficial."

"I'm listening," Mara said, taken aback. Lavinia smiled as she led the way back to the Wingling nest home.

"Now that I am free from Queen Codruta, I *do* have plans to kill Valistaran, and they are all centered around you."

CHAPTER NINETEEN
AN UNEXPECTED NOMINATION

Mara's reflection gazed back at her with rote obedience, following her every action. This was the first time she had allowed herself to peer into her bedroom mirror to examine the physical changes of her transformation in several weeks. There were rumors in Thanatanos that Sangorans had no reflection in mirrors, but she was pleased to see that as a Wingling, at least, she still did. She didn't know if that idea or the very fact that she had her own bedroom was more preposterous. She scoffed and wondered what other stereotypes about Sangorans were false.

She tucked her hair behind her ears and turned to look at the appendages jutting out of her back. They would eventually shape into leathery wings that would allow her to be free and fly through the skies, but for now, they were simply sore, pinkish limbs that resembled handless arm stumps up to the elbow. She had a small amount of control over them now, and she reasoned that she should practice controlling them as they grew.

They were still ugly.

She had come to terms with the fact she was no longer human. It was one sure thing in a life of uncertainty and constant anxiety. But was she actually Sangoran?

"Who are you?" she whispered, staring her own reflection right in the eyes for a long moment. She hung her head.

She glanced at the crumpled sheet of parchment on the floor next to her feet and scooped it up, scanning the page to remind herself when she must be ready. She had been invited, or perhaps commanded, to appear before the council of governors—the Mistresses of Dusk.

The letter introduced the council's purpose as the queen of Sangora's ruling council. Mara had only skimmed the lengthy note explaining that each member was assigned to govern one of the seven Sangoran states, and that they wanted to meet her. She racked her brain but could find no logical reason why they would want to do so. Perhaps something concerning the incident with the Walkers or the slave breakout? It had to be something to do with Lavinia's plans.

She wadded the parchment into a ball once more and tossed it into her closet. She withdrew the striking black dress from the corner and pulled it on behind the partition despite the fact she was alone in the room. She stepped out to look at herself in the mirror.

"Oh, damn."

Mara couldn't stop staring at how well the dress accentuated her figure in all the right places. It also allowed her growing wings to hang down her back, while from the front, she appeared normal. Human—if that's what 'normal' meant anymore.

The corner of her mouth twitched, and she began to smile. She had gained some weight back over the past couple weeks, so she didn't feel or look as sickly as she had in the camp, and Elena had cut and styled her hair. For the first time since she arrived in Sangora, she felt beautiful. Maybe, she thought, even the ugly wing stumps would someday soon be beautiful too.

For a moment, she thought of a man who would have loved to see how the dress fit; she thought of so many things that she never told him, but then a feeling creeped into her heart that she was all too familiar with, although one she'd never reserved for him. Hatred.

She felt her pulse race, and she fell to the ground, smacking her knees hard on the polished stone floor. She held her head in her hands as she rocked back and forth. He betrayed her—he was the reason for all her suffering. She screamed and heard the mirror shatter, and tiny fragments of glass showered to the ground. She felt a hand on her shoulder, and she whirled around to see Elena, her loving caretaker, who said nothing as she stroked Mara's hair.

"I'm sorry," Mara said, hyperventilating. "I didn't mean to— I didn't, I really didn't—I'm sorry, Elena…"

Elena nodded and continued to try to soothe Mara's nerves. Mara looked around and saw that much of the room was littered with debris, and the furniture now resembled piles of kindling.

"No one is mad at you, dear," Elena said. "Now—let's get you ready for your meeting with the council. It is soon, after all."

Mara ignored Elena's comment and looked around the room. "How did I do this?"

"You know, not many people have appeared in front of the Mistresses of Dusk. They must have some honor for you, to be sure!"

"Elena. Answer me—please."

Elena sighed and surveyed the wreckage around the room. She helped Mara to her feet and held her close, letting the weary girl lay her head on her soft shoulder.

"We had this conversation only minutes ago, dear. The healers think the trauma you experienced, or perhaps something else going on in your brain, has caused you to have some memory loss and some emotional and mental distress, to put it lightly. When you're in your fits, you can't control your new powers and…" Elena trailed off as she saw tears rolling down Mara's face. "All will be alright, dear. I'm sure whatever the council has in mind for you will help. Please do try to believe me."

Mara forced herself to form a smile, and she wrapped her arms around Elena in a real gesture of affection.

"Thank you, Elena," Mara said. "I hope I didn't hurt you."

"No, dear! Although you have done me a favor by smashing your mirror. It reminds me of how much like my mother I've started to look!" Elena said. Mara laughed through some tears and smoothed out the folds of her dress.

"You're not old yet, Elena," said Mara.

"Hopefully someday, sweetheart."

"I'm ready to go," Mara said, taking a deep breath. Elena nodded and took her arm and together they exited the chamber.

"You look absolutely breathtaking, dear."

Elena accompanied Mara out the front gates of the building where they found a cart pulled by several black horses. It reminded her of the slavers' prison carts, and she hesitated.

"My, my, they've sent you a driver. Good luck, dear," Elena said, and pulled Mara close before whispering. "No one could tell you've been crying, by the way, if you were wondering."

"I *was* wondering—thank you, Elena," she said with a sniffle.

Lavinia emerged from within the vehicle and stepped out, leaving the door open for Mara, who stepped up into the cart. She glanced up to see Lavinia and Elena share a quick embrace before following Mara inside. She sat down and groaned.

"Damn. You're still alive," Lavinia said to an ancient Sangoran sitting across from them dressed in the most beautiful gown Mara had ever seen. Mara tried to count the number of precious gems on the woman's dress, headpiece, and fingers, but she was distracted as woman began to speak.

"I am Mistress Delia of the council of Mistresses of Dusk. I simply wanted to meet you before the meeting of the council," she said, holding out her hand, a ring held out toward Mara. Mara guessed that the woman wanted her to kiss the ring, but she refrained, much to her disdain. Delia's face resembled that of a skeletal vulture, and her wispy hair looked like straw sticking out from under her headdress. "I hope you know that no matter what happens, you will always be below me."

"Until you keel over, and we put you in the ground," Lavinia said. "Oh, Delia. How I long for that day when I get to open a bottle of Opikorla on your gravestone.

"The nerve!" Delia exclaimed.

Lavinia turned to Mara. "You're probably wondering why you have been summoned."

The cart gave a lurch and began to move.

"It's crossed my mind," Mara answered. She watched Delia adjust the rings on her fingers as if there was some way to make them even more noticeable.

"You've been nominated to become a Mistress of Dusk."

"What? Why?!" Mara exclaimed, wiggling her wing nubs so that they were visible above her shoulders. "By who?"

"By me. I know that a Halfwing has never been given such an honor, but it isn't like there's a law saying that it can't happen," Lavinia answered. Delia scoffed as she examined her jewels.

"There are *those* who disagree," Lavinia said, glancing at Delia. "You will be given a task, Mara. Whatever it is, you must take it, and you must succeed. Am I clear?"

Mara nodded, and Lavinia sat back against the corner of the cart to get more comfortable. She closed her eyes and made sure to take up more than her half of the bench. Delia indeed took notice and sneered at Lavinia, who clearly didn't care.

"I suggest you get some sleep. It's a short path to Valistaran's Palace in Bukaral, but I'm not sure when you'll have the chance to sleep again," Lavinia said without opening her eyes. She said no more and was soon fast asleep, despite the bumpiness of the road.

Mara sat in silence for the remainder of the ride as Delia seemed content in her own delusional world of proud vanity.

Sooner than Mara had expected, the carriage stopped, and the side door next to Lavinia opened, letting moonlight pour into the cart. Lavinia almost fell on top of Delia as she jolted awake. Mara half stood to climb out, but Delia gave a cough and pushed past her, stepping from the vehicle with a surprisingly graceful stride.

"She hates you because you're prettier than her, even with all those gems," Lavinia said as she gestured to all of Mara. "It's a whole thing."

"Oh, thank you," Mara said, taken aback.

They emerged from the cart to see columns of human soldiers lining the street and gathered at the entrance to Valistaran's palatial fortress. Mara felt their gaze upon her, and she realized how self-conscious she was of her wing nubs in the backless dress. Lavinia and Delia guided the confused Halfwing up the stairs, following a crimson carpet that had likely been rolled out for this occasion. Mara remembered that crimson was not one of the colors of Talohira, and thus it must be in honor of the Sangoran guests. Who was she kidding? It was the color of blood. Of course, it was.

As the two Mistresses of Dusk and their Halfwing guest approached, the guards turned ninety degrees and held their spears high into the air, allowing them safe passage. As they neared the front gates, the sound of a great windstorm broke the solemn procession. Dozens of figures materialized out of thin air in a flurry of dust and ash, blades drawn and swinging.

They cut a bloody swath through the line of disoriented guards, spinning through their enemies with deadly accuracy. The captain ordered his men to attack but was felled by one of the Walkers who delivered two slashes across the chest with twin hook-shaped blades.

As soon as they had appeared, they were gone, at least twenty of Valistaran's men dead or bleeding on the stairs. Many of the remaining guards formed a wall of spears around Delia, Lavinia, and Mara. Lavinia unsheathed her sword and Mara grabbed a fallen spear from the earth.

"What is happening?" Mara asked.

"Your old friends," Lavinia said. "The Walkers. Be ready!"

There was another flurry of black smoke, and the Walkers reappeared, their leader at the fore of the onslaught. His blades danced through the guards with ease, and he launched himself toward Mara. Lavinia lashed out, but the leader of the Walkers vanished before her strike fell.

"Ronin!" Mara cried in defiance. "Show yourself!"

He appeared behind her with his hooked swords high above his head. Mara was ready for him and thrust her spear under her arm, striking him in the chest with the blunt end of the weapon.

She whirled around, but he was prepared, lashing out with both weapons. The way he dodged the weapon seemed to be part of a choreographed dance; the sickle swords caught the shaft of her spear and in one motion, he had disarmed her.

Mara thrust her palm forward, and a bolt of electricity escaped her hand, striking Ronin in the stomach. It threw him backward onto the stairs and immediately a dozen guards were upon him. Several of Ronin's men lay dead upon the stairs and Mara raised her hand once more in defense of her life.

"You are lost," Ronin said, his voice ethereal against the now silent night, "and how the world shall now have reason to mourn." He vanished into black smoke that faded on the wind.

His final words echoed in the night air, sending shivers down Mara's spine. She looked to Lavinia, who had a look of betrayal etched on her face. It vanished, much like Ronin, as soon as she saw Mara looking at her.

"Are you okay?" Mara whispered. "What's wrong?"

"Nothing."

She and the guards ushered Mara into the fortress with Delia trailing behind before the Walkers could appear again. Their cryptic message and Lavinia's brief expression haunted Mara, and she made a mental note to bring it up again.

"He went straight for you," Lavinia said. "Not for me or for our walking treasure chest over here." She gestured toward Delia, who simply looked annoyed that they had been attacked. She showed an utter disregard for the loss of life that had occurred.

"Why?" asked Mara.

"It seems *Lord* Ronin Jakoni is aware of something we are not," said Lavinia. The way she said lord was laced with venom.

"Just before I was made Sangoran, I remember someone saying I was compatible with—I don't know—I thought they meant I was compatible with becoming Sangoran, or to give me powers, but then Ronin mentioned something about curing the Sangoran race or a cure *for* the Sangoran race, or something— I'm not sure which he meant—"

"Slow down, girl," Lavinia said. "We need to go."

At that moment, Mara wondered who exactly had been the one responsible for saving her from death atop the tower.

The guards led them through the palace to a high chamber at the top of a tower with several archways allowing access to the sky. At the center was a moon shaped table between two sets of tiered seating on opposite sides of the room, much like the one in Doftaan. There was a second rectangular table set up juxtaposed to the crescent shaped one; three other Sangorans sat behind it with one empty seat, to which Lavinia motioned for Mara to sit. She did so and attempted to hide her pitiful half wings upon noticing the powerful sets of wings on the others.

The guards lined the edges of the chamber, and hundreds of Sangorans flew into the room upon the signal to enter. They soared through the archways and took their seats on the tiered benches. Several Talohiran humans entered the council room to witness the proceedings as well, joining the others in the stands. As the last of the Sangoran and Talohiran citizens got settled, Lavinia signaled to close the archways, and the soldiers stationed there sealed them off with retractable steel grates.

Mara examined the Sangorans in the stands. They were all clad in fine apparel, perhpas important figures from all over the country. Lavinia and Delia took their seats around the crescent shaped table with the other Mistresses of Dusk. Lavinia gave no eye contact to Mara, as if trying to conceal their alliance.

"We recognize Mistresses Lavinia and Delia. We welcome you to this session of the council's meeting," said a voice from somewhere in the room. Delia seemed put off that her name was not mentioned first, and Mara felt a growing dislike for her.

"We also recognize Ladies Draguta, Lacramora, and General Anca the Nightmare of Thanatanos seated alongside the Halfwing Mara," the voice rang through the chamber again.

Mara wondered if the striking contrast between formality and informality during the proceedings was part of Sangoran culture. She thought it odd that the leaders did not use any of the women's surnames, and the fact that the common people took their seats before their leaders confused her, but she knew customs had to be different in her new home. She vowed to learn those norms and practices in order to survive and even thrive here. If she was going to stay, that was. But how could she ever go back to Thanatanos like this?

Soon the wide double doors at the rear of the chamber opened once more, and a column of three more Mistresses of Dusk entered the room.

"We now recognize the Mistresses of Dusk Ihrin, Raluca, and Florenta." The others took their places around the crescent table as Florenta's minions set the massive woman's platform down at her spot before taking their seats in the stands.

A second door opened opposite the one the Mistresses of Dusk had entered from, and the entire chamber stood.

"Hail High King Valistaran Talohir, Uniter of the Nation of Talohira and Tribes of Sangora!" the announcer's voice rang through the chamber.

Everyone in the room placed their hand over their heart, and Mara took notice to follow suit. Valistaran took his seat on a throne facing the others. His crimson cloak was a gesture of goodwill to the Sangoran nation, and in his hands, he held a jeweled scepter. He sat down, pushing his cloak out of the way.

"I have called this special session of the Council of Dusk in order to discuss the nominations for the positions of Mistress of Dusk. As of today, I will not be naming my new queen."

Everybody in the stands whispered to their neighbors, for they were eager to discover both who would be their queen and who would become a Mistress of Dusk. Valistaran cleared his throat and spoke with great authority.

"First, we shall hear the case of Lady Lacramora of the tribe of Dashga. After which, we shall hear from Lady Draguta of the people of Terman. Third, General Anca of Krim's case shall be heard. Lastly, we shall hear the case of why a Halfwing from Thanatanos, Mara Bartunek, should join the council. Let it be known that two of these four shall do so," Valistaran said. "There shall be eight Mistresses of Dusk, and in time one shall be named queen of Talohira and Sangora."

He looked toward Lady Lacramora as a cue for her to speak. Lady Lacramora stood, and Mistress Raluca did the same.

"Lady Lacramora has been a prominent leader among her people for nearly a decade," Raluca said. "Her contributions to Sangoran society have included an improvement to the standard of living in the impoverished sector of the State of Dashga, which I govern, as well as the complete extermination of the Walkers from our state, a feat which has been accomplished nowhere else except Karpaska." Raluca and Lacramora took their places. Mara hoped that she would get to be as silent as Lacramora, but she rather doubted it.

"Lady Draguta," Valistaran said. Draguta and Delia stood.

"Lady Draguta has led a successful campaign against Laniras itself," Delia said. Mara glanced at Lavinia who shook her head with a scoff. "She was influential in the establishment of the work camps to construct the building for the new, future government sector, and other—"

"Mistress Delia, does Laniras still stand?" Valistaran asked.

"It does, my lord," Delia replied, her voice scratchy.

"Then do not make the mistake of claiming success over it in order to convince me that your *second* choice for Mistress of Dusk should earn such a position. Lady Draguta, are you aware that your spokesman did in fact nominate Lady Lacramora before yourself?"

"No, my lord," Draguta replied. Valistaran said no more, and both Draguta and Delia took their seats. Mara wondered if Valistaran shared her and Lavinia's dislike for Mistress Delia. She felt that Lacramora's case was much stronger than Draguta's, anyway. A sentiment shared by many, as evident in the murmurs and whispers around the room.

Next, General Anca stood up. Anca was a warrior and built with broad shoulders and tight muscles. She would stand at least a head above most people in the room, but as Florenta raised herself to her full height, she dwarfed even the general. Mara estimated that the woman had to be over two meters tall and nearly as wide.

"General Anca, the Nightmare of Thanatanos, has been at the fore of our armies for many years. Although she has not yet taken Laniras, she has leveled cities in the name of the king and in the name of Elafris and the Goddesses while defending Sangora's borders from all enemies."

Mara glanced up at the mention of the name of Elafris, the one called the Fallen, who dwelled in the Afterworld. She wondered to what regard he was held in Sangora and Talohira.

"I care not for the Thannish old gods *or* the women you worship," Valistaran said, "but General Anca has indeed been a loyal and powerful tool in my hand. For this reason, I may keep her at the head of my armies, rather than the head of a table, with all due respect to you, my general."

General Anca nodded, and she sat down. She did not seem the type for politics anyway. Valistaran turned his attention to Mara, who was distracted and taken aback. She quickly stood, breathing heavily as she tried to calm her nerves. Lavinia stood and walked away from the table to stand near Mara.

"Mara Bartunek has not been among us for long. Many of you shall say that makes her a problem. *I* say the complete opposite. She has power and a certain resolve that I have seen in very few. I'm not the only one. The Walkers see it in her as well. The attack which occurred only moments ago was launched against her, and not against me or Lady Delia." Mara saw Delia sneer as Lavinia used the wrong title. "Never have the Walkers been so bold to make a brazen assassination attempt within the grounds of the palace."

"An interesting argument," Valistaran said.

"Halfwing—no, *Lady* Mara, is a proven warrior and a most resourceful woman. Within the slave camp, I witnessed her escape attempts, and I noted how she acted within its walls. She is a born leader, a valuable ally, and as staunch of a soul as I have ever met. I have never seen anyone give others hope as she does." Lavinia sat, and Mara followed suit.

"Lady Mara, I am not finished with you," Valistaran said. She stood back up. "It is true that you are originally from Thanatanos. Many Sangorans are originally Thans, but you were one who did not come here by your own free will. You were forced into this life. Forced into a new body. You have had our cultures thrust upon you, and I must know now and forever more, if you do swear your allegiance to the Sangoran Nation and to me, High King of Talohira and Sangora."

No words came to Mara's lips, and she glanced toward Lavinia, who gave a slight nod as if to tell her what to say.

"I do," Mara said. "I was betrayed by my friends and allies from the slave camp—so, yes." She felt her nerves rising, and she could feel an anxiety attack coming on. She bit the inside of her cheek in order to try to keep calm. It didn't help.

"And now—a task for you all. I know of Anca's prowess in battle, but I have yet to see your own leadership tested. You will plan an assault on the city of Nitra from the newly liberated city of Vudapas. It is my hope that you will take the city, but your simple survival may prove your worth," said Valistaran. Mara glanced toward Lavinia, who gave her an encouraging nod.

"May the most bloody survive," said the high king as he strode from the chamber. "I wish you all success."

CHAPTER TWENTY
NITRA FALLS

Lightning illuminated Mara's legion of warriors; thunder clapped overhead like a war drum of the Sangoran goddesses, and her heart seemed to beat in her chest just as loud. At that moment, she wondered just how she had reached that point in her life. Mere months ago, she was thinking of ways to overthrow the enemies that enslaved her, and now she led an entire host of them into battle against the kingdom she once called home.

Home. A strange idea. She was between two of them now, and yet she did not belong in either of them. Unwelcome in both. An outsider. A stranger. Hated by all, it seemed. Then how could she betray that which cast her out? Whom could she betray but herself?

Her own experience told her that a friend's knife could dig deeper than any stranger's, tearing away any allegiance to a people or cause. She now had no loyalty to anything other than her own survival. To herself. And at that moment, she made up her mind that she would not just endure life but overcome it. Conquer it. Control it.

In the weeks since her meeting with the council, her wings had developed to the point that they could suspend her for a short time before she grew too exhausted. Her new limbs ached for days after she tried, as they currently did. It was slow progress, but progress, nonetheless.

Ladies Draguta and Lacramora led legions borrowed from other generals in the Sangoran army, but General Anca led her own more experienced troops. Every Sangoran knew the purpose of the campaign: not only to take the city of Nitra, but to prove the tactical worth of each of the candidates to Valistaran Talohir.

The horde of Sangoran warriors halted a half a mile from the walled city of Nitra, resting for the first time since launching the assault from the city of Vudapas. They had flown through the night in order to cross the border into Thanatanos.

Due to her improved eyesight since her transformation, Mara could see the outlines of men lining the ramparts of Nitra's wall, even in the dark. She was getting used to many of the changes, including her wings, but she still bit her bottom lip with her sharpened teeth whenever she ate.

They weren't visibly any different from a human's, of course, but it was still the least favorite of her changes. She ran her tongue along the newest wound as if doing so would take her mind off the battle that would soon commence. She shook her head; why was she thinking about a hurt lip now?

She watched Thannish soldiers hoisting large boulders into the baskets of trebuchets set upon the bulwark to protect the city. Erected below them were vicious ballistae and pots of boiling liquid ready to make short work of any Sangoran foolhardy enough to come near the walls.

Mara shook her head. Didn't they know Sangorans could fly?

Her army stood motionless behind her, awaiting her command, as did those that followed Draguta, Lacramora, and Anca. Hours ago, she and the other nominees sent a convoy with a message for the city's leaders. Mara thought the message was simple, if not a bit clichéd: Surrender to Talohira or be destroyed. She'd given different orders to her troops, however.

She had given orders that they were to allow all civilians to evacuate and were to avoid engaging them at all costs.

Even Drahomir, the coward that had betrayed her could understand the original message, and she hoped that he was one of the few that would stand and fight so that she could return his treachery tenfold. Her mind drifted to Aleksander, for although she was determined to seek revenge, she wondered if she would be able to kill him. He too had betrayed her on that fateful night upon the tower, after all. And what about Pol? Rehor?

She shook off the thought as a trio of sturdy war horses galloped forth from the wide gates leading from Nitra. They bore the viridian banner of Thanatanos and were accompanied by the returning Sangoran envoy. Mara cracked her knuckles as she walked out to meet King Romiton's messengers. Draguta and Lacramora followed, but Anca stood still before her troops, as if taking notes on how the others performed in this exercise.

"I bring word from Crown Prince Xanthurias, son of King Romiton Romus," said the foremost of the company. His horse trotted up next to the group of potential Mistresses of Dusk, putting him a few feet higher than them. He dismounted and unrolled a short scroll.

Mara flinched at the mention of the prince's name.

"I assume you received our message?" Mara asked.

Draguta chuckled and Lacramora smirked. The man said nothing in response and began to read.

"May it be known to the powers that be in Sangora and Talohira that the city of Nitra will not bow down to the hosts of blood. We are prepared to defend the innocent and oppose tyranny wherever it may show its face," read the messenger, giving a nervous glance up at the Sangorans. "Although many settlements have fallen, the nation of Thanatanos will stand firm as a constant light against the darkness. Signed, Crown Prince Xanthurias Romus."

He rolled up the scroll and waited for a response.

"You may tell your beloved prince that brave words have no power over the blade. We will bleed dry each and every man, woman, and child that does not flee," Lacramora said. Without further warning, she thrust her dagger up into the man's chest. "And that includes you."

At the same time, Draguta pounced upon the other soldier, tearing at him with razor sharp claw attachments on her gauntlets. The third messenger galloped away, sounding a horn. Lacramora took after him, unfolding her leathery black wings to take flight.

Mara's stomach twisted as she beheld the needless murders.

"No, let him go," Draguta shouted. "Let him warn the city. Let him tell them what they face!"

"Lady Mara, as soon as we cross the wall, take the western region. Can you do that?" Lacramora asked.

Mara felt resentment growing in her chest. Who was Lacramora to order her to do anything?

"I'll do what I need to do."

Lady Lacramora raised her bloodied dagger over her head and screamed a Sangoran war cry. The Sangorans following her mirrored her action, sending the countryside into a cruel cacophony of blood-curdling screams. Mara thought to herself that she would have to show such leadership if she were to become a Mistress of Dusk.

Without another second of hesitation, she took flight, spear raised high above her head. She was the first to advance upon the city of Nitra, and her host of Sangoran warriors followed behind her in like manner. She only hoped they would remember her orders not to harm civilians.

The hordes of Lacramora, Draguta, and Anca were close behind, descending upon the wall in a dark wave. The men upon the walls pushed the tanks of boiling oil over, scalding many of the Sangorans as they attempted to fly over the wall. Mara yelped as a massive ballista arrow skewered one of the warriors flying to her left.

Her fatigued wings could barely take her high enough to crest the mighty bulwark of the city, and she began to fall. She cursed under her breath and hurled her spear through one of the few small glass windows in the wall. She swooped into the chamber, finding a guardhouse filled with armor clad soldiers ready to defend their home.

Mara lurched forward, drawing a dagger from her waist. Many of her followers pushed their way through the small arched window as well, crawling into the room behind their leader. Mara advanced, plunging her dagger into a man's shoulder before scooping up her fallen spear. The Sangorans tore through the room with the ferocity of dragons, felling any soldier that impeded their progress. They were not without losses, however, and many of her own fell by the blade.

"Get this door down," Mara ordered. It was barred from the other side and would not budge. "Any and all who have powers, blast it on my mark. One, two—three!"

Several bolts of electricity and balls of flame collided with the door, reducing it to rubble. Mara pushed through the settling dust and over the twisted iron and splintered wood, finding herself within the wall of the city. She remembered coming to Nitra long ago to deliver a shipment of grain with her father and marveling at the construction of the mighty, double thick walls, which offered greater security for those inside.

If her father could see her now.

"They keep more soldiers within these walls," she said as she remembered what she had seen so long ago. "The narrow passageways take away our main advantage of flight, so they could overrun us. We need to find an exit as soon as possible."

"Then we shall fight our way through until we find the prince himself, Lady Mara," said one of her warriors.

"What is your name?" Mara asked the brave woman.

"My name is Vasilica, my lady," she answered.

"I want you by me at the front of our assault—your heart will inspire those around you," she said then addressed one of the others. "You—send word to those behind. I want this wall cleared out before the rest of our troops continue into the city. Now—raise your spears and take down this city!"

Down the narrow passageway, Mara saw a group of soldiers advancing, several of which hefted heavy crossbows. She could hear another group behind them; they were trapped on both sides. As a shower of crossbow bolts felled those around her, Mara screamed in her fury and instinctively let out a burst of telekinetic energy that sent the darts clattering against the walls and ground.

Vasilica shot forth like an arrow, letting her spear guide the way. More Sangoran warriors flooded through the guardhouse door into the passageway, and Mara spurred them onward. Half of her troops attacked one group of soldiers while those following herself and Vasilica crashed against the wall of shields and pikes guarding the crossbowmen. Several of Mara's warriors perished against their foes' weapons, but Vasilica broke through their ranks by tearing at their unprotected faces with the metal, razor sharp claw attachments on her fingers.

Mara winced as a blade pierced her wing, but one of her followers slew the attacker. Her soldiers fell one after another, and she realized that if they didn't meet back up with the rest of their troops, they would all perish. Her followers faced similar losses against a second wave of fierce Thannish soldiers, but her few powered people hurled bolts of electricity and flame into their foes. Still, they did not break.

She launched a weak burst of lightning from her palm, striking the nearest man in the chest while two other Sangorans cast flames toward their foes; the fire caught on the soldiers' cloaks and spread across the straw scattered across the ground. The flames swept over several of the dead that lay upon the earth, creating a temporary break in the chaos. Mara leaped into the air and flapped as hard as she could, making it over the soldiers and the wall of smoke, her dwindling group of followers close behind.

"I see a door ahead!" Mara cried. "Keep going! We can meet up with the others outside!" This was not going well, and she knew it. Together, she, Vasilica, and the other six remaining warriors raced for the opening, leaving the battle behind. They turned as sharply as their wings would allow and shot out the archway up into the open sky. The horrific sound of battle greeted them as the silver moon and orange flame bathed their faces in their light.

They soared over the conflict toward the hilltop fortress at the center of the city. Many houses were ablaze, and the empty market was littered with corpses, human and Sangoran alike. A moment of regret and remorse filled Mara's heart, but it was soon overrun by feelings of revenge, betrayal, hatred, and the need to survive. She would be stronger than those below, whatever it took. Her heart ached with the agony of a tortured soul, but still, she pressed on.

"Make for the open patio there, just above the courtyard!" Mara shouted as one of her followers was riddled with arrows and plummeted toward the ground. She could make no sense of the chaos and was unable to distinguish her army from the rest of the frenzied Sangorans below. Her six remaining followers would have to do.

They landed upon the patio on the second story of the fortress. The garden there was serene—a strange moment of peace, untouched by the madness outside the palace. Mara strode toward the double doors and Vasilica shattered the beautiful glass panes with the butt of her spear. It was easy to open the door after that, and they strode inside unopposed.

"Where are they?" Mara wondered aloud. "Shouldn't the fortress be more guarded than the rest of the city?"

"What is our plan, Lady Mara?" asked one of her followers.

"Find Prince Xanthurias. If we can kill him, we will without any doubt prove ourselves to Valistaran and the council," she answered. They strolled through the castle looking for any indication of the prince or any palace guards.

"Perhaps they evacuated the palace," suggested Vasilica.

"This is a fortress, just like the palace in Laniras," Mara said, shaking her head. "I wonder—"

A bolt of cyan energy tore through the nearest Sangoran, splattering the wall behind her with dark gore as her body slumped to the ground. Mara whirled around with wide eyes to see the silhouette of a warrior eight feet tall standing before her.

Mara stood motionless, unsure of how to act, but then Valakor, the General of Thanatanos, stepped forward, the metallic thud of his boots echoing throughout the room.

He said nothing as he raised his weapon, a long scythe with a vicious, yet elegant blade. He advanced slowly, but they were all immobilized with unsurety and fear to flee.

"Where is the prince?" Mara demanded.

"He is not here, for he fights alongside his men. He does not hide in his tower as they lay down their lives. You, however, show great cowardice in coming here to hunt him as a trophy for your fallen king," Valakor said, readying his scythe.

Mara shot into the air and Valakor unleashed a bolt of blue energy from his blade toward her. She flipped in the air, and Vasilica and the others darted after her. Valakor sliced one of her warriors clean in half with a swing of his scythe; both halves of her body hit the floor, and he unleashed another stream of cyan flame from his weapon toward Mara, who threw herself out of the way, striking the ceiling in the process.

Mara and her followers shot around the corner like startled birds. Valakor's heavy footfalls echoed throughout the hall after them as she tumbled against the floor and came to a stop near a set of double doors marked as a hospital wing.

"Don't you dare!" Valakor roared, slicing one more of Mara's soldiers in half.

She pushed her way into the room to escape Valakor's onslaught but was surprised to find that the hospital was not empty. It was filled with injured and sick citizens of Nitra, who screamed in horror as she entered the room.

They shut the doors behind them as Mara strolled into the chamber of healing, the eyes of dozens of scared civilians locked on her. She strode to the end of the chamber.

Her heart leaped from her chest, and she barely believed the lies her eyes told her, but after a brief moment of doubt, there was no mistaking it—it truly was Drahomir in the hospital bed before her. Fortune smiled upon Mara, and her mouth twisted into a dark smile. Even if she failed in her quest to find Xanthurias, today would be a personal victory.

"Please, please don't kill us," said someone in a bed behind Mara. She turned to her followers and held up her hand, a signal to stay their weapons.

"My orders stand. They all survive," Mara said. "All except this one."

Her three followers obeyed, standing guard at the door should Valakor break through. Mara grabbed Drahomir by the front of his hospital gown and pulled him from the bed despite his weak attempts to strike her. The onlookers screamed, and he groaned as she slammed him against the floor, twisting his legs in the bed sheets. A look of confused horror crossed his face.

"You didn't think you'd ever see me again, did you?!" Mara shouted, kicking Drahomir in the ribs.

He crawled toward the door on the opposite side of the room, and she let him go. She found a strange sense of empty enjoyment in her victory as the traitorous coward squirmed away. Drahomir tried to crawl away, slumping against a pillar.

"Why me?" Drahomir asked.

"I've asked myself the same thing a lot over the past months," Mara said, pulling the dagger from her belt. She kneeled next to her former friend and grasped his wrist. "So, I'll ask *you* instead, Drahomir. *Why me?*"

"Mara?" he whispered as the realization of her identity dawned on him. "By Elafris, what did they do to you?"

Mara slashed the blade across his arm, drawing a crimson line of blood. A cut for a cut. He cried out and jerked away from her, rolling onto the floor. He inched away out the far doorway, and she stepped on his back, pressing him to the ground.

She could hear Valakor pounding on the hospital door.

"They? *They* did nothing. This is all *your* doing."

"Please, Mara. I'll tell you anything. I can find you Aleksander. It was his plan to betray you in the first place!"

She could tell he was spouting whatever lies he thought would help him survive. She understood the thirst for survival.

Mara ignored his pleas and plunged the dagger between his ribs. He roared in pain and threw his legs into the air, trying to punch and kick Mara, but to no avail. Blood soaked his healing center gown, and his face grew pale.

"Mara, stop!" a familiar voice echoed down the staircase. That voice. It resonated in her soul, and her rage manifested in crackling lightning around her head, limbs, and wings.

She looked up and beheld Aleksander standing before her, sword drawn. Hanna, Shanthah, Josman, and Kamil were close behind with their own weapons in hand. Hanna gasped and placed her hands over her mouth in shock. Mara raised her wings and held her spear aloft, lightning crackling around her hands.

"Mar…" whispered Hanna, tears streaming down her face.

"He deserves this," Mara said through her own tears, glancing down at Drahomir. "You all do! You left me to die!"

"They had no way to get to us! Damn it, Mara!" yelled Drahomir.

"And maybe that makes Mara right," Aleksander said. "Maybe we all deserve this. But you don't, Mara. This isn't you."

"I've killed more than you know, and you should be next," Mara answered as she pointed her spear at Aleksander's heart.

"Revenge will bring you to a place where there is no turning back. Sure, you killed in war, but not—" He was cut off as Mara stabbed Drahomir once more with the tip of her spear.

"You have *no idea* what I've done before *and* after that damned slave camp!" Mara shouted. She stumbled back, tears streaming down her cheeks. She pressed her hand over her mouth in shock and despair. "How could you forget me?!"

As she let her guard down, Valakor appeared and tackled her through the window behind Drahomir. Her three followers raced after them as they plummeted downward.

"What took you so long?" Mara shouted, blackening his armor with jolts of electricity as they fell. It was a genuine question, for the warrior had been right behind them. Valakor lashed out with his scythe and caught onto a window frame, using it to swing into the window and out of view.

Mara plummeted toward the ground and at the last moment gained control of her wings just enough to save herself from the fall. Her followers landed next to her, and she glanced around, finding herself in the courtyard of a ruined church.

She thrust her spear into the earth and slumped next to it as hellish fire engulfed Nitra. She felt panic overtaking her, but she had to fight it off. She shut her eyes and tried to breathe.

"Lady Mara," said Vasilica, "look!" Mara obeyed, as if she was not the one in a position of authority. She followed her lieutenant's gaze and saw Prince Xanthurias leading a group of now homeless citizens of Nitra away from the chaos.

"Take him," Mara ordered. "But let them go."

They shot toward him, and Mara limped after them on foot. She winced at the gash in her leg where the window's broken glass had sliced her flesh. The citizens fought Mara's soldiers with rocks, broken blades, or whatever they could find, but they were pushed back by their long Sangoran spears.

Prince Xanthurias drew his blade and with several of his guards and a vicious yell raced toward Mara, who echoed his cry and shocked him with a sudden burst of electricity. The tenacious prince got to his feet, and his blade met Mara's wing, cutting a hole through the thick skin. Vasilica and the others dueled with the prince's royal guard as Mara faced her prize.

Mara screeched and slammed Xanthurias hard in the chest with both wings, knocking him to the ground. They were both exhausted but fought with a ferocity that burned as bright as the flames that consumed the city. She leaped upon the prince as he drew a knife from his belt and embedded it in her side just near the hipbone. She clawed at his face, and he brought his fist up into her sternum, knocking her backward. The prince stumbled to his feet and brought his sword around, which clashed against the shaft of Mara's spear.

She lashed out again, and at the same moment Xanthurias punched her in the jaw, spinning her around and knocking her spear to the dirt. She recovered just in time, landing a well-timed jab to Xanthurias's face with a bloodied fist. He struck her in the stomach, and she slammed both fists against his ears before he tackled her to the ground.

She called out for help, but her followers were still locked in combat. Many of her allies had been driven away, but a vast portion of the fallen city was a glowing inferno. As Xanthurias pommeled her face with punches, she saw thousands of refugees fleeing through the streets.

"Tell them to let the refugees go!" Mara screamed at one of her followers, who shot into the sky at her command.

Mara twisted beneath the prince just as Xanthurias brought his weapon down to plunge it into her heart. As it came down, Vasilica slammed into the prince, knocking him off Mara as a group of eight Sangorans with bloodstained weapons emerged from the ruined church.

Vasilica held Xanthurias at bay as Mara rallied her forces; holding her sword aloft, she cried, "To me!"

She limped toward Xanthurias with her bladed wings outstretched. The prince parried a blow from her left wing and then slammed her in the sternum with a heavy fist. She fell to the ground, and he whirled around, beheading a Sangoran soldier with a slash of his regal blade.

The prince's golden sword was like a light shining through the darkness as he hacked through both wings of one Sangoran warrior before twisting around to block a blow from another.

He brought his elbow around into the throat of his nearest foe and then plunged a dagger into the neck of the next. He danced around them and regained his balance, stabbing the now wingless Sangoran through the heart.

"Back!" called Mara, and the others shot into the sky, retreating from their certain death.

Mara shot toward Xanthurias, tackling him into the dirt one last time. The two wrestled to gain advantage over the other, but the prince cried out as Mara's dagger pierced his chest. His eyes widened, and he went limp. Mara stumbled backward in disbelief and collapsed against a ruined bit of wall.

Two emotions filled her heart: hope for a future without war, but also remorse and regret at what had to be done to bring to pass such a future. Blackness closed in on her. What was happening? This had to be a nightmare. Without warning, images of Drahomir, Aleksander, and the others shot into her head. She began to panic and screamed into the night; broken memories of a time between her betrayal and this dark moment filled her mind—it seemed like years ago, but it was surely impossible.

The prince was dead. Both sides of this conflict believed they were right and fought for the freedom of their people—for people they loved. So, what difference did it make if she slew Valistaran or Xanthurias? Both, even? She seemed doomed to a life as a weapon, no matter what side she was forced into. She got to her feet and stumbled toward a priest standing alone in the ruins of the church. Did he think himself a sentinel that could defend the ruined building?

"I sense the sadness in your heart," the priest said. "There is hope yet remaining for you, friend. You have not resigned yourself to Elafris quite yet."

"Have revenge and murder not already done that?" Mara asked through tears. "If not, they are the price I have paid for whatever position I gain from this damned campaign."

"And with that position, what will you do?" he asked. Mara said nothing for a long while. The priest once again spoke up. "I hope that with power, you will bring peace and find redemption. You are never lost, daughter of Sangora. Never."

"There is a song," Mara said after a few moments, dragging her spear through the debris of the chapel. "A song my mother wrote. It's a simple tune."

"Why are you telling me this?" the priest asked.

"Because I need you to play it for me," Mara said, pressing her spear into the back of his neck to get him to move.

"But the stairs—I cannot reach the organ," he said in protest. Mara said nothing but grasped him under the arms and shot into the air, dropping him onto the crumbling balcony that held the massive pipe organ. "The tune?" he asked.

Mara hummed the hauntingly beautiful tune, and the priest played along.

"Thank you," Mara said. She didn't know why.

The tune of her mother's lullaby filled the world as the battle continued in the distance. Nitra's army was all but defeated, and the prospect of reinforcements was bleak. By the time word reached Laniras that Nitra had fallen, Mara and the others would be long gone.

She sang to herself in a soft voice, struggling to get through the song without tears, her words drowned out by the booming pipe organ.

Whatever it takes, my—my love
I'll hold your heart with mine
And from your side—from your side, ne'er I'll depart
Even when—even when my heart breaks, my dove
There with you… Yes, there I'll be.

She sobbed through each line of the song and turned around, her heart thundering in her chest as she saw the silhouette of a lone man standing in the ruins of the church. She knew her plan had worked as soon as she heard him finish the second verse of the song in time with the music.

Whatever it takes,
my dear sweetheart
For both our sakes
far from death's black dart
There with me, yes, you'll be
Whatever it takes.

Aleksander stepped out of the shadows, sword drawn and bloodied. Had he followed her all the way here from the tower? Mara thrust the end of her spear into the earth and looked at Aleksander with disdain and sadness. She tried to cling to the remorse she felt earlier but seeing him seemed to drain it from her heart. Lightning flashed high above them, followed a moment later by a mighty crash of thunder. The heavens began to weep upon the fallen city, a soft lullaby that soothed the roaring flames.

"You have no idea why I distrusted you and not the others when I first met you in the slave camp," she said, taking a step toward him. Aleksander said nothing as he stood there, his leg still bleeding. "It's because it was you. All those years ago—that boy. It was you. I knew it all along. I knew it couldn't be a coincidence that you just *happened* to be in my slave district. You weren't called Aleksander back then—but that name I knew you by wasn't your real name either. It couldn't have been. I know that now."

"I have no idea what you're talking about," Aleksander said. "Mara, let me help you. Talk to me. *Please.* I'm begging you."

She blasted his sword with a bolt of lightning that separated blade from hilt and rendered her former friend defenseless.

"Don't play me for a fool, Aleksander. You betrayed me on that tower just like you betrayed my family and the people I loved. You are the reason so many of them died. Don't you dare tell me you don't remember. I didn't want to admit it until now, but how could I not, now? You *know* why they came to Cineca!"

Aleksander knew he had to think fast if he wanted to survive this encounter. He fought to remember, but it was in vain.

"Mara, you know I wish I could. I can honestly tell you that I don't remember what happened. Please, tell me. I was trying to help you get out alive in that tower. If I did something that made you think I betrayed you, I am so, so sorry."

Mara gave one hysterical laugh and shook her head, slamming her spear into the ground as all mirth and mercy drained from her face.

"Do you know what that cuff we found does?" Mara asked. Pure loathing was carved across her striking visage. Aleksander remained silent as to not provoke her. "The building Drahomir found it in isn't The Cage. No, Aleks—the cuff itself *is* the cage. It's a Mind Prison. Put it on someone's wrist for a few seconds, and it's like they spent months in their own private cage in their mind. One minute, and they're trapped for a year. How long did you leave it on my wrist?"

A horrible realization washed over Aleksander and all hope seemed to drain from his heart. "At least twenty minutes."

"Twenty years!" Mara shouted. "Twenty! I was trapped in my own mind for twenty years, Aleksander! Don't you dare say now that you didn't betray me!"

Tears streamed down her beautiful, tortured face.

"I am so sorry," Aleksander said in shock. "I—I had no idea—"

"You used to represent *hope* to me," Mara said. "I had hope you'd come back. You meant something to me once. And that's why I'm not going to kill you right now." She turned away from the burning city, intent on leaving him there. "But the next time we meet, I won't be so merciful."

"Don't walk away like this," Aleksander whispered, stepping over the hilt of his damaged blade. The inferno that danced around him to the tune of Mara's mother's song echoed more than the death of his people. Indeed, it heralded the end of hope itself. He could utter but one word.

"Why?"

Defenseless. For the first time since their final kiss, nothing else mattered. Nothing. Splintered images of memories shattered by betrayal and loss, corrupted by the foul grip of time and change began to creep into his mind.

"You know why," she replied, the orange and crimson of dancing flame reflecting across the glistening, crystal blue of her eyes, "and so do I."

All seemed to succumb to the shadows. All except those eyes. Those eyes that once shined with hope. Those eyes that once meant so much more but now only mirrored the death and fire that consumed the earth.

"I do," he replied, his voice faltering. He collapsed to his knees as if he were begging, his greaves clanking against stone. "But we can't let it end this way. Please, Mara—"

"It already has."

Disembodied screams and bloodcurdling howls murdered the eerie silence. A shiver crawled down his spine as he tried to stop himself from watching her walk away. Wings as foul as the accursed night's sky unfolded from beneath her cloak, which, tattered as the faith of the dying, seemed to wave as a banner against hope and love.

Together with her last remaining lieutenants, into the midnight sky she disappeared. Gone in the red moonlight, leaving thousands wounded and thousands more bled dry by the dreaded watchers of night.

CHAPTER TWENTY-ONE
FALLEN SON

Aleksander awoke from his dream in a cold sweat. His heart thundered within his chest as he scrambled for a moment to remember where he was. The hospital bed in Laniras felt like the silken linens of a king's bed compared to the pathetic cots in the slave camp, which were all he knew. His friends from his district and other allies lay wounded in nearby cots around him.

They had won their freedom from the slave camp and survived the invasion of Nitra, but at great cost. Many of their allies had given their lives, but one person weighed more heavily on Aleksander's mind than any other—not a life that was taken in the traditional sense of death, but taken, nonetheless.

His dream was about her, but not as they used to be. He saw her face and heard her screams, the vivid image of the burning city imprinted into his mind. Mara wasn't dead as they had assumed.

No, her fate was much worse. He closed his eyes and once again succumbed to exhaustion.

The day came and passed, and the pale gold light of the dying sun gave little warmth to the cool spring evening. Everything it touched seemed to radiate a faint glow, causing the world to seem somehow softer, as if the world were allowing its people a moment of reprieve from the chaos.

Aleksander and his friends were gathered now for the funeral for Prince Xanthurias, which would soon begin. He would be laid to rest alongside his grandfather Jaromir and his other fallen ancestors in a tomb beneath the palace in Laniras. The fallen in Nitra and those who died freeing the prince as well as the slaves would also be honored during the service.

Dignitaries from all over Thanatanos were gathered to pay tribute to the fallen son. However, it was the masses of common folk that crowded outside the walls of the open-air chapel that displayed just how beloved Xanthurias was. The roof of the church was open, allowing the sky to shine into the room, despite the slight chill of new spring.

"I wish that I had known him," Hanna said to Shanthah.

"You would have loved him," Shanthah replied. "No prince has ever had a way with the people as Xanthurias had. Or such a way with the ladies."

"Yeah, not impressed," Hanna said, scooting closer to Shanthah with a smile.

Aleksander sat in silence next to his friends, arms folded, and ankles crossed; he could not help but think that he *did* know

Xanthurias, and he cursed his mind for not remembering him. Josman, Kamil, Mara's brother Pol, and Rehor sat on the white wooden bench behind the trio, and all of them bore visible wounds. Drahomir alone was absent. He had survived but was in critical condition.

The events of the past few days had been heavy on each of them. Other than Aleksander, Mara's fall to the darkness had the most profound impact on Hanna, Pol, and Rehor. Pol and Rehor had bonded in the healing center, and their new friendship was at least one spark of happiness that had emerged from the nightmarish embers of despair.

"I don't know what to feel," Pol said, staring at the front of the chapel. "I just feel numb."

"You know, sometimes there are moments that time just stops—or seems to," Rehor said, twiddling his thumbs. "There's nothing but you. You are just so defeated, and the world knows it. The universe just *lets* you be numb. But do you know what is so beautiful about those moments? They are when you truly start to heal. And I believe that this peaceful moment under the sunlight is one of those times for many of us."

"If we were in a bar, I'd drink to that," said Josman.

"Unfortunately, we're in a church," Shanthah answered.

"There's no rule saying you can't drink in a church," Hanna said with a laugh and a wink.

"*No, I think there very specifically is,*" Kamil replied to each of their minds.

Aleksander smiled to himself as he watched Hanna grab Shanthah's hand. Another spark of happiness.

An ensemble of musicians playing various instruments signaled the beginning of the procession and the service.

Hanna glanced at Aleksander who was staring into nothing.

"Hey—are you okay?" she asked in a whisper.

"I'm doing just fine, why?" Aleksander said with a feigned smile. She scowled and slugged him on the arm.

"Are you lying to me?" she asked.

Aleksander was quiet for a moment. "Yeah."

"I know. You're a horrible liar, you know that? You're blaming yourself for what happened to Mara *and* Xanthurias. Stop it. That does no one any good."

Hanna squeezed Aleksander's shoulder and gave him a quick side hug as the musicians' beautiful music floated around the room. The melody made the group feel safe, reassuring them that an army of Valistaran's men was not going to burst through the chapel's doors, and a horde of Sangorans was not going to ambush them through the roof.

Safe, for the first time in so long.

The doors at the rear of the chapel opened, and a group of men in golden armor entered the chamber carrying the prince's closed coffin. Prince Verahim Romus led the procession, flanked by several members of both the Royal Guard and Court of Thanatan including Hokkod, Bovin the Minotaur, Valakor, Manitrius, and a few others Aleksander didn't recognize. Shanthah declined to join them, choosing to sit with his friends.

All in attendance stood, watching the coffin holding the prince's body pass by. King Romiton Romus entered last, following the procession as it made its way to the front of the chapel. When the king deemed it appropriate, his men placed the prince's coffin upon a raised dais. He took his place at the front of the room behind a pedestal and motioned for his subjects to be seated. His lined face and graying hair caused by the stresses of loss and duty gave him the appearance of a much older man.

"It's a strange thing to be at a funeral for someone you don't know," Hanna whispered to Shanthah, who nodded and slid his arm behind her. "Should I cry? I'm a very ugly crier."

"I promise I'm worse," Shanthah whispered back.

First, Verahim, the new crown prince and only living son of King Romiton, spoke of his fondest memories shared with his brother and late mother. When he concluded, Romiton stood next to the coffin, placing his hand on it for support. He spoke of his son's daring deeds and the contributions he had made to ensure peace, emphasizing his bravery and strength in defending the kingdom. When he finished, several other dignitaries left their remarks as a tribute to Xanthurias.

The speeches were soon over, and the prince's casket was carried away, accompanied by a second procession. This time, everyone in the church followed behind the fallen prince toward the place where he would be laid to rest forevermore.

With his mind on Mara, Aleksander watched the casket and the parade that followed it until it disappeared into the city. He and his friends decided not to accompany the group to the actual burial, electing to head to a nearby pub instead.

On the way there, Shanthah approached Aleksander, whose cloak was billowing in the light breeze.

"Did you notice they didn't seem to talk about Xanthurias himself very much? They talked about his noble deeds and heroism but not about what he was like," Aleksander said.

"I served as one of his personal guards a couple times," Shanthah said. "I was telling Hanna a little while ago that he was a good man. Quiet, but strong. He fought for the people he loved. You know, you actually remind me of him quite a bit."

"I'll take that as a compliment," Aleksander said, his mind on what Hanna had said about blaming himself. "Don't be so quick to say that, though. Who knows who I used to be?"

"Does it matter, really?" Shanthah asked with a shrug. "I'll keep up my praise until I see otherwise. Anyway, we're almost to the tavern, and I always say that your true self always comes out after a few drinks. I tested it many times in my university days."

"You didn't go to university!" interjected Hanna.

"The university of life, Hanna," said Shanthah.

Hanna winked. "Not sure you have one of those either."

As they approached the door of the tavern, Aleksander simply watched his friends enjoying one another's company. He heard Hanna's laugh echo through the streets as someone made a joke, and he wondered what it was, but he was just happy to see his friends joking around again. Safe. Happy.

His thoughts turned to Mara, and he hoped she too was happy, wherever she was, but her words haunted him. Shanthah clapped his friend on the back, and the friends entered the warmth of the tavern's welcoming halls.

CHAPTER TWENTY-TWO
THE UNCHAINED

Thick curtains of rain swept across Bukaral. The deep black thunderheads painted over the noonday sun gave the world the appearance of a dreary midnight; the storm over Nitra had evidently not rained itself out on its path into Talohira. Canvas awnings had been erected all over the center of the city near the royal palace in order to keep bystanders, humans and Sangorans alike, dry. The spring rain was an expected truth to be dealt with, and it was prepared for as such.

Hundreds of thousands of Sangoran and Talohiran citizens were gathered in the streets of Bukaral, and those lucky enough to be standing near the royal palace would be the first to learn the identities of the new Mistresses of Dusk. The humans were, of course, outnumbered by the vast hosts of Sangorans interspersed throughout the crowd while many more perched on whatever surface they could to see over the crowd. The

Talohiran men and women came out of duty to their king, but the Sangorans came out of love for their queen.

Not used to seeing so many Sangorans in their city, many of the humans were paranoid and nervous with the future of the alliance between the two peoples so uncertain since the queen's unexpected assassination.

Lavinia, Ihrin, Raluca, Florenta, and Delia, the five remaining Mistresses of Dusk, sat enthroned in ceremonial robes as they sat upon elegant, high-backed chairs on one of the palace's many balconies. A pair of massive double doors behind them burst open, and Valistaran emerged in his crown and a white, ceremonial military uniform covered in colorful medals and a sweeping cloak. A trio of hooded Sangorans accompanied him; their identities were hidden from the crowd. He raised his hands high above his head and wasted no time beginning his speech.

"I trust that I am not alone in saying that I don't want to be out in this weather any longer than we need to." The king's comment was met with laughs throughout the crowd, but they were silenced as he raised his hands. "Citizens of Talohira and Sangora both, I stand before you on this momentous day to name those who shall join my council as new Mistresses of Dusk. Just as the dusk comes before the night, so too do the Mistresses of Dusk come before those called the Children of Night. They shall share the responsibilities of ruling over and protecting all of the wonderful people of Sangora."

He gestured for the three new Mistresses of Dusk to step forward, and they took their respective places beside him.

"As your new Mistress of Dusk to govern Doftaan, I present to you Mistress Lacramora of Dashga!" Valistaran exclaimed, and Lacramora removed her hood. Much of the crowd cheered, and Valistaran wondered if they were members of her own tribe. "For your leadership and influence in the battle of Nitra, I hereby name you Mistress Lacramora, regent of Doftaan and despoiler of Nitra! Do you accept this station and the duties that accompany it?"

"I do accept," Lacramora said. "I vow to lead Sangora into victory against Thanatanos—never again shall we meet defeat at their hands, my king."

Valistaran nodded and placed a silver circlet upon her head.

"Next, I present Mistress Anca, Nightmare of Thanatanos! Mistress Anca has long been one of my most trusted generals in the campaign against Thanatanos," Valistaran said. "Today, she is named Mistress of Dusk for her contributions to our united kingdoms. She will continue in her capacity as a general but shall have added influence and authority where it is needed. I hereby bestow upon you, General Anca, the rank and title of Mistress of Dusk as my regent and governor of your home state of Krim."

"I thank you, my king," Mistress Anca said, bowing.

She said no more and stepped forward to accept her unique silver crown. It looked out of place upon her head, as if she should be adorned in battle armor and a helm instead of robes and a crown. The crowd began to murmur amongst themselves, but Valistaran held up his hand, and a hush fell over the crowd.

"It is with a heavy heart that I must also confirm the rumors of the murder of my dear Queen Codruta. Only my council and a select few were aware of the exact circumstances. Over the next week, a special week-long Sangoran death festival will be held in central Doftaan," said Valistaran. "Because of our great loss, one of the Mistresses of Dusk will become my queen. In time, I shall announce who I have chosen. Therefore, today I will reveal to you an eighth Mistress of Dusk. I present to you Mistress Mara Bartunek, the Unchained—Mara Bartunek, Prince's Bane!"

The Unchained.

Mara's heart leapt as she took a nervous step forward and removed her hood. She waved to the crowd and to her surprise, she was met with thunderous applause. Valistaran continued, saying, "Mistress Mara has done that which many have tried, and all have failed. She has slain Prince Xanthurias Romus, first son of King Romiton Romus of Thanatanos! For this deed alone, I bestow the rank of Mistress of Dusk upon you, Mara Bartunek. At this time, I shall not bestow upon Mistress Mara regency over any region of Sangora until I choose my queen."

Mara stepped forward, and Valistaran set a circular crown of silver upon her head. The elegant silver ring shined like the moon in the night's sky as it rested upon her hair as dark as raven feathers. Her heart thundered in her chest, but it was not a feeling of panic, but rather one of excitement. Joy. She raised her hands once more to meet the applause of what now seemed to be the entire country and only one thought rang through her mind: How the hell was this happening?

A smile spread across her face, and even with her hair billowing wildly in the wind, she bore a certain majesty standing before the people. *Her* people. The words filled her mind. She extended her growing wings above her head, as pathetic as they currently looked, and pressed a fist to her forehead—a traditional Sangoran gesture of respect, she was told. Every Sangoran in the crowd mirrored her action with cheers of victory and hope. Even the humans in the crowd hooted and hollered for her upon hearing her accomplishment.

"Under the leadership of Mistresses Lacramora, Anca, and Mara alongside their fellow mistresses already serving, I vow to you as your king that Laniras itself will fall! No more will that jewel of Thanatanos vex our people. I announce to you today that we are close to bringing this war to a close!"

His words were met with even more jubilation. Valistaran motioned for his new Mistresses of Dusk to sit, and they each took their places with the others behind the king.

Mara felt a strange feeling of fondness growing in her heart for the Sangoran people, one that she wanted to nurture. She had never felt such a love for her former home as she now did for this strange new place.

However, she still harbored a deep disdain in her heart for Talohira and its slavers, and she wondered how that would influence her new role as Mistress of Dusk. She remembered at that moment the memories filled with sadness and grief that she had experienced in both Thanatanos and Talohira.

There were good times, of course, but they did not sit at the forefront of her mind these days.

In contrast, Sangora had welcomed her with open arms since her transformation, despite the violent nature of how she got there. If this was to become her home, she would embrace it.

Valistaran continued his impassioned speech about the three new Mistresses of Dusk and the future of Talohiran and Sangoran relations. Mara thought that several parts of the speech felt clichéd, as if it could be given at any important diplomatic ceremony. She smiled, nonetheless, welcoming the applause that followed regardless of the content of the king's words.

Mara's thoughts swam away from her, leading her back to what had happened in Nitra. The image of Aleksander and the others in the ruined church filled her mind, and she wondered if they had survived the conflict. Aleksander. Pol. Rehor. Hanna. Shanthah. Josman. Kamil. Even the image of Drahomir's face appeared in her mind.

She also wondered what had happened to Draguta, the other Sangoran that had been nominated for her new position. She dozed off for a moment, but her mind snapped back to reality as Valistaran ended his speech and turned away from the crowd, and she wondered if she had somehow napped through the entire speech. How long had the king been speaking? She felt as if she had been asleep for hours, but she knew it could have only been a couple minutes. Right?

Both Anca and Lacramora followed the king away from the balcony, and she hurried after them, pretending to know what the king had said. Valistaran turned to the three new members of his council as they walked inside; he raised his hands in a celebratory gesture, and a smile appeared upon his face.

"Congratulations are in order," he said. "Mara and Lacramora, as newcomers here, feel free to explore the fortress. You are now allowed access to wherever you may desire to wander except into my personal chambers, of course. Feel free to visit the royal library, the archives—or my favorite, the kitchens. When you are ready, I will have someone show you to your chambers until you return to your respective states."

Anca bowed to Valistaran and wandered off. Mara laughed as she noted that the battle-hardened general seemed exhausted and nonplussed over all the pompous events of the day. She guessed that the general was intent on leaving it all behind, heading straight for bed. However, Lacramora seemed more excited to explore the great fortress of Bukaral and uncover any and all luxurious comforts that she had gone the rest of her life without.

"You said something about a royal library?" Mara asked, a hint of hesitation in her voice. The sound of Lacramora's footsteps faded into nothingness as Valistaran strode down the opposite corridor without a word. Mara remained where she stood as he walked away before he glanced back over his shoulder.

"Well, are you coming?"

CHAPTER TWENTY-THREE
DUSK IN THE LIBRARY

Not expecting the king to show her the way to the library himself, she half walked, half flew to catch up with him. Valistaran's imposing height made his stride much longer than Mara's, who struggled to keep up. After a while, she remembered that she had wings and decided to fly in order to match the king's pace.

"It has been far too long since I have had the time to read a book," said Mara, trying to speak in a proper manner. She felt silly and winced, hoping the king did not take notice, but she caught a cheerful smirk on his face.

Valistaran led Mara through the castle to the grand library. They passed a statue of a bearded man holding a sword and the king said, "I trust you recognize Talohira's greatest hero?"

"I'm sorry, no."

"You'd be a liar if you said you did. To be honest, I have no idea who this man is. The palace decorators do what they want, and I pay them for it—it's always been something that made me laugh," said Valistaran with a wink.

They walked down another hallway, and they stopped in front of a massive painting of the sea between Talohira and Kurash. In the image, golden light shone down through a storm on tempestuous waters as a boat struggled to keep afloat.

"This one, though—this one I brought in myself," said Valistaran, admiring the artwork. Mara examined it and felt an unexplainable connection to the painting, as if she was the boat on the stormy sea, and the light was the hope for a better future. Hope that Rehor once spoke to her about.

"I like this one," said Mara in a soft tone. Valistaran smiled but said nothing more as he motioned for the guards standing outside the wide doors of the royal library to allow them entry.

"You know, in my opinion, there is nothing more dangerous or powerful than a woman who reads," the high king said. "When you return to Doftaan, you'll find a second, smaller royal library there ready to welcome you."

Mara smiled and together they entered a vast sea of bookshelves beneath the painted sky of a vaulted ceiling that seemed so high that she wondered how there could be room for anything else in the rest of the palace. Bookshelves lined every surface, and some towered so high they were unreachable by non-Sangorans unless they had a very high ladder. Even then, it would be precarious to climb so high. An enormous staircase snaked its way up the center of the library, leading to more hidden knowledge for six more floors.

"Where do I even start?" she whispered, trying to take it all in at once. "I could stay in this room forever, die here, and be completely happy with my life."

"Something you and I have in common," he said. "And, might I add, something that you will find that you do not share with the other Mistresses of Dusk—if Mistress Florenta even *can* read. Well, I must depart. Enjoy yourself, Mara. Never in your lifetime will you be able to read them all, so choose wisely."

The king turned with a flurry of his majestic cape, leaving Mara in awe. The door slammed behind her, jogging her back to reality. She gazed upon the face of a grandfather clock standing next to the doorway. Nine-fifteen.

The new Mistress of Dusk wandered to the first bookshelf on her left and grabbed a book at random. Its cover was bare, but its spine read: *Forgotten Languages of the Deadlands: An Incomplete Grammar.* She smiled and flipped through the pages of the tome.

"*Kaixo…*" she repeated, knowing with certainty that she had mispronounced the word. She had wanted to learn a new language since she was a little child. At the time, she'd learned a few phrases from a Sangoran girl a Thannish family had adopted.

Perhaps it was her mind's way of expressing her desire to run away. To be free. To escape. She never had the chance, but perhaps in her new home she would find the time to master Sangoran if her new duties allowed it. She closed her eyes for a moment and took a deep breath before setting the book back on the shelf. She turned back to the clock and shook her head in disbelief, for there upon its face, the hands indicated nine-fifty.

"It must be broken," she said to herself. "I'll have to tell the king." She chuckled, for never before had she spoken with a king, let alone been on terms to tell him that his clock was broken. She accumulated a large pile of books to read, scanning each one before deciding on another. Every so often, she would drift off and then wake up still holding a book.

The new Mistress of Dusk felt a sudden wave of exhaustion flood over her, and she decided that she should get some sleep; she vowed to return in the morning if she was not needed for something else. The doors opened before she reached them.

"Ah, Mara," came Lavinia's smooth voice from the darkness. "I've been looking for you. I wanted to congratulate you."

"Oh, I'm sorry," Mara replied. "I just wanted to take a quick look at the royal library."

"As is your right. But Mara, a quick look? I've been trying to find you ever since the ceremony. You must have been in there for hours," Lavinia said. "I ran into the king who told me that you two parted ways in the library, so I decided to check for you here one last time before giving up."

Mara was at a loss of how to answer, and her mind shot back to the mysterious speed of the hands on the clock. It now read twenty minutes after three. Was it possible that she really had been in the library for such a long time? As she stood there in confusion, Lavinia grasped her forehead without warning.

"What are you doing?" Mara asked, feeling Lavinia's grip tighten on her skull. The more experienced Mistress of Dusk did not reply for a moment as she examined Mara's pupils.

"Back in the slave camp—were you sent to The Cage?" Lavinia asked. "I didn't think you were, but—"

Mara's memories exploded in a flurry of painful emotions, and she fell screaming to her knees. She did not realize that the shrieks were escaping her own throat until Lavinia stroked her hair to calm her nerves.

"I'm sorry," Mara said as she sat up. She realized she had somehow managed to lie flat on the floor against the wall.

"Yes, I thought so," Lavinia muttered as she took Mara's wrist in her hands. She examined the puncture wound in her flesh next to the long scar from Drahomir's knife. "This is what I was afraid of. Mara, to explain what's happening to you, you need to understand how the magic of The Cage works."

"Okay," Mara said with hesitation.

"It's also called a Mindprison," Lavinia said. "A horrible invention of a fallen people in the Deadlands."

"The Deadlands? Really?" Mara asked in awe. She'd heard of the wastelands beyond the borders of the four countries, but nothing more than that. "The name fits. For every minute it's on your wrist, you're trapped in your own mind for a year, right?" Mara asked, pulling away from Lavinia's grasp. "I know. Someone put it on me for at least twenty minutes."

"And what are you going to do to that person?" asked Lavinia. "Do you want revenge? Maybe I can help you if you help me—would you like to punish whoever did this to you?"

A tear rolled down Mara's face as she gave a feeble nod and mouthed the word, "Yes."

"You understand its basic purpose, sure, but there's more to it. If a mind is subjected to that kind of torture, it will have lasting effects—scars, if you will," Lavinia said. "In rare cases, the victim can relapse into the Dreamstate brought on by the Mindprison even when it isn't in use. Essentially, it will extinguish your mind like a matchstick in a hurricane, and it'll feel like you traveled hours through time. Because, well, you kind of did."

"So, you're saying, what—I time traveled? There have been a few times where I've blacked out and hours have passed—"

"Obviously not, Mara. It only felt that way. I sat here with you for a few hours as you lay unconscious on the floor. I even had time to fetch a book for you from the library to help you understand more about what is happening."

"How do I fix this?" Mara asked, feeling her heart pound in her chest. "I can't keep blacking out!"

"Read the book," Lavinia answered in a soft voice. "Perhaps you can't cure what's happening, so you will need to learn how to harness these relapses. You will be able to overcome the fainting in time. You know what, Mara? I am exhausted. I'm going to head to sleep now, and I suggest you do the same."

Mara nodded and Lavinia unfurled her great black wings. The Mistress of Dusk gave a nonchalant wave goodbye and soared down the corridor, leaving Mara alone.

She must have blacked out again, because when she glanced up at the clock, it read seven-thirty. She swore under her breath and slumped against a bookshelf, cradling the tome to her chest.

The exhausted woman forced herself to stay awake as she flipped to the page that Lavinia had marked for her by folding over the page. She could sleep when she was done. She glanced at the page and examined confusing diagrams and skipped over mathematic equations and scientific explanations of matters that she did not understand. She turned to another chapter Lavinia had marked for her with what looked like a page from another book. The chapter explained how to treat the fainting episodes that accompanied the effects of The Cage's torturous magic.

The text went on for pages and pages about psychological conditioning and diet suggestions for training the brain not to have an episode. She flipped through more pages, stumbling upon a passage Lavinia had marked with yellow ink.

"A rare and unintended side effect of a Mindprison is the ability to slip in and out of the Dreamstate at will. The effect does not manifest when individuals subject themselves by choice to the dream-torture, although in any case, any sane individual would never do so.

This ability can prove invaluable if the individual is able to control it. This can give the individual the ability to think, plan, and calculate for extended periods of time while only taking a moment in the real world with little to no fatigue. When controlled, torture is replaced with a boundless potential.

Even more interesting is the phenomenon that occurs when entering the Dreamstate. One will notice that they are not nude while in their torture-dream but are wearing the exact clothes that they

"Never in my lifetime, huh?" Mara whispered to herself, referring to Valistaran's last words to her. She rocked back and forth in a combination of excitement and exhaustion while cradling the book. She decided exhaustion was the more likely of the two, given the fact that she kept talking to herself. "If I can do what it says in this book, maybe in only a few months…"

She trailed off and clapped her hand over her mouth. She glanced around the chamber in an excited frenzy, once again not knowing where to begin. However, before she could decide, she succumbed to another episode brought on by the Mindprison's magic, and then was claimed by the blackness of sleep upon the cold stone ground.

CHAPTER TWENTY-FOUR
SMILES AND BIRDSONG

Hanna rustled the weather-beaten leather flap of the tent as she pushed her way outside, allowing the pale morning light to illuminate her face. The makeshift dwelling was much too small for all eight of the travelers to rest in comfort, so both Aleksander and Josman had elected to sleep on the ground outside. She stepped over Josman's snoring form and laughed, remembering his complaints the night before that the combined body heat was going to kill him, and that Aleksander claimed a drunk Shanthah had tried to cuddle him. Both were of course obvious lies in order to give the rest of the company the chance to sleep in relative comfort.

She couldn't sleep with all of Drahomir's tossing and turning; she assumed he was reliving some horrible memory from the camp, and she empathized with him. It had become a norm for those in the group to cry out during a nightmare, and the others would understand and be kind enough to ignore it.

She now sat upon a boulder to take in the peaceful solitude of the morning's stillness. The weather was beginning to warm, and the spring rains were less chilling, a welcome change; faint rays of golden light streamed through the clouds over the mountains, and the first birds of morning were beginning to sing their cheerful tunes, free from the wars of men.

The friends were on their way from Laniras to Josman's family home in Melnik, a day's travel north of Laniras. He had offered them a place to stay until they could find somewhere in the city to live or to return to their hometowns.

They had vacated their hospital rooms in Laniras to make room for the flood of refugees from Nitra and other surrounding towns. The wounded seemed to outnumber the healthy in Laniras, and so the group chose to leave. The night's sky was clear, and to the delight of those watching, occasional shooting stars had darted across the inky blackness.

Now that morning was beginning to wake, Hanna's thoughts turned to food as she dangled her feet from the boulder into the shallow creek that flowed past their campsite. Her ragged boots were piled in an unceremonious heap on the ground next to the chilling water.

The grand capital city of Laniras loomed behind them in the near distance, glowing in the early morning's light. She heard footsteps in the grass behind her, and she turned to see Shanthah approaching with a sleepy smile. He climbed up onto the rock beside Hanna, who scooted to make room.

"Hey, you," she said, splashing the cool water with her feet.

"And hello to you," Shanthah replied. "Couldn't sleep?"

"I did. I just wanted to come outside. Look how beautiful it is right now!" Hanna said, staring out into the misty morning.

"Yeah," Shanthah said, looking at her with a soft smile as she closed her eyes to take in the pleasant air. "Absolutely beautiful."

She turned her head toward him.

"Do you think things are better now?"

"What do you mean?"

"Just, in general. We survived the camp and whatever the hell that was in Nitra. Do you think things are better now?"

"Things got better for me the day you and I started to get to know each other," Shanthah said. "Did you know that?"

Hanna's heart leapt, and she smiled again with a small nod.

"The feeling's mutual, Mr. Kalen."

"And that feeling is…"

"Shan." She closed her eyes. "You know."

She leaned in, and their foreheads touched as the distance between their lips closed.

"Oh," Shanthah whispered, his face breaking into a smile.

And then, they were kissing on that beautiful, bright spring morning filled with birdsong beside the creek. All they had, and perhaps all they needed, was this new feeling.

"You know, the camp would have been a lot more fun if we'd done that earlier," Shanthah said.

Hanna kissed him again, squeezing his hand.

"I can't stop smiling."

"Then don't," Shanthah replied, brushing her hair from her face back behind her ear. "Because I can't either."

At that moment, Shanthah pulled a necklace with a small, green gem from his tunic. It gave off a soft glow and was humming like a bumblebee. He let out a small groan.

"What's that?" Hanna asked.

"General Hokkod gave it to me as the new leader of my squad of the Royal Guard, if that's still what we all are," Shanthah said. "It's all very vague. It lets me know when he needs to speak to me."

"I thought we were all going home," Hanna said.

"Laniras *was* my home," Shanthah said. "Still is, I guess. I have a sister there, you know. You'd like her. Is your family still in Vudapas?"

"Umm, yes and no," Hanna said. Shanthah cocked his head. "They all live in the Vudapas central graveyard now, so I don't really visit much to be honest."

Guilt filed Shanthah's chest for making the comment.

"Maybe we could visit together. I'd like to thank the people who raised such a great Hanna, even if they can't hear me."

Hanna smiled. "It was the slavers. My entire family and someone else." Her voice faltered. "My—my Viktorija."

"Oh," Shanthah said, pulling her close. "I'm so, so sorry."

"It's okay. Well, no it isn't. But I have my Shanthah now," Hanna said as she rubbed his back. "Right?"

"Right," Shanthah said with a nod. "He's not going *anywhere.*"

"I haven't told anyone else," Hanna said. "No one knows. I'd appreciate if—well, you know."

He pulled away and made a motion as if locking his lips with an invisible key.

"Of course. And it sounds like Viktorija had *exquisite* taste."

Hanna laughed as she played with the necklace around Shanthah's neck. "Well, as much as I love this moment, I think it needs to come to a close."

"But I don't want it to," Shanthah said. "Ever. But General Hokkod *did* tell me he wasn't likely to summon me, or you know, us, if you all still want to be part of my squad."

"I've got no other plans," Hanna replied.

"Perhaps we should wake the others."

From nearby, they heard Josman groan, "We're awake."

"Speak for yourself," Aleksander muttered.

Josman got up and headed into the tent, stumbling inside like a bear into its cave awoken from its hibernation too soon.

"I think Josman has us covered," Shanthah said as the sounds of the sound of everyone else waking up filled the tent.

"If they won't let me sleep, none of you can either," came Josman's voice from inside the tent. Pol's groans were the loudest. In a few moments, Pol, Kamil, Rehor, and Drahomir emerged from their shelter, and Shanthah explained the situation regarding the Royal Guard's summons to them.

"If they're sending you on some kind of mission, you had better take your entire Royal Guard squad with you," stated Pol. "That's what we are, right? I'm ready for more adventures."

"You don't want to go home?" Josman asked. Pol shrugged.

Kamil gave a thumbs-up to show his agreement with Pol, but Drahomir seemed slightly irked at the comment but shuffled back and forth as if trying to make up his mind.

"I mean, that'd just mean going back to working a normal job and having a boring, normal life," Drahomir said. "But who wants to do that? Count me in, I guess. If not just this once."

"*Whatever happens, I'd like to stay together,*" Kamil thought to the others with his power as a Mindspeaker.

"I can't go back to my ma and pa without Mara," Pol said. Rehor patted him on the back.

"I'm with my family," Aleksander said, gesturing to the others. "Probably. Who knows."

They all let out a collective. "Aww."

"Well, let's get this tent down," said Josman, pulling a stake up out of the ground. The others began to help, but Hanna stepped forward and placed a hand on Josman's shoulder.

"What about you, Jos?" she asked as the others worked on the tent.

"You know the story you just told Shanthah? You know, the one I definitely wasn't supposed to hear?"

"Yeah?"

Josman shrugged. "There's nothing for me in Melnik."

She wrapped him in a tight hug.

"You two going to help?" Drahomir asked. "Just like Josman to say, 'hey Drahomir, come help,' and then do nothing."

"Says the boy who has only pulled up one stake," Rehor said with a booming laugh.

Aleksander looked up for a moment to take in the beautiful morning. He hoped the dramatic colors of the sunrise were not caused by smoke and the fires of war.

Hanna had been practicing her telekinetic abilities whenever she had time, and she made use of them to help take down the tent. When it was complete, Josman packed it into the back of the wagon the Court of Thanatan had lent them as Kamil guided their two horses to be hitched up.

They set out, and a couple hours later, the group reached the main gates of the palace in Laniras only to be stopped by a pair of guards holding long spears. Shanthah showed them his gem, and they let the squad inside.

CHAPTER TWENTY-FIVE

A NEW MISSION

"So, they let the rest of us in because *you* had a glowing gem?" Hanna asked. "Security in Laniras seems lax."

"Yeah, how do they know we aren't murderers and thieves?" Pol asked. "We could be."

"Well, are you, Mr. Bartunek?" asked Rehor.

"No," said Pol, shrugging.

"Pity. We'd be much more interesting if you were, right?" Shanthah replied with a wink.

Kamil chuckled, but Drahomir did not look amused as they followed Shanthah down a flight of steps that led to a great underground amphitheater.

Dozens of men and women sat around the room. Most looked like they'd seen far too many battles, but others held the air of politicians that had not never carried a blade in their lives.

A few empty seats that looked grander than the rest were positioned upon a stage at the front of the room for the leaders of the royal guard and Court of Thanatan. Shanthah led the group to an area with enough empty seat for all of them. They were not all right next to each other, but it was the best they could find. Shanthah motioned for a man to scoot over so that Hanna could sit next to him. The man did so with a scowl.

"You know, Shanthah, if you're always this late, you're never going to find a good spot," Hanna teased.

"Sometimes sitting in a 'bad spot' is beneficial in these meetings," Shanthah replied, shaking his head.

"Now *that* is the truth," Rehor said.

Aleksander, Hanna, and Rehor joined them while Drahomir, Kamil, Josman, and Pol were scattered across the row behind.

The room fell silent as General Valakor, the massive, armored spirit warrior entered the room through what Aleksander guessed was one of the few doors in the kingdom high enough that he did not need to duck to enter. The warrior sat in one of the throne-like seats on the stage, and soon enough, the room was filled with chatter once again.

"So, what is he, exactly?" Hanna wondered aloud.

"That's Drahomir. I know he's ugly, but you don't have to make fun," Shanthah replied. Hanna gave him a disapproving look. "Ok, ok, sorry. Valakor is one of the leaders of the Court of Thanatan. Remember Itrus?"

"Yes, but I mean, what *is* he?" Hanna said.

"You can't just ask what people are," said Shanthah. "It's very rude, Miss Samsa."

"Shanthah," said Hanna with two raised eyebrows. A warning sign not to cross her again.

"Okay, sorry. Again. They're important leaders and warriors whose spirits were transferred into those huge suits of armor. Some kind of technology from the Deadlands," Shanthah said.

"You haven't heard the legends?" Josman asked, leaning forward. "About Valakor and his eleven brothers who were granted immortality by Thanatan himself?"

"You are forgetting the most important details," Rehor chimed in. "Valakor and eleven others—there is some debate on if they were his actual brothers and sisters, mind you—were powerful warriors in the service of our lord, Thanatan. There was a vicious battle that claimed all of their lives, but they alone held off thousands of the minions of Elafris the Fallen. They sacrificed their lives to buy the ancestor of King Romiton, Nezamysl, first king of Thanatanos, time to escape, saving the future of our kingdom."

"*Is it true?*" Kamil asked to their minds from the row behind.

Rehor shrugged. "Probably not, no. But legends are often more interesting that reality, are they not?"

"All that matters is they're basically indestructible and on our side," Josman said.

"Not indestructible," Hanna said with a somber tone, thinking back about the death of Itrus not so long ago.

"No, not indestructible," Rehor said. "And not all on *our side*. Out of the original twelve, only a handful remain. Seven were seduced by the Fallen's tricks, and he claimed their souls. If my math is correct, that leaves only five left to serve their true master. Of those, three were lost when the Deadlands fell. We know the fate of Itrus, and the sole survivor sits before us."

"So, what happened to the others?" Aleksander asked. The others leaned in, excited to get more of the story.

"No one knows for sure," Rehor said, shaking his head. "Perhaps, the Court of Thanatan does, but there are rumors of them. Perhaps, Valistaran keeps them for his most nefarious purposes—assassinations, special missions, and the like."

Everyone within the amphitheater stood as King Romiton Romus and his son Verahim, younger brother of Xanthurias, entered the chamber. They were accompanied by several members of the Court of Thanatan, including Hokkod, Bovin the Minotaur, Manitrius, and several others they did not recognize. The king stood behind a podium upon which he placed several documents printed on thick stacks of parchment.

"I have assembled the Ministry of Diplomacy, all squads of the Royal Guard, and the Court of Thanatan today for several matters of important business. First, I have news regarding the war efforts in Talohira. Second, I will have General Hokkod discuss a diplomatic mission to Kurash.

"For those unaware, a recent rescue operation in Talohira resulted in the death of Lieutenant General Itrus as well as many others. However, I am happy to report that more were rescued than were killed. The purpose of King Talohir's camps were not to build his cities and grow his power, but to lessen ours. He used the camps to gather individuals from Thanatanos with magical abilities. Long have those gifted with powers been a valuable resource to our kingdom, and Valistaran has been systematically enslaving and killing them."

Aleksander glanced at Shanthah, who raised his eyebrows in surprise. Aleksander was aware that his friend could turn invisible, that Hanna had the ability to control objects with her mind, that Kamil was a Mindspeaker, and of course that he could produce flames, but if everyone in the camp was there because of their abilities, what secrets did the others keep? Did Valistaran somehow know something they did not?

"Next, I bring news from the sieges. The siege of Vudapas in Talohira has ended, with great losses on both sides. The city walls have fallen, and it is no longer a stronghold to Talohira, but it has not returned to Thannish hands.

"I need not remind you of the bold attack on Laniras and the surrounding villages that was thwarted not a week prior to this meeting. Rebuilding has already begun, and citizens displaced by the destruction will be rehoused. I will not speak of my son's death today.

"Word has reached Thanatanos that Valistaran's alliance with the Sangoran people, or Night Witches as they are known in these parts, is beginning to crumble. His wife, the queen of Sangora, was killed in the same battle as Itrus. He has yet to choose a new queen to maintain the alliance but has selected several new members of his council. It was these new council members that led the assault on Nitra."

Mara's face and the burning city haunted Aleksander's mind as Romiton mentioned the battle.

"King Valistaran Talohir has offered me a deal to unite our kingdoms under one banner to end this war, but I see this as nothing more than surrender. We must do that which is of most use to our people, but when more details and information emerge, we will discuss further. At the same time, intelligence suggests that Talohira is seeking to strengthen ties with Kurash. General Hokkod, I now turn the time to you to discuss our new mission there to beat them to their new ally."

He turned from the crowd and sat in the seat next to Prince Verahim, and Hokkod approached the podium. The warrior looked slightly out of place on the stage, for he was clearly more comfortable in war than diplomacy. The king seemed exhausted, and Aleksander wished he could help somehow. Although he couldn't relate personally, he knew the loss of a child must be horrible to any father, even a king.

"The king has elected me to lead an expedition to the desert nation of Kurash to seek an alliance. Since the beginning of our conflict, Kurash has been neutral and refused to take sides. There have been Night Witches entering the capital city of Tal-Ahosh in great numbers, and the nation has informed us that it will entertain talks for new alliances after Queen Codruta's death.

"Therefore, we will be undertaking a diplomatic mission to the capital city of Tal-Ahosh in Kurash, where we shall hold a forum between our two great nations with their leaders, including the Supreme One who is named Kadir, the Grand Judge, and regional and religious leaders have all agreed to meet with our delegation. We will need any and all who speak Kurashic to join us, as our embassy there is too small to handle this many talks in such a short time. Are there any here who do?"

Kamil got to his feet and raised his hand. A dozen or so others did the same. Hokkod motioned for them to stand. The squad all turned to give him encouraging smiles. Romiton stood once more, and Hokkod stepped aside.

"Does it count to say Kamil speaks Kurashic if he can't speak?" asked Hanna. Shanthah gave her a disapproving look.

"Now who's being disrespectful?" asked Shanthah.

"You're a bad influence."

"I would also like to invite all those with powers, including those rescued from the slave camps to join us. The Supreme One holds magic, as they call powers, of all kinds in high regard, and those who have them will be able to protect the envoy as well."

Shanthah motioned for his new squad to stand. Seven others in the chamber did so as well. Hokkod called on several other squads of the Royal Guard and diplomats not assigned to Kurash to stand as well. Discussions on the topics to be discussed in Kurash were led by the Minister of Diplomacy, a man named Gabriel Johanek, but the squad stopped listening, instead speaking amongst themselves.

"Look how short he is next to Valakor," said Aleksander in a low voice. Shanthah laughed.

"Look how short you both are *always*," said Hanna. She punched Shanthah in the arm playfully. "Yeah, I said it."

Minister Johanek and King Romiton discussed other logistical issues and topics of discussions.

"Anyway, I can't take any more of Hanna's insults. I'm ending this meeting."

Hanna tried not to laugh, but a loud snort broke through. She hid her face in shame, and Shanthah turned to hide his own laughter as Aleksander did a better job in concealing this most inappropriate fit of laughter.

"Hanna, that was *so* loud," Shanthah whispered.

"One last comment as you depart to prepare," King Romiton said. "I would like to ask those who are not joining us now to volunteer their hands to help in the destroyed towns. In the coming days, we will have more information on those efforts. Thank you all for your service. May Thanatanos guide us."

"You guys, we're going to Kurash!" Pol exclaimed. "That's *not* what I thought would happen! We get to see the world! I might even get to see the camel people Mara used to tell me about from the stories! They're real, right?"

"There aren't many left, but we'll see!" Rehor said in response as they all stood to leave. "And for future reference, they're called Dromedarians."

"Is what I said offensive?" Pol asked, putting his hand over his mouth. "I'm so sorry!"

They group of friends all filed out of the room with dreams of their next adventure that would begin in the new week. For the first time in so long, they all joked with one another and smiled as they left the chamber.

CHAPTER TWENTY-SIX
JUST LIKE WE USED TO DO

The entire world felt like an oven. Sweat dripped down the high king's brow as he rode along a dusty street lined with curious Kurashian citizens as they watched the arrival of the Talohiran dignitaries.

Along with his diplomats and negotiators, he brought with him General Anca and twenty of his own elite guards. Anca wore a traditional Sangoran shroud over her armor to protect her skin from the scorching sunlight as she rode her horse next to the king. She would be his only representative of Sangora during the meetings—choosing her, the greatest Sangoran general, rather than a diplomat, to join his entourage was a conscious choice. A message, even. However, the official Sangoran ambassador stationed in Kurash would still join them later.

Valistaran's reasons for the expedition were threefold. First, he wanted to beat the Thans to an alliance with Kurash. Second, decades ago, he had heard that the three all-knowing Kurashian elders, known as the Secret Keepers of Kurash, held information about a mysterious weapon so powerful that none would dare oppose him. It was said that it was one of the reasons that the land west of Thanatanos and east of Sangora had gained the name of 'The Deadlands.' He'd tried to find it in his youth but had ultimately given up. He wanted to try again.

The third and final reason he made a point to cross the sea between the two countries was to visit someone that dwelled in Kurash—someone he had not seen in many, many years. He was more nervous for this encounter than any of his other official plans, although there was neither risk of death nor negative geopolitical ramifications. He shook the thought from his mind as his caravan neared the palace at the exact center of Tal-Ahosh.

The architecture of the Supreme One's temple and the surrounding city was unlike anything back home. While Doftaan in Sangora was covered in high spired towers of black stone and onion-shaped domes, and Talohira boasted more stately architecture, everything in Kurash simply felt *massive*. Everywhere he looked were huge bubble-like gilded domes, colorful mosaics, huge obelisks and walls, and spires thinner than those in Sangora like towering spikes of gold.

Valistaran stood in awe every time he saw the temple, wondering how its creators had managed to create it. It was built as a temple to Kurashian gods, and remained as such, but also housed the ruler of Kurash, the Supreme One known as Kadir.

Valistaran's caravan reached the gate of the palace's outer wall. There, they were met by a party of servants, who led the group's weary horses away. Another servant who looked more important than the others approached the head of the caravan and addressed the king himself.

"High King Valistaran Talohir, Uniter of Nations and ruler of Talohira and Sangora, we salute you, and the Supreme One who is called Kadir welcomes you to Kurash," said the servant, dropping into a deep bow. He spoke in flawless Thannish, the language of both Thanatanos and Talohira. He had only the slightest accent that gave his voice a certain warmth.

Valistaran dismounted his horse and mirrored the bow then said in Kurashic, "Ben shukrarim siz." *I thank you.*

"His majesty speaks our humble language, oh how wonderful!" said the diplomat with more excitement than he perhaps should have. "Ben siz shukrarim tsok!" *Thank you as well.*

The servants took Valistaran's steed and the rest of his delegates' horses and led them to water.

"The Supreme One has planned a feast in your honor. It has been long since a foreign king has visited our lands," he said. Valistaran thought to himself that the heat was probably the reason for the lack of visits but said nothing.

"And when will negotiations begin?" Valistaran asked. "I apologize for being so upfront, of course."

"Your highness has nothing to apologize for, as this is the reason for your visit. The Supreme One knows that you are weary from your trek here. He wishes you to rest and, in the morning, he shall meet with your company. You will be informed of tomorrow's events later tonight. Shall we lead you to your chambers?"

The servant seemed to say this in one breath, yet never seemed out of wind, for he continued speaking while exhaling; Valistaran recognized this as a distinguishing characteristic of a native speaker of Kurashic, one that he was never able to master in all his time spent in the country's capital.

"Take my men to their quarters and my beasts to the stables. I wish to explore Tal-Ahosh and admire her beauty. As most people would, I prefer sightseeing to politics," Valistaran replied.

"Do you wish for an escort?" asked the servant. Valistaran shook his head with a polite smile. "Then your men and beasts will be well taken care of. I shall have people waiting for you near the gates upon your arrival."

"Thank you," Valistaran said. "I apologize again, for I never asked your name."

"Ah, yes—I am Umut," said the servant. His introduction seemed awkward, as if he was not used to using his own name as a servant in the Supreme One's palace.

"Thank you Umut," said the king with a nod. Umut and his fellow servants led the rest of the caravan into the Supreme One's luxurious home, and Valistaran pulled the hood of his tunic over his dark hair as he set off alone. Although the sun was now dipping behind the horizon, the heat lingered. The king felt a trickle of sweat roll down his spine as he passed a market.

A couple of orphan children stood in his path, their dirty hair matted and their clothes dusty. They looked up at him with great, big, brown eyes, and he knelt next to them. Without saying a word, he dropped a gold coin into each of their palms. He saw tears roll down their cheeks as they hugged his legs before running off, shouting words of thanks and joy.

Valistaran wondered for a moment if Mistress Mara had yet used her newfound ability to learn any of the many languages of Kurash. He envied her, for although he spoke some Kurashic in addition to his native Thannish, he would love to study a third language. He'd never quite mastered Sangoran.

He strode through the streets, which were now far less crowded than they were when he had arrived. He took no time to explore. He had spent enough time in Tal-Ahosh in his youth to memorize the winding paths and twists and turns of the city. He enjoyed taking in the breathtaking beauty of Tal-Ahosh, but he had a far more important task to complete.

Valistaran soon arrived at a small home on the ground floor connected to several others. A tattered awning of blue and white stripes hung over the door, upon which he gave three sharp raps. He heard a scuffle from inside, but there was no answer. He knocked again. He hesitated before going to knock a third time, but he heard the latch turn and the door swung open.

The remaining bit of sunlight illuminated the face of a woman with dark, tanned skin, striking black eyes, and shoulder length hair. Her plain, yet beautiful face showed signs of a woman who had lived through years of stress and anxiety but held strong. She said nothing as she looked him up and down.

"May I enter?" Valistaran asked.

"Word on the street is that the High King of Talohira is in town to meet with Kadir," the woman said in Thannish. Valistaran noted the casual use of her leader's name.

"Word on the street is wrong—to an extent. Can Val Talohir come inside?"

"He can," she said, her smile playful. "The king can't."

"Thank you, Alia."

Valistaran stepped over the threshold, and she closed the door behind him. She motioned for him to sit on the old sofa at the back of the tiny room. He sat near the armrest which seemed to welcome him as an old friend.

"Why don't you use some of the money I sent you to move somewhere more comfortable?" Valistaran asked.

"Like a palace in Talohira?" Alia asked. "No thank you."

"You know that's not what I meant."

"And how would you find me if I moved?"

"You could at least make yourself more comfortable here."

"I'm perfectly comfortable, Val." Alia scowled. "I give that money to people who really need it—just like we used to do."

"All of it?" Valistaran asked with a perturbed expression.

He examined the room, and a deluge of memories came flooding back. For a moment, the mantle of royalty was lifted from his shoulders, and he was simply young Val again.

"Do you know why I'm here?" he asked.

She sat down in a ratty cushioned armchair across from him and folded her legs beneath her bottom.

"Not much happens in your side of the world without at least rumors trickling down here," she replied. "Your queen is dead."

"She is," Valistaran replied to the abruptness of the comment. It stung, but he said nothing else, waiting for the woman to speak again.

"You know how I feel about you. About the war. About everything—what do you want me to say, Val? That I discovered where that legendary weapon is you've been after all these years? It doesn't exist. Or maybe that I want to leave my life here and come be royalty around a bunch of snobby Sangorans and watch you bleed your country—and Thanatanos—and Sangora dry?"

"No," was all Valistaran could muster as a response.

Alia was silent for a moment. She cocked her head, and her expression seemed to soften. She sighed softly with a mirthless smile, the face made when laughing replaces crying, but the emotions remain.

"You're here to ask for my permission to take a new queen. Again," she said after a few moments. Valistaran did not say a word. His silence confirmed her question. She smiled and crossed the room in only a couple strides then plopped down next to him.

"Is she better than the last one?"

"Yes."

She took his hand in her own and placed a soft kiss upon his cheek. He smiled but suppressed it to hide his emotions as a king must often do. Sometimes, he hated being king.

The sound of movement in the back room made him glance up. Someone had come in the back door. Was it an intruder? An assassin?

"Go for it, Val," she said, teary-eyed but smiling. Happy. Valistaran saw someone emerge from the other room, hesitate for a moment, and then dart back out the door.

"Who was that?" Valistaran asked. The woman got up and crossed the room, her back to the king.

"He's no one," she replied with far too much abruptness.

"Who was that?"

"I think it's time for you to go," she said. The king stood, obeying her wish. She blocked the way to the back room.

"So it seems," Valistaran said. "Goodbye, Alia. Thank you."

"It was good to see you, Val. Really. Stop by before you go home, won't you? I want to know what's going on in your life. We'll have dinner and talk."

"Just like we used to do."

Alia nodded, but no more words were shared.

She shut the door behind him. He passed the orphan children again but had no intent of imparting his wealth this time. He swept past them toward the palace, his mind racing between what had just happened and a conversation that had transpired three days prior with Mara Bartunek, the new Mistress of Dusk.

From where he sat upon the hill, he could see the palace of Tal-Ahosh in all its beauty, illuminated by the fading evening and countless fires within. The High King of Talohira looked out over the city of Tal-Ahosh and slid to the ground, alone.

He was overwhelmed with a hurricane of conflicting emotions as he placed his hand over his mouth in shock.

Two words escaped his lips.

"My son..."

CHAPTER TWENTY-SEVEN
THE POWER OF KNOWLEDGE

THREE DAYS EARLIER

A crimson droplet of blood fell from the silver dagger. Mara winced as she squeezed her palm, letting the fluid collect at the bottom of a glass vial. She had discovered several new types of powers while practicing the use of her ability in the library, and not only that, she had also discovered detailed instructions on surgeries to enable her to use other powerful new powers. She also found that there was nothing actually magical about them despite what others said. It was science, and nothing more. Science she could learn to harness.

And she had nothing but time to do so.

Her current read was about blood types; some people were compatible with certain types of abilities, and others not. If someone tried to give themselves powers they weren't compatible with, their body would reject them like a horrible, fatal allergic reaction. For whatever reason, she had been compatible with every single one, just as she'd been told.

Aleksander could create and control fire. Hanna was a Telekinetik. Others could teleport or control the elements, but *knowledge* was her power. When she had been converted into a Sangoran, the scientists had performed a similar ability-inducing surgery on her as a test to give her the power to create lightning, but soon, her knowledge would allow her to do so much more.

She had been practicing her abilities to control the Dreamstate to read several thick tomes on arcane sciences and studies of genetics to learn just how powers worked; her discovery was that these abilities were not random occurrences brought about through mutation or a blessing from the gods but were passed down through bloodlines just like hair or eye color.

This shocked her, for she believed that powers were something that only appeared in random individuals. She would have to order Talohira and Sangora's magicians and scientists to examine her blood for any signs of latent abilities she could activate. She pocketed the vial of blood and continued reading, making sure not to get any blood on the books.

The two abilities that intrigued her the most were Mindspeaking and telekinesis. She had feared that her doctors would need to cut into her skull to examine her brain and unlock the powers of the mind, and nothing seemed more terrifying.

However, according to one heavy book on the matter, all that was required was a complicated chemical substance to unlock the latent potential in compatible brains.

Within the day, she had ordered her scientists to create the requisite substances for her to develop several powers. After a horrendous migraine, she was able to begin testing her new abilities by reaching into the minds of the other Mistresses of Dusk. What secrets could she now unearth?

She heard the door of the library creak open and then swing shut with a soft thud; she looked up to see Valistaran striding across the wide expanse of the dark room with a fireball in his palm to light the way.

"How do you read in here with no light?" asked the king, using the fireball for light.

"I don't need light where I go to read these books," said Mara, pointing at the side of her head. "Besides, I can see in the dark now. I'm a Night Witch now—"

"I'm surprised you use the term 'Night Witch.' Is it not held as a derogatory racial slur?" asked Valistaran, knowing full well that it was. Perhaps he phrased it in such a way that Mara wouldn't feel embarrassed for using the word. Mara shrugged.

"Maybe I deserve it."

"I come with a question," said the king. "I am leading an envoy to Kurash tomorrow to discuss an alliance with their leader, the Supreme One."

"You want me to come with you," said Mara without even reaching into his mind.

"If you would like."

"Bring Anca. She's itching to get out of here," replied Mara. She sensed a hint of disappointment in the king's mind but neither of them mentioned it.

"By chance, have you come across anything in this library of a mythical weapon hidden in the frozen lands?" asked Valistaran.

"If you're looking for a mythical weapon in frozen lands, Kurash is the wrong place to look," answered Mara. Valistaran did not reply but waited instead for a response. "No, I haven't."

"What about the Secret Keepers of Kurash?" asked the king.

"Something about them, yeah. They are Mindspeakers in Kurash that have a constant connection with their leader—that Supreme One you spoke about. They know the entire history of humanity or something, right?"

Mara asked. She had skimmed through a short section on the topic while reading a book about Mindspeaking.

"You are correct. But have you come across what information they keep?" Valistaran asked. "I have come to realize that this library is lacking in books of history."

"I noticed," said Mara, "but history is boring. It's the future that I am looking forward to, and how I can make it mine." Mara cocked her head and grinned. "You think the Secret Keepers know about your mythical weapon, don't you?"

"I do."

"So that's why you're going to Kurash," said Mara. Valistaran nodded. "And there's another reason—a woman named Alia."

"Ah, you're a Mindspeaker now?" asked Valistaran. "Be careful, my mind is a dangerous place."

There could be no other way that Mara knew that name. He would need to be more careful to guard his thoughts around her.

"Not a very good one. I can't always filter out all the noise."

"Something I will do well to remember," replied the king, tapping his forehead.

"I once loved someone too. A boy who came to my village. I didn't see him for years, and when I did, he had completely forgotten who he was—and who I was," lamented Mara. "Let's just say that things didn't work out for us either."

Valistaran replied, "are you so different?"

"What do you mean?" asked Mara.

"If that boy from your village, not the man he became, mind you—what would he say if he saw you now? Have you forgotten who *you* are?"

Mara considered the king's comment for a long moment and hesitated before speaking. "Actually, I think I'm beginning to know who I am for the first time in my life. It's weird to say, but ever since I came to Sangora I have felt like I am remembering myself—remembering something I've never experienced. Does that make any sense? No, of course it doesn't…" She trailed off, closed her book, and set it on her pile.

"You have quite the pile of books there," said Valistaran, sitting on the stone floor across from the new Mistress of Dusk.

"I think all good people should have a long to-be-read list. Mine is probably just too long for my own good," said Mara. Valistaran laughed; it was a merry sound, one not unlike Shanthah or Josman's. Mara examined the king's face for a moment before saying, "you used to give children coins with Alia."

"My very fondest memories."

"Let me turn your question back at you. Have you forgotten the man who gave those poor children coins, when you yourself had few to spare?" asked Mara.

Valistaran was silent for a moment, a faint smile on his face. He nodded and replied in a soft voice, "an intriguing question. One that I must think about."

"Well, you'll have lots of time to think on your way to Tal-Ahosh, right?" said Mara.

"I have another question for you. One that *you'll* need to think about while I am gone," said Valistaran.

"What's that?" asked Mara.

"I would like you to become my queen," replied the king. Mara's eyes widened in surprise, and she had nothing to say. She glanced at him, her mouth hanging open in shock.

With that, he bid Mara farewell without receiving an answer, leaving her alone with her thoughts in her endless jungle of books.

CHAPTER TWENTY-EIGHT
THE EMPIRE OF THE GOLDEN SUN

The delegation from Thanatanos was seated upon ornate cushions on the ground of the Supreme One's vast diplomacy chamber. Beautiful columns decorated with a motif of golden vines and suns lined the circular chamber, and vibrant mosaics covered every wall. The Supreme One himself would soon join his guests and negotiations would commence.

Shanthah's new squad had been nervously chatting while waiting for the meetings to begin, discussing their abilities. So far, Rehor, Drahomir, Josman, and Pol still hadn't discovered their powers.

Their conversation died down as the wide doors opened, and a column of diplomats and soldiers entered the chamber bearing the flag of Talohira, a banner of three horizontal stripes of azure, deep blue, and black overlaid with a white, upside-down sword.

As they found their seats, Valistaran and Mistress Anca entered, and one of the Supreme One's servants showed them to their cushions across from King Romiton. The Supreme One would sit between the two kings with his servants behind them. Aleksander counted two vacant cushions in the Talohiran section. Were two of his guests late?

"Well, there he is," Aleksander muttered. "The reason for all our troubles."

Although he had seen firsthand the evil their enemy had wrought, he could not deny the air of majesty, power, and raw authority that the high king exuded.

The doors opened once more, and a man clad in glorious robes entered the room; his exquisite clothing reminded Aleksander of the deep blue of the sea, and the white trim resembled the crashing of waves.

His skin gave off a warm glow as if it had absorbed the sunlight above, and there was no mistaking who he was. The Supreme One, Kadir, flanked by several of his finest warriors, sat upon his cushion between the rival kings of Thanatanos and Talohira.

A contingent of eight other warriors stood at attention behind him brandishing what looked like the long, curved blade of a scimitar set upon the shaft of a spear. They were heavily armored, and from the chest up they resembled camels, complete with the animal's signature hump on their backs.

"There are your Dromedarians, Pol," said Shanthah. Pol seemed delighted, and he nodded in excitement.

"With enthusiasm, I welcome you to Tal-Ahosh this day. All of Kurash has celebrated the possibility of peace in your lands, and I am honored that you would choose our humble city as the forum to foster such relations. I hope that you enjoyed the banquet in your honor last night," The Supreme One said.

Aleksander was surprised at how human the Supreme One's speech was, and then he laughed to himself, for despite the man's magic and majesty, the man was indeed a mortal human being.

"This chamber is a circle, and we sit upon the floor for a reason. No man in this chamber is above his brother, and all who desire shall have the opportunity to speak," the Supreme One said. "I recognize each of the nations represented here today: Thanatanos, Talohira, Sangora, and Kurash, as well as the many tribes, states, and peoples of all creeds that constitute them."

Aleksander watched as the servants spread out around the circle in order to translate for those who did not speak Thannish, the common language between Thanatanos and Talohira.

"I have granted High King Valistaran Talohir the first right to speak in our assembly," continued the Supreme One. "Afterwards, King Romiton Romus shall present his ideas. All must have their turn to present their side of this conflict. Let us kindle peace amongst our cultures here today."

"Thank you, Supreme One," said Valistaran, bowing his head. "Before I present my ideas for an alliance and truce, I must announce that two of my trusted diplomats have disappeared, and we suspect that—"

"There will be no accusations here," said The Supreme One. "This is a diplomatic session, not a trial before the Grand Court. Your friends will be found. Your ideas, High King?"

A fiery explosion shook the chamber.

A shower of debris rained down from the ceiling, giving the delegates in the chamber little time to react; the Supreme One raised his hands, and a glowing shield of sunlight appeared above those immediately near him, including Valistaran, Anca, and Romiton, but several others were crushed by chunks of brightly colored stone and twisted metal.

A second blast echoed throughout the chamber, and everyone scrambled for safety. Shanthah screamed and pulled himself to his knees just in time to see a huge chunk of stone falling directly toward his head. With no time to move, all he could think was that he hoped death wouldn't be too painful. A moment later, when he hadn't been crushed, he opened one eye to see the debris floating in the air above him.

"Move, you beautiful idiot!" Hanna shouted; she had caught the rubble with her mind and stood behind Shanthah with trembling, outstretched hands. He scrambled out of the way, and the wreckage crashed to the ground, smashing the beautiful, intricate mosaic tiles where he had been moments before.

"Thank you, gorgeous!" Shanthah said with a grin.

Hanna tried to return the smile, but she stumbled and collapsed. Using her powers had drained her much of her energy.

"Woah, there!" Shanthah caught her just in time andpulled her along before making his way toward the door. He passed Rehor, who had been knocked out by the blast just as a third explosion sounded in the distance. He hesitated for a moment, knowing that he might not be able to save them both. Just then, he caught a glimpse of Josman's wide silhouette through the smoke.

"Josman!" shouted Shanthah. "Josman, over here! Save Rehor!" Josman ran in the direction of his friend's voice and almost tripped over Rehor's unconscious form on the ground. He pulled the man onto his back, and they ran from the room as a fourth explosion boomed nearby. Josman helped a Talohiran diplomat to his feet, and they fled from the chaos.

Elsewhere, Aleksander climbed over a pile of fallen rubble trying to see through the smoke. His friends were nearby when the first blast hit, but they were nowhere to be seen.

"Shanthah!" he called over the chaos. "Josman! Hanna! Pol! Kamil? Rehor?!" He tripped over someone's leg and hit his face hard on the ruined floor, and a Kurashian soldier helped him up.

"*Aleksander! Help me!*" He heard Kamil's distinct mental voice echo over the chaos around him.

"Where are you?" Aleksander asked; yet another blast echoed in the distance. The word 'help' echoed in his mind, and he decided to try to free the person under the boulder. He heaved with all his might to push the debris off the helpless individual and pulled him to safety.

He lit a flame in his palm and saw Kamil, covered in dust and blood, smiling back at him. His friend had a deep gash on his forehead and blood was dripping into his eyes, but he was alive.

"Kamil?" Aleksander asked. "Oh, thank Thanatan. Come on, let's get you out of here."

"*Where are the others?*" Kamil asked.

"No idea. You're the only one I could find!"

He pulled Kamil's arm over his shoulder and the two hobbled toward a hole in the wall to escape. A group of survivors pushed past them in a stampede, knocking them over, and leaped through the gap. Aleksander crawled forward, and his fingers brushed a soft cloak covering a fallen body. He lit another ball of flame, and through the dust and smoke he saw the face of King Romiton.

"Oh no—ooooh no," Aleksander said, eyes wide in shock. "Kamil, help me get him out of here!"

The two pulled the king from the ground, and they made slow progress toward the gap. He drew painstaking breaths, but he was alive. Kamil pushed through the pain of his injured leg, and Aleksander climbed over into the hole in the wall to help the others up.

"I'll pull King Romus up and over, and then I'll pull you up, okay?" Aleksander asked. Kamil nodded, and together they got the king up through the gap. Aleksander dropped Romiton as gently as he could then helped Kamil climb up as well.

"*I can sense others going this way,*" Kamil thought in Aleksander's mind, pointing through the dust. Aleksander nodded, and they draped the king's arms over their shoulders to carry him away.

They found themselves in a corridor that led to the lower chambers. Romiton stirred, and Kamil collapsed to the ground in a combination of exhaustion and pain. Romiton groaned and gave a feeble stir.

"Kamil, are you alright?" Aleksander asked. The mute man nodded and crawled over to Aleksander and the king.

"Yes, I am alright," Kamil said. *"You good?"*

"Yes, I'm fine," Aleksander said. "Let's hope the king is, too. We've got to get moving."

Romiton opened his eyes and pushed himself to his hands and knees with a deep cough. Aleksander and Kamil steadied him, and the three men supported each other as they walked.

"Where are we?" King Romiton asked, staring into Aleksander's face. "What happened?"

"There was an attack on the council chamber. We don't know who died and who escaped, but we need to get you to safety, your majesty. The explosions haven't stopped, so we are still in danger. I'm Aleksander, by the way, and this is Kamil."

"Romiton," said the king, as if the others did not know who he was. Aleksander chuckled.

"Were we fools to believe that no one would attack a meeting with the leaders of Thanatanos, Talohira, Sangora and Kurash?" Kamil asked, speaking to each of their minds.

"Yes, we may be," said Romiton. "However, only fools do not try for peace. We would have been even greater fools if we stayed holed up in our castles and let our people kill one another."

He helped Kamil limp toward a large window in the middle of the hallway that had not been shattered. They glanced outside to see parts of the city on fire.

"Who could have done this?" Aleksander asked. "Who would threaten the lives of their own people just to get ahead in the war?"

"Sadly, there are many who would do such a thing. I want to believe that it was not someone from Thanatanos, but I fear that I may be wrong. There are many who oppose the war and suffer because of it, but there are others who gain from it and want it to continue," Romiton said. "I was hoping today would be the day to end all of it."

Aleksander folded his arms and looked out the window. He hesitated for a moment then looked to the king. "Do you think that's who did this?"

Before Romiton could answer, the sound of footsteps echoed through the corridor. The trio hid themselves by pressing against the wall behind a massive circular pillar then waited in silence as a group of armed men in Thannish uniforms walked right by them. Aleksander started to follow the group, but Romiton grabbed his arm with a wild shake of his head.

"He was seen escaping from the Supreme One's chamber after the explosion. He can't have gotten far," said one of the men. His accent was Thannish. Not imposters, then.

"Maybe they're trying to make sure you're alive," Aleksander whispered to the king. Romiton shook his head.

"He's sure making this harder for us. Why couldn't he have just died in the explosion?" asked one of the guards.

Romiton raised an eyebrow as if to say, "I told you so," and Aleksander nodded in return. Kamil creeped around the pillar and the others followed, making it around just in time.

A second group of men clad in Talohiran colors emerged from a door where they had been standing a moment before.

They waited for the men to leave before Aleksander helped Kamil hobble through the door, and Romiton led them up a flight of painted stone stairs riddled with debris. Kamil limped along, and Aleksander made sure he was alright before they moved on.

"There are some very important people in Kurash," said Romiton. "I fear for their safety. This way."

They through a doorway that led to a long bridge connecting that part of the palace to a high spired tower.

"Care to fill us in?" asked Aleksander. "Who? Valistaran? His general?"

"No. The Secret Keepers of Tal-Ahosh are said to know the entire history of the human race, although with an understandable bias toward their area of the world," replied Romiton. "That includes the existence of some very powerful magical items that could end this war—ones that Valistaran has long desired."

They took cautious steps across the bridge, for the intricate wooden lattice work surrounding the walkway was ablaze, and smoke and flame seemed to fill the sky. A long, deep blare of a horn sounded repeatedly over the city, a signal to warn of danger and to seek shelter.

Aleksander glanced down to see healers tending to the masses of wounded people in the streets below. Flames covered much of the center of the city, and despite efforts to put them out, they were spreading.

As the trio crossed the middle of the bridge, a fireball erupted from beneath the walkway. They recoiled and covered their faces with their arms as the intense heat washed over them.

"Go!" Romiton cried, urging Kamil and Aleksander forward. A second hellish blast engulfed Romiton in flames just as Kamil and Aleksander got out of the way.

Aleksander leaped into the flames and pulled Romiton along; the fire scorched their bodies, racking them both with incredible pain. He groaned as his skin began to tingle, and the burns instantly started to heal, just as they had when he had first awakened with no memory.

King Romiton collapsed in pain as the inferno dissipated, but Aleksander had saved him from being burned alive. The king's hands and arms were blackened, and he wheezed for air.

Aleksander wheezed as he helped the king to his feet to limp the rest of the way across the bridge, and they followed Kamil through a ruined doorway.

"*Come on!*" Kamil's thought was as much of a shout as it could be.

"I would call you a fool to step through fire, but it seems to me that I am lucky to know such a fool," said Romiton as they shut the door behind them. "Your burns are already healing. You must be a Dragonsoul."

"A what?"

"A fire-thrower. We heal faster from burns. It's part of our power," said Romiton with a wink. "You, me, and Valistaran."

Aleksander gasped as he watched the king ignite a ball of flame in his palm as his blackened began to fade to pink.

He turned just as Kamil collapsed to the floor, rubbing his wounded leg. Romiton and Aleksander knelt next to him for a moment of reprieve.

"We shouldn't linger," Kamil said.

"I think that explosion was no mere coincidence. A trap—proof that whoever did this doesn't want anyone to come in or out," said Romiton. "I have an idea. Kamil, friend, you can speak to our minds. Can you also hear the thoughts of others? I need you to find the Secret Keepers."

Kamil shook his head and tried to stand, grimacing as he put weight on his leg.

"I've never been able to before."

"Focus your thoughts around the tower. Try to speak to the minds of anyone inside. The Secret Keepers are also Mindspeakers, and if they are up there, you will be able to contact them," Romiton said. Kamil nodded, and closed his eyes, tried to contact the Secret Keepers with his Mindspeaking abilities.

Kamil's face twitched every few seconds then his eyes shot open after about a minute of strained effort; he scrambled to his feet and ran up the spiral staircase, leaving the others behind. Romiton and Aleksander hurried after him, tripping several times as they tried to dodge flames and debris in their haste.

"The Secret Keepers are in danger!" said Kamil to each of their minds around the bend in the staircase. Aleksander tried the door at the top of the stairs as they reached it, but it was locked. A moment later, there was a click, and the door swung open. Although apprehensive, Aleksander stepped through the doorway as he unsheathed his blade.

"*I told them to unlock it,*" Kamil said, limping over the threshold. "*They know we're friends.*"

Romiton shut the door behind them, and they stepped into the chamber. All three gasped as they found themselves in a dense jungle; the sound of distant birdsong and screeching monkeys replaced the sound of the chaos in Tal-Ahosh, and as Kamil shut the door, the Empire of the Golden Sun had all but disappeared. Thick foliage covered the ground and only a faint bit of light escaped the canopy above.

"Where are we?" Aleksander asked. "How?"

He turned to find the door, but it had disappeared. Kamil reached out with his mind once more but failed to find anyone there. Romiton stroked a long-leafed frond, making the branch bounce; droplets of due fell from the plant, and he rubbed the moisture between his fingers and took in a deep breath, smelling the world around him. He shook his head, pacing back and forth.

"It's an illusion," Romiton said. "A precaution."

"But Kamil said they know we're friends," Aleksander said.

"*True. But we're not alone.*"

His face twitched as they pushed through the trees and discovered a foggy glade. Rain began to fall in the clearing as a trio of birds squawked overhead, and the trio backed into the jungle for cover. Aleksander squinted through the curtain of black rain that had appeared and thought he caught a glimpse of someone standing in the middle of the clearing; he stood there like a statue waiting for something to happen—another trap?

"*Someone's out there,*" Kamil said, his mental voice a whisper.

"The Secret Keepers?" asked Aleksander.

Romiton shook his head and drew his silver blade.

"Stay here," the king said, "and stay down."

He emerged from the jungle and approached the other man. The wind played with each of their cloaks, waving them like the flags of their people.

"You will not find the Secret Keepers, Val," Romiton shouted over the rain. Valistaran turned to face Romiton, his sword already unsheathed. "I knew I would find you here."

"You haven't called me that in a long time, *friend*. If you are blaming me for the attack on Tal-Ahosh, we had nothing to do with it," Valistaran said. He did nothing to stop the illusion-rain from running down his stern face.

"Then who?" Romiton asked.

"You are here in Kurash for many of the same reasons as I am. But are we here in this tower for the same purpose as well?" Valistaran asked. Romiton looked around and gestured to the jungle. "No, I know we're not really here. We're still in the Secret Keepers' tower. They're very powerful, Rom. They can make you see things. They can trap you here forever if they want to."

"They must have sensed your intentions," said Romiton. Valistaran advanced slowly on Romiton, his sword sweeping through the tall grass.

"Mine?" asked Valistaran with a smirk. "Or yours?"

"Tell me, what do you plan to do when you find them?" Romiton asked. "When you find that damn weapon?"

"What indeed?"

"We decided long ago not to pursue this foolish dream!" Romiton shouted. "Don't you *dare* go through with this!"

Valistaran lashed out with his drawn blade, and Romiton swung his own upward to meet it. Valistaran whirled around with an aggressive slash at Romiton's head, but the blow never came, and Romiton found himself standing near the doorway of the Secret Keepers' chamber outside the illusion. Valistaran stood near him, his sword held high overhead—still trapped, for now.

Aleksander and Kamil collapsed as they too were released from the vision. Aleksander glanced up to see three elderly men and two women in beautiful robes with intricate designs standing around Valistaran.

"We cannot hold him forever, for he is of strong mind," said one of the Secret Keepers to each of their minds.

"We cannot hope to hold High King Talohir forever. Help us, Aleksander. Help us, Romiton. Help us, Kamil."

Aleksander drew his blade and looked toward Valistaran.

"We could kill him right now," Kamil said. *"It's what he deserves."*

"If we kill him, this entire attack would seem like a plan to assassinate him," said Aleksander. "We're going to have to outrun him and hide the Secret Keepers. He wants them, not us."

"Our hold on his mind will begin to weaken as soon as any of us leave the room. Can you protect us?" asked one of the Secret Keepers.

"To my last breath," the king replied as Aleksander opened the door on the opposite side of the tower.

"You're more valuable than us, King Romus. Go," Aleksander said. "I'll hold him off."

King Romiton smiled and shook his head, staring intently at Aleksander. "No, no. That isn't true. Let me speak to him."

Aleksander and Kamil did as they were told, stepping out onto another bridge that connected to the main part of the beautiful temple. Romiton watched Aleksander leave for a long moment before turning back to Valistaran.

Two of the Secret Keepers lowered their hands and followed Aleksander and Kamil outside. Valistaran's still form convulsed, and the remaining three Secret Keepers strained to keep him frozen, their faces twitching with the strain of their powers.

Aleksander helped one old woman cross the bridge while Kamil assisted another down the single step onto the walkway. The next two climbed down by themselves, leaving one of the remaining Secret Keepers with Romiton to keep Valistaran trapped in the illusion, but the king was beginning to stir again, his muscles twitching and eyes darting between the two men.

With one of the Secret Keepers safe on the other side of the bridge, Aleksander and Kamil turned back to help the others. Aleksander cried out in surprise as he saw Valistaran break from his mental bonds and lash out in a circular motion, sweeping a flaming blade across the chests of the old man holding him back. Romiton's blade clashed with Valistaran's as the man's body hit the floor.

"Get them to safety!" Romiton cried, locked in combat. Aleksander and Kamil obeyed, bursting through the door to guide the four other Secret Keepers away.

Romiton threw a ball of flame onto the rug beneath Valistaran's feet, igniting it in an instant then swung his blade around to parry another blow from his foe.

A bolt of black flame shot past Romiton's head, blasting one of the old women in the back and throwing her from the bridge.

The king of Thanatanos bathed the floor below Valistaran in ethereal flame then let his fury ignite, creating an explosion that decimated the side of the tower and sent Valistaran flying across the room; he collided with the wall and struck his head against a burning bookshelf, its books ablaze.

Romiton was upon his enemy in a moment, and he punched him hard under his chin then once again just above the eye. Valistaran blasted Romiton in the chest with all the flame he could muster then clambered to his feet. They each roared in agony, their flesh charred and blackened and black and golden flame flashing all around.

Romiton groaned in pain and stumbled against the wall. He turned just in time to parry a blow from Valistaran as the ceiling nearby collapsed. A ball of black fire struck Romiton's forearm, making him drop his kingly blade. Valistaran raised his sword to strike off his foe's head, but Romiton got to his feet and clenched one fist, immobilizing Valistaran in a pillar of flame. He unleashed all the flames his body would produce, bathing Valistaran in an unearthly white glow.

Valistaran roared in agony, retaliating with an explosion of his own dark hellfire. The tip of the tower exploded in a blazing shower of debris, and both kings collapsed through the weakened floor. Valistaran's shoulder struck the edge of a stair, and Romiton tumbled past him. Neither of the men stirred for several minutes.

Their charred skin began to fade to pink as their bodies' abilities began to heal the burns. Valistaran was the first to stand, and he staggered out of the burning tower, coughing.

Bleeding from a wound on his temple that his abilities couldn't heal, Romiton limped after him, knowing what would happen if Valistaran captured the Secret Keepers. He hoped beyond reason that Aleksander and Kamil had helped them hide.

He emerged from the stairs, his charred body a reflection of the inferno below. He launched a weak fireball toward Valistaran, who was already crossing the bridge. It struck him just above the small of his back, knocking him to his knees.

Nearby, Aleksander glanced out a window to see the two kings now standing upon the bridge facing one another. He could tell they were saying something. Yelling, now.

He watched in horror as Valistaran let forth a stream of hellish flame toward Romiton, striking him in the chest; the king of Thanatanos was thrown from the bridge and plummeted downward, lost in the smoke and flames.

Aleksander's heart thundered in his chest. He could not find the energy to scream; there was no escape from their hiding place at the top of the second tower, and Valistaran had managed to both cross the bridge *and* kill King Romiton.

"We need to find another way out," said Aleksander, beginning a frantic search for another exit. Kamil smashed a window with a brick and motioned to the others.

"*Out here!*" said Kamil.

Aleksander helped the two old men and last surviving woman out the window and then followed them onto the narrow ledge. One of the men needed extra help, but they made it outside just as a dark fireball zoomed past, singing the rearmost Secret Keeper's side. He almost fell from the tower, but Aleksander steadied him. All three were wounded now, and Aleksander swore under his breath.

"Go!" cried Aleksander. They climbed over the mosaic of colorful ceiling tiles and scooted down the roof, knowing that Valistaran was close behind.

"Can you climb?" asked Aleksander.

The Secret Keeper looked at him with a blank stare.

"*Hal 'ant tasaluq misin?*" asked Kamil to the man's mind, translating Aleksander's question. The man nodded and replied to Kamil in their language, then they began their decent.

Aleksander helped the second man over the ledge, but the third was far too feeble to make the drop. Valistaran emerged from the chamber and plunged his blade through the man's back then kicked him off the roof. He fell broken near Kamil.

Completely exhausted, Aleksander hurled a blazing sphere of flame toward Valistaran. The shocked king stumbled backward, nearly falling from the roof as Aleksander brought his fist around into the king's face.

He blasted Valistaran with two fireballs then leaped from the ledge onto the next level of roofing, knocking off several of the beautiful blue tiles.

Valistaran sent a roaring inferno after him, and Aleksander had to shield his neck from the debris that followed. The king sent another fireball past Aleksander, striking one more of the Secret Keepers in the back.

"Kamil get them out of here!"

Kamil tried to force him to stand, but it was no use. The man was dead. Aleksander threw two fireballs toward the king, but they missed their mark. Kamil pulled the two remaining Secret Keepers along as Aleksander raced away from his foe for better footing.

"Stop!" cried a firm voice. A moment later, a shower of arrows rained down on Valistaran, and two of them stuck into his flesh. He cried out in agony and collapsed to his hands and knees.

Valistaran unleashed a blaze of hellfire at the soldiers, who scattered before retaliating with more arrows. As the group engaged the king in battle, Aleksander and Kamil helped the two Secret Keepers climb through a doorway back into the palace just as a shower of debris rained down from the battle above. A heavy beam struck Kamil on the side, and he plummeted downward to another level of roofing.

"Kamil!" Aleksander shouted. No answer.

Aleksander helped the two Secret Keepers lie on the floor for a moment of rest then peered over to see if Kamil was alright.

"I'm alive. Get them away from Valistaran!" Kamil's voice echoed through Aleksander's mind.

One Secret Keeper was bleeding from a wound on his back, and he had twisted his ankle, which was swollen and discolored. The other wheezed in pain and gripped his blood-soaked side. Aleksander feared their fate would be far from pleasant.

"Where can we go? I need to save you," said Aleksander, coughing into his hand.

Blood.

He groaned.

"You do not need to save us. You must save the secrets that we hold," said the female Secret Keeper. The other man did not speak Aleksander's language but reached for Aleksander's forehead.

"What are you doing?" Aleksander asked as the other Secret Keeper did the same.

He felt a surge of pain rack his skull, and he collapsed. The world was spinning. His vision blackened, and he could neither see nor hear. He crawled in order to find the old man and women and grasped their hands. The world came back into focus, and he could tell one of the man was already dead.

"How interesting and fortuitous…that the man who forgot everything…must now remember all things. Only you could have saved our knowledge," said the last Secret Keeper. *"Truly, the gods prepared you for this moment."*

His grip on Aleksander's hand slackened, and then he too was gone, his eyes vacant.

Aleksander's mind swirled and then exploded with a million broken memories that were not his own. Pain like that of a lightning bolt in his head brought him to his knees, and then blackness claimed him.

CHAPTER TWENTY-NINE

THE NEW KEEPER OF SECRETS

Aleksander's convulsing muscles prevented him from standing. He stumbled over to a high-backed chair in the corner and slumped into it, the horror of what had just happened still sinking into his mind. He had no idea how long he had been unconscious, and he realized that his trembling hands as well as his torso were covered in blood. Whether it was his own or that of the Secret Keepers, he had no idea.

The Secret Keepers' words echoed through his mind. They had granted their knowledge to *him*, somehow forcing every single one of their memories into his head. Apart from his spasming muscles, he felt no different and had no idea what implications this newest update would have upon his life.

One thing he did know was that Valistaran would soon be upon him, meaning he had to flee. He pushed against the arms of the chair, forcing his legs to cooperate. He wobbled over to the window and saw that Kamil was gone, and the entire group of Kurashian soldiers were dead on the roof. Valistaran was nowhere to be seen. That could only mean one thing.

The door behind Aleksander crashed inward and splintered in a shower of wood and flame. The smoking remains smoldered on the floor as Valistaran stepped into the room. He examined the dead Secret Keepers and then turned his stern gaze to Aleksander who collapsed against the wall.

"What did they say to you before they died?" Valistaran asked. It was a demand, not a question.

"Nothing," Aleksander lied. "They bled out before they could tell me anything—and you know what? I think I'll try to do the same rather than tell *you* anything."

"Aleksander, is it?" He gestured to Aleksander's scar.

"You know me?" he asked, perplexed.

"She talks about you, you know," Valistaran replied. "And Aleksander, she *despises* you."

"What?" Aleksander whispered.

"And how disappointed she would be to see you here, having murdered these sacred men and women. If she could see you right now, she'd—"

Aleksander stumbled to his feet and punched Valistaran square in the jaw before he collapsed. The king was taken aback for a moment but said nothing, simply letting out a small chuckle.

"Before you kill me—was this you?" Aleksander asked, gesturing out the window at the flames. "All of it."

"If I was behind this attack, you would all be dead. This attack was clumsy. Chaotic. Someone is sending us all a message. Now, Aleksander, I am going to ask you one more time. What did the Secret Keepers tell you?"

Aleksander bumped against the window as he tried to stand.

"It's been nice to meet the High King of Talohira, but—"

Aleksander hurled a ball of flame and lashed out with his sword at the same time, shattering the window behind him. He flung himself from the ledge and felt the window's fragments bite his skin as he plummeted toward the ground. He hoped in silence for either a soft landing or a painless death.

He struck a thick fabric shade awning which broke his fall, but when he hit the pavement, he could tell it was not enough. Pain shot through his body, and he had heard several sickening crunches when he struck the earth.

Something, if not everything, was probably broken.

He was thankful for the crowd that had gathered, and he crawled between their legs. He glanced upward to the tower to see Valistaran standing alone in the window, his cape billowing in the warm night breeze. Kamil. Where was Kamil?

He groaned as he forced himself to his feet. He turned back, and scooped up his fallen sword and slid it into his belt. He caught a glimpse of a troop of Kurashian soldiers pushing through the crowd, and he felt a wave of unease sweep over him. All eyes in the crowd were fixed on him, the man that had just fallen from the high tower.

He pulled his hood over his head and hobbled in the opposite direction. As he passed an alleyway, a hand burst from the shadows and pulled him into the darkness. His reaction was to fight, but a petite Kurashian woman with piercing eyes pressed her finger to her lips to indicate silence, and they hid against the wall. Aleksander hoped to whatever gods were listening that she was an ally. Most of her face was hidden by a shroud, and he caught a glimpse of a long, curved dagger strapped to her belt.

"They are looking for you," she whispered, pointing in the general direction of the troops.

"Were you too?" asked Aleksander, his eyes wide.

"The Supreme One sensed the deaths of the Secret Keepers as soon as they died."

"How do you know that?" Aleksander replied. "I didn't kill the Secret Keepers, if that's what you're implying."

"I know, as do you, who the real murderer is. To answer your question, the Supreme One is one of the most powerful Mindspeakers ever born. He just sent a mental message to every single Kurashian in Tal-Ahosh to find you."

"Again, why me, if Valistaran is the murderer? And again, how do you know Valistaran is the real murderer? Are you going to help me?"

He had a million more questions, but he bit his tongue.

"I know Valistaran better than most. Better than anyone, actually. I know why he came here. An alliance was never his priority—just a ruse to hide his real intentions."

"What do you mean?" Aleksander asked.

Another group of Kurashian soldiers filed past, and she became quiet. When they were gone, she spoke again.

"The Supreme One must have had some kind of image or impression of you when the Secret Keepers died. Their mental connection with him was very powerful, and you must have done something to affect that connection somehow. Were you the last thing they saw, or something?"

"Something like that, yeah."

"That'd do it."

Aleksander knew without a doubt what the disturbance in the connection was: the Secret Keepers had transferred their entire collective consciousness into his mind. He said nothing of the matter to the stranger and hoped the Supreme One could not see through her eyes or read his mind wherever he was. Perhaps, though, he would see the truth if he could. Had the Secret Keepers doomed him by making him take their place?

"Quick, this way." She led him down the alleyway when she assumed it was safe. After a few turns she guided him to a small, unremarkable home up the hill. She checked over her shoulder to assure they were not being followed and went inside.

"Thank you for your help, mysterious strange woman," said Aleksander. He grimaced, knowing the words did not come out how he wanted them to.

"You are welcome, strange man. My name is Alia. Sit."

He did as he was told, plopping down on a tattered sofa on the edge of the quaint room. The woman said something in Kurashic, and a dark-haired young man entered. They conversed for a moment and the boy nodded.

"We can hide you from the soldiers and get you back to your people," said the boy. Aleksander thought that he couldn't be much older than Pol.

"Thank you," said Aleksander, "but forgive my asking, who are you two?"

"You can call me Karim," said the boy.

"I'm Aleksander. And why aren't you handing me over to Valistaran and the Supreme One, Karim?"

Alia sat next to Aleksander and took his arm. She took a deep breath as she began to examine it.

"At one time, I probably would have. Now, well—that's a long story," Alia said. "One for another day, perhaps."

"So, what now?" Aleksander asked.

Aleksander felt a tingling sensation spread from where Alia's hands were pressed on his skin, and the pain dissipated.

"Oh, that's nice," he said as a cooling sensation spread across his arm. "How?"

"I'm a healer," Alia said, wiggling her fingers. "Obviously."

"Ah. More please," Aleksander replied with a laugh.

"Well, they are going to be looking for you for a while. They think you killed the Secret Keepers, and that seems like a motive enough to attack the council chamber as well, don't you think?" asked Alia. "Because of that, anyone associated with you is probably a fugitive as well—do you know where any of your friends or allies are? I'm assuming you're not here alone."

Aleksander's stomach sank as he realized he had no idea where any of his friends, including Kamil, who had been with him during most of the chaos, were now.

"No. My friend Kamil was with me when the Secret Keepers died, but I don't know what happened to him or the others."

"We'll help you find them," Karim assured him.

"Thank you. They're resourceful, but I won't be able to stop worrying about them until I know they're safe," said Aleksander.

Alia continued healing the lacerations and burns with her abilities as they conversed. He didn't realize he had sustained so many injuries during the conflict. He marveled at how his skin sewed itself up at her touch.

"How many are you?" asked Alia.

"I think eight, other than me?"

"Names?" Karim asked.

"Let's see. Shanthah Kalen, Josman Faros, Hanna Samsa, Apolinarius Bartunek, Drahomir Zimov, Rehor Toth, Kamil Ramzi, and Mara Bartunek."

He realized that Mara's name had slipped out before he could stop it.

"Okay," Karim said. "Say those again when I actually have time to write them down."

"Sorry." He repeated the names, and Karim nodded as he jotted them down.

"I'll ask around."

"We were trapped in Valistaran's camp to eliminate the powered people in Thanatanos and were somehow thrown into this mess. I'm really not sure how we became involved in a diplomatic mission or anything that has happened, but none of us have been home since."

"Ah, yes. I am *well* aware of those slave camps," Alia said.

For some reason, Aleksander felt at ease and that he could trust his two new allies, despite knowing nothing about them. He decided to keep talking to build a relationship with them.

"And where is home?" asked Karim.

"Some of them are from Laniras in Thanatanos. Others are from small towns. Kamil, who I mentioned, is from Kurash—"

"You," Karim said. "Your home."

"I'm not really sure," Aleksander replied. "I know, that's weird, but… Cineca, I think."

He couldn't get Mara's face out of his mind as he said it.

"What do you mean?" asked Alia.

"Long story short, I lost all my memories up to the time I was thrown in the Talohiran slave camp," said Aleksander. "Don't ask me how or why. No idea."

Alia sighed. "Well, my powers can heal broken bones, mend wounds, leech out infection, and sometimes even cure disease. They don't *always* work with issues of the brain, but I can try to mend your mind, if you'll let me."

Aleksander hesitated. What if there had been some darkness that needed to be hidden within his mind? Alia did nothing, but the conversation piqued Karim's interest.

"No. As must as I want to, there might have been a reason for it," Aleksander replied. "Thank you, though."

"Do it," Karim urged him.

"Now, now. Leave the strange man alone," said Alia. "I would advise you to sleep. You'll need your energy. I'll be sure to have breakfast ready for you in the morning."

"Thank you both."

Alia pulled a moth-eaten blanket from a small chest in the corner and threw it over the sofa, covering Aleksander's head.

"Use this tonight. You can sleep on the sofa. If it gets too hot in here, which it will, you can use the blanket as a pillow instead. Goodnight, Aleksander."

She exited, leaving him alone. He pulled the blanket off his head, and he collapsed onto his side, unconscious within moments. Alia came back into the room and upon seeing him asleep, kneeled next to him.

"You must remember. If I'm right, I am so, so, sorry, but this is more important than you realize," she whispered into his sleeping ear as if trying to justify her action.

Although it could take months for his mind to heal and his memories to return, she prayed to the Kurashian gods that her abilities would have some effect in restoring what she believed he must remember. She placed her hand on his forehead and closed her eyes. He convulsed for a moment before his breathing returned to normal, and he lay still.

CHAPTER THIRTY
LORD OF THE WALKERS

As morning broke, a whisper swept through the streets like a cool breeze; it was soft in tone, but fierce in message: "*Gather.*"

Into every mind in the city the whisper came, intruding into the private thoughts of the day's earliest hours. No one questioned the command or from whence it came. They all knew. The Supreme One of Kurash sent his command to every mind in the city.

While the Supreme One was a just and kind ruler, his summons were rare. Failing to obey the command could result in harsh punishment, and before the sun reached its highest place in the sky, a great multitude was gathered near the ruined palace, many eager to hear the words of their leader.

Aleksander, Alia, and her son Karim were in attendance, knowing that whatever information the Supreme One presented would be crucial in planning how to act next.

Perhaps Aleksander's comrades had been apprehended, and he hoped the Supreme One would mention something about their incarceration so he would know where to look. The trio positioned themselves at the back of the crowd just in case someone called attention to them.

The Supreme One and several other leaders were seated on beautiful thrones upon a gargantuan, golden stage outside the gates of the palace. To the surprise of many, Valistaran and General Anca were seated at the right hand of the Kurashian leader. Representatives from Thanatanos were absent, a bad sign for the survivors of the Thans' delegation to be sure.

When he was ready, Kadir stood before the multitude and motioned for Valistaran to join him. He spoke in Kurashic, and Alia translated for Aleksander as he spoke. The absence of an official translator indicated that this message was one meant for Kurashian ears only.

"More blood of the children of Kurash has been spilled in the past day than in the past two hundred years. Such an act of..." Alia trailed off and asked her son for the correct translation and then continued, "Such an act of—uh, cowardice or treachery will not be ignored, and those responsible will be found and punished to the highest extent of our law."

The Supreme One paused for a moment as if he were choking back tears then continued. Alia readied herself for another round of translation, taking a deep breath and trying to block out background noise by plugging one ear.

"Over five thousand souls were cut—or, more like severed you know, by force," said Alia, trying to use the correct Thannish verb then tried to hurry through the couple lines of the speech she had missed, saying instead, "something about being severed from this world, sent to the underworld—" She stopped translating for a second to catch up with the Supreme One's quick speech again before jumping back into the translation. "Among the dead are the three Secret Keepers of Kurash, and along with them, the history of our people and that which came before them. However, there were many witnesses there, and the assassins responsible have been identified."

Alia sighed in relief as her ruler paused.

"Do you want me to translate?" whispered Karim. Alia scowled, and Karim backed off. They both forgot to translate for a moment, and Aleksander understood why, for two of the Supreme One's camel-headed Dromedarian soldiers had unfurled a banner with a colossal image of Aleksander's own face imprinted on its canvas. Paintings of the faces of his allies were printed below, although much smaller.

"Not ideal," Aleksander muttered into Alia's ear.

With a nervous glance around, he pulled his hood lower over his eyes. Karim stood in front of him, trying to be surreptitious enough to hide him from view as Alia continued the translation.

"This man is known as Aleksander. He's from Thanatanos and is responsible for the deaths of our Secret Keepers as well as thousands of other innocent men and women. His—" Alia paused her translation for a moment.

"What's wrong?" Aleksander hissed. "My what?"

"I—the word isn't coming, you know…" she turned to Karim in a panic.

"You know, it's like that feeling when you…" her son said, trailing off. "Like maybe arrogance? Or selfishness?"

"No, that's more like *ahnania*." Alia said, and Karim nodded. Alia snapped to indicate that she figured it out, and said, "It's a Kurashic word that doesn't translate. Like pride and cowardice, with a bit of what Karim said too."

"Okay, I get it. Aleksander's proud and a dirty coward. Keep going," Aleksander said. Alia nodded and continued.

"Basically, they blame this Aleksander for the attacks last night," Alia said. She was careful not to use the pronoun 'you' as to protect his identity from those potentially listening.

"What are they going to do to him?" Aleksander bit his lip.

"Oh, execute him, of course," Alia replied. The Supreme One sat, and Valistaran stepped forward to speak. This time, a translator conveyed the message in Kurashic as Valistaran spoke.

"It is with great sadness that I address you this day," he said. He paused for the translation to finish. "However, a light in the darkness is that the Supreme One has agreed to an alliance with Talohira. For too long war has spread across my lands, but now with your ruler's blessing, peace can now blossom in the heart of Talohira. The terms are simple. He will not send soldiers into Thanatanos to atone for the bloodshed of last night, but he will send warriors to help defend from their ruthless attacks against my people. My nation's treasury will fund the construction of a great system of aqueducts to bring life from the sea beyond Tal-Ahosh into the desert city of Yeni Kudus and beyond."

There was a murmur from the crowd, and Valistaran continued. "I know that Kurash has not gone to war in many hundreds of years, but I welcome any man or woman who wishes to help defend freedom and end this hateful war. I applaud and thank you for being the ones to step up and help end the conflict. I applaud the Supreme One's goodness in refraining from brutal retaliation against Thanatanos, even though their delegation here was responsible for the attacks last night."

"What a wolf," Alia whispered. Aleksander nodded.

"A chest of gold will be given to any man or woman that brings us this Aleksander alive. We believe that he took something of great value from the Secret Keepers."

It was at this moment that Alia pulled Aleksander away from the crowd. Karim made sure no one around was watching, and the trio hurried down an alleyway. They made their way toward Alia's home, but the clanking of an approaching group of armed guards gave them pause. They turned back to see that a second group of soldiers was marching in a line from wall to wall up the alleyway to prevent anyone from passing by.

The warriors began calling to them in Kurashic, but Aleksander ignored them, trying in vain to discover an avenue to freedom. An arrow clattered against the cobblestone near Aleksander's feet. A warning. Nerves began to set in, and panic threatened to freeze him on the spot. He glanced upward to see a trio of archers in the windows above, their bows ready.

"You're not fighting your way out of here," said Karim.

Alia raised her hands and began speaking to the soldiers in rapid Kurashic. The soldiers' voices became increasingly aggressive, and Alia's speech quickened, raising her hands in defiance.

A sudden arrow whizzed from the tower, but it didn't seem to have any particular target, breaking against the stone wall on the other side of the alley. Aleksander looked up again and saw that the group of bowmen had disappeared. In that moment, the warriors closed in on the trio; Alia and Karim both screamed, and there was a burst of black smoke all around them that obscured their vision. When the smoke cleared, the group of soldiers lay incapacitated on the ground.

"What in the world?" Aleksander wondered aloud.

"Best not to ask. Run!" Alia exclaimed. She took his arm, and the trio sprinted toward her home. They burst through the door, and Alia locked it behind her.

"We don't have a lot of time," said Karim. "We need to get some supplies and get out of here. Whatever got those guards might be after us next."

Karim and Alia went into the back room to gather supplies while Aleksander stood dazed in the living room. He turned around and gasped as he came face to face with a man draped in tattered rags from head to foot. The man had not entered the house with them through the door.

"Do not be afraid," he said. "You are in no danger."

"I won't let you hurt them," Aleksander said.

"My name is Lord Ronin Jakoni. I am here to ask for your assistance," the newcomer stated. His eyes gleamed yellow from beneath his wrappings and his skin was pale, as if he had never seen the light of day. His accent was Sangoran, but no wings stretched forth from his back. Were these the Walkers that his he had heard mention of in the slave camp?

Alia appeared from the back room and dropped the supplies she had gathered for their escape. A juicy plum rolled across the floor and Lord Ronin Jakoni stooped over to pick it up. He handed it to Alia and turned back to Aleksander.

"No, no, no," said Alia. "Go away, Ronin. We will not help you. You are extremists. Terrorists. You are not welcome here."

The Lord of the Walkers did not acknowledge Alia's comment, adamant on delivering his message to Aleksander.

"Before Valistaran Talohir slew the Secret Keepers, they told you something. I need you to be honest with me when I ask you: what did they tell you?" Ronin asked. Aleksander looked at Alia as if to ask her if they could trust this stranger. She shook her head, but Aleksander turned his attention back to Ronin.

"They made me the new Secret Keeper of Kurash," answered Aleksander. Alia covered her face with her hands and groaned. "I'm telling you this because you aren't accusing me of murdering them. I assume, perhaps wrongfully and stupidly, that I can trust you."

"Your friend does not trust us," said Ronin. "I shall have to work to build her trust. Have you discovered the power of your new calling?"

"No," admitted Aleksander. He realized that they had transferred all their knowledge to him, but he couldn't summon a single image of their memories to his mind.

"Have you told anyone else?"

"No."

"You will soon begin to remember things that you have never experienced. Things from hundreds or even thousands of years past. Do not take these thoughts lightly, for they are the secrets that have been forgotten by all but a few. By all but you."

His words sent a chill down Aleksander's spine. Alia bit her lip, knowing that Aleksander would soon start remembering his own past as well as memories forced upon him by the Secret Keepers.

"Valistaran knows that. Doesn't he? That's why he's after me. He knows that I know something he wants to know?"

"Exactly. King Talohir seeks—" Ronin said, but Alia interrupted the Lord of the Walkers.

"A weapon of legend hidden in the frozen lands of the north," Alia said, finishing the stranger's sentence. Ronin seemed taken aback, and Aleksander smirked at the Walker's surprise. "I always thought that it didn't exist, but now I'm not entirely sure."

"The weapon he desires is not in the frozen lands, no. You are correct about that—but it does exist," said Ronin.

"So—what do you need from me?" asked Aleksander.

"I need you to help me find it so that the world does not burn under Valistaran's hand," Ronin replied. "Believe me, friend Aleksander, if he finds that which he seeks."

Aleksander made a mental note to remember to cover his scar more carefully.

"And when you find it, what will you do with it? Which side are you on?"

"There are no sides in this conflict. There are only survivors and those unlucky enough to escape it. I simply wish to be part of the first group. When I find the weapon, I will destroy it. No man or king should ever hold the power to end so much life."

"What is it?" asked Karim, who had been listening from the other room.

"I do not know, only that it is a weapon from ancient days," said Ronin. "Death follows in its wake. Our adventure will likely take us far from Thanatanos to the lands known as the Deadlands."

"Wait a minute," said Karim. "Did this thing make the Deadlands *into* the *Dead*lands?"

"I believe so," said Ronin. "Because of your new position as Secret Keeper, you are the only one who will be able to lead us to it. You will save more lives than you can imagine."

"And what of Aleksander's friends?" asked Alia.

"What of them?" asked Ronin.

"They are missing. I haven't seen them since the attack on the Supreme One's palace," said Aleksander, his thoughts snaking back to Alia's comment about the Walkers being extremists and terrorists. For a moment he wondered if Ronin was responsible for the explosions but admitted that his assistance might be the only way out of Kurash.

"Then perhaps I shall make a deal with you. You promise to help me where I can, and my men shall ensure the safety of your friends," said Ronin.

Aleksander looked to Alia, who still looked apprehensive, although Ronin's mention of wanting to destroy the weapon had softened her expression.

"Then to the Deadlands it is," said Aleksander, taking a deep breath. "Let's save the others and end this war."

CHAPTER THIRTY-ONE
THE WINDOW BREAKS

The newly crowned *King* Verahim's coronation had been a somber, unceremonious occasion, one that would not be remembered in the pages of history for its flair or celebration. Due to the circumstances, there were no great festivals, and because of that, he wondered how long many of his citizens would believe his father was still alive.

The lone surviving member of the royal Romus family line crumpled a sheet of parchment in his fist and tossed it to the ground. He hurled his thin golden crown across the chamber in a fit of rage and collapsed into his father's empty throne—no, *his* throne. The new king looked up to the messenger and sighed, massaging the bridge of his nose.

It had been a week since the ill-fated diplomatic expedition to Kurash, and instead of returning to his own country, the High King of Talohira had walked unimpeded into Laniras—into the very heart of Thanatanos itself.

"Today of all days—is nothing sacred?" Verahim asked. "Valistaran is a fool if he thinks these threats will frighten our people into surrender. Send him word none will support him."

Verahim's advisor, a hunched, balding man with a sparse beard took a deep breath before addressing King Verahim. "My lord, with all due respect, much of the kingdom already does. Many have lost respect for the crown—you saw in that message that he is promising them peace, protection, and relief from your father's taxation. In Talohira, his people can believe in whatever gods they wish to believe, not just in Lord Thanatan. He's forming a government of the people."

"He's establishing a senate and reforming his government in Talohira, yes, but when will it take power? When he is dead? When all of Thanatanos is burned to the ground and its people in chains?" King Verahim asked. "His new imperial sector itself is being built by slaves! It's a front, I tell you!" He spat toward an eastern facing window. The direction of Talohira. Bukaral.

"Well, like it or not my lord, he is here. He has the support of Kurash—he took for himself the alliance we wanted to forge. We simply cannot stand against the combined forces of Talohira, Sangora, *and* Kurash. You know that, my liege."

"You can always stand up to people like him. He is a bully like those from my youth tormenting my brother Xanthurias, who should be king. I didn't stand for such behavior then, and I will not do so now," said Verahim. His advisor hesitated for a moment at the mention of the fallen prince's name. Both men knew Xanthurias would have been crowned king, had he survived the war.

"My lord, I—" said the advisor.

"The banners of Talohira will never fly over the city of Laniras," Verahim said, slamming his fist on the table.

"Then perhaps, the people of Laniras will leave in chains."

"You sound like you support Valistaran. I shall have any of my people with pro-Talohiran sentiments to be expelled."

"It isn't that I support him or his ideas, but I am tired of this war. Everyone is, my king. It's already claimed the lives of your brother and now your father too. No one else needs to die for the sake of war—we want peace to flourish," said the exasperated advisor. "This might be the only way out. Your mother, Queen Rose, may she rest in peace, would have agreed."

"Do *not* bring her into this. We could find peace with one more death."

"You want Valistaran's head on a spear. That will just aggravate them more, my lord. Don't make him a martyr."

"Get out," said the king, pointing to the door. "You served my father well, and for that, I won't expel you quite yet. Go."

His advisor bowed and left the chamber without a word. Verahim sighed and scooped up his crown. Valistaran's messengers had sprung the surprise that their king would soon arrive, giving him no time to prepare—the tactic of a coward.

He stormed from his throne room and made his way to the council chamber where he would attempt to make negotiations with Valistaran. He entered the chamber earlier than expected, surprising the assembled diplomats and generals inside. He sank into the seat at the head of the opulent, oval table with a glum expression and without introduction.

He threw his hands into the air with exasperation.

"So?" he asked. "Where is the usurper?"

General Hokkod of the Court of Thanatan was seated to his left while that to his right was empty, reserved for the crown prince. However, because of recent events, there was no such person. There was only a young, reluctant king with no heir.

"My lord," said Hokkod in salutation. "When King Talohir arrives, he will outline his terms for the end of hostilities to follow-up negotiations in Kurash. He has requested permission to address the people of Laniras." He hesitated for a moment before saying, "It has been granted."

"By whom?" asked Verahim, slamming his fist on the table. His face was red from both the harsh sun of Kurash and his intense anger.

"By your father before his death," replied Hokkod.

King Verahim looked around the chamber at the faces around the table and shook his head in disbelief.

"Valistaran made the request even before our voyage to Kurash," said Hokkod.

"Without my knowledge?" asked Verahim. Before Hokkod could react, the doors at the other side of the chamber burst open, and Valistaran and several of his own advisors filed into the room. Mistress Mara Bartunek stood at his right side, and the rest of the Mistresses of Dusk followed behind them. Even the corpulent Florenta was carried on her platform into the chamber.

"Lord Valistaran," said General Hokkod in acknowledgment of the foreign dignitaries. The entire room stood, except King Verahim; did Valistaran think this such a decisive victory that he must bring the entire ruling council here? Valistaran smiled and bowed to his rival, sitting across from him but saying nothing.

"Well? Are you going to speak?" asked Verahim. "You brought all of *them*? The Mistresses of Dusk have *never* stepped foot in this palace."

Valistaran ignored the comment. "It is customary to wait for permission to speak. Thank you, your majesty, King Verahim Romus," Valistaran said in a calm tone. He unfolded his hands and addressed the representatives of Thanatanos. "Esteemed leaders of this fair country, I bring you tidings of peace."

"You bring nothing in your wake but death," scoffed Verahim. Valistaran shook his head and continued.

"A great king of old once declared that, 'we must come to see that the end we seek is a society at peace with itself, a society that can live with its conscience.' King Verahim, if our society can live with its conscience when this war is over, I will count us all blessed, but that will not happen if we continue to enforce peace by the sword and the bow."

"Can you live with your own conscience, King Talohir?"

"No. And that is why when this conflict is ended, I am establishing a new government elected from the common people to rule over our joint country," said Valistaran.

"Joint country? So, you do wish to unite Talohira, Sangora and Thanatanos," said Verahim.

There was an audible gasp around the room.

"I wish to unite the *world*, my dear king. A world at peace. There are those who believe that all of Talohira simply wishes to conquer. To see the world in chains, or to rule over its brethren in Thanatanos, its sisters in Sangora, and even those who dwell elsewhere beyond our maps. These twisted lies are spread by those who would do the same to our great nation."

"So, what are you saying?" asked King Verahim. "Are you demanding that we hand our lands and people over to you? There is a difference between an alliance and an occupation. Indeed, you must see that!"

"My dear king, are you so blinded by hatred and addicted to your new power that you will not allow your own people to *choose* if they would like to enjoy their freedom and safety? While I sit on the throne of Talohira, there will be no invasion. No occupation," Valistaran asked. Verahim scowled at his opponent, who then added, "Your father knew what had to be done."

This seemed to be the last straw with Verahim. He slammed his fist on the table and stormed from the chamber, knocking his chair to the marble floor with an echoing clatter. Valistaran frowned and pressed his fingers together. The diplomats and negotiators in the room glanced around at one another, unsure of what to do next without their king.

"I lament that King Romiton is not here to participate in negotiations," said the High King of Talohira. "If he were, peace would soon be upon us."

Hokkod, now the highest-ranking person in the room, watched as Valistaran strode to an open window. He glowered at the foreign king but kept silent.

Those assembled in the chamber began to stir, not knowing if Verahim was coming back. Hokkod glanced around to the different Mistresses of Dusk until his eyes settled upon Mara's face. Her features were familiar to him, but he couldn't quite recall her name. It wasn't until she spoke that the horror of her identity dawned on him.

"Our king still has a message to deliver to the people of Thanatanos," said Mara. The other Mistresses of Dusk nodded.

"Mara?" Hokkod whispered to himself, recognizing her as one of those that had accompanied him on the ill-fated expeditions into Bukaral and Doftaan. How then, had she become the terrible Night Witch that now addressed the room?

"That I do," said Valistaran regarding Mara's statement.

General Hokkod sighed, knowing everyone was waiting for his response now that he oversaw the meeting in the king's absence. Perhaps at least now the diplomats would be able to address one another without fear of retribution.

"I would not allow a murderer and liar to address the people if it was not Romiton's wish," said Hokkod with a sigh. "But because of that fact, I will allow you it. We will send word for the people to assemble near the palace to hear your paltry words."

"Thank you, general Hokkod. I hope that peace will bloom this day," Valistaran replied with a smile and a nod.

"Watch your words, king, or I promise that you will not see the next sunrise," Hokkod said in a dark tone; Valistaran chuckled and bowed his head.

"I'd expect nothing less," he said.

Hokkod sent messengers from the room to spread the message throughout the city. Another runner exited the room to blow the massive horn in the highest tower, a signal to summon the people of the city. Word would then spread by word of mouth to those on the outskirts and outside the city wall.

Valistaran bowed and departed alongside Mara and the rest of his followers. Hokkod shook his head as he watched them leave, and Mistress Lavinia glanced over her shoulder to blow a kiss, a barefaced sign of a challenge. He and his diplomats left the chamber to prepare for Valistaran's speech.

CHAPTER THIRTY-TWO
SLEEP WELL, MY LOVE

Much later, Valistaran stood upon the balcony in silence as the sunset cast the stone city into an eerie orange glow. Hours had passed since the tense meeting's abrupt end, and thousands of confused citizens of Thanatanos were now gathered below.

Standing behind him were each of the Mistresses of Dusk except Florenta, who was far too large to fit through the narrow doorway. Mara was at his right side, and on the other side of the balcony stood King Verahim and his generals, Hokkod and Valakor. Valakor stood motionless and statuesque, but Hokkod seemed nervous, for he fidgeted as if they were all on display.

"People of Thanatanos," boomed Valistaran, his voice somehow amplified by the shape of the palace. It carried to all those gathered below and would be relayed to the rest of the crowd. "I appear here before you to usher in an era of tranquility between our nations. I beg you to see reason and heed my words, for we must live together as brothers or perish together as fools.

"I propose something simple: a new nation forged from the broken shards of two fallen peoples. I know the pages of history are soaked in the blood of those we love. I offer you now an escape from this nightmare. Any who wishes for peace are welcome in Talohira whether you choose to unite or not.

"There are harbingers of death among us who are responsible for the deaths of your humble king, your dear prince, my beloved queen, and more. They are a hidden flame that threatens to consume the safety of *our* home. They stole forbidden memories from the wise men of Kurash of an ancient weapon to extinguish the flame of peace that we wish to stoke."

Valistaran allowed the crowd to calm down before continuing. "Long has marriage been a binding promise in both of our cultures. Today I proclaim Mara Bartunek of Thanatanos as queen over the united nations of Talohira, Sangora, and if it will have her, Thanatanos. Until the new nation is established, will you have Mara Bartunek, a native of Thanatanos and Mistress of Dusk over Sangora to be your queen?"

He looked over the crowd, and to his satisfaction, the weary citizens of Laniras began to kneel. He raised his hands high into the air and much of the crowd cheered while the rest booed and hissed. The High King of Talohira smiled as he watched a third of the crowd kneel. Mara was unaware of the proper protocol and raised her hand in a simple and awkward wave.

"I will now have *Queen* Mara Bartunek say what she will."

She took a deep breath and hesitated for a long moment.

"You don't know me, but for too long, I have felt sorry for myself, but I will no longer play the role of the victim—today, I choose to be a queen," said Mara. The crowd below cheered as if they shared her sentiment. "Though my life has been painful, I know now that pain will lead to peace. There is no other way."

She winced, hoping her words didn't sound as cringeworthy as she thought they did. There was cheer from below, so, maybe her words had resonated with the people after all.

"I shall depart myself now to apprehend these fanatics before they reach the instrument of our destruction. Their deaths, your vote, and the wedding between Mara and myself, between our nations, will mark the end of this war and shall usher in a new age of peace!" He raised his hands into the air and even more of the crowd roared in approval. His entourage followed him away, but Mara was the last to depart as she took in the scene, for it was something she never thought she would see.

Many of the late king's Royal Guard and his elite warriors, the Court of Thanatan, were assembled in the chamber behind the balcony for security. Shanthah had been allowed to bring one member of his squad, so he had elected to bring Hanna.

She nudged him in the side and gestured with her head as Valistaran and his followers had left the balcony Shanthah nodded and gripped her elbow to acknowledge her message and guide her out the side passage just as Valistaran exited. When he was sure they were out of earshot, he turned to her.

"Are you up for an adventure, Miss Samsa?" he whispered.

Hanna put her hand on her chin as if pretending to contemplate the proposal.

"Why, Mr. Kalen, I do believe that I am," she replied. The duo grinned at one another as they made their way down the corridor. Shanthah took a deep breath, and then turned invisible.

"You know, I'm still not used to that," Hanna said.

"Says the girl who can literally pick things up with her mind. I've been practicing, and I think I can make you invisible too."

"I prefer being able to see you," Hanna said with a smile and a wink. "Because, yum."

Shanthah grinned back as he grabbed her wrist, and she too faded from the world. She put a hand on her cheek and touched her arm to make sure her body was still tangible then let out a sigh of relief. A moment later, the duo reappeared.

"So, what's the plan?" Hanna asked as they made their way toward Valistaran's entourage.

"We're going to follow Valistaran wherever he goes and stop him from getting that weapon he wants. It's obvious that he's after it too, right? Stay close, or they'll be able to see you," said Shanthah. He grabbed her hand, and they vanished once again.

"Vague, but let's do it," Hanna replied.

They sprinted down the hallway to cut off Valistaran's group. Hanna stumbled several times, realizing that running while invisible was more problematic than she would have thought; her auburn hair became visible several times as she lost contact with Shanthah, but she held his hand tighter, hoping no one had seen.

Voices echoed from the corridor ahead. Valistaran's group was close, but they managed to reach the intersection of two hallways before Valistaran did, and they waited in invisible silence as the Talohiran king's group filed past.

"Should we try to find Josman or another one of our friends?" Hanna asked. "We could use a good fighter."

"No time. He might lead us to them if *we're* the hidden-flame-harbingers-of-death-and-chaos, though. I did kill his queen…"

He trailed off as he and Hanna joined the group of foreign dignitaries, stepping unseen alongside the Mistresses of Dusk. They maintained enough distance that they wouldn't be touched, but the Mistress of Dusk named Raluca stopped in her tracks looked in their direction and reached out toward them as if she had somehow sensed them. Shanthah and Hanna both took a deep breath and stopped. She shook her head and moved on.

As the group continued, one unmistakable Sangoran in particular lagged behind even as Raluca departed. She too stared in their direction, but there was no confusion on her face as was upon Raluca's. For a moment, Shanthah wondered if they had become visible. Mara banished her sad expression and followed the others too.

"Mara," whispered Hanna, tears rolling down her cheeks. "I can't believe it." Shanthah nodded, a gesture that went unseen. The procession left the palace and boarded a caravan of black carriages pulled by massive horses.

"Ready to hitch a ride?" asked Shanthah. Hanna squeezed his hand to indicate, 'yes.' She couldn't keep her eyes off Mara; unlike Raluca, she had absolutely sensed them.

Shanthah and Hanna waited in silence as Valistaran's followers packed into the vehicles. As the door shut on the rearmost carriage, the duo leaped onto the back platform and then onto the top of the cart.

They pressed themselves between the many supplies strapped to the roof, completely hiding them from view. Shanthah groaned as they became visible.

"Snug, but I don't mind one bit," Shanthah said. "If they find us, I'll make us invisible, but I can't keep it up too long."

"I know a pretty fun silent activity for the trip. Well, it *can* be silent," Hanna said, snuggling close. "It involves lots of kissing."

"I would very much like to participate!"

Hanna giggled and shushed him, pressing her body on top of his as she kissed him deeply. Shanthah ran one hand through her wild, auburn hair as he enjoyed the feeling of her lips on his own. He managed to maneuver his other arm around her in the confined space to rub her back and hold her close.

His heart leapt as she ran her hand up his side under his tunic and stopped on his toned chest. Hanna bit her lip and pulled away for a moment with a sultry grin, but at that moment, the horses gave a sudden jolt. Both Shanthah and Hanna's eyes went wide, and their faces collided with a long groan.

"Oww."

"More later, yes?" he asked as their groans turned to laughs.

"You can have all the Hanna you want when we're not at risk of breaking each other's faces."

"Can't wait," Shanthah replied. "I guess I'll stay up and keep watch. Try to get some sleep, okay?"

"My hero," she said with a wink. "Promise you'll try too?"

"If I can," Shanthah replied.

"Good. We can smash faces again later, then."

She stole another long, lingering kiss then laid her head on his chest with a content sigh.

Several hours later, she rubbed her eyes as she awoke. The sun too was waking, sending its rays of light over the mountains.

"We drove through the night, but this isn't Talohira."

"Are you kidding? What do you mean?" Hanna asked, craning her neck to peer behind their vehicle. "Where are we?"

"We're still in Thanatanos, but we're way west of Laniras, near the sea. I don't think we're going to Talohira, Hann."

"Elaborate?"

"It would be easier, much easier, to reach Talohira by land than by sea," said Shanthah. "So, wherever we're going, it'll be our next grand adventure together."

"Hey, I've never complained that you never take me anywhere nice," Hanna said with a smile. "Plus, we're going to stop Valistaran—somehow."

Shanthah nodded. Hanna wondered to herself what exactly it would take to do so. She peeked up over the barrels, and as Shanthah tried to pull her back down, she beheld hundreds of Sangoran and human soldiers alike filing into three large ships. Near the closest one, she caught a glimpse of five eight-foot tall, armored beings overseeing the army before them.

"They're those spirit warrior things like Valakor and Itrus!"

"So, they really are on Valistaran's side," Shanthah said.

"You doubted it?" Hanna asked.

"They haven't been seen in a long time. Whatever we've stumbled into—this is *big*," said Shanthah. He grabbed her hand, activating his invisibility powers. The duo disappeared as Shanthah thought out loud. "There are at least five still alive on their side—we'll see for how long that lasts."

Their carriage stopped, and Shanthah led Hanna off the roof but paused just as several soldiers emerged from within. He took her hand and led her away from their foes toward the ships moored at the dock. They snuck unseen past the five Spirit Warriors and clambered over the gangplank.

Hanna followed Shanthah onto the vessel, her eyes glued to the warriors behind them. Four of them were around the same imposing height as General Valakor, while the last was several feet taller and much bulkier; in its hands, it held a gigantic mace. Hanna shuddered as she wondered if they'd have to fight it.

The two invisible stowaways snuck into a room filled with supplies and plopped down on the floor behind a large pile of barrels. They became visible again when the coast was clear.

"Might as well get comfortable, right?" Hanna asked, cuddling against him.

"Is it later yet?"

"Later meaning more time for more Shanthah-Hanna lovin', yes?" Hanna asked. Shanthah nodded with a wide smile. She shook her head. "I don't think that's a good idea right now. It's your turn to get some sleep, Shan. You're gonna need it."

She pulled an empty sack over him as a blanket, kissed his forehead, and then guided his head down onto her lap as a pillow.

"Hann and Shan against the world," he muttered.

"Hell yeah," she whispered, playing with his hair as he nodded off. "Sleep well, my love."

CHAPTER THIRTY-THREE
FACELESS

Brackish droplets of seawater sprayed Mara's face as she stood at the bow of the lead ship. She loved the feeling of the salty sea air against her wings, which she had extended behind her like a cloak in the wind. As the ship pulled up to shore, she watched her followers attempt to moor the vessel against the rocky shore, dropping both anchors. No dock adorned the inhospitable coast, and the jagged rocks threatened to pierce the ship's wooden hull as it crashed against them.

Mara peered through the darkness, trying with great difficulty to discern why an island with such a dangerous coast would be their destination. No towers or cities adorned the island, so whatever her fiancé's prize was must be hidden underground.

She extended her leathery black wings and soared into the tempestuous sky before flipping backward in midair to land near the helm of the ship. The helmsman saluted his queen but said nothing as he and his crew tried in vain to steady the tossing ship.

A gruesome sight was strewn on the deck, for before her lay three of the corpses of the Secret Keepers of Kurash, their bodies bound as if for burial. Three Talohiran Mindspeakers were in a deep, trancelike state with their hands on the heads of the three dead men. Their concentration was absolute, and Mara didn't dare disturb them.

Because of her time in the royal library and her special ability granted to her by her time in The Mind Prison, Mara had discovered how to grant herself the ability to Mindspeak, although she was much less talented than the three attending to the dead Secret Keepers.

Although the Kurashians were deceased, Valistaran's Mindspeakers could still retrieve fragmented images from the fading minds of the three men. Mara wondered just what horrible things they were seeing in the minds of the dead.

Valistaran's crew had used that information to lead the ships to this god-forsaken island far off the coast of Thanatanos. Mara wondered if it was here that the king would discover his prize.

"So, where are we headed?" Mara asked the nearby crew.

A nearby human soldier saluted her. "There is a small village of some kind hidden in a cove ahead. We'll start there."

Queen Mara glanced across the black, choppy water to see the other ships slamming against the rocky beach too. Ropes unraveled from the sides of the ship, and Valistaran's soldiers began to repel down the side of the hull while a swarm of Sangorans simply fluttered through the rain to the shore.

One thing gnawed at her anxiety: before embarking on the journey, she had clearly sensed the presence of Shanthah and

Hanna with her new abilities. Recognizing someone's mental presence was not a particularly advanced technique, and she had spent enough time with the two that she was sure she was not mistaken. She hadn't sensed them since that moment, but she wondered if they were planning some kind of revenge.

She didn't want her own vengeance against Shanthah or Hanna, but if they were here, maybe that meant Aleksander or Drahomir were too. A frown spread across her face at the thought. Why hadn't they come back for her? Why did they abandon her? They created her. Because of what they did, she was now the queen of an entire nation.

A terrified, unsure queen.

However, thinking of the change she could make as queen, she considered forgiving and even thanking her former friends for what they'd done, but her mind summoned memories of the Cuff of the Mindprison on her wrist and of Drahomir betraying her to save his own life.

She began to scream.

She fell to her knees, breaking the concentration of the three Mindspeakers and the helmsman alike. Panic swept over her as the crew hurried toward her side.

Without warning, she shot into the blackened sky and then spiraled toward the water. Her heart thundering in her chest, she flapped her wings hard and soared toward the coast, the salty spray splashing over her face.

As she landed on the jagged rocks, her mind's eye caught a glance of both Shanthah and Hanna hurrying to shore. And then it was gone. Brief, but unmistakable, just like before.

Mara tried to find them again but failed to locate them in the crowd of human and Sangoran soldiers that now swarmed over the beach. She set herself down on some jagged black rocks and cursed under her breath. Why had her king led such a massive invasion force here? What opposition could *possibly* await them on this island?

Not far away, Shanthah and Hanna scrambled over the sharp points of black stone that littered the unforgiving coast. They followed the flow of soldiers, being careful not to venture too close to avoid detection again.

A flash of lightning illuminated a small village nestled in the craggy cliffs of the cove. They hadn't seen it from the ships, but they both felt determined to beat Valistaran's men there.

Hanna squeezed Shanthah's invisible hand as they made their way toward the scattered buildings, clambering over a ruined and moss-covered cobblestone wall. They hurried to the back of the tiny village to investigate before the crowd arrived, remaining invisible all the while.

Valistaran's forces reached the village and entered each of the buildings, searching for something unknown.

"Do you think they know what they're looking for, or do you think they're as clueless as us?" Shanthah asked.

"*More* clueless than us," Hanna replied.

Soon, a call echoed through the cove and spread throughout the small army. Listening as hard as they could, the duo overheard that a trapdoor had been found in one of the dwellings that led into a dark cavern beneath the earth.

Hanna guided Shanthah in the direction of the building with a trap door and creeped up to the side of the crumbling house to peer into a glassless window caked with green moss.

Shanthah slowed, the toll of maintaining their invisibility beginning to drain his energy. The duo could see that many of Valistaran's troops had already disappeared into the darkness of the cavern, and more were filing through the trapdoor. More still stood watch outside, but seemed apathetic, as if guarding the entrance from no one.

"That cave has got to be huge if that many of them fit. Let's see if we can find another way in."

Hanna nodded her invisible head, and the two creeped alongside the building. They surveyed the cliffs behind the homes and located what looked like a narrow cave leading into the mountain.

"Look up there, think it leads to the same place?" asked Hanna, hoping to herself that she was wrong so that she would not have to climb.

"Can't see where you're pointing, Hann," Shanthah said, reminding her that they were invisible. "Oh. But I think I do see it. It's worth a potentially life-threatening try, right?"

They traversed the rain-soaked crags of the cliffs until they reached the spot that Hanna had pointed out, becoming visible again as they entered the cave.

"Too bad Aleksander's not here. He could make us a fire," said Shanthah. "I sort of forgot we can't see in the dark."

"While Aleksander *could* be our fire, *I* fortunately brought some supplies. You're welcome," said Hanna with a smile.

"What would I do without you?" Shanthah asked.

"Die, probably."

She produced a small vial of dark liquid from her pack then ripped a wide strip of fabric from the bottom of her long tunic. She dipped the fabric in the liquid and handed it to Shanthah as she scooped up a broken tree branch the length of a human arm.

She took the oil-soaked rag back and wrapped it around the stick before rummaging through her pack again to locate her fire making supplies. She used a small tinderbox to ignite the rag which burned with a bright orange flame.

"You're a miracle," Shanthah said as she gave him the torch.

"I know. I'm not sure how long this will last, but it'll have to do. You're carrying it. Don't drop it."

As the descended into the cave, it seemed empty save a few bats that squeaked and flapped away from the torchlight disturbing their sleep. The steep stone corridor twisted back and forth, leading deep into the heart of the earth. They followed the cavern for what felt like several miles in complete silence.

A strange, unearthly groan echoed softly through the cave. Hanna stopped, and Shanthah bumped into her. She brought her finger to her lips, and he nodded as the sound of muffled screams followed the previous noise. Hanna bit her lip.

"We're too far to go back now," Shanthah said. "We'll be okay. Maybe."

"Maybe?" asked Hanna.

"Alright, I promise," said Shanthah, grinning in the torchlight.

He kissed her on the forehead, and she smiled; her eyes flickered in the torchlight, but the moment had to end, and they ventured onward. At that moment, two things happened at the same time. The ground collapsed beneath their feet, and a deafening boom rocked the entire cave system. Shanthah and Hanna screamed as they plummeted downward into the darkness in a shower of rocks and dust. They groaned as the dust settled, and the distant sounds of screaming intensified.

"Hanna! Are you okay?" groaned Shanthah.

"Nope. Dead," she replied, scooping up her torch, which was fortunately still burning.

He could feel tiny pebbles pressed into his palms and winced as he brushed them away. He glanced up just in time to shove Hanna hard out of the way of a massive boulder tumbling down the slope behind them; the chunk of stone filled the cavern with dust, and Hanna stumbled to her feet, disoriented. Several Sangorans lay dead around them, crushed beneath the pile of boulders. She scooped up the torch and looked around.

An unearthly groan echoed through the cave and seemed to reverberate within their very minds; the sound was echoed by a deep feeling of dread and panic, one that did not dissipate with the groans. Hanna helped Shanthah to his feet and then pointed the torch in the opposite direction of the haunting noises.

"Your choice. Toward the rest of the Night Witches or whatever is making that sound?" asked Hanna.

"You're letting me choose? How thoughtful," answered Shanthah, who started in the direction of the horrible groaning.

"Wait, seriously? *That's* what you're picking?!"

"I thought it was my choice, though?"

"Yeah, but it was the wrong one," Hanna said.

"I assume they brought this entire army to kill whatever's making that sound. So maybe, as much as I hate to say this, we're going to need to go toward it—oh, and my invisibility isn't going to do us any good down here, so, be careful, okay?"

Hanna nodded, and the duo began down the path, but soon stopped as they heard footsteps up ahead. The pattern of the steps strange: Fast, slow. Fast, slow. Fast, slow. Whatever side the person was on, they were limping. Shanthah motioned forward, and they continued onward, despite the horrible chorus of groans that now permeated the air at all times.

As they turned the corner, the injured individual came into view—an injured Sangoran hobbling slowly along on a broken leg. Both of her wings were ripped to shreds, and her clothing was soaked in crimson blood.

Shanthah knew that Sangorans had better night vision than humans, but she was still just as terrified as he was down here. As they approached, the Sangoran stopped to greet them, believing that they were part of Valistaran's force.

"Where are the others? Mistress Lavinia ordered the ceiling be brought down on those—those things, but when the dust cleared, I was alone! They must have left us. Thank goodness you came," said the wounded Sangoran, pressing her palm into a vicious gash on her side to staunch the bleeding.

"Here, sit down," Shanthah said, helping the Sangoran to a sitting position. He cut a strip of cloth from his traveler's cloak as a makeshift bandage and began to dress the wound.

"I'm sorry. I'm no doctor, but it might just stop the bleeding," said Shanthah in an apologetic tone. Hanna pushed his hands away and saw to the woman's wound. The Sangoran let out a short scream as she did so.

"You're okay now," said Hanna, keeping pressure on the wound. "We won't hurt you. Tell us what's ahead."

"Horrible things. They ripped us apart," the Sangoran replied in a shaky voice, raising what was left of her wings. Just as she said this, a shadow shot past, and a horrifying groan filled the air. There was no breathing, no gnashing of teeth or growling, only the horrible, disgusting sound and an overwhelming feeling of dread and agonizing hunger that accompanied it.

And then the monster was upon the trio. Shanthah's blade sang as it escaped its sheath and sliced through flesh on the humanoid creature's chest but spilled no blood. The monster stumbled back and then lurched forward again.

Shanthah caught a glance at the creature's face, or rather, where its face should have been—in place of eyes, a nose, and a mouth was just a slab of albino flesh smeared with crimson blood; Shanthah nearly vomited as he realized that its sparse hair was matted to its body with a gruesome amount of blood.

And then it was gone. Hidden in the shadows. No one moved. Whatever the thing was, it used the shadows to hide, and worse, it knew how to kill. The Sangoran screamed as three-inch claws pierced her throat.

She fell dead before Shanthah and Hanna could even scream. It sliced at the dead Sangoran woman's body and rubbed its bare face in the wound as if trying, but unable, to consume her flesh.

The creature's all-consuming, voracious hunger permeated their minds; the faceless monster could not eat, and they could somehow sense its frustration as it tried in vain to devour the mutilated Sangoran.

Shanthah lashed out with his blade, and the creature retaliated by slashing at his arm with its claws. He dodged, but it leapt upon him, tearing his cloak to shreds. He thrust his blade through his foe's shoulder as the creature turned to Hanna. He hacked through its arm, which fell twitching to the ground; both Shanthah and Hanna stumbled back in disgust.

Hanna recovered from her initial shock and grasped a small, sharp stone from the ground then hurled it toward the monster. She caused the stone to accelerate with her mind powers like an arrow, piercing the monstrosity through the forehead. The faceless creature fell dead, but no blood spilled from its wounds.

"Did you feel that?" Hanna whispered.

"The hunger?" Shanthah asked. Hanna answered with no more than a faint nod. "Yeah—yeah, I did."

"It doesn't have a face. Why? Do you think these things are Mindspeakers?" Hanna asked in horror. "How else would it sense us or make us feel like that?"

"Did you see it trying to eat her?" Shanthah asked, shuddering. "What did we get ourselves into, Hann? We've gotta go. If you're right, they can sense us much more easily than we can sense them. We aren't getting out the way we came in either."

"Why didn't it bleed?" continued Hanna. "How does it survive if it can't eat? And why doesn't it have a face?!"

"Let's hope we never have to find out."

They left the dead Sangoran behind and continued onward, hoping they were going in the correct direction. The only sound over the silence was their own breathing and footsteps. And then suddenly, the groaning returned. Not one voice, but hundreds.

Was it in their mind or could they hear it with physical ears?

They sprinted through the cavern, their torch throwing shadows in strange directions in the eerie shifting light. The groans intensified, and the footsteps of the creatures behind them sped up to match their own pace.

Five more of the emaciated creatures blocked their path, each with a face smeared with blood and hair matted against their pale skin. They slowly stood silently in their path, and Shanthah raised his sword.

"Just a few days ago I was complaining about Josman's snoring and now I'm—I'm here?" Shanthah said as the creatures began to advance on them.

"Yeah, life's funny, but let's survive this, okay?" said Hanna, scooping up a few more sharp stones from the ground.

The emaciated creatures broke into a sprint toward them. Shanthah hacked the head off the nearest monster with a vicious blow as Hanna launched one of her stones into the throat of the next. One of the monsters tackled Shanthah, but Hanna planted a rock in the back of its head before it could disembowel him.

Shanthah thanked her and kicked the creature in the chest then stabbed it in the back. It did not rise.

"Where are the others? There were five, right?" Hanna wheezed, turning to find their attackers. They were nowhere to be found. She drew her own borrowed sword, taking Shanthah's shaking hand in her own.

They proceeded with caution down the passage and turned a corner into a cavern so vast that their torchlight could not find the end of the darkness. At the far side of the emptiness stood an obelisk emanating a dim, cyan glow. Looming behind the obelisk was another cave lined with stalagmites and stalactites that resembled the maw of a horrible beast.

Shanthah hit the ground hard. Hanna whirled around and slashed her blade down the back of the creature's head to the middle of its back then, with another blow, severed its left arm. She was not as skilled as Shanthah with the blade, but the principle of hacking and stabbing was easy enough. The creature collapsed to the ground and Shanthah stumbled to his feet.

"Thanks," he said, pointing toward the glowing obelisk. "I think we found what Valistaran's looking for. Come on."

Hanna gazed toward the dim glow but was distracted as the wounded Faceless cut her calf with its sharp claws; she stumbled backward, and it began pulling itself toward her with one hand. She cried out in pain and with her telekinesis hurled a small stone through its blank face. She fell to the ground clutching her wounded leg as warm blood trickled between her fingers.

"Trim your damn fingernails!" Hanna shouted at the dead creature and kicked it in the head. "Shan! Help!"

Shanthah was instantly at her side and helped her to her feet. Together, they limped toward the obelisk, which resembled Hokkod's Telepillar, in the center of the room. As they neared it, the darkness behind them was dispelled by a disorderly group of at least two dozen Sangorans accompanied by ten of Valistaran's soldiers brandishing torches and blades. Hanna gripped the back of Shanthah's arm as they realized who was leading them.

"Why hello," said Mara. "I knew I sensed you earlier—but it has been a while, hasn't it?"

At the queen's right was the Sangoran named Vasilica, who had aided her in the battle of Nitra and thus gained her position as Mara's lieutenant.

"Yeah, I don't think we've seen you since you stabbed Drahomir—and killed Prince Xanthurias—and burned Nitra to the ground," said Shanthah. "Fun times, right?"

"I told Aleksander that the next time I saw any of you I wouldn't show you mercy," Mara said, extending her wings to reveal that they were tipped with sharp blades. Her Sangoran followers did the same, and some brandished an assortment of spears, swords, and long daggers.

"Hey, listen," said Shanthah, backing up toward the glowing pillar upon the mound behind them. "After all we've been through, can't we let bygones be bygones? I don't know what in the world happened between you and Aleksander and Drahomir, but we had no part in whatever that was. And aren't we even, now that you've killed what, a few thousand of our friends? I'm pretty sure—"

He stopped talking mid-sentence and vanished.

Mara's head shot back in surprise as he did so. She heard his footsteps sloshing in the shallow water surrounding the pillar, and she shot toward Hanna with a flap of her powerful wings.

Hanna was ready. With her telekinetic abilities, she summoned four sharp stones from the moss-covered ground and levitated them before her face, trusting that Shanthah would do his part.

"Mara, don't do this!" Hanna shouted.

"You're here to stop us," Mara said. "They said you'd be here to kill me. Why, Hanna?!"

Mara landed and brought her bladed wings down, but Hanna launched one of her rocks like an arrow toward the queen of Talohira and Sangora. Mara spun out of the way just in time, and the stone embedded itself in one of the other Sangorans, who collapsed into the shallow, murky water.

The mass of soldiers moved in, and the glow of the obelisk cast an eerie light on the battle as Mara and Vasilica soared around it. Valistaran's soldiers charged, and the rest of the Sangorans launched into the air as one. Hanna stood as a lone sentry against the forces of darkness, launching stone after stone into the host advancing toward her. She felled a soldier with a stone to the chest then planted another in the throat of a Sangoran about to slash at her with mighty, bladed wings.

The woman's corpse slammed against the mossy rocks beside Hanna then tumbled into the water where her bones would lie forevermore.

She summoned several more stones from beneath near her feet. Mara screamed and landed next to her. Hanna drew and raised her blade just in time to parry a blow from the queen's armored right wing. Her other wing swung around, but Hanna was too slow to defend herself, even with her mind powers.

The blade on Mara's wing glanced off something invisible, and she realized that Shanthah had defended Hanna from her onslaught. Hanna rushed forward, blasting Mara backward with her telekinesis and then leaped upon her, sword in hand. Mara's wings launched up and inward like a colossal trap, but Hanna grabbed each of them with her mind and forced them down.

"Mara, stop!" Hanna shouted.

"Why didn't you come back for me?!" she screamed back.

Hanna yelped as Mara's fist collided with her chin. In an instant, Vasilica and another Sangoran soldier grasped Hanna's arms to carry her away, but Shanthah severed the leg of Vasilica's companion, who struck the rocks nearby and was still. Vasilica swooped around toward her invisible foe, watching his movements in the water.

Anticipating where his sword would come from, the Sangoran lashed out with both armored wings as well as her own twin daggers to utilize four potential attack points. Her readiness threw Shanthah off guard, and he stumbled through the shallow water. Vasilica's attack missed, but only just, her blades mere inches from Shanthah's throat.

The nine remaining human soldiers stood in a circle around the pillar, not daring to get too close to the invisible warrior or within range of Hanna's onslaught while the cloud of Sangorans soared around them. Perhaps they were allowing Mara and Vasilica the honor of slaying Shanthah and Hanna, or perhaps they were too terrified and confused to advance.

Mara caught hold of Hanna's arm and dug into it with her the metal claw attachments on her fingers. Hanna screamed and lashed out with an instinctive sweep of her blade, breaking Mara's hold. She spun around and launched two sharp stones straight at Mara, who brought her wings around, blocking the attack with the thin layer of armor on the back of her wings. She threw herself again at Hanna, knocking her to the ground.

Close by, Shanthah dueled the tornado of Vasilica's blades. The Sangoran warrior could see his footsteps in the shallow water, but he was at a loss as to how she kept parrying his blows. He knew he was too predictable, and he knew he'd have to be less so if he were to survive.

As Vasilica advanced upon him again, he hurled himself backward on the rocks, and all four of her blades missed their mark. He lay still on the mossy rocks around the pillar as she splashed through the water and onto the bank.

"Advance!" cried Mara as she knocked Hanna's blade from her hand. "Help your queen, you cowards!"

"Can't do it yourself, you—" Hanna was cut off as Mara blasted her backward with a weak bolt of electricity. She struck the ground hard and groaned as she felt blood trickling from a wound on her forehead.

She did not see the tears rolling down Mara's cheeks.

The swarm of hesitant Sangoran and human soldiers hurried to their queen's aid as Vasilica stumbled over Shanthah's invisible leg. He leaped to his feet and at the same time slashed upward, drawing a line of crimson from her hip and up her side. She screamed in pain but lashed out with all four blades, pinning his tunic to the ground and then punched him in the chest.

"Agh!" he cried out, trying to pull away.

At the same moment, Hanna used her mind powers to summon her sword toward Mara. The blade shot through the air at the queen who had no choice but to hop away from Hanna. Hanna took this time to leap to her feet as her sword clattered to the rocks a few feet away.

"You know what, Mara?" Hanna shouted. "You're in bed with the devil, and I don't mean Elafris!"

The way in which she emphasized Mara's name was laced with poison. Mara was about to strike her, but a horrendous groan filled the cavern, and every combatant froze. Hanna and Mara exchanged a knowing glance, and they backed away from each other, bringing their duel to a pause.

"Around us!" Mara cried then looked at Hanna and said in a low voice. "This isn't over, but you know as well as I that we aren't getting out of here if we don't work together now."

With only the groan as a warning, hundreds of dark shapes emerged from the shadows, illuminated both by the soldiers' torches and the glow of the pillar in the center of the chamber. Many of the Faceless were smeared with fresh blood, and their incessant groaning seemed to fill the entire world.

The mass of creatures lurched forward at once, using their Mindspeaking powers to stalk their prey. They were faster and more agile than any of the terrified soldiers, and they covered the distance between them in seconds. Shanthah knew that invisibility would no longer aid him, and he materialized next to Hanna, sword in hand. They both felt the toll their powers were taking on them, and they each separately hoped that they would be able to fight their way out of the cave.

"I'm sorry for bringing you into this," Shanthah said.

"What else would I be doing tonight?" Hanna asked with a scoff and a wink. "Maybe next date, something more normal like dinner, yeah?"

"Boring."

The horde of faceless creatures swarmed through Valistaran's soldiers like water loosed from a dam. They cut through the king's men in a spray of blood and viscera, but flight gave the Sangorans an advantage. As the humans fell, so too did their torches, plunging the cave into darkness, apart from the eerie glow emanating from the obelisk.

Hanna, Shanthah, Mara, and Vasilica stood around the pillar, slicing into the creatures as they advanced. Their bodies piled on the rocks, but still the endless tide kept coming from all sides. Hanna bumped into the pillar and something within it clicked and began to hum; something had activated within. The light that it emitted intensified, bathing the chamber with light.

The savage creatures with no faces were no less terrifying in the light. If possible, the realization that they were in fact there, and not just a nightmare in the dark, made them even more horrible. That, and the fact that they could now see just how many of the creatures surrounded them.

"Around me!" Mara shouted again, and her cloud of Sangoran warriors slashed at their foes with bladed wings to create a perimeter around their queen. They fought the monsters off as well as they could, giving Mara, Vasilica, and their temporary allies a moment of reprieve.

Shanthah took that moment turn invisible and slam Vasilica against the pillar just as she tried to stab him with her four blades. Mara retaliated by slamming the armored side of her wings against Hanna's head; the force of the attack knocked her from the pile of boulders around the pillar, and she crumpled to the ground. The Queen of Sangora turned to Shanthah, who rematerialized and raised his sword to slay Vasilica.

"Stop! You have to know you won't get out of here without me," said Mara just as Shanthah plunged his blade into Vasilica's side before vanishing again.

Mara cried out and raked her terrible, metal claws down Shanthah's invisible back, feeling them tear through the man's flesh. Although he was invisible, the blood still soaked her claws crimson. She heard him stumble, and he materialized against the pillar. She made her slow advance as her host of Sangorans fought off the oncoming death that was the faceless creatures.

One resounding word from Hanna's mouth filled the queen's ears as she raised her bladed wings to slay Shanthah as he lay bleeding, and possibly dying, against the glowing pillar.

"No."

Hanna had regained her footing and emerged from behind the glowing obelisk with murder in her eyes. She held out her trembling hand and everything that lay on the ground around her, including stones, pebbles, and fallen weapons rose into the air. Hanna's hair began to flow upward as if she were standing in the midst of a great storm, and her clothes rippled in the flowing energy that was her raw power.

She focused on Mara. Or rather, she focused inside of her. On her bones. Her organs. Her blood. She clenched her fist and Mara screamed in agony as Hanna tightened her grip on Mara.

The queen of Sangora tried to call out but was unable to form words; she took a painstaking step forward as if she were walking through a thick bog, but Hanna extended her bent fingers, and Mara felt her body begin to rip itself apart. Hanna and Mara both screamed as Hanna's abilities drained her energy and pushed the queen's blood through the pores of her skin.

"Never! Touch! Him! *AGAIN!*"

She opened her hand and Mara's screams filled the chamber; blood ripped through her pores, but something stopped Hanna's onslaught. Shanthah was on his feet, and he was now clutching something at the top of the pillar. As he turned the gem on the top of the device, a rush of cyan energy erupted from the ground around them.

"No!" cried Mara.

Shanthah's surprise had slackened Hanna's hold on Mara, and although the queen was now dripping with crimson, she was alive. The Faceless broke through the swarm of Sangorans and raced toward Shanthah, Hanna, Mara, and Vasilica, who were now all unsure if they would escape the encounter.

"Hurry!" cried Shanthah.

As he said this, a half dozen Faceless swarmed him. Hanna leaped through the air, pushing away as many of the creatures as her mind powers allowed. Another Faceless wrapped its bony fingers around her ankle, and its horrendous groans filled her mind. She tried to grab it with her mind powers, but nothing happened. She cursed under her breath and stabbed the beast in the face, but another wrenched her sword away from her grasp, leaving it lodged in the monster's skull.

The Faceless grabbed Mara's wings and cloak, pulling her into their ravenous swarm, and she disappeared beneath the writhing pile of emaciated bodies.

Hanna kicked the creature off and crawled forward, grabbing Shanthah's bloodied leg. She trembled, unsure if he was still alive, but she hoped and prayed for the best. She launched herself forward, catching Shanthah's tunic as the Teleportation Pillar's energy pulled them both away. As she dematerialized, she caught a glimpse of Mara blast her way free of the Faceless in an explosion of lighting with hatred etched on her face.

"Tell Valistaran that we don't fear his whore queen!" Hanna screamed. She heard one more word escape Mara's throat.

"PLEASE!"

And then they were gone. Light replaced the darkness, and the smell of the sea filled their nostrils.

They were alive. They had escaped. Against all odds, the pillar had whisked them to safety. Hanna found herself hoping that Mara and Vasilica had managed to escape, but as she glanced around, she didn't see them anywhere. No one deserved to meet their fate against those vile creatures—especially someone she had loved like a sister.

She sobbed into her hands until she regained her composure. Many dead bodies lay strewn on the grassy hillside around them, pulled along by the pillar's magic.

She counted herself lucky that Shanthah was trained on how to operate a Telepillar, but what fate had they abandoned Mara to? She shook the thought from her mind.

After a short, frantic search, she located Shanthah lying still against a gnarled tree. She grabbed his face and shook him, trying to get him to wake up. She cursed herself for not learning how to treat the wounded.

"No, no, no," Hanna whispered, fearing the worst.

Shanthah stirred, and a weak cough escaped his throat. His wounds seemed to have stopped bleeding, and she wondered if the Telepillar's magic had somehow sealed them up.

"Is there…a healer here…?" he muttered.

"No, no, it's just me. Just me. But I'm going to help you," Hanna said, clutching Shanthah's hand. "I'm here, my love."

"…Because it must have hurt…" he said.

"No, I'm fine, I'm just worried about you. I—"

"…When you fell out of heaven."

She punched him in the shoulder for the tacky line, and he gave a coughing, hacking laugh. She smothered his forehead with kisses and held him close, cradling his head in her lap and stroking his hair. Even as he lay dying, he was cracking jokes.

Hanna glanced out to the sea and beheld two large ships sailing toward the cove. One of Valistaran's ships had capsized, and its ruined remains crashed against the rocks. She hoped that the newcomers would be friendly and then sighed in relief as she saw the flag of Thanatanos tied to the top of the mast.

"We made it, Shanth! We're safe, see? Look, ships! Shanth? Shanthah!"

CHAPTER THIRTY-FOUR
SINS OF THE FATHER

The two ships from Thanatanos crashed over the white-capped waves toward the accursed island. The storm was fading, but the sea was still choppy enough to threaten these warships helmed by the best captains in Thanatanos.

For the past few days, Aleksander had lain low while staying with Alia and her son, who had located Kamil and reunited him with Aleksander.

During that time, Aleksander had begun to remember brief flashes of his past, but they slipped from his mind like a fading dream. Because of this, he had trouble discerning which of his memories were real and which were memories implanted by the Secret Keepers; some were more vivid than others, but his background was still cloudy.

However, with help from Kamil's Mindspeaking abilities and Alia's guidance, he had discovered the memory that led them to the same place as Valistaran: the island that held a way to access the weapon so mysterious that most people on the ship doubted its existence.

Aleksander, Kamil, Alia, and Karim had set out immediately. They had visited the Thannish embassy in Tal-Ahosh, who had arranged a ship to help them reach the Thannish vessels before they got too far. Hokkod welcomed all of them with open arms. They had hoped to find Rehor, Drahomir, Josman, and Pol while they were there, but the embassy had already sent them back to Thanatanos where they'd be safe until they could reunite.

They were now most worried for Shanthah and Hanna, as it wasn't like them to disappear without telling the others. The embassy hadn't seen them, and Hokkod had headed a short-lived search party to find them, but it became more dangerous for them to stay, so they had to give up on their search.

It had been a whirlwind few days, and Aleksander and Kamil sat exhausted on the deck of Hokkod's ship with Karim. The other vessel was filled with members of the Court of Thanatan and the king's Royal Guard.

Clapping his hands on his thighs as he stood, Aleksander excused himself to find something to eat before they dropped anchor at the island, leaving Kamil and Karim alone together.

Karim looked nervous as the two ships approached the island, and Kamil could not help but ask why, opening his mind to speak to the young man.

In doing so, he inadvertently stumbled into a memory at the fore of Karim's mind that he wished he had not discovered without permission: Karim was not his true name. Feeling as if he had intruded into something private, he withdrew his mind.

He hoped his new friend had not noticed, but Karim looked up and chuckled.

"I guess with a Mindspeaker on board, I wasn't going to be able to hide my identity, right?" Karim thought, knowing Kamil could still hear him. Kamil smiled, grateful that Karim had not been offended by his trespassing.

"Your secret is safe with me," Kamil said to Karim's mind. *"But now that I know who your father is, and that you are named after him, I can't help but say that this complicates—well, everything."*

"I have never met Valistaran," said Karim in his thoughts to Kamil and then said aloud, "He is my father, yes, but all I share with that man is my name."

"Do you see yourself as Karim or Valistaran?" asked Kamil.

"My mother and people we really trust call me Valis. I don't particularly like the name Karim, but it is a very common name in Kurash, so I don't stand out. But you know that, you're Kurashian."

"And am I one of the people you trust?" Kamil asked then with a wink said, *"Probably for the best. It'd get confusing for others since our names are so similar."*

"Well, I guess I *have* to trust you now. So, yes. You can call me Valis. No one will overhear you anyway," said Karim out loud, or as Kamil now knew him, Valis. "My secret is why I chose to come on this expedition in the first place."

Kamil nodded in understanding, a sign that he would not betray his young friend's secret. As the ship sloshed over the waves, they caught a glimpse of two individuals on the island's craggy face near the coast. Valis could see them through the dense fog, but they seemed like ghosts.

"My father's men?" asked Valis.

"*I don't think so. They don't look like soldiers. Grab the helmsman's spyglass,*" said Kamil. Valis leaped to his feet and located the spyglass strapped next to the ship's helm.

"I need this," he said. The helmsman gave a listless nod.

Valis peered through the brass instrument and took a moment to locate the two figures on the island. He did not expect to recognize them, so he was not disappointed. He handed the spyglass to Kamil, who put his eye to the instrument and gave a hearty laugh.

"*Well, well. It looks like we have some friends on the island. Only the gods know how they beat us here,*" said Kamil, an overjoyed expression on his face. He sent a mental message to Aleksander, and he sensed his friend's excitement as he scrambled back up to the top deck.

As the ocean kicked the ship upward, Kamil lost sight of Shanthah and Hanna who were now limping toward the beach; he could tell that Shanthah was wounded, and Hanna was supporting all his weight as they made their way to the coast.

Through the glass, Kamil saw several humanoid creatures emerge from cracks in the rocky cliffs. At first, he thought them to be Valistaran's men, but then he recoiled as he examined the creatures.

They appeared to be walking, emaciated corpses with pale bodies smeared with crimson. War paint, maybe? He examined them closer and dropped the spyglass to the deck. It rolled away as waves rocked the ship and dread filled his heart. Not paint.

Blood.

"What's wrong?" Valis asked aloud, scooping up the glass. "Are they my father's men or not?"

"*They don't have faces!*" Kamil said to his friend's mind.

Valis put the spyglass to his eye and beheld the horror his fellow Kurashian had seen. Valis swore in Kurashic and Kamil nodded in agreement.

"Your friends are going to need help," said Valis, and Kamil nodded again, eyes wide. As they hurried to a lifeboat tied to the side of the ship, Aleksander emerged from below deck.

"Aleksander!" exclaimed Valis as Aleksander and Alia approached.

"I know, I know, Kamil told me!" Aleksander called as a sailor helped him ready a lifeboat. He climbed in and held out a hand to help Kamil aboard. Valis turned to Alia as if to ask for permission, and she raised an eyebrow.

"It's rude to keep them waiting, kid," Alia said.

"Really?" Valis asked. "I was expecting—"

"They'll need you," Alia said, offering a quick hug. "Go!"

Kamil and Aleksander helped him and the sailor aboard while Alia and another sailor lowered the vessel to the waves.

"Come back safe, or else!" Alia called.

The ocean threatened to claim them the moment the little vessel touched the waves, but Aleksander and the crewman rowed them ashore with surprising ease and skill.

"*Perhaps in your forgotten life, you were a pirate,*" mused Kamil.

"Probably my favorite theory yet," said Aleksander aloud with a smile. "Do you see Shanthah and Hanna?"

He was unable to locate them through the dense fog and feared that their friends had already been overtaken, but Kamil pointed to a spot on the rocky cliff face as they made it to shore.

"Stay with the ship," Aleksander said, and the sailor nodded.

"Gladly, sir!" he replied. "It'll be ready for your return!"

A horrendous groaning and an unexplainable sense of dread and agonizing hunger filled their minds as they neared the cliffs. Out of nowhere, one of the emaciated, blood-stained creatures leaped from the cliff, emerging from the fog with claws outstretched and covered in blood.

As it lunged toward him, Aleksander blasted it back with an explosion of flame. Its charred body hit the rocks, and for a moment, he thought it was dead, but it stood as three more faceless monsters appeared out of the thickening fog.

"Be ready!" Aleksander called.

"*I can sense them,*" Kamil answered, using his powers as a Mindspeaker to locate the Faceless that surrounded them.

"How many?" asked Valis as he backed away from the three Faceless that stood still, waiting to pounce.

"*We're surrounded,*" thought Kamil. "*There are dozens of the things. I'm going to try something new—I'm going to let you into my mind so that you can sense what I sense and see where they are.*"

"Why aren't they attacking?" asked Valis.

The three men stood back-to-back-to-back in a triangle, waiting for the monsters to advance. Both Valis and Aleksander could now sense how many of the Faceless were surrounding them and judge their location within the fog.

"I can't focus on fighting them and revealing them, so Aleksander and Karim you're up," thought Kamil.

As their minds met, Aleksander could sense Valis's thoughts, including that of his true name.

"Valis?" Aleksander asked aloud. Kamil smacked himself in the face, knowing his actions had revealed his new friend's secret.

"I'll explain later," said Valis. "Don't worry about it, buddy."

Kamil nodded in apology.

They could sense the Faceless inching toward them through the fog, and Aleksander buffeted the line of creatures with a shower of hot sparks from his palm. Their groaning intensified, and the circle closed in on the trio.

"Got any tricks of your own?" Aleksander called, and to his relief, Valis replied with a thin bolt of lightning from his palm that seared the flesh of a Faceless just out of view. "Perfect!"

"Look out!" called the Thannish crewman near the lifeboat as Valis and Aleksander both blasted the same monster as one.

They turned to see the sailor stab another through the chest, but that didn't stop its advance. It kept inching toward him, the blade digging deeper and deeper into its body. He withdrew the weapon and hewed down the creature by chopping out its legs, but still, the creature advanced, pulling itself forward. It grabbed the man's wrist and used it to propel itself upward, slashing out his throat in a spray of blood, and then he was lost in the fog.

"No!" the trio all screamed, but before they could help the man, the horrible beasts were upon them in earnest.

Kamil felt a pair of jagged claws rip into his calf, and he lost concentration. Both Aleksander and Valis faltered for a moment, disoriented in the fog without his shared sight. In an instant, they were both overtaken by the Faceless.

"They knew our plan!" Valis screamed.

Flashes of lightning and flame lit the fog as they tried in vain to slow the tide of Faceless. Valis dropped just in time to dodge a set of claws mere inches from ripping out his throat.

As it leapt at him, Kamil smacked it in the face with the end of an oar hard enough to snap its neck, and it stumbled then lurched forward toward him. Valis blasted it through the chest with a bolt of lightning, and it fell, smoldering, to the ground.

Meanwhile, Aleksander cast up a wall of flame that charred the flesh of a group of the beasts as it ran toward him; a horrendous smell filled his nostrils, and he had to stop himself from retching as the monsters ran about, still ablaze.

As Kamil regained his footing and concentration, it was as if someone had lit a lamp, dispelling the shadows from a dark room. They could see each of the Faceless, and just how outnumbered they were.

More importantly, they were able to locate Hanna and Shanthah's mental presence in the fog.

"Valis, get the boat ready!" Aleksander shouted.

He pent up flames for several seconds before letting them explode from his body, sending a pillar of flame high into the sky to show Shanthah and Hanna the way back to them.

He watched Hanna appear from the mist soaked with water and blood, her auburn hair matted against her face. She limped over the rocks toward Aleksander's makeshift beacon levitating Shanthah's unconscious body beside her.

"Aleksander!" she screamed. "Help!"

Kamil and Valis loaded the dead sailor's body into the lifeboat as Aleksander hurried toward Shanthah and Hanna. He summoned a shield of flame around him, scorching the creatures that dared venture too close.

"Hanna!" he called. Kamil's help was weaker so far away from him, but he managed to find her. She broke down sobbing and collapsed into his arms.

"It's okay. I've got you. I've got you both."

He supported Hanna as she levitated Shanthah, and they made slow progress toward the shore.

Kamil's voice rang in his mind. *"I'm keeping you hidden from their minds, but hurry! I can't keep it up much longer!"*

As soon as they made it to the lifeboat, Kamil collapsed, and the effects of his powers vanished. The Faceless swarm moved as one, and Aleksander pushed the boat off before clamoring in.

Two Faceless managed to claw their way on board, but Hanna dispatched them with two well placed stones. She clutched Shanthah's hand.

"He's dying!" she cried. "Aleksander, Kamil, please! Help him! I can't—I don't know what to do, and—I can't lose him!"

"My mother is aboard the ship!" Valis exclaimed.

"Okay," Hanna said. "I—what? I don't care—"

"She's a healer!"

"Okay, I do care!" Hanna exclaimed.

Aleksander and Valis rowed with all the strength they had left, and soon, they made it back to the ship. The crew hoisted them back up, and they hurried Shanthah aboard first.

"Be gentle!" Hanna sobbed. "Please, be careful with him!"

Alia pushed her way to the front of the group and checked for signs of life. "Everyone, back up!"

She began to coax his wounds to close with nothing more than a touch. They watched in awe as she manipulated his body to heal itself and stave off death.

Aleksander kneeled next to Hanna and pulled her into a one-armed hug, and together, they watched Alia mend their friend's broken body. When she was finished, she turned to Hanna.

"It's okay, friend," she said, placing a hand on Hanna's cheek. Hanna felt her anxiety melt away, and she wrapped Alia in a tight hug. "You got him to me just in time. He had minutes, seconds, even, left. I convinced his body to speed up production of blood, so he is going to survive."

"Thank you, thank you, thank you!" Hanna grabbed Alia's face and kissed her right on the lips multiple times before pulling her back into a hug.

"Oh!" Alia gave a bright laugh. "He's lucky he has you. Keep him warm, keep him happy, and keep him from exerting himself. Can you do that? He'll be good as new in a couple hours."

Hanna nodded, tears in her eyes. "Yes, I can do that."

The first thing Shanthah saw when he opened his eyes was Hanna's face smiling down at him.

"Hann…"

"Don't scare me like that again, mister. I won't *always* be around to save you," she said. She hesitated for a moment, then added, "No, I will. I'll always be there for you."

"I know." His words were little more than a breath, but he managed to tap a finger to his lips and then press it against hers too. She smiled and kissed him on the forehead.

"They're going to keep you safe and help you get better, okay, love?"

He nodded, closed his eyes, and squeezed her hand. When he pulled away, there was a small gem in the palm of her hand. Hokkod's crew took him away, and Hanna turned to the others.

"What were those things?" she whispered. "They weren't human *or* animals. I saw them die and get right back up again!"

"They—they were a disease. A virus," said Aleksander with blank eyes, staring into nothingness, or perhaps into everything all at once. Hanna waved a hand in front of his face. Nothing.

"What?" Hanna, Kamil, and Valis all asked at once as Aleksander's attention snapped back to the present.

"He is the new Secret Keeper of Kurash," Alia said loud enough only for the others to hear. "He sees the past."

"What?" they all repeated.

"I'll explain everything," Aleksander said. "It's been—well, it's been a long few days. They gave me their power and—"

"Ah, so you didn't kill them after all?" Hanna interrupted with a wink, and Aleksander laughed. "You know, there are wanted posters all over Tal-Ahosh for you, right? Shanthah was jealous. He said it isn't fair, and that he wants one too."

They all laughed, and then Aleksander explained the entire situation regarding the Secret Keepers.

"So, does that mean you know what this is?" Hanna asked.

Aleksander gazed at the gem Shanthah had given her.

He had flashes of masses of people using Teleportation Pillars to travel vast distances, and the huge, man-made cavern beneath the island, but nothing more.

"It guides the Teleportation Pillars," Aleksander said as if recalling the face of an old friend. "Like the one we used before."

As Kamil, Alia, and Valis spoke with one another in Kurashic, Hanna pulled Aleksander aside. Tears filled her eyes.

"Listen, Shanthah and I just fought Mara under the island. I know how you feel about her, and—Aleks, I think we just killed her. I am so, so, so sorry."

"What?" Aleksander managed to say. "She's—"

"I didn't know how to tell you. I still don't know if it's true. You didn't want to see her like this, though, Aleks."

"I've seen her since—well, you know," Aleksander said. "We were all in Nitra, after all..."

"Right," Hanna said. "Listen, if you want to talk, I'm here. She was my best friend too. And I know it's not the same, but..."

He took her hand and in a soft voice said, "What? Hanna—of course it is. We both loved her, and I think in a way, part of us always will."

They embraced for a long moment until General Hokkod emerged on deck with several other members of the Court of Thanatan, including Bovin the Minotaur.

"I think you're up," Hanna said. "I can't do this. Can you?"

She handed the crystal to Aleksander, who took it with a nod.

"It's okay. Go be with Shanthah—I'll see you later."

She squeezed his shoulder and departed, and he approached General Hokkod with the Telepillar's gem in his palm.

"Where in the name of Thanatan did you get this? How?"

"It was Shanthah and Hanna. It makes Teleportation Pillars work, right?"

"If Shanthah was involved, perhaps I don't need to ask *how*, although I do wonder. And no, the gem doesn't power the pillars, but it does hold coordinates for their use," said Hokkod. "But the question is—to where?"

"If King Talohir wanted it, perhaps it leads to the weapon he's been searching for," said Aleksander.

Hokkod stared at Aleksander with an intense gaze as if trying to figure out what exactly Aleksander knew, and how he knew it.

"Perhaps. We will speak later," he said at last. "All hands, set sail back to Thanatanos!"

The crewmen motioned with large colorful flags to the other ship to follow them home, and soon, the two vessels from were free from the fog surrounding the island, and the sun soon shone down upon them.

"Your friends have saved many lives this day," said Hokkod. "But we aren't out of this yet."

He pointed to the Talohiran ships setting sail in the distance.

"Do we have enough forces on board to fight them?"

"We shouldn't need to fight," Hokkod said. "But if they do engage us, much of the Royal Guard and Court of Thanatan are aboard the other ship, and Valakor, Bovin the Minotaur, and Manitrius are here with us. We will be quite safe."

"I'm not sure if that's ever true anymore," said Aleksander.

Hokkod chuckled and leaned on his long spear for support.

"How are you and your friends enjoying your time in the Royal Guard with Shanthah? It seems that trouble has followed you for the past few months, and you've always spit in its face."

"You know, when he asked if we'd join the guard, I thought we'd do a lot more *guarding* of *royals*," said Aleksander with a laugh. "Is that not in the job description?"

Hokkod shrugged. "If you're stationed in the palace, sure, but if you're on assignments elsewhere, it's more or less like this."

A sudden shower of debris exploded from the hull of the other ship. Aleksander stumbled to the starboard side of their vessel to see, staring open mouthed as a second explosion ripped through the aft of the ship and several survivors jumped into the waves, but it seemed that most of the crew was below deck.

"Lower all lifeboats immediately!" Hokkod shouted. "Search the ship! If one of our ships is targeted, they both are!"

Just as he said this, a portion of the port side of his ship exploded, sending wood and metal into the sea. Most of the crew members were already on deck and survived the attack, but several dead members of the royal guard and Court of Thanatan found their fate in a watery grave. At that moment, a final explosion rocked the other vessel, and its fiery wreckage sank beneath the sea. Other than those that were scrambling into the lifeboats, there could be no survivors.

Hokkod, Aleksander, Alia, Valis, and Kamil sprinted below deck to see the open space where much of the hull of their ship should be.

The gap in the side of the ship was high enough that seawater did not pour into the ship, but Aleksander groaned as he watched the vessel's main mast collapse like a felled tree into the ocean. The ship rocked, and everyone held on to whatever they could until it steadied itself.

Valakor and Bovin appeared behind them. The massive minotaur was holding a struggling man clad in Thannish armor.

"Ah, what have we here?" asked Hokkod, pressing the spear into the man's neck. "Not one of ours."

The man opened his mouth wide to see that his tongue had been cut out. He then spat at Hokkod, who didn't flinch. He pressed the spear's point deeper, drawing blood.

"Valakor, find Manitrius and see to the survivors," said General Hokkod. "They should be boarding soon."

"I'm a healer," Alia said. "Can I be of service?"

"Yes, go with Valakor," he responded, staring at Bovin's captive. Valakor and Alia hurried to the upper deck to receive the survivors.

"*Who are you?*" asked Kamil, reaching into the man's thoughts for any clues of what had happened. The man smiled and the smell of something burning filled their nostrils. Hokkod realized that the man's flesh and clothes were smoking; heat radiated from the man's skin, which felt as hot as a pot over a fire.

Hokkod thrust the man toward the gap in the hull. The heat that poured from his body made the room feel like a furnace; the man gave a horrible cry as Bovin's axe thudded into his chest, throwing him overboard. As he disappeared under the waves, what looked like a tiny sun appeared in the blackness of the sea. The explosion sent shock waves through the water but did no damage to the ship's hull.

Everyone could now clearly see the masts of Valistaran's twin ships on the horizon. One of the three had been lost to the storm, but the others were gaining on their position. With the main mast destroyed, their enemies would soon be upon them.

"Prepare for an attack!" shouted Hokkod. "The only way we're getting home is if we fight them off and sail back to Thanatanos on their own ship!"

Within the hour, the Talohiran ships surrounded the smaller, ruined vessel. Each crewmember on Valistaran's ship had their weapons drawn; there was no longer any intention of peaceful discussion on Talohira's part, despite Hokkod's earlier words.

Valistaran himself stood at the front of the ship.

"Prepare to be boarded!" a soldier called from the other vessel. The king's men dropped the gangplank and secured it with hooks on ropes. Hokkod said nothing, knowing that if he protested, Valistaran's men would attack. Kamil shared a knowing glance with Valis as the king strode onto their ship.

Valis let out a deep breath, hoping and praying that his mother would stay hidden, wherever she was now. He had no idea if his father would be merciful or ruthless if he saw her.

Valakor and Hokkod were the first to meet Valistaran and his men as they boarded the ship. Bovin snorted as the king strode past him, and for a moment, the minotaur gripped his axe as if fighting the temptation to remove the king's head.

"Give me what you found under the island, and I will let you sail away to safety," Valistaran said in a mocking tone, gesturing at the remains of the ship, which was now sticking up out of the waves at an odd angle, clearly taking on a considerable amount of water. Valakor planted the butt of his vicious scythe on the deck of the ship in a gesture of defiance toward the king.

"Our war ends now," Valakor replied, his voice cold.

"Our petty strife ended the moment your people bowed to me," said Valistaran. "However, it is clear to me now that some knees need forcing."

A torrent of dark flame erupted from Valistaran's outstretched hands, and in a split second, Hokkod had activated the magic inside his shield. A cyan burst of pure energy erupted from the piece of armor, creating a spherical wall to protect his allies. The flames fizzled, and the shield dissipated, and at that moment, Valakor leaped toward the king, his scythe overhead.

Valistaran drew his blade and brought it around in a curtain of flame, deflecting the massive Spirit Warrior's scythe, which arced around again to slice out the king's knees. Valistaran leaped backward and his men flooded the ship, engaging the remaining members of the Court of Thanatan and the Royal Guard.

The clash of swords accompanied flashes of powered fire and lightning as the two sides battled. Valistaran's five warriors in armor like Valakor's appeared on the deck of their king's ship. Hokkod caught a glimpse of them and sighed as he wiped blood from his cheek. He could not tell if it was his own, but the adrenaline in his veins helped him fight on, even if it was.

Valistaran's spirit warriors cut down all that opposed them with no mercy. The fifth of Valistaran's monstrosities stood even taller than Valakor and held a massive mace high over his head; with a crash, he smashed it through the deck, causing a group of screaming warriors to fall through the floor.

Hokkod leaped over a fallen ally, thrusting his spear forward at the king as Valakor grappled with one of the armored giants. and Bovin dueled the biggest of the enemy Spirit Warriors.

"Kallus, crush them," Valistaran ordered.

Hokkod activated his shield again, creating an impenetrable wall of energy between his men and their foes. Kallus, the massive, mace-wielding Spirit Warrior, brought down his vicious weapon again and again against Hokkod's energy shield.

"Brace yourselves!" Hokkod shouted as the shield broke, sending bolts of lightning into the crowd instead of shards of glass. At that moment, Valistaran glimpsed Aleksander's face.

"You!" he exclaimed. "Take him. Now!"

Aleksander readied two fireballs, and Hokkod scrambled for his fallen shield just as one of the spirit warriors dropped through the hole in the ship wielding two twin scimitars. Hokkod's shield was lying a few feet away, but he could not reach it in time.

As the newcomer brought his weapons down, someone emerged from a burst of black dust wielding two hooked swords of his own. Lord Ronin Jakoni of the Walkers appeared and deflected both weapons and then vanished in another puff of black smoke. The Spirit Warrior stumbled in confusion and then cried out in surprise as a bolt of flame struck it square in the face.

Not taking this moment of reprieve for granted, Hokkod scooped up his spear and shield and hurried forward. Close behind him were Aleksander, Kamil, and Valis who stepped forward without weapons, but ready to make use of their powers.

"Where did you come from?!" Aleksander shouted as Ronin Jakoni reappeared atop the warrior's shoulders and wrapped both of his hooklike swords around their foe's neck. Hokkod activated his energy shield to blast the Spirit Warrior backward.

The combined efforts of Hokkod, Ronin, Aleksander, Valis, and Kamil's mind powers incapacitated the warrior long enough for the hulking form of Bovin to bring his axe down, cleaving the warrior in two just as Ronin's blades severed its neck. Aleksander watched in amazement as bluish flames burst from the wreckage of the warrior's false body.

Aleksander regained his footing and glanced upward, swearing under his breath. In the sky above, he could see a swarm of Sangoran warriors circling over their ruined ship.

"Hokkod, the Telepillar—did the Court of Thanatan bring it on this voyage?" Aleksander asked.

"Yes, it is in the captain's quarters, but it won't do us any good if we don't know where it'll take us," replied Hokkod. "May Thanatan bless us that its destination is safe."

"Kamil, go!" Aleksander said, tossing him the gem then he and the others reengaged Valistaran's forces. Kamil caught it and scrambled up a ladder.

"After him!" shouted Valistaran.

Kamil burst through the doors of the captain's quarters, which were already ajar. Several dead crewmen, including the ship's captain and other soldiers lay dead throughout the room.

A gaping hole in the back of the ship let a warm sea breeze that tickled his face. On the floor was the Teleportation Pillar. It was on its side, but seemingly undamaged.

"I don't know what I'm doing!" Kamil thought, hoping Hokkod could hear. *"Hokkod!"*

"That's okay, buddy. I do," said a familiar voice. He turned to see Hanna, Shanthah, and Alia standing behind him.

"*Shanthah! Thank the gods!*"

Hanna used her powers to hoist the pillar upright, and Shanthah set the gem in its face. He manipulated the gem by touching its surface, and it lit up as it obeyed his command.

"Just got to undo what I did to get us out of the cave, and…"

The device began to hum and bathed the sunlit room in cyan light. Aleksander and Valis reached them just as Shanthah activated the machine.

They heard several thuds outside the chamber, and Mistress Lavinia and Lieutenant Vasilica entered the room flanked by three other Sangoran warriors.

"Oh, hello," said Shanthah as the pillar began to glow. "We're busy now, can you come back later?"

Ronin Jakoni and two of his Walker minions appeared between them as well, their weapons raised.

"Ronin!" Mistress Lavinia shouted.

The Lord of the Walkers turned in surprise as Mistress Lavinia thrust her twin wingblades through both of his followers' chests. She then turned to him and punched him in the jaw.

"Lavinia, we can talk about this!"

Just before she landed a killing blow against the Lord of the Walkers, everyone in the cabin was vaporized in a flash of green and teleported away to wherever the gem decided to send them; a beam of light as thick as a tree ripped through the ship and shot into the sky, decimating the room. The beam expanded and pulled everyone within its reach toward an unknown land.

The last thing Aleksander saw before it did was Mara as she entered the room. Their eyes locked, and then they were gone.

Half of the Thannish ship's hull was missing. Valistaran's foes as well as many of his own forces had been teleported away. As he realized he'd been left behind, his rage manifested in a roar and a burst of black flame.

He clung to a chunk of the mast to avoid drowning and motioned to his men who had salvaged a lifeboat. His queen and her Mistresses of Dusk would have to see to it that the weapon was procured, and their enemies destroyed. Aleksander was gone, and so too was the knowledge of the Secret Keepers. Only one thing remained in his mind, and that was the destruction of Laniras. His soldiers grasped his arms and pulled him into the lifeboat which began to make its way back to their ship.

"Your orders, my king?" asked one of his men as they pulled him into the lifeboat.

"We return to Bukaral. From there, we will burn Laniras to the ground."

Terror struck him as a deep groan filled his mind and he was filled with a horrible, insatiable hunger. First, one gray, clawed hand emerged from the sea and clutched the side of the boat, and then there were more. The creatures splintered the craft within seconds, and Valistaran felt the waves crash over him.

The Faceless pulled him down into the crushing blackness, and the last thing he saw before all went black was the flaming wreckage of the Thannish ship and his own men setting sail without him.

CHAPTER THIRTY-FIVE
THE DEADLANDS

For what seemed like an eternity, green light was all that existed, and when it disappeared, everything was falling. Confused combatants, thousands of gallons of seawater, and the fiery debris of half a ship rained down from the sky.

Most everyone was screaming, but many were in shock, too taken aback to know how to react to this bizarre turn of events. Only those who were within the captain's quarters were aware of what was happening, but even they had no idea where they had been transported.

Very much alive, Mara and her Sangoran followers darted across the sky in a frantic attempt to intercept Valistaran's soldiers before they struck the ground. At the same time, Ronin Jakoni's followers, the Walkers, were using their limited powers of teleportation to transport their Thannish allies from the sky to the ruins of a forgotten city nearby.

Many were not lucky enough to be rescued. Dozens of soldiers in the colors of both Talohira and Thanatanos met their fate as they crashed against the earth. Several died before hitting the ground from heart attacks caused by sheer shock, sparing them from an even more painful death. The unluckiest were those that met their fate against the earth.

Aleksander's heart threatened to pound hard enough to burst from his chest, but the sound of a sudden burst of black smoke eased his fears, yet adrenaline convinced him that he was still not safe. The shadows engulfed him, and Ronin Jakoni himself wrapped his arms around him, and together they disappeared in another flurry of shadowy smoke.

What remained of the doomed ship and its hapless crew crashed against the ground with a cacophony of screams, splintered wood, bones, and metal. And then there was silence.

Ronin grasped Aleksander's shoulder and performed a quick visual inspection to make sure he was uninjured, or at least alive. The mysterious Lord of the Walkers turned away and looked over the expanse of the ruined world around them. Aleksander expected Ronin to inspect the rest of the wounded, but then assumed he had only earned special treatment because of his role as the new Secret Keeper of Kurash.

"Are we—Ronin, are we in the Deadlands?" Aleksander asked. The name fit the desolation of the blackened ruins that stretched far past the horizon.

"Yes, I believe it is. But perhaps not the Deadlands that we are familiar with surrounding Thanatanos," Ronin said in a cryptic tone. He began to walk away.

"No, no. Come back. You're going to explain that comment," Aleksander called, following close behind the Lord of the Walkers. "Ronin!"

"You hold the secrets of your race in your mind, and you expect *me* to explain?" Ronin scoffed. "Wherever we are, our world is behind us. This land—this is a new world—and yet, an old world. It holds more secrets than we can scarcely imagine. The weapon is here."

"How do you know?" asked Aleksander. Ronin gave no response, as if Aleksander's question did not merit one.

However, Aleksander felt that Ronin's words held truth. He could not tell if his trust in the Walker was genuine or just because he had saved him, but Alia had told him that Ronin Jakoni was a violent extremist and not to be trusted.

The ruins of the city around them were overgrown with vicious thorns and vines that choked the crumbling, burned out buildings. Weeds had long since replaced what were once vast roads wide enough for entire teams of carts to turn around. Aleksander wondered what kind of weapon could have destroyed this civilization. Could Valistaran use it to annihilate Thanatanos just like this? Was this the future of Laniras?

"I need to find my friends," said Aleksander.

"Your friends are safe," was Ronin's entire response.

"How would you even know that?"

Ronin ignored him. Ahead of them, Ronin's followers were busy setting up a makeshift camp in a building that was at least partially intact, although the architecture was completely foreign to Aleksander.

His mouth opened in awe as he saw the remains of a castle that he deemed had once been beautiful. Not a fortress like in Laniras, but an elegant, welcoming place. A long, ruined bridge led through an arched gateway into the wide, inner court. The walls around were dotted with several high towers capped with conic spires of faded blue.

The highest of these towers stood just off center behind the main windowed bulwark on the front of the castle. The entire palace remained beautiful despite its crumbling stonework and ruined edifices. He felt a strange draw to the castle and hoped it was not a trap of some sort.

"Why are we not setting up camp in there?" Aleksander asked aloud. No one seemed to pay attention to him, and Ronin disappeared in a shadowy burst of smoke, leaving him behind.

"Yeah, good talk, Ronin!" Aleksander called, knowing he couldn't hear him. He grumbled under his breath as he set off in search of his friends.

He located Shanthah and Hanna after a short search and joined their conversation. He could read the emotion on his friends' faces but knew all was not well.

"Hey, pull up a seat," Shanthah said, gesturing to a nearby pile of crumbled bricks. Aleksander sat next to them and felt the exhaustion of the past weeks wash over him.

"We're responsible for this," said Hanna in a hushed voice. "We brought everyone here, but we don't have any idea how to get us back."

Aleksander realized that amid the chaos, he hadn't even considered a return journey. He sighed and rubbed his temples.

"If Ronin and Valistaran were both headed here, someone must have a way," Aleksander said. "What about the pillar?"

"You know where Hanna's going with this. We don't have any idea where the Telepillar even is, and I'm sure not walking back to Thanatanos. It's probably in the wreckage of the ship, but that's where Mara and her people are," said Shanthah.

Aleksander nodded. He had assumed the wreckage was closer to their position, but Ronin's men must have transported them farther away than he had thought.

"We're going to have to launch an assault on them then. If it's there, they know. We can't let them use it or they'll leave us behind," Aleksander said. "But the good thing is that they won't do that any time soon. They're here for the same reason as Ronin—they want to find the weapon."

"So, let's get to the pillar and leave them here with the weapon before they do the same to us," said Shanthah. "If they have no way back, let them have it for all I care. But if you do want to search for the weapon, I for one think that we'll find something in there."

He pointed at the blue tipped spires of the nearby castle.

"I think that's why Ronin's people brought us here too," said Aleksander. "But if it's filled with those walking corpses…"

"How would they know?" asked Hanna. Aleksander hesitated for a moment before speaking.

"Because *I* know," Aleksander replied, feeling somewhat like Ronin in his cryptic answer.

"Secret Keeper stuff?" asked Hanna.

Aleksander nodded but was unable to explain more.

"Then we have an advantage," said Shanthah.

"Unless they have a Mindspeaker reading my memories—or the memories of the Secret Keepers. I can't keep them straight anymore. I don't know which memories are my own, and which ones are implanted," Aleksander said. "So as usual, my head feels like a bowl of porridge."

"My sympathies," said Shanthah. "So, porridge-brain, shall we?"

"What about Kamil? And Alia and her son? Or Hokkod? We'll need help," said Aleksander.

"I agree—I'm not in the best condition thanks to those things we found on the island," Shanthah admitted.

They continued to plan their search of the castle as they began their search for their missing friends, agreeing to say nothing of their plans to Ronin or his men.

Not too far away, Mara sat before a set of ruined gates leading to a long road. From her position by the wreckage of the ship, she could see the beautiful, ruined castle at the center of the ruined city. The rest of her forces were preparing for the inevitable battle with her former allies, but she was taking a moment of rest to escape an inevitable, crippling anxiety attack. She, too, was a victim of exhaustion, and the moment of reprieve was welcome. As she sat with her eyes closed, she sensed a familiar presence behind her.

"Mistress Lavinia," she said without looking up. She was too spent to say anything else.

"So formal," said Lavinia as she sat next to her queen.

"Yeah. Sorry," Mara said.

"You're a queen—you don't have to apologize for anything anymore. What's on your mind, my friend?"

"This place. I recognize it," said Mara. "I read about it in the grand library in Bukaral. They called it the most magical place in the entire world. It's rumored in legends that the people who created this city actually *created* magic. I found references to a nearby city to this one called the City of Angels, and not far away is one they called the City of Sin—what kind of place is this?"

"Then, maybe, as the center of the most magical place in the world, this is where the weapon that our beloved king wanted so badly is," said Lavinia.

"I don't doubt it for a second."

"Then what's your plan?" asked Lavinia. Mara did not answer. "You can speak your mind. He's not here, you know."

Mara knew she was referring to Valistaran.

"I thought of what you said months ago," Mara said.

"About my plan to kill the king?" Lavinia asked.

Mara looked around to make sure no one heard what they were talking about, and she grabbed her friend's shoulder.

"I want more."

"I knew you would," said Lavinia, knowing what her friend was referring to. "Power feels good, doesn't it?"

"I know how we could do it. Announce that he died at sea trying to retrieve the weapon. He's probably dead anyway."

"And if he's alive and comes back?" asked Lavinia.

"Do you really think he could be?" Mara asked.

"I plan for *everything*."

"Then we kill him again," Mara said, answering Lavinia's original question.

"You want Sangora to rule over Talohira?" asked Lavinia.

"It's a country forged from war," said Mara. "We could help them adjust until they can become truly independent.

"So you want to *free* Sangora?" asked Lavinia.

"Well, I mean—Talohira's been nothing but warlords and slavers for so long, and they conquered Sangora—shouldn't Sangora reclaim what's ours? I mean, why should a bully of a country like Talohira keep a mighty nation like Sangora under its boot?" Mara asked.

"Interesting thoughts—but would all of Sangora rally behind you?" asked Lavinia. Mara could tell that this was a leading question, but to what end? Lavinia always had her own motives, and Mara knew that.

"I am their queen," said Mara.

"So were past queens killed by their own people. Just promise not to become those that came before you. There will always be those who choose not to follow you and forcing them to do so will *not* end well. Believe me, I've seen it firsthand. Do you think Florenta's forces would follow you?"

"I get what you're saying," said Mara.

"You know, Mara, Belokej the Talohiran slaver once killed someone I loved. And yes, I'm capable of that emotion."

"Who?"

Lavinia's expression grew soft.

"My sister. Her name—her name was Sveta."

"I'm so sorry," Mara replied. "What did you do? But what does that have to do with anything? I'm sorry—that was insensitive."

"What I *did* isn't important, but Belokej will never try anything like that again. The point is—I stole the respect of those around him. His cronies in the camp don't respect him, but they *do* fear *me*. Queen Codruta knew how to do the same. She died right before your conversion, but there are rumors that she discovered how to force us all to love her. Just like—well, just like the queen before her."

"Force us?" asked Mara. "But you just said it wouldn't end well if I did the same."

"Do not use that power against your people, but against the other Mistresses of Dusk? Have fun. Before her death, even I loved Codruta. Now, though—I realize that it was just the Queen's Control. I hate her, Mara, and I always have. As much as Belokej," Lavinia said, her voice a mere whisper. "If you are going to take your rightful place as queen of Sangora, you might need to discover this power too. You might even prove me wrong and end the war, like you said."

"So, I will need to find the source of Codruta's power and ensure Valistaran's death in order to rule over Sangora," said Mara. Lavinia shrugged.

"He's *probably* dead. But if not, he's supposed to become your husband. Another path to power. Are you willing to go through with that?" She watched the conflict grow on Mara's face.

"He is good to me, I guess," said Mara with a shrug of her shoulders and a look of dejected consternation.

"But I know you don't love him. Think about it. I engineered this, I admit, but I want you to be happy," replied Lavinia. "You could be the one who truly ends the war. You could be the hero of Thanatanos, the hero of Talohira, and the savior of Sangora."

"I could bring everyone together again."

"You could bring everyone together again."

"But why me?" asked Mara. "Why don't you do this yourself?" In response to this question, Lavinia thought to herself for a moment before speaking.

"I see a lot of you in a younger me. I also see a lot of you in Valistaran and vice versa, but there is a distinct difference between the two of you," said Lavinia.

"Which is?"

"There are two powers in this world, Mara, and two only: order and chaos. Valistaran maintains order around him, but at his core is darkness—chaos. There is chaos around you, yes— there always has been and perhaps always will be, but at your core, there is light. Order," Lavinia said before softly adding, "Hope."

"What about you?" asked Mara, cutting her off.

"I'm all chaos, all the time, babe."

"*That* is an understatement," Mara said with a laugh. "But I'm not sure I understand."

"You will."

Mara continued to gaze toward the ruins of the great civilization but said nothing.

Lavinia broke the silence by saying, "A time is coming, my queen, when you need to choose who you want to be."

"What do you mean?"

"When Valistaran named you queen, you said you could choose to play the victim of life's treachery or choose to overcome it. Be a queen. Choose that every single day," said Lavinia. Her tone was authoritative, yet kind. "*Our* queen. Redeem us."

"I know," said Mara. She was silent for a moment before abruptly changing the subject. "I've been studying the languages of the Deadlands, you know. A lot of them."

"Oh," said Lavinia. "Why?"

"It takes my mind off everything. I know it's weird, but it's interesting to me. It soothes me. Like a little secret."

"I'm no stranger to secrets," Lavinia said. "If it's something you love, it isn't weird, though." She turned toward the ruined gates of the city. A string of words in an old script was scrawled in faded paint on the massive wall over the front gates.

"Let's see how good you've gotten then," said Lavinia with a wink. "What does that say?"

She pointed upward to the forgotten language painted across the entrance to the city. Mara squinted to make out the faded paint and what the combination of letters and words signified. She hesitated, understanding all but the last word in the sentence.

"Celebrating two hundred years of magic. Welcome to Disneyland."

CHAPTER THIRTY-SIX
THE FALLEN WAKES

Everything seemed unnatural. The castle itself felt artificial, as if the sturdy yet crumbling stone walls were erected simply for show rather than as actual defensive bulwarks. Aleksander, Shanthah, Hanna, Kamil, Alia, and her son Valis made their way through the palace, wondering who once lived in such a strange place. The stench of decay lingered in the forgotten halls, and Valis walked with his tunic over his nose.

Hanna discovered a dust covered tome set upon a pedestal and swept her hand across its pages; colorful images of knights, princes, and princesses adorned the aged parchment. She paid it no more heed, and the group continued up a short flight of stairs. Light poured through a damaged stained-glass window, bathing the room in muted jewel tones that danced as the clouds above moved across the sun.

The group found several more archaic tomes placed in nooks around the room, and Hanna marveled at the strange displays of unrealistic statues lining the chamber as she helped Shanthah limp along.

"What is this place?" asked Aleksander to no one in particular, brushing his fingers over the hideous visage of what looked like a statue of a witch with an exaggerated nose.

"*Not sure, but I don't think anyone else has been here in a while,*" said Kamil to the minds of his friends.

"By what I remember about the outside of the castle, I think these stairs probably lead up to the tallest tower," said Alia.

She pointed up the spiral staircase nearby. Shanthah raised his sword and paraded up the stairs as fast as he could manage with Hanna supporting him.

"Forward, ho, men!" he called to the others in an exaggerated voice like the brave leader of an exploratory force. Hanna stopped and cleared her throat with an exaggerated cough which prompted Shanthah to say, "forward ho, women, too, sorry!"

Shanthah looked to Hanna for approval; she nodded and helped him along once again.

The others followed close behind until they reached a wooden door of solid construction. Aleksander reached for the doorknob, but Kamil grabbed his wrist and jerked it away.

"*I can sense someone inside,*" said Kamil to the minds of the entire party. "*The presence feels like the lull in a conversation where you know someone wants to speak but does not—I don't know what lies behind that door, but we are not alone.*"

"Are we in danger?" asked Hanna.

Kamil reached out with his mind to contact whoever stood behind the door.

"*No. Whoever is behind this door is not responding. Asleep or unconscious, maybe,*" replied Kamil.

Shanthah put his finger to his lips and turned the knob. His stomach leaped as the handle turned, expecting the door to be locked. He pushed the door open, and the group made a slow advance into the chamber at the top of the high tower.

Dozens of skeletons of long dead men and women were strewn across the floor. Many of the skeletal fingers were still wrapped around strange looking black and silver objects that seemed to be some type of archaic weapon; at the far side of the chamber stood a metallic cylinder with a dusty glass window upon its face. Tubes extended from the bottom of the structure and several blinking lights flashed just below the glass.

"Is our friend inside?" asked Shanthah.

Kamil nodded, his heart pounding.

A somewhat apprehensive Valis was the first to venture forward this time and brushed his hand across the dusty glass to expose the pale white face of a sleeping man. Whoever was in the glass pod must have been inside for a very long time, judging by the state of the bones strewn about the chamber.

"Who are you?" asked Alia in a hushed voice.

"Is it a prison?" asked Aleksander.

Valis stumbled over a skeleton and glanced down, noting that the forehead of the skull had been crushed in as if pierced by an arrow. Doing a quick scan of the room, he realized that each of the skulls in the chamber were desecrated in the same way. Kamil had noticed the same as he crouched near a pile of bodies.

Aleksander traced his finger along the glass and down the side of the tube. He stopped as he touched a flashing green light next to a small indentation. Without much forethought, he decided to press his finger into the hole. There was a click and a soft beep, and the light began to flash yellow.

"There's another one on this side," said Shanthah, pointing at another indentation next to a green light. Curiosity overwhelmed the entire party, and Kamil pressed the button.

"Wait! What if he's not a friend?" exclaimed Alia.

They ignored the one voice of reason in the room as the green light turned yellow to match its twin, and then in unison, both lights glowed a brilliant red.

There was a hiss and the glass window slid upward into the metal pod. A dense fog spread across the floor, flowing off the man's body like smoke as he thawed. The man slumped forward, and Aleksander and Shanthah caught him. Hanna gasped as the man's eyes shot open, and he scrambled away from those that had freed him. The man collapsed to the ground and crawled away from the group.

"Wait, stop!" Aleksander exclaimed.

The man didn't even seem to hear him as he pulled himself across the floor. Kamil grabbed the strange man's arm and pulled him up. He was nearly as thin as the faceless creatures on the island, and it was therefore easy to lift him to his feet.

Aleksander looked into the man's eyes, which seemed to dart around the room but looked at no one in particular. His pupils were so dilated that the blackness seemed to engulf the cool blue of his eyes, but soon they returned to normal. His breathing slowed, and he allowed Aleksander to support him.

"Do you understand me?" asked Aleksander. The man looked him in the face with no response.

"What's your name?" asked Shanthah. "I—AM—SHANTHAH." Each word out of his mouth was slow and loud.

The man's eyes glazed over for a moment before he spoke.

"I am—I am Daniel," said the man.

"You speak Thannish!" exclaimed Hanna.

Alia and Valis helped Aleksander lay Daniel on the ground between a few skeletons then looked the man over. His body was covered in lacerations and blue bruises that had somehow not healed during his time in the pod.

"Lay still. I can help you," said Alia, placing her hands upon Daniel's wounds. He sighed in relief as the pain subsided and the injuries seemed to mend themselves.

"Ah, you have one of my gifts," said Daniel with a chuckle to himself. "Fortunate for me, eh?"

"*Your* gifts?" asked Alia.

She paused, an air of nervousness evident in her voice.

She, like all the others in the room could recall the old tales of Thanatanos that said Elafris the Fallen, God of Darkness, Lord of Chaos, and Bringer of Death was also the deity who brought powers into their world, calling them his gifts. Aleksander lit a ball of flame in his palm as a precaution.

"That's what I always called them—the gifts I gave to our soldiers. How wrong I was. How very, very wrong," said Daniel. "He called them that too. Yes, yes. Some are useful, like my ability to translate languages instantaneously, or your gift to heal wounds—but others? Oh, dear—for those crimes, I have paid dearly."

He looked at Aleksander's burning hand.

"What exactly were your—" Aleksander paused for a moment. "Your crimes?"

Daniel glanced around the room. For the first time he seemed to notice the skeletons and the foreign garb worn by the strangers.

"How long have I been asleep?" he asked, glancing around the ruined chamber.

He hurried to the pod and pressed a button near the window. A moment later, a glassy square lit up with lights to the astonishment of all in the room but him. He tapped a few places next to illegible scribbles of text on the magic box and then sighed.

"So? How long?" asked Shanthah with a sarcastic tone.

"Oh dear. Longer than I had hoped," said Daniel. "Nearly four hundred years? No, that can't be right. This model of Lifepod is only meant to function for a maximum of—"

"Four hundred years?!" exclaimed Hanna, glancing at Shanthah, who had disbelief etched on his face.

Daniel hurried to the window and gazed out over the ruined landscape. He shook his head in inconsolable sadness and fell to his knees in grief.

"You okay buddy?" Shanthah asked.

The others gathered around him.

No one spoke as Daniel wept near the ruined glass window. After a few moments, he stood and turned to them. He pointed to the desolation outside and shook his head.

"I am so sorry. This was me," he whispered. No one spoke. "I helped create the forces that caused this. They told me this would happen. I should have listened—"

He spoke to no one in particular, but everyone in the room felt frozen by an unspoken feeling of unease. The strange man grimaced and collapsed to his knees while holding his forehead. Hanna and Alia hurried to his side, but the men stayed back.

"They are coming," said Daniel, cradling his body with his arms and rocking back and forth. "Is he awake as well?"

"Who?" asked Aleksander in a tone of caution.

"I lost my connection to him some time ago, but I could sense that somehow his mind was connected to mine. If I'm awake, he must be—or soon will be," Daniel said.

"Who?" Shanthah cocked his head in annoyance at the man's cryptic words. Daniel hurried back to the window.

"Perhaps he is already here."

"You lost a connection to *him*?" asked Alia, placing her hand on the man's back. "What do you mean? Who?"

"I lost our mind link. I tricked him into it. I had to track him, Alia. I had to know where he was," Daniel replied. Alia glanced at Aleksander with a nervous expression. She had not mentioned her name, yet the man knew it.

"Who is he?" asked Hanna again.

Before Daniel could answer, a half dozen bursts of black smoke filled the chamber, disorienting the already confused occupants. Daniel stumbled backward as Ronin Jakoni, his right-hand soldier Emil, and four other Walkers appeared around him.

Aleksander expected a battle to ensue, but Ronin and his followers knelt before Daniel, holding their swords before him across their outstretched palms. An act of fealty. As soon as Ronin stood, a deep groaning filled the world—one that Shanthah and Hanna could remember all too well.

Hanna snapped around as she caught a glimpse of the faceless creatures swarming up the stairwell. Shanthah cursed as he slammed shut the wooden door and barred it with a tall lamp from the corner. As Shanthah barricaded the door, Aleksander peered out the window. His mind shot back to some forgotten memory, and he knew not if it was his own.

He, or someone else, had been here before. Whoever's memory this was had spoken to Daniel. This bizarre sense of déjà vu felt vivid and real, and he eyed the man with piercing curiosity. He was familiar, like a friend that he had not seen in years but still loved. He shook his head. This had to be a memory from the Secret Keepers of Kurash. He snapped back to reality as the Faceless began slamming against the door, intent on mutilating all that breathed inside.

As the creatures burst into the room, Aleksander hurled a ball of flame into the crowd as Ronin's followers held their hands aloft. Hanna shot a small stone into the neck of one of their foes and then all of reality went black. And then it was not—they were no longer in the chamber. Black smoke spiraled around them like smoke before giving way to dim torchlight.

"What?" Valis and Hanna both shouted at the same time.

Shanthah groaned, dusted himself off, and got to his feet.

The Faceless were nowhere to be seen.

"Where are we?" asked Shanthah as he counted heads. Hanna, Aleksander, Alia, Valis and Kamil. Good. Everyone was there. He did not care to count Ronin or his followers.

"We combined our powers to save you from certain death," replied Emil, Ronin's second in command. "You're welcome."

"Okay, but again—where are we? Is this underground?" asked Valis, noting the lack of windows.

"*Oh, they're definitely going to try to murder us,*" Kamil mindspoke to his allies. Shanthah chuckled.

"*Yeah, no doubt about that,*" Aleksander replied, knowing Kamil could sense his thoughts.

Torches flickered above, illuminating Ronin as he stood alone near a massive metal gate blocking a wide tunnel.

"Beneath the castle. My son loved that place," said Daniel. "The most magical place on Earth, they called it. Makes sense that no one would look for an arsenal underneath the ruins of a theme park, right? I had it moved here when, well…"

"Underneath a what?" Hanna asked.

Alia's heart dropped. Did Valistaran's fabled weapon exist after all?

The entire group watched as Daniel pressed small flat buttons on a panel near the metal gateway. The sound of hissing steam and crunching metal filled the chamber as the doors spun around each other and then split, opening the way forward. Ronin pushed Daniel forward, and he led the group through the empty portal.

"My lord, what are the creatures that attacked us?" asked Ronin as he walked beside Daniel. Aleksander raised an eyebrow and glanced at Shanthah upon hearing the honorific bestowed upon the stranger.

"A weaponized form of a particular virus," said Daniel. "Definitely not an accident, though, like in movies. Oh, no, they released this on purpose. It caused entire populations to turn into those undead, soulless things—horrible weapons. They dismantled cities brick by brick until nothing remained. It got out just before my son was killed. They had a purpose, but everything went wrong, oh—"

No one pressed for more information, but everyone wondered what kind of purpose the creatures once had. Despite not understanding the implications of what Daniel had said, the group chose to follow him. They came to a second, smaller, gate as the tunnel narrowed, and a shared feeling of claustrophobia began to set in. Daniel approached the panel to open the gate and shouts filled the chamber.

"They found us," said Hanna, whipping around.

The low groan of the Faceless overwhelmed the Sangorans' screams as the two groups met in battle. Daniel turned to address his allies just as an arrow whizzed through the air and pierced his abdomen. He collapsed and cried out in agony; Ronin and the others encircled him then disappeared in a cloud of dark smoke.

"Are you serious?" asked Shanthah as he pounded on the heavy metal gates. "Come back here, you useless—"

He turned to the nearby panel and pressed the small, flat buttons at random. A red light began flashing above them, and he backed away from the buttons like a child caught sneaking sweets as Hanna helped Daniel lie against a wall.

Horrendous shrieks and groans from afar accompanied by the flashing red light painted the scene with an eerie, evil ambiance. The sound of Mara's troops and the Faceless monstrosities that chased them drew nearer as Aleksander had another sudden jolt of déjà vu at the sight of his scar.

"I can get us in," he whispered as memories flooded his mind. He stumbled toward the gate, his head swimming.

"What? How?" asked Shanthah. "The Secret Keepers wouldn't have known about this place!"

"Just do it!" Hanna cried, but Aleksander collapsed.

"What is happening? Get up, man! Sleep later!" Shanthah shouted. "Get us in there!"

As if in a dream, Aleksander could see the gates in his mind. Another vision provided by the Secret Keepers of Kurash, perhaps? Whoever first experienced the memory he was now reliving stood next to both Daniel and the late King Romiton Romus. The king watched Daniel type a string of letters on the buttons then turn to the owner of the memory. This wasn't a dream implanted by the Secret Keepers—no, this was his own.

"The Walkers are right behind us. We've failed. I know we're not going to reach the weapon before they find us, and I fear that I may not make it back here before the end of the war. You know what you must do," said Romiton.

"You'll have to wipe our memories," Aleksander, before he was Aleksander, said. "If they take us, they'll be able to find it."

"But you must remember!" said Daniel. "I know they're going to take *me*, so you must—"

"Daniel, you need to do this," Romiton ordered.

As Daniel entered the password into the machine to close the doors, Romiton drew a knife and carved each letter of the password into Aleksander's arm, then began to do so on his own.

"If I'm killed or Thanatan is able to awake before I do, I pray that the memory of how to return here will return to you."

"And if not?" asked 'Aleksander.'

"Then heaven help us. This knowledge will be lost."

"Perhaps it's for the best," 'Aleksander' said. "If we get through, I'll destroy all the databases you talked about so they can't bring that technology back."

"Go back to your Lifepod. They can't know you're already awake," Romiton ordered. "I can't believe we didn't make it."

"I'll erase all our minds, then," Daniel said. "Godspeed."

'Aleksander' took a deep breath and grimaced as he wiped the blood from his scar.

A-L-E-K-S-A-N-D-E-R

He thought of everything he'd lose when Daniel wiped his mind, but most of all, he thought about *her*.

His vision became blurry and disoriented as the Walkers banged on the door. Romiton collapsed as Daniel erased his mind with his powers then activated a handheld device that teleported the king away. Then, 'Aleksander' felt his own mind go blank as Daniel grasped his forehead before his world too melted away in a flash of green.

And then it was all replaced by blinding light and flame.

The modern-day Aleksander's eyes shot open to see his friends locked in combat with Mara's forces. As the vivid memory echoed in his mind, he stared at the faded scar upon his arm and got to his feet, disoriented. He cursed and knew his friends would have to take care of themselves until he could finish with the keypad.

Something tackled him as he scrambled toward the panel; he lit a ball of flame against the head of his Faceless attacker and crawled over its writhing body. He pulled himself up and typed the letters into the keypad.

The door lurched, and the metal screamed as it opened halfway, revealing a massive chamber on the other side. The malfunctioning door shook, and a violent, scraping sound filled the corridor as broken, unseen gears crashed against each other.

A mighty bolt of lightning sizzled through the air, followed soon after by a deafening thunderclap. As Hanna recovered from the temporary blindness of the lightning's brightness, she turned to see a Sangoran enshrouded in crackling electricity flying straight at her; she stumbled over a dead Faceless creature and hit the floor. The Sangoran sliced a knife across Alia's calf then shoved her to the ground, continuing toward her foes.

Hanna rushed toward Alia and hurled a stone at the Sangoran, who deflected it with a strike of her powerful wing. Mara's voice filled the chamber, but she remained unseen. The

Faceless were concentrating on her forces for now, giving the others a moment to recover.

"Mistress Lacramora, regroup!" the queen cried.

Mistress Lacramora ignored Mara's order and flapped in the air above Hanna, ready to strike. Hanna acted first, crying out as she thrust Lacramora across the chamber with her powers. The Mistress of Dusk struck the wall, and then Hanna sent a rock through her throat, and she fell to the ground in a ruined heap.

"Go!" Hanna shouted.

The others wasted no time climbing through the gateway. Kamil had sustained several deep wounds, Valis was bleeding from both arms, and Alia had a deep gash from Mistress Lacramora's blade. She helped them climb through as Shanthah slipped unseen as an invisible bringer of death to defend them.

Aleksander typed his name on the keypad again on the other side, and the doors slammed shut, crushing a Sangoran soldier and two Faceless that had tried to follow them through. Shanthah slid to the floor against the cold metal of the gate in relief as Hanna cried out in exhilaration.

"What was that?" asked Valis. "How did you open the gate?"

"I thought it was something from the Secret Keepers of Kurash," Aleksander said, unsure of how to explain the truth.

"What did you see?" asked Shanthah. "What happened?"

"But it wasn't their memories. I was here. *I* was here with King Romiton and Daniel."

"He didn't seem to remember you, though," Hanna said.

"He erased our memories, even his own," Aleksander said.

"So did you remember who you are?" Shanthah asked, gripping his shoulder. Aleksander shook his head.

"No."

Alia sat nearby as they talked, her back turned to the group. A relieved smile crossed her visage. She hadn't known exactly what Aleksander needed to remember, but at that moment, she was eternally grateful she'd healed his mind. She said nothing.

"Let's just say, I'm not Aleksander," he said, holding his arm aloft. "I think the real Aleksander is Daniel's son—you know, the one that he mentioned. The one that died."

"Then who will you be?" asked Hanna in a low whisper.

The sound of Sangorans trying to save themselves from the Faceless slamming against the gate drove fear through each of their hearts.

"Well, I don't think the original owner of the name needs it back, so until I remember, I'll still be Aleksander."

"You knew about this place then. Before you forgot everything, you knew where the weapon was hidden," said Valis.

"*I can't wait to find out more about your story,*" said Kamil to Aleksander's mind. "*I hope we live to hear it.*"

"We bet that what you forgot was important, right? Do you owe me some gold now?" asked Shanthah with a wink.

They delved deeper into the chamber and soon found themselves standing upon metal scaffolding that lined the outside of the circular room with several more levels beneath and above them. Aleksander and Shanthah peered into the darkness of the seemingly bottomless pit below while Hanna backed up.

"Nuh uh," she said. "I don't like heights."

The darkness at the bottom of the chamber was dispelled in short bursts as hundreds of blinking lights showed the way down the spiraling scaffold.

"What is this place?" whispered Valis as he and Hanna helped support Alia on her injured leg.

Ronin's distinct voice echoed upward, and a laugh, not one of humor, but of triumph, soon followed.

"Ronin!" Aleksander called. "How the hell did he get in?!"

He led the others downward, dispelling the darkness with a ball of flame in his right hand. At last, they found Ronin, Emil, Daniel, and four Walkers near another arcane panel of buttons.

"You used us!" Hanna shouted.

"Yes, but for your own good, damn it," Ronin replied. "I just needed you to open the door. Our powers made the rest easy."

Uninterested in speaking further, he returned his attention to whatever it was he was doing.

"Ronin, what is this place?" shouted Aleksander.

"I regret that necessity has made you an instrument to guide me here, Aleksander," said Ronin. "But I do not apologize. I, one of the Immortals, will save this world from the evil that your people have for so long embraced. I do not expect you to understand now, Aleksander, but perhaps in time, you will remember."

Aleksander caught Daniel's gaze as the man typed on the massive keypad. As he did so, the floor at the center of the chamber began to spin and then spread apart just like the gateway in the tunnel.

The group watched in both fascination and horror as a pointed monolithic tube of painted metal rose from the opening in the floor. Lights flickered on and off in the chamber, allowing glimpses of the fabled weapon. It was a long, cylindrical device of some kind covered in strange markings in a forgotten language, and multiple metal fins extended from its body.

Ronin gestured in triumph to his prize as he turned back to the group. "Thanatan is returning, Aleksander, and we must be ready for him." Aleksander made eye contact with Daniel, who drew something from his pocket and placed it on the machine.

With that, Ronin and his followers raised their palms; in a tremendous burst of energy and smoke, they disappeared from the room, taking the forgotten weapon with them. Aleksander hurried to the control panel and hit switches and levers, turned knobs, and even tried typing his name into the panel. Nothing interesting happened.

"They played us for fools," said Alia, slumping to the ground. She pulled a spool of bandages from her pouch and began dressing her wounds. Hanna stooped over to help.

Aleksander reached for the object that Daniel had placed on top of the machinery. "I watched him put this here…"

It was a small gem embedded in what resembled a long-necked candlestick. Shanthah smiled and pulled the item from Aleksander's grasp.

"Ah, Hanna. Look what we have here," said Shanthah in a tone of mock expertise.

"Ah, yes. What we have here is a mess-up-your-life stone which will take you somewhere you don't want to go, and you'll almost surely die obtaining it," said Hanna. "How many of these have we found now, Shan?"

"Two now, if I can count correctly, Miss Samsa."

"It's just like the one we found on the island full of Faceless, but what's this part here?" asked Hanna, grasping the protruding part of the device.

"It's a portable Telepillar," said Aleksander. "He used it in my vision and used it to send me back to Thanatanos right after he erased my memories."

"Does anyone else get the feeling that Ronin's men think he is—" started Kamil to each of their minds.

"Elafris, the devil himself?" finished Alia. "I don't believe that they are incorrect." Shanthah struggled to make out the double negative to make sure he understood Alia's statement. It was a normal grammatical construction in Alia's native Kurashic, but it did confuse Shanthah for a moment.

"I think you're right, and I think the Secret Keepers agree," said Aleksander, memories of the name Daniel Elafris trickling into his mind.

"You think that squirrelly little guy is the *devil?*" Shanthah asked. "I don't buy it."

"If Elafris has been awakened, and his followers have a weapon strong enough to even stop Thanatan..." thought Kamil, trailing off.

"In my memory—the one where King Romiton carved my—sorry, Aleksander's name, that is, into my arm—they said that Thanatan was returning. They must know something that Ronin does as well," said Aleksander.

"Why didn't Romiton ever say anything about this?" Shanthah asked. "Something's afoot, and I don't like it."

"He must have lost his memory, just like you," said Valis.

Shanthah pressed on the gem, and it began to glow. A burst of green energy filled the chamber, pulling Aleksander, Shanthah, Hanna, Kamil, Alia, and Valis to safety, or so they hoped.

They hit the earth hard as they reappeared. The transition from darkness to blinding daylight sun stung their eyes, but as Aleksander's vision returned well enough to see where they had been transported, his heart dropped. The teleportation stone's magic had transported them back to the surface of the Deadlands, not home; Aleksander cursed, knowing that meant they were still in danger. Shanthah discarded the ruined device.

"Guess it only works once."

They were standing before the wreckage of their ruined ship, surrounded by the horde of Sangorans locked in combat with the surviving members of the Court of Thanatan. The wreckage of the ship concealed them from view, but they all knew that it would not do so for long.

"Why couldn't it have just sent us home?" Hanna asked.

"Because we didn't ask it nicely," Shanthah replied.

Aleksander peered over a hunk of gnarled debris just in time to see Valakor sever the neck of an opposing Sangoran in mid-flight.

"*Well, at least we aren't alone,*" Kamil thought to the others. Shanthah joined Kamil and Aleksander as they peered around the wreckage, and he laughed.

"Nope, just a tad outnumbered, right?" Shanthah asked with a wink. "But seriously, we've got to get out of here. Alia, can you heal our wounds?"

"Can I? Obviously. Do I have the energy to do so? Maybe not," she replied. She began her work.

Shanthah's eyes caught the glint of something glowing beneath the splintered bits of wood, and he motioned for Aleksander and Valis to help him shift the debris as Alia healed Kamil's wounds.

"I think I know what Valakor's fighting for," he said. "Fortunate for us this is where Daniel's machine sent us, eh?"

He wrapped both hands around the Telepillar and with his friends' help, hoisted it upright. The magical artifact from times gone by pulsated with a dim glow, even in the daylight.

"Maybe Daniel's device just sent us back to the nearest Telepillar, then," said Hanna. Shanthah nodded in agreement. "We need to help Valakor. Is he alone?"

She peeked her head around the wreckage, glimpsing Hokkod as he speared one of his foes through the stomach. At the same time, Bovin the Minotaur swept a trio of Talohiran men from before him with a mighty swing of his axe while Manitrius fought at his side.

"I think those four are all that are left of the Court of Thanatan," Aleksander said. "Let's go!"

Aleksander climbed atop the pile of debris and with a yell, hurled a ball of flame into a crowd of Sangorans. The fire dissipated before reaching his foes, but it achieved what Aleksander hoped it would do.

It bought Valakor, Bovin, Manitrius, and Hokkod a moment of reprieve. General Valakor caught sight of Aleksander standing upon the wreckage, and he spurred his remaining forces onward.

Vanishing from sight, Shanthah sprinted from cover. Only the splashes of his feet were visible in the ankle deep, murky water as he made his way toward Valakor and the other survivors. Hanna joined Aleksander atop the wreckage, leaving Kamil, Valis, and Alia behind to guard the Telepillar.

Bovin bellowed in agony as a woman with a spear pierced his thick hide from his left. He spun around and shattered the wooden shaft with his elbow before raising his axe. An arrow slammed whizzed his back as he brought the weapon down upon his attacker, splitting the soldier in two. Hokkod leapt around Bovin, felling the archer by slamming the edge of his shield into his skull with a sickening crunch.

Valakor raised his scythe toward Aleksander, and he, Manitrius, Bovin, Hokkod, and the few remaining men that followed them sprinted toward the ship's wreckage while Aleksander, Hanna, and Valis used their powers to cover their escape. Every so often, a soldier would fall to an unseen hand, and Aleksander knew that Shanthah was indeed part of the fight.

"Secure the pillar!" cried Valakor as arrows clattered against his armor. Hokkod was using his shield as an umbrella against the rain of arrows while Bovin treated the darts like annoying bee stings but was otherwise unfazed.

"It's here!" called Hanna. "Come on!"

"*What should we do?*" Kamil asked directly to Valakor's mind.

"Activate it!" Valakor shouted as a bolt of energy struck him in the back. A dozen or so dark shapes shot up from the tunnels; Mara and her followers had escaped yet again, but it was evident they had sustained heavy losses.

Mara rallied the remainder of her forces, and they soared over Valistaran's men toward the enemies guarding the Teleportation Pillar. Aleksander's heart pounded, and his stomach dropped as he caught sight of her, and he wondered how the beautiful, fierce woman he once knew and loved had become their greatest adversary in such a short time.

A bolt of cyan light erupted from the pillar as Alia limped forward and placed her palm on the gem on its face. She stumbled backward and was not engulfed by its teleportation light, but she could feel it drawing her in.

Valakor, Bovin, and Hokkod guarded their last four men as they scrambled up and over the embankment of debris. They were all injured, but alive, and they would live to fight Mara's forces another day.

"Hurry!" cried Hanna, who was growing exhausted from deflecting arrows with her mind. She collapsed from the strain of using her powers and tumbled from her perch. Her fall was softened by an invisible someone who held her close.

"I've got you," Shanthah whispered into her ear.

Mara landed alone beside Aleksander, her bladed wings folded against her back. They locked eyes, standing still for a long moment as the others fought. Mara reached out for him, her weary eyes full of defeat, but then, once again, their world was engulfed in cyan light before they could speak.

Everything exploded.

Chairs were sent flying across the room, and the long table around which King Verahim and his advisors were seated was blasted into the ceiling. Everyone in the chamber scrambled backward as cyan light filled the room, and then a Minotaur, dozens of Sangorans, a spirit warrior, and many more humans appeared from nowhere. Even chunks of what seemed to be a decimated ship's hull appeared through the portal, crashing through the far wall.

"What the hell?!" the king exclaimed.

The room erupted into further chaos as the Sangorans turned on the humans, hacking at them at close quarters with knife tipped wings. Mara took advantage of the confusion and clawed her way out of the fray toward King Verahim himself.

The king drew his shining silver blade and thrust it through her wing, piercing flesh. He roared in his rage as he grappled with his brother's killer; the two tumbled to the floor as someone smashed a chair over Mara's head as she attempted to tear out Verahim's throat, knocking her to the ground.

"Good job, Apolinarius!" called the king.

Mara whipped around, and her heart seemed to stop. Her brother—her own little brother. Disbelief filled her soul as Pol stood above her brandishing a short sword.

"Pol?"

And at that moment, she was not a queen, but a worried older sister. Pol's eyes took in his sister's transformation, and he stepped backward in shock, unsure of what to do.

The chaos continued around them, and then a misdirected ball of flame and a bolt of lightning struck the north wall. The brick exploded outward, revealing the view of Laniras below and the blue sky above.

Mara leaped to her feet and ignored the throbbing pain in her wing as she shot toward the Telepillar.

The mind has a funny way of bringing up memories at inopportune moments, Mara knew, and this was one of those times. Amidst the chaos and death around her, she thought of what Lavinia had told her. She had to choose who she wanted to be. She had to choose to overcome—to be a queen.

She struggled to lift the pillar but exerted the limits of her new telekinesis powers and hurled it from the open wall before racing down out after it. All of her remaining soldiers followed close behind.

The artifact struck the ground, and a burst of fiery energy exploded from all sides. Strange, chaotic lightning crackled around it. What was she doing? She had no idea how to harness the pillar's magic, but she had seen it used several times.

Once in Sangora, when she had been betrayed by Drahomir. Again, when she was double crossed by Shanthah and Hanna. Breaking free of her thoughts, she slammed her palm into one of the gems on the pillar. As she did so, she focused her Mindspeaking abilities into the gem as she pictured Bukaral's grand library. A bolt of crimson light engulfed her.

CHAPTER THIRTY-SEVEN
THE EMPRESS OF BLOOD

The Telepillar exploded as Mara appeared near the palace in Bukaral. She collapsed, coughing, to her hands and knees. Where were her allies? Was she the only one who survived? That's how it should be. She needed none of them. And yet, she craved their companionship. Where were Lavinia and her new lieutenant, Vasilica? Perhaps the crimson energy had transported them to Sangora, but she knew they would most likely be imprisoned.

She had to save them. They were the only ones she had left.

She pushed the thoughts out of her mind, telling herself she was nothing like Drahomir or Aleksander—nothing. She vowed to save her friends. She could do it, for she was the queen of Talohira and Sangora—

Or was she?

Her impending marriage hadn't happened, and she couldn't control other Sangorans like Codruta could. She would have to fix that if she wanted to maintain her throne, she knew. She got to her feet, the Telepillar nowhere to be seen.

Its energy had cracked the street where she appeared, and several confused bystanders gawked at her. A woman held a small child in her arms and shielded her from the Sangoran that had just materialized out of nowhere. Mara despised the look of fear and disgust on the woman's face, and she averted her gaze.

No one should look at her like that. She was a queen.

Perhaps, the woman would someday tell that child of the day that she thought she had seen Queen Mara Bartunek. That *maybe* it *could* have been her.

As she walked away from the scene, she thought of her title, for she felt it was wrong. A queen was only subservient to a king, wasn't she? And if the king was dead—she'd just be called a dowager queen, further relying on a man to legitimize her position. She was the head of an entire empire, not a kingdom.

Empress Mara Bartunek—yes, that sounded better. For some reason, she considered what her caretaker Elena had told her about blood and purity in the Wingling home.

Mara Bartunek: Empress of Blood.

She took flight, wincing with every flap of her wounded wings, but she soon glided on an air current that carried her to Valistaran's palace. No—her palace, although she much preferred the one in Doftaan. She would have to stop thinking of herself as Valistaran's second in command. But that's not what she was either.

He had turned her into his weapon. An attack dog, and nothing more. She still wondered for a moment if he had somehow survived, but she shook off the thought.

She landed on a balcony that she knew led to a chamber just outside the grand library. Lavinia had mentioned Queen Codruta's ability to control the rest of their race, and the thought of how to reproduce the power was nearly consuming her.

During her time amongst the books, she had found hidden secrets of arcane science in old, dusty tomes taken from the Deadlands. She had forced Valistaran's magicians, or what those in the Deadlands would have called scientists, to perform operations on her in order to use different abilities. She'd do the same to learn Codruta's power.

She entered the grand library and hurried to the section where she had found the most information on powers from the Deadlands. Aleksander betrayed her by trapping her in her own mind for twenty years, but unbeknownst to him, she had gained the ability to enter her Dreamstate where every minute in the real world equaled one year in her mind, and at that moment, she thanked Aleksander, wherever he was now.

She paused, distracted by a pile of language books, which she had been able study and master using the Mindprison. She had studied Sangoran and Kurashic, but others from the Deadlands as well, including an ugly one called English, and two beautiful ones, Ukrainian and Romanian, two of the ancestors of Sangora.

"I have time," she told herself with a shrug, picking up a book at random. While thumbing through it, she discovered that her own native tongue, Thannish, had descended from a language called Czech, or perhaps one called Slovak. There was some debate, of course.

She set it down, telling herself to focus—no, she was the Empress of Blood, and she could spend her time however she wanted. And what she wanted was to read about languages.

According to a book about the Kurashic language, during a great war, millions of refugees from a group of countries flooded into another called Turkey. She laughed, for she knew that in that harsh, ugly English language, a turkey was a fat, flightless bird. The mesh of cultures and languages had resulted in Kurash.

She picked up her favorite book of all, the tome containing all the secrets of the Sangoran language. She smiled as she thumbed through it. She must have read it and the entire Sangoran—Thannish dictionary a dozen times, but she still loved it. Sangoran, similarly to Kurashic, had arisen refugees fleeing to one location. The people and their languages, including Ukrainian, Romanian, Bulgarian, Belarusian, Hungarian and several others had blended to create Sangora and her language.

She looked at some of her other favorite books, grammars on Lithuanian, Finnish, and the next one she planned to learn, Kazakh. They felt like friends—secrets no one else knew.

She read for a few hours in the real world then forced herself to walk away to continue her search for information on Codruta's ability. No more getting sidetracked.

"No more languages until you finish, miss," she said.

To an outsider, when in Mindprison's mental state, she would appear to spend several seconds or minutes at a time in a meditative state on the floor holding books close to her chest.

However, she was really spending days, months, or even years at a time in her own mind researching their contents.

At long last, she discovered a book in that ugly English language entitled, "A Treatise on Honeybee Pheromones and their Application in Biowarfare." A lengthy title with too many words she didn't understand yet. However, it piqued her interest, and she cracked it open, scanning the table of contents.

Mara felt the book would lead her in the correct direction, and she lay on one of the library tables and slipped into her

Dreamstate. When she awoke a few seconds later, she threw the book to the floor and scrambled to the shelf to find another.

Her excitement grew as she read more and more about a power called the Queen's Control. At one time, soldiers in the Deadlands were given special genes and glands from honeybees so that they would be more obedient to their commanding officers. Was that genius or barbarism? Mara did not know. Were Sangorans a similar experiment in the Deadlands to give soldiers the ability to fly? Or to give them night vision, or maybe turn them into living weapons—just like Valistaran had done to her. If those things were true, what on Earth were those faceless creatures beneath the island supposed to be? Or Minotaurs?

Mara continued to chapter twelve, where she found that when these honeybee pheromones were combined with telepathic Mindspeaking abilities, mere influence and suggestion could be twisted into imperative command. Control. A fabricated affection, even.

The chapter detailed organic technology called "radio receivers" that were grafted into primitive Sangorans' wings to hear orders from commanding officers. Was this why the Walkers severed their own wings and sacrificed the beautiful gift of flight, so that past queens could not control them?

She found another written specifically on Sangorans, wherein she discovered the people of the Deadlands had used a far more simplistic and barbaric term for her race: 'Bat people.' There was another that sounded better, but she didn't know quite what it meant: 'Chiropterans.' A picture of a Sangoran with a bat-like face stared up at her. Surely, they hadn't looked like that, right?

If these scientists had created these abilities to gain power for their kingdoms, then where were they now? At long last, she located a thick tome in a section requiring special clearance, which she ignored, with the title, "The Fall of Humanity." It seemed like an appropriate place to start. A great war had ravaged the land and ended the civilization that had created powers. But then where were their buildings? Where was the proof that they had lived there? And then she found it: a passage on faceless creatures that dismantled entire cities and killed everyone inside. She rolled onto her back, back atop the table, to keep reading.

She discovered a set of laws long since forgotten that forbade the mention of the war. The goal of the laws was to let the knowledge of what had transpired fade away with the generation that had caused it. Their descendants would have no idea what had transpired. She stared at the words in disbelief.

Whoever had wanted to cover up the war was successful, as she was unaware of any of it. Perhaps this book was mere fiction? She knew that she may never know. But the weapon that Valistaran was looking for—the weapon under that forsaken castle in the Deadlands—the Faceless—were they all remnants of that great and fallen civilization? How were they connected?

"Focus, Mara," she said. "Fo—cus."

She turned her attention back to her real goal of uncovering the secrets of the Queen's Control. She found another book entitled, 'Queen Mandibular Pheromone in Chiropterans' and remembered seeing mention of that particular pheromone in the other book on honeybees. She chose not to enter the cuff's mind-state, for she wanted her victory to seem real.

It was more about the artificial organ in each of the wings of the queen Sangoran. Like a honeybee, she could use her pheromones to control the rest of her kind to do many things.

These pheromones were powerful alone, but useless at a distance. However, when combined with the powers of a Mindspeaker—yes, she already read that in the other book. But how were queen Sangorans chosen if the organ was synthetic? It must have been implanted, she determined.

She continued reading until she felt that she understood the science behind the artificial honeybee pheromone organ in the wings of the queen. In other, more gruesome words, in the wings of Valistaran's dead queen, who had also discovered this ability.

Mara wasted no time. She took the book with her and shot through the window toward the royal graveyard not far from the palace. She soared over the guards who stood as sentries outside the gates and made her way to a beautiful mausoleum engraved with the words, 'My Beloved Queen Codruta Talohir' over the massive arched doors.

"Wow," breathed Mara aloud.

Valistaran had *loved* Queen Codruta. Would he have ever loved her as much, or was it merely a political decision? She didn't care anymore. He was dead. The empire was hers.

She blasted the door open with a bolt of lightning, and the metal gate swung open, its lock broken. She stepped foot into the mausoleum. It was lit by a large circular window at the height of the chamber that let a ray of sunlight or moonlight illuminate the stone box that held Codruta's remains.

Mara took a deep breath, ignoring her own pleas of guilt and regret as she blasted the coffin with several bolts of lightning until the stone gave way and broke. She struggled to lift the heavy slabs away from Codruta's body with her telekinesis and then smiled as she saw the former queen's face.

"Hello, my queen," she whispered as she rolled the corpse over within the grave.

She drew a short knife and carved into the shriveled arm of Codruta's wing. She gasped in pleasant surprise as her knife met metal. She was relieved that there was no blood in the preserved wing and that cutting through it was like cutting through a dry husk of corn.

She extracted the artificial organ that created the pheromones, replaced what remained of the stone lid, and soared from the chamber. She vowed to have Codruta reburied.

The Empress of Blood returned to the palace, this time entering through the front doors. The guards let her past as they recognized her as Valistaran's bride-to-be, although they were visibly nervous about the fact that she was covered in blood.

She pushed open the heavy doors to her empty throne room and approached the gilded seat from which Valistaran had ruled. Codruta's throne seemed to have been destroyed, somehow. She dropped onto the throne and traced her finger along the intricate designs on the armrest then reached into the pouch on her hip.

As she sat in Valistaran's throne, she promised herself that she would not be cruel like Valistaran and so many of the other Mistresses of Dusk. The slave camps would have to be shut down, obviously. She sighed and buried her face in her hands.

"I hate this place," she whispered as tears streamed down her face. "I hate it, I hate it, I hate it."

She decided then that she would leave Talohira behind and live in Doftaan. Perhaps, she'd transport Bukaral's entire library to Doftaan.

She didn't know what to do next.

She set out for the palace scientists and magicians. When she arrived at their laboratory, she explained her plan, showed them the information in the tome, and they agreed, whether out of fear, respect, love, or something in between to help her.

She lay in a hospital bed and took a deep breath as they injected her with some type of potion. She began to drift off, but she knew that when she awoke, she would have all power over Sangora. She would be more than a queen. Mara Bartunek, Empress of Blood…

The last thing her mind's eye imagined before she lost consciousness was the disappointed face of her little brother.

CHAPTER THIRTY-EIGHT
CLOUD OF WAR

Lavinia was a master strategist, and many events that had transpired in both Sangora and Talohira during the past few months had been to her design. This turn of events, however, was not part of her grand strategy. She suddenly found herself, along with several of her comrades, in the Thannish palace surrounded by the king's men.

Her eyes darted to the gaping hole in the wall through which Mara had escaped. For the briefest moment, a spark of doubt creeped into her mind, and she wondered if her efforts in helping Mara to become queen had been in vain, but she shook the thought. She would survive this to see her plans fulfilled.

After Mara's escape, the fighting ended in favor of King Verahim's forces, much to the dismay of the defeated Sangorans. Even those with powers knew when they were defeated, and they had surrendered. When Verahim had finally collected himself, he turned to address his men.

"Send these Night Witches to the dungeons," he ordered with a wave of his hand. "They have no place here."

"I would esteem a king such as yourself above using such bigoted words," Lavinia said, cooperating with the members of the royal guard placing shackles on her wrists.

Verahim scoffed. "I am above everything now, thanks to you and your people. Who do you think you are addressing?"

"A boy on the same path as Talohira's dead king."

"Take her away," Verahim ordered.

He said no more, and the surviving members of the Court of Thanatan escorted Mistresses Lavinia, Vasilica, and the other Sangorans from the room to the dungeons.

"So few survived," whispered the king, almost to himself.

"On both sides," Aleksander said, drawing the king's glare.

In all, only three men other than the surviving members of the Court of Thanatan and Shanthah's ragtag squad. In essence, The Court of Thanatan was no more—a shard of its former glory and power. The King's Royal Guard was now similarly decimated, leaving the king nearly alone.

"As one of the last remaining members of the Royal Guard, the duty to report to you what has happened falls on me. We offer you our services," Shanthah said, bowing his head.

Aleksander watched Shanthah closely, reading his expression. He had come to know the man well enough over the past months to recognize his apprehensive expression. What was Shanthah planning?

"It seems I would be a fool to reject you," said King Verahim as he clapped his ally on the shoulder and gave a curt nod to Aleksander in thanks.

He did not show any indication of acknowledgment to Hanna, Alia, Valis, or Kamil. Verahim motioned for the group to follow behind him, and Kamil reached into Verahim's mind, finding no traces of intended malice or offense.

"As the council chamber is no longer usable," he said as he motioned to the ruined chamber, "we will convene in the dining hall. I need to know exactly what happened on your mission."

Shanthah nodded. "Of course, my lord."

For the first time since their reappearance in the council chamber, Pol greeted Aleksander, clapping him on the back.

"It's so good to see you! Josman and Drahomir are here too. We've been so worried for you all, and I can't wait to hear where you've been!" Pol exclaimed.

Aleksander smiled and opened his mouth to answer, but Verahim interrupted.

"Apolinarius, please run ahead to arrange the room for us."

"Pol! We've missed you, buddy," said Shanthah, ignoring the king's command to greet his friend. Hanna waved, and Pol returned both gestures before bowing to the king. Obedient to Verahim's order, he hurried ahead to the banquet hall.

"I did not want to speak too much of Queen Mara Bartunek in front of the boy," said Verahim, apprehension evident in his voice as he clasped his hands behind his back.

"Well, if she comes up, you can always have him leave, but I think he deserves to know the truth," said Shanthah. "My lord, the Sangoran terrorist Ronin Jakoni betrayed us. He helped us locate the weapon Valistaran was after, but when we found it, he and his men took it and vanished. It's in their possession."

Aleksander stayed silent, watching the king's reaction. He could tell Verahim's interest was piqued, but whether it was by mention of Ronin Jakoni or the weapon, he did not know.

"Ronin? And the weapon? What was it?" asked the king. Shanthah shook his head and shrugged at the same time.

"*Something from ancient times in the Deadlands,*" said Kamil.

"He said that Thanatan was returning, and we need to be ready when he does," said Shanthah.

"Very curious," said Verahim. "A fairytale, but if true, good for us. What news of Valistaran Talohir and Mara Bartunek?"

"You saw for yourself that Mara survived," said Shanthah.

He glanced at Aleksander but said nothing.

"Dead, we believe."

"Then we have cause for a feast!" said Verahim, smiling at the group. Valis and Alia were both silent, and Aleksander wondered what they were feeling.

Pol welcomed them as they reached the banquet hall. Verahim sat on one side of a long table, while Shanthah, Aleksander, Kamil, Hanna, Alia, and Valis each slumped on the opposite bench.

They each felt the exhaustion of the past few days set in as they finally had a moment to rest. Pol sat on the bench behind them.

"My father and I have spoken with Ronin Jakoni before. He has appeared to me several times, always with cryptic warnings about Sangora or Talohira. I have always considered him an ally, albeit a mysterious one," said the king.

"So, you trust him?" asked Alia in an incredulous tone. "He is considered an extremist in both Sangora and Kurash."

"Yes, but I trust that man with my life," replied Verahim. He hesitated for a moment before continuing. "Before the voyage to the Deadlands, he met with me one last time. I am still troubled by the meeting."

"He told you about Thanatan and the weapon," guessed Shanthah. The king nodded.

"He didn't tell me exactly what the weapon was," said Verahim, stroking his chin. "I won't tell you what he told me, but what he said was deeply troubling."

"You knew he was there, then," said Alia. She exchanged a furtive glance with Hanna.

"Yes. And although his actions seem—" Verahim paused to think for a moment, searching for the appropriate verbiage then glancing at Alia, said, "to use your word, extreme, I would not be so quick to believe that he means us harm."

At that moment, Pol rushed to the doors of the banquet hall, and in strode Josman, Drahomir, and Rehor. The young man ushered them in, and they took their place behind their friends, who welcomed them with wide smiles. They each understood that the time for proper greetings would come after the king departed.

Pol filled them in on the details they had missed as the king continued, and Hanna turned to give an excited wave to her friends. They each smiled and waved back.

"You don't believe that he's going to destroy us all with the Deadlands' weapon?" Shanthah asked.

"No, not unless we get in his way," said Verahim. "He's Sangoran. Let him kill his own kind, for all I care."

"We can't trust him," said Alia, shaking her head. The king ignored her comment and turned back to Shanthah.

"There's more," said Shanthah. "We discovered a man in the Deadlands by the name of Daniel. Ronin believes that Daniel is…" The king leaned forward in expectation as Shanthah's words trailed off.

"He believes that Daniel is Elafris himself," said Hanna.

"The Fallen God?" Verahim asked. "Ronin truly does dabble in myth, doesn't he?"

"I don't think the theory is implausible," said Shanthah. "But his role as a god is probably overstated just a little bit."

Verahim nodded in quiet understanding, and Hanna glanced at Shanthah in exasperation; he squeezed her hand in acknowledgment but kept his eyes on the king, expecting Verahim to be surprised, but he did not even seem fazed.

"He mentioned to me that he hoped to locate Elafris before Thanatan returns," said Verahim. He began to speak again, but a loud flurry of horn blasts sounded in the distance. War horns. The entire party got to their feet and rushed to the banquet hall's windows to try to see what was happening outside.

As Pol withdrew the curtains, a horrible sight came into view. A dark cloud veiled the horizon, obscuring the sun, and at once, the king and his allies realized that thousands of Sangorans were swarming over the countryside toward the city of Laniras.

Alia covered her mouth in shock as the blackness settled upon the hills outside the city's walls.

"Did they know Mara was here?" asked Pol.

"No way," said Aleksander. "This has to be a planned invasion separate from what was going on in the Deadlands."

"Aleksander is correct. I know military strategy, and that would take weeks to organize," said Josman, speaking for the first time since arriving as he pointed out the window.

"Send for Hokkod and Valakor," King Verahim said to Pol. The boy leaped to his feet, eager to fulfill the mission for his king. "By the way, you never said what happened to Valistaran."

"He went down with his ship," Alia said.

"Perhaps this is his last act against our great nation, then," said Verahim. "I am needed elsewhere, but please, let us discuss Mara Bartunek later when her brother is not present."

"Yes! Go, we understand," said Aleksander. Verahim said nothing more as he turned down another corridor.

The tense air of the meeting seemed to follow the king as he departed, and despite the ominous host of Sangorans outside the city, the mood in the banquet hall turned to one of levity.

"Well, hey you three!" Shanthah exclaimed, finally free to address Josman, Drahomir, and Rehor. "Feels like it's been four hundred years!"

"Oddly specific," said Josman with a chuckle as he pulled Shanthah into a bear hug.

"Not really, no," said Hanna, thinking back about how long Daniel Elafris had been frozen as she wrapped her arms around Josman's huge frame.

"Get in here," said Shanthah to Rehor and Drahomir.

Rehor smiled as he joined the circle of hugs. Drahomir seemed reluctant, but Hanna pulled him in, and Shanthah gave him a friendly punch to the shoulder.

"I hear you have been on quite the adventure," said Josman.

"All the while *you've* been sitting here in a comfortable castle in Laniras, eh?" Shanthah laughed, but Josman shook his head.

"A comfortable castle in Laniras is the perfect place for a coup to overthrow the king," said Rehor.

"You planned a coup?" Shanthah asked. Josman laughed.

"While you were gone, we discovered a plot to kill King Verahim, and he said he'd even think about giving us places in the Royal Guard," said Josman in a nonchalant tone. "Pol is one of the king's official messengers now. He is ecstatic! We'll have to tell you about it sometime—no time now."

"Looking forward to it! I can tell he's enthusiastic about it," said Aleksander with a laugh. Catching up with their friends lessened the mood of oncoming doom.

"About the Royal Guard— someone, maybe the same person as in Kal Ahosh, planted Dragonsouls that blew themselves up, destroying one of our ships and disabled the other—long story short, we were teleported from an island with Faceless monsters to somewhere in the Deadlands with even more of the creatures and, well—" Shanthah said, but the horn outside sounded once more. As everyone hurried to the windows to watch the Sangoran forces nearing, Hanna grabbed Aleksander's arm and pulled him away from the rest of the group.

"I said I'm here to talk, remember?" Hanna said.

"Of course," replied Aleksander. As their friends spoke, Hanna took a deep breath and took his hand in her own.

"Mara's going to be out there," she said. Aleksander avoided eye contact, but Hanna snapped her fingers, and he met her gaze.

"Yeah, I know."

"She's going to be looking for you. Remember what happened back in Nitra?" Hanna said in a voice of warning. "If it comes down to it, and I think it will, could you fight her?"

Emotions swirled in his head as he thought of the young woman through which they had all survived so much only to have her torn away from their lives.

"I don't know," Aleksander said, glancing toward the window. "Hanna, I don't know what to do. I'm scared I'll have to."

"She loved you. Really. We girls talk about everything. I hope she won't want to fight you, either."

"How I felt—or how she felt—that doesn't matter anymore. She's made up her mind, and I think, well—before the end, we're going to face a lot more pain, and I'm not going to pretend like I don't know that."

His voice was soft, and he fought off tears.

"Aleks, I am so sorry," said Hanna. Aleksander responded with a sad smile. "I wish we could save her. I really do."

"On the bright side, we might not have to worry about it," he said, gesturing with his head toward the window and the invasion force outside.

"If we die?"

"Yeah."

"Way to look on the bright side, buddy," Hanna said with a smile and slugged her friend in the shoulder. "We sound like Drahomir talking like this."

They shared an amused grin, but she could see the tears in his eyes. She wrapped her arms around him for as long as he needed, letting him cry on her shoulder.

"Thanks, Hanna. You are the best," Aleksander said when he pulled away.

"I know." She smiled, and they rejoined their friends as they gazed out the window.

Far below, the garrisons of warriors in Laniras were deploying all over the city, lining the walls and other strategic positions in the streets and buildings. Soldiers were ushering citizens into the fortress at the center of the city while still more set up the defenses.

"This is going to be bad," Shanthah said. The others nodded.

Valis got to his feet and cleared his throat to speak.

"Um, everybody? I—uh, I have something to say," he muttered, and the others turned to him.

"For those of you who don't know me, my name is Valis— Short for Valistaran. He's my father. I just wanted you to know where my allegiances lie. I mean, it was bound to come to light."

"My father was a milkman," said Josman. "Doesn't mean I was."

Valis smiled as the others nodded, offering kind words of support; he was surprised at the acceptance that he felt from each of them.

"I can safely say that you are one of us," said Aleksander.

"*A misfit, just like the rest of us*," said Kamil with a smile.

"Well, Valis, what do you say we replace the current king of Talohira with someone else—someone more fitting of the title of king?" said Josman with a smile. "I've learned quite a bit about coups during my time in Laniras. Wanna start one?"

He winked at the young Valis who grinned but shook his head.

"Are we ever going to hear that story?" asked Shanthah.

"Well, there we all were," Josman said, starting the story. As he spoke, everyone in the room wondered if they would live to see the next sunrise.

CHAPTER THIRTY-NINE
FURY OF THE EMPRESS

How dare she?!

In her fury, Mara had ordered her own release from the medical center in Bukaral after hearing of Mistress Delia's betrayal.

With the king dead and Mara absent, Mistress Delia had claimed the throne of Sangora and the title and power that accompanied it. She even had the audacity to officially announce that the king and queen had been murdered during their voyage to the Deadlands.

Mara would play that to her advantage, knowing that if the people thought Valistaran was dead, it would be easier for her to kill him herself—if he was still alive, of course.

Delia had ordered Mara's armies to make way for Laniras, the capital of Thanatanos, the same place that Mara was now flying at near breakneck speed.

She had ordered a cart and driver to take her most of the way toward the capital of Thanatanos and had been traveling for the better part of two days; her drivers had alternated so that they never had to stop, and she ate, drank, and slept on the way to conserve her strength. They only stopped a couple times during the entire journey.

At long last, she became too antsy to wait any longer.

"Stop, please," she called to the drivers. Soon, the vehicle came to a halt.

"Yes Empress?" asked the driver.

"You've taken me far enough. Thank you very much," Mara said. "I think we're close enough for me to fly the rest of the way on my own."

"I wish you luck, Empress."

"Please, take a couple days to recover. You've driven me far, and you deserve rest," Mara said.

"Yes, thank you, Empress," the driver replied. She nodded, and he spurred the horses onward, turning the cart around to head back to Bukaral. She unfurled her mighty wings and took flight in the direction of Laniras.

The sun dipped below the horizon, and day melted into dusk as crimson and indigo painted the sky. She watched her reflection in the glassy water as she soared over a calm expanse of the mighty Viltava river. The dramatic sunset caused the mirror-like surface to seem as if it were a river of fire burning its way through the countryside toward Laniras, and she smiled, thinking of a lake back in Cineca that had looked the same.

Fitting. The countryside was already burning in Delia's wake, but Mara would reclaim her forces and once again assert herself as empress of Sangora. If she withdrew Delia's forces, perhaps it would create new bonds of trust between their nations. She played with the idea. Delia, however, would die no matter what happened.

The lights of Laniras were visible in the distance, surrounded by an innumerable horde of dark shapes—the forces that Delia had usurped from her during her absence. It wasn't her entire army, but it was a sizable force. She glided over the camps of mixed Sangoran and human warriors and landed near the nearest crimson banner of Sangora marking a commanding officer's tent. She dropped her exhausted wings to her sides in relief.

"Come outside," she ordered in a low whisper, using her newfound abilities of the Queen's Control for the first time since leaving the medical center. A compliant commander pushed through the tent's flap and met Mara's gaze with rapt attention. She looked confused, as if pulled from a deep sleep.

"You will tell me where to find Mistress Delia," said Mara, with a look of pure hatred.

"Queen Delia's camp is at the center of our forces," replied the commander. "It would be my pleasure to lead you there."

Mara smiled. Her experiment had been successful. Not only did she have complete control over the woman, but she also seemed to *want* to serve her true empress, just as Lavinia had said.

"Thank you, commander," said Mara.

The commander's wings unfolded and she soared toward Delia's position with Mara trailing just behind her. The usurper's tent stood grander than the others and was surrounded by human and Sangoran soldiers alike. The camp was set upon a low cliff that overlooked what may soon become a battlefield.

She willed Delia to appear, testing the telekinetic influence of the Queen's Control. The traitorous Mistress of Dusk appeared from the tent, and her Sangoran guards turned to flank her. Mara glared in their direction and willed them away.

"Mara!" Delia exclaimed. "What are you—"

"I am your empress," said Mara. Delia took a nervous step backward in fright, disbelief etched on her pale visage. "Say it."

"You are my empress," said Delia with a smile. Mara circled the woman as the campfire nearby flickered in the darkness.

"Are you going to tell me what is happening here?" asked Mara. She stared at the traitor with contempt.

She crossed her arms and awaited the reply. Delia seemed to fight against her control, but after a few moments succumbed, just as they all would.

"We assumed that you were dead. I was going to take Laniras in your honor," said Delia. Her response was terse as she was forced to speak when she did not desire to do so.

"I see that even with my new powers, you can still lie to me," said Mara. "Tell—the—truth."

She emphasized each word with fierce animosity.

"I claimed you were dead," said Delia.

"But did you think I actually was?"

"No."

"So, what would happen if I claimed *you* were dead?" asked Mara. "What would happen if *my* armies saw that *I* am alive?"

"I do not know, my queen," said Delia.

"What you've done does not sit well with me," Mara stated. "You are hereby stripped of your title and office as Mistress of Dusk."

"There were rumors that you had designed the same plot against High King Valistaran Talohir," said Mistress Delia.

She seemed both defiant and compliant, as Mara's order to tell the truth was still affecting her.

"Who told you that?" asked Mara, pointing at Delia with a razor-claw attachment on her finger.

"There was no rumor—I overheard you speaking with Mistress Lavinia," said Delia, straining against Mara's control. "I know your magic, *Empress* Bartunek. I fought against Codruta's control, and I will do the same to you."

"Step from the cliff."

Mara's abrupt order filled her mind, and it took all her energy to resist. She took an awkward step toward the precipice. Mara could see Delia's determination and knew that she was fighting for control, but in the end, Mara's willpower overcame the traitor's resolve.

The queen of Sangora watched her fall, but she did not smile. She thought that killing Delia and taking back her forces would make her feel better, but she felt no different.

"Your orders, my queen?" asked the commander.

"Call off the siege. We're going home," said Mara. "Send word to Laniras about what happened and spread the word that I am once again in charge, and Delia is dead."

"Yes, empress."

She entered Delia's tent and collapsed upon the cot inside and soon lost herself to the comfort of sleep. She was awakened sometime later by the clash of swords and the echo of screams. She pushed herself up to a sitting position as a Thannish soldier ripped open the flap of her tent with three more standing behind him. A dozen or so dead Sangorans lay outside.

Mara let loose a bolt of lightning into the stomach of the nearest human soldier, blasting him out of the tent. The others scrambled through the opening while others sliced through her tent to reach her. She took one deep breath through her nose then screamed in her fury.

"We were *LEAVING*!" she roared, and lightning streamed from her arms, each of her fingers, and the tips of her wings. The deafening thunder that followed her raw power heralded the deaths of all her attackers as blinding lightning decimated the tent. How did they even reach her?

None survived. She stood alone in the crater that had been Delia's tent, charred bodies of the traitors loyal to her enemy scattered all around her. A cool breeze played with her dark hair, and she collapsed to her knees. She had vast legions that surrounded her, thousands that would die for her and follow her to the ends of the earth, and yet she was alone.

So very, very alone.

CHAPTER FORTY
THE HIDDEN FLAME

Three long weeks had passed since Mara withdrew her order to end the siege. Although no blood had been spilled since the initial attempt on Mara's life, the capital city was surrounded by her loyal followers. During that time, Thanatanos had made several more assassination attempts, and word had reached Mara that the Thannish armies had burned four Sangoran towns near the border to the ground, solidifying Mara's decision to stay.

Her forces had stalled all trade to and from Laniras, cutting off the capital's once constant flow of food from the farms. Many of the people of Laniras were already starving as it was, but now, most markets were closed due to a combination of fear of the looming horde and the fact that shopkeepers hoarded what little food remained for themselves. Despite its many walls, the city had not been prepared for a siege.

The only contact with the city was a declaration sent by the Empress of Blood. Within the note, Mara proclaimed her wish to end the war, promising safety for all that would surrender. If Laniras did not surrender or yield control to Sangora within two weeks' time, her forces would fall upon the city if it did not first collapse from want of food. The allotted time had come and gone, and the citizenry was restless. The people of Laniras wondered if the extra week was supposed to give Laniras more time to prepare or a way to bleed them dry.

Every soldier left in Laniras was armed and ready for the imminent bloodshed. Thousands of archers lined the walls, and hundreds of rapid-fire ballistae had been erected upon rooftops to send any airborne Sangorans to their deaths. Laniras was starving, but ready to fight to the bitter end.

Far from Mara's tent, Aleksander examined the chipped sword he had been issued and sighed, knowing how poorly many of the defenders had been equipped. He was sitting with the others in the palace dining hall, which had been converted into community sleeping quarters for soldiers and refugees alike, and he and his allies had volunteered to help defend the chamber. He, Rehor, and Josman sat near a window, ready to wake the others if the siege broke and the army advanced. Their friends were asleep, or at least pretending to be.

"You know, I'm getting sick of all this," said Josman. "I have *never* been so tired."

"I know what you mean. When this is all over, I'm settling down somewhere in the countryside where my only worries will be eating, sleeping, and taking care of some good dogs," said Rehor. "They're good company, you know."

Aleksander laughed, but motion outside the window caught their attention. What he saw was inevitable, yet it still seemed impossible—the army outside was at long last advancing upon the walls of Laniras.

He hurried to where Shanthah, Hanna, Alia, Valis, Pol, Kamil, and Drahomir were sleeping and shook them one by one. They remained quiet as they awoke, not wanting to spread panic to those that slumbered nearby, but each of them knew why they had been awakened. Battle was upon them.

"Well, every day can't be the best day, right?" muttered Drahomir as he watched the approaching army.

"But that means that every day can't be the worst day either," said Rehor with a wink. The corner of Drahomir's mouth twitched into a smile, and he nodded in agreement. When they were all awake, they strapped on their weapons and armor and peered through the gaps in the barricade.

They were assigned by the king to help protect the innocents within the chamber. There was only one entrance, but they were all aware that the far wall's high windows were also vulnerable to airborne Sangorans, and they had been barricaded to prevent entry. Outside, soldiers were hurrying along the corridors, readying last-minute defenses.

"You know groups like us in the great stories always have epic sounding names," Pol said. "I think we need one."

"You are right about that, my boy," said Rehor, trying to keep the young man from being afraid. "Even in the great legends that come from the Deadlands, groups of heroes had names that made them legends. Think of what we should be called, Pol. I'm sure you'll think of something fitting."

"What about—what about The Hidden Flame?" asked Pol. "Valistaran called us that anyway. What do you think?"

"I absolutely love it," Josman said with a hearty laugh. "Let's burn them to the ground, just like he said."

The others nodded in agreement, with Shanthah and Aleksander the most enthusiastic about the name, feeling that it described their powers well.

Rehor winked at Pol just before an explosion rocked the eastern wall of the city, bringing them back to reality. They could see the flames and smoke even from here.

Pol bit his lip, and his limbs began to tremble, but Rehor patted his shoulder to assure him that everything would be alright. Smoke trailed from a bright fire on the city's wall; through the light of the flames, they could see Sangorans clad in black armor soaring over the burning bulwark.

A squad of archers let loose a volley of arrows with deadly accuracy, felling a dozen Sangorans, which plummeted to the ground into disfigured shapes upon striking the earth.

"So, what do we do, just stand here and wait for them to get in?" asked Drahomir.

"Would you prefer to be out there?" asked Shanthah, gesturing with his sword. Drahomir shook his head and backed off. At that same moment, the sound of shattering glass filled the corridor, and a swarm of Sangorans poured into the hallway outside the chamber.

"There you go, Drahomir," said Hanna, who went to work with her telekinetic abilities to swirl the shards of glass into a whirlwind of jagged death; the Sangorans shrieked as the glass tore into exposed skin, spraying blood over their companions.

Aleksander launched two fireballs in quick succession toward their foes as Hanna continued her attack, and Valis felled one of the flying soldiers with a bolt of lightning.

Kamil reached forth with his powers and touched the Sangorans' minds, allowing himself the ability to sense their intended actions. He relayed this information to the others, who used it to their advantage.

"They're looking for the king!" thought Kamil to the minds of his allies as he intercepted a stray thought from one of the Sangorans.

As Hanna, Valis, and Aleksander held off the horde of Sangoran warriors, a second swarm burst through another window not far away. Shanthah swore as he turned toward them. "I'm going to have a word with whoever designed this place!"

Drahomir sheathed his blade and drew a bow from his shoulder, nocking an arrow. He let it fly, and the projectile struck a Sangoran in the back of the neck, causing the rest of the group to advance on him.

Josman raised a heavy mace in his friend's defense as a Sangoran swooped down toward them. He crushed the warrior's leg as it clawed at his face while a second lunged at him with a spear as his back was turned. The blade pierced his cloak but shattered against his shoulders.

Josman struck the ground hard and groaned in pain then whirled around, slamming his mace into his attacker's stomach. As two more swooped down toward Alia and Valis, Josman roared in protest and caught one by the wing with both hands before slamming her, flailing, to the ground.

Valis unleashed a weak arc of electricity from his palm, frying the face of the second Sangoran, which crashed into the stonework behind him. Aleksander gave Valis an encouraging bump of his fist before hurling another fireball into the crowd.

Alia hurried to Josman's side and placed her hands where his wound should be. She allowed her healing powers to seep into his back, struggling to keep up with him as he dueled with a Sangoran armed with bladed wings. Alia knew how long it took to heal a stab wound, but there was nothing left to heal.

"You aren't even bleeding!" exclaimed Alia. An arrow whizzed past her and splintered against Josman's back as he slammed another warrior in the chest, confirming Alia's suspicions. "You have magic skin!"

"What?!" Josman shouted as Shanthah finished off an attacker with a stab to the heart. "I don't have powers!"

"Clearly untrue," said Shanthah.

"Well, Valis, I bet your father regrets imprisoning a bunch of powered people in one place!" said Shanthah, smiling at Hanna, who stood nearby him twirling glass around her hands with her mind powers. "Josman, what do you think? Is there any way for us to barricade those high windows?"

Josman shook his head. "Not unless Hanna can float someone up there to fix the barricades!"

There was another crash from within the banquet hall, and they rushed back inside. The few guards still stationed in the room were locked in combat with the Sangorans that had broken through the tall, narrow windows. The civilians screamed, trying to run from their attackers.

Rehor and Alia ushered the terrified people into the corridor.

"Get those tables over the windows!" cried Aleksander as he and Valis hurled flame and lightning into the swarm. Their attacks scorched a few wings and limbs but killed no one.

The soldiers began to push the tables upright, but a Sangoran hamstrung one of them with a sweep of her spear. The other guard stumbled and dropped the long banquet table, which smashed to the ground.

Aleksander and Valis continued their assault with fire and lightning as Hanna once again joined the fray, launching glass and fallen chunks of wooden debris at their foes. All the while, Shanthah, Drahomir, and Josman hurried forward to assist the soldiers who were barricading the lower windows as Kamil, Pol, Rehor, and Alia helped the noncombatants get to safety.

A bolt of lightning ripped through the smashed window, burning a hole through a soldier's chest. Valis retaliated with his own beam of electricity, which was followed by a shriek.

"Nice shot!" Aleksander called.

The remaining soldiers helped Josman and Shanthah lift the massive oak tables over the windows and piled chairs over the bulwark to reinforce them as well as they could. While they worked, Aleksander and Valis defended them from the small horde; at last, they managed to fight the creatures back.

Hanna strained herself to lift another large table into the air with her mind and place it in front of the high windows, but without proper fastening, it would likely not stay up long.

In all, ten civilians and as many soldiers lay dead on the floor. Alia saw to the wounded, but only one of them had survived. The Sangorans outside hammered against the makeshift barricade while the survivors within the room pressed against the unstable bulwark to keep it from falling.

"Get these barricades secured!" shouted Josman.

Aleksander, Drahomir, Shanthah, and the soldiers worked on repairing their barricades, but then for a long moment, the entire world went completely silent.

No words.

No fighting.

No breathing.

Utter silence, until a deep, authoritative voice filled the minds of everyone in the room.

"*I am awake.*"

Everyone in the chamber glanced around, unsure for a moment if they had heard or imagined the words, and if the others had as well. Shanthah was the first to speak, uttering the thoughts of all.

"You all heard that, right?" he asked.

The civilians and soldiers alike nodded and shared furtive glances with one another. The soldiers continued their work securing the barricade as Aleksander and the others regrouped.

"What was that?" asked Pol.

"It must have been Thanatan?" asked Hanna. "What Ronin said. Oh my goodness—"

"All my life I thought that would be a good thing, but now I'm not so sure," said Rehor.

The Sangoran soldiers seemed to have moved on from trying to force their way into the windows of the dining hall.

"Why did they stop?" asked Aleksander, realizing for the first time that the pounding on the barricade had ceased. "Definitely not because of our quality workmanship."

He gestured to the pile of wood and debris.

"They must have found another way in with less *us* in the way," said Hanna as Aleksander made his way to the nearest window and shifted a chunk of wood to peer outside.

What he saw filled him with despair. Plumes of smoke trailing from pillars of flame all over Laniras. The cloud of airborne Sangoran warriors still loomed over the city, and the main gates had been breached by massive battering rams, meaning the Talohiran foot soldiers had entered the city as well.

Aleksander watched a brave ballista operator spray a group of Sangorans with bolts from his mighty weapon but was soon overtaken by bolts of lightning cast from an unseen foe as he ran out of ammunition.

"Hanna's right. They did manage to get in somewhere else," said Alia, pointing at windows all over the palace that had been smashed in.

"We're getting destroyed out there!" cried Pol, continuing to survey the scene. "What do we do?"

Aleksander's stomach dropped as he saw Valakor and Hokkod locked in combat with their winged foes upon the palace's rooftop. Aleksander wondered where Bovin the Minotaur and Manitrius were and hoped they hadn't already fallen. The last remaining members of the Court of Thanatan were outnumbered, yet still fighting their way to the tallest tower.

"Hokkod and Valakor are pinned down out there," explained Aleksander. "I don't know what they're doing, but some of us need to stay here."

"You're our boss, technically, right?" Pol asked.

"Drahomir, Kamil, Pol, Rehor, and Josman will stay here. Kamil, find the injured with your powers, and bring them to Alia," commanded Shanthah. "Meanwhile, Valis, Aleksander, Hanna, and I will use our abilities to help fight."

No one questioned his direction and did as they were told. Kamil sensed the minds of the wounded outside the room, and together with Pol and Rehor, led them into the banquet hall so Alia's healing hands.

Meanwhile, Shanthah, Hanna, Aleksander, and Valis creeped down the hallway. They found it abandoned, other than the corpses that lined the passageway. They made their way around the corner and Shanthah led them through a smashed window onto a ledge outside the palace.

"Hanna, can you get us up there?" asked Aleksander.

"You're all pretty heavy but I can try," said Hanna. "And no, Shanthah that is *not* a fat joke."

Shanthah raised his hands with a smile on his face.

"Valis is the lightest. Get him up there, and he can help us up," suggested Aleksander.

"And we'll boost you up so Hanna has less distance to throw you," said Shanthah, cupping his hands together. Aleksander did the same, and Valis stepped into their hands, and then they hoisted him up as high as they could.

"Comforting. Never been thrown before like—"

He cried out as Hanna tossed him into the air, and as she did so, he caught hold on to the lip of the roof and pulled himself up, throwing his legs over the side to safety. He reached down, ready to pull the next person up.

Aleksander and Shanthah boosted Hanna as high as they could, and Valis grabbed her hand. He pulled her up and then together, they helped both Shanthah and Aleksander up as well.

"Good job, Hann," said Aleksander.

Hanna nodded in appreciation, her breath heavy and energy waning, but she had a smile upon her face. Shanthah grabbed her hand, and they darted across the roof toward Valakor and Hokkod's position.

Not far away now, they watched Valakor blast an entire group of Sangorans to their deaths with a shock wave of pure energy from the blade of his scythe. At that moment, Hokkod emerged from behind his ally and thrust his spear into the neck of a Night Witch before severing the wing of another, sending it plummeting to the ground far below.

The two generals were now surrounded on both sides as more of the swarm flocked toward them. As they hurried to join the fray, Aleksander and Valis launched flurries of flame and electricity into the crowd while Shanthah vanished, hacking unseen at his foes. Hanna stayed back to cast sharp pieces of debris, roof tiles, and rocks at their enemies.

It was just the distraction the two warriors needed; Valakor beheaded several Sangorans as if he were reaping wheat as Hokkod made a break for the tower. A bolt of lightning struck Valakor in the chest, knocking him backward, and half a dozen Sangorans were upon him at the same time, making him drop his scythe over the precipice. He roared and two short dagger blades appeared from beneath his armored vambraces.

Valakor spun around, disemboweling two of his attackers while Hanna peppered them with bits of debris that stuck into their flesh, knocking them from the roof. Valis struck one of Valakor's assailants with a bolt of lightning from his palm while the Sangoran horde overwhelmed him.

"Go, help General Hokkod!" cried the Spirit Warrior as Aleksander, Hanna, Shanthah, and Valis raced toward him, climbing up to the next level of the palace's roof to join the fight. He nodded in appreciation, but as the smoke shifted, through the flames that now engulfed the palace, they all saw a lone Sangoran striding out of the smoke toward Hokkod.

Mara.

Hanna grabbed Aleksander's arm, a look of sadness and fear on her face. He nodded, let out a deep breath, and they turned to face her together.

Mara's furious barrage of lightning illuminated the night, and Hokkod raised his magical shield to deflect the blasts, roaring in defiance as he protected Aleksander and Hanna from the onslaught of death-bringing light.

Hanna concentrated all of her attacks on Mara, ripping chunks of ceramic tile from the roof to cast at her former friend. The lightning ceased as Mara used her own limited telekinetic abilities to shield herself from the attack while an aggressive Sangoran warrior pinned Aleksander against the wall.

Hokkod took this moment of reprieve to emerge from behind his shield and lunge at the empress. Mara extended both wings as Hokkod's spear neared her chest, and she let herself fall from the roof of the castle before shooting back up into the sky. She arced around and plummeted toward Hokkod, who thrust his spear upward just as Mara unleashed a web of lightning. They both cried out in rage as Mara had to throw herself aside to avoid being impaled, and white-hot energy peppered Hokkod's body.

An armored Sangoran struck Hanna from behind with the shaft of her spear, breaking her concentration, and she hit the ground. Aleksander wrestled his attacker's knife away from his neck and burned the soldier's forearm; he twisted the blade from his attacker's grip, and Valis blasted the woman with a bolt of lightning.

"Hanna!" Aleksander shouted, tossing her the knife. She caught it with her mind just as her attacker attempted to spear her through the abdomen. She forced the blade downward from the soldier's neck to her hip in a line of dark blood. All the while, Shanthah was clearing the way up ahead. He too was beginning to tire, as his faint outline was now visible, his invisibility waning.

Nearby, Hokkod turned just in time to see Valakor being dragged over the edge by dozens of Sangorans. He could see Valis, Aleksander, and Hanna fighting their way toward him, and he swore under his breath, knowing that if he died, they were the city's last chance for salvation.

Hokkod whipped around to see Mara standing still before him, the wind playing with her hair; she held her hands together near her waist with a look of exhausted defiance on her face.

The General of the Court of Thanatan leapt toward her, and she cried out as she brought her blade-tipped wings forward, impaling the general through the abdomen on either side. At the same time, she screamed in agony as his blade pierced her side just above the hip.

Mara stumbled backward and collapsed just as Hokkod did. She jerked the blade from her side and dropped it to the level below. Hokkod reached for his golden shield, but the Empress of Blood blasted it with a bolt of lightning, sending it clattering to the level below next to his spear.

"Aleksander! Bring my shield to the bell tower!" he shouted, hoping his allies below could still hear him. Hope drained out of his body as his blood did, and he slumped over as he tried to get to his hands and knees. Mara stood above him amidst the smoke and flames, her bladed wings outstretched and covered in crimson.

"Aleksander won't help you," Mara said. "Just like he won't help *me*."

With a mighty cry, she brought her wingblades down, piercing both sides of his chest. With his last breath, he grabbed her head and pulled her toward him with such force that she had no time to react. The top of his gleaming, golden helm struck her face with a crunch and a spray of blood. Crimson dripped down her visage, and she stumbled backward, disoriented.

Hokkod died with a grin spread across his face, and then he was gone. Hanna, Shanthah, and Valis focused their energy on Mara's forces as Aleksander raced for Hokkod's fallen shield, but their enemies began to overwhelm them as they rallied to their empress.

"Mara, please! We can convince them to give you amnesty," cried Aleksander. "We can save you! Please, come back! We can do this—whatever it takes, we can do it!"

"I'm not looking for your forgiveness, and I do *not* need to be saved!"

Holding her side, Mara dove from the rooftop before Aleksander could grab the shield just as he ignited two balls of flame in his hands. With no words shared between them, Aleksander unleashed a torrent of brilliant fire, and Mara raised Hokkod's shield.

The flames washed over its golden face, and Mara screamed as the heat became unbearable. Tears filled her eyes, and she cried out as she unleashed a flash of white lightning from her wings, disorienting Aleksander enough to give her time to recover.

Aleksander composed himself just as Mara slammed the edge of Hokkod's shield into his chest, throwing him hard against the roof, his head striking the tiles. He groaned and turned onto his side to grasp Hokkod's fallen spear, swinging it up just as Mara brought her boot down. She kicked the shaft of the weapon hard before swinging the shield down toward Aleksander's chest.

She cried out in confused surprise as the shield stopped just inches from his sternum; she looked up to see Shanthah supporting Hanna as she focused all her mental energy on the shield. Mara let out a bloodcurdling scream, sobbing, as Hanna telepathically wrenched the shield from her arm with a sickening crack.

Aleksander leaped to his feet, spreading a wall of flame between himself and Mara. The Empress of Blood looked up, holding her broken arm, tears streaming down the grime and blood on her cheeks. The distraction gave Aleksander and the others time to flee, and Shanthah scooped up Hokkod's shield.

The soft rain dampening the world became a torrent and extinguished Aleksander's flames. Mara stumbled after them, trying in vain to figure out how to hold her arm and the deep wound in her side at the same time. With tears in her eyes, she took a step, and with her good arm, sent a bolt of lightning toward her former friends.

The force of the blast sent Aleksander through a stained-glass window with a shower of glass, and he was lost to view.

"Aleks!" Shanthah shouted but got no response.

"There's no time!" cried Hanna. "They're gaining on us—they'll catch you, even if you're invisible. I'll hold them off, okay?"

"No, come with me!" Shanthah said, rematerializing as he glanced upward with a groan. They had fought off what seemed like an entire horde of Sangorans only to see a coordinated vortex of winged bodies descending upon them from above.

As the swarm descended, Shanthah pulled Hanna close as if in an intimate dance and looked into her eyes for what he hoped would not be the last time. He smiled, his eyes shining with love and hope. She returned the expression, despite their approaching fate.

"Really, now?" Hanna asked with a grin.

"Probably should have said this before we were about to die, but—I love you, Hanna."

"It's fitting," replied Hanna. "And of course, I love you too."

She winked, and then Shanthah's lips locked around hers as certain doom barreled down toward them. She took his hand as he pulled away.

"Don't you dare die," she ordered through tears. He smiled, saluted, and vanished along with Hokkod's shield. "Now *GO!*"

He looked over his shoulder as he raced toward the bell tower to see Hanna fighting for her life—for both of their lives. No, for the lives of everyone in Laniras, even though they had no idea why Hokkod wanted them to bring his shield to the bell tower.

With the courage and ferocity of a dragon, she telekinetically tore jagged shards of tile from the roof and sent them hurling through the sky, drawing the Sangorans' attention away from Shanthah and the shield. Valis joined her, sending up bolts of lightning to keep them from Shanthah.

As the horde of Sangorans descended on them, Shanthah leaped to the next level of the roof and sprinted toward the high bell tower, completely unsure of what to do when he reached it. Utter exhaustion began to set in, and he screamed as an explosion rocked his world, and he was thrown forward several yards. He crashed to the ground but stumbled to his feet and kept going. He took a deep breath. They weren't defeated—not yet.

Another blast tore through the ceiling nearby, and a great ball of flame bathed his face in horrendously scorching heat. He glanced over his shoulder and cursed as he saw Mara limping slowly toward him. He could no longer see Hanna, and he began to weep.

"No, no, no," he whispered as he tried to vanish, but the strain caused him to collapse. Parts of his body became translucent, but in the end, his powers failed him. He crawled away from Mara, knowing they were both spent.

"Shanthah! Give it—give it to me," Mara called.

Shanthah ignored her pleas, pulling himself up with a drainpipe leading up the bell tower. He groaned as Mara's telekinesis pressed him against the wall, and he dropped Hokkod's shield.

"No," he said, trembling. "Mara, no…"

He kicked the shield with all his might, sending it from the rooftop. Mara approached Shanthah and raised her bloodied wingblades.

"Mara…"

Mara did not respond, glaring down at the man with both defeat and trepidation. Shanthah pointed with one finger, and Mara followed his gaze to see someone enter the bell tower carrying Hokkod's shield which gleamed in the light of the flames before disappearing into the building.

The Empress of Blood turned to Shanthah; her nostrils flared, and she shut her eyes tightly. She shook her head, and half-walked and half-flew after the stranger with the shield, leaving Shanthah alone on the roof.

She took the stairs as quickly as her exhausted form would allow until she came to the top where she found a vaulted ceiling that held an ornate bell. She glanced around the room to find the lone man left standing against her forces.

Pol.

He hurried toward the bell as a swarm of Sangorans pushed their way through the open archways. They clawed at his flesh, but still he pressed on; he swung the shield around with enough force to kill one of the assailants, leaving a deep gash in her forehead.

Dozens of Sangorans filled the room, lashing out at Pol with knife-tipped wings and vicious claws, but he cried out and placed the shield into the mouth of the bell, and a bright white light exploded forth, engulfing the chamber. The blast vaporized Pol's enemies nearest him and decimated the rest of the chamber.

Mara ducked behind what remained of a wall and covered her eyes as a brilliant stream of pure energy poured forth from the bell and Hokkod's magic shield; the flow of blinding white light curved outward in a spiral that cut through the horde of Sangorans. Pol stood as the final defender against the swarm and kept the shield pressed tightly against the bottom of the bell, and although it burned his hands, he never faltered.

The burst of energy flowed from the tower, disintegrating any Sangorans it touched; it created a dome that expanded around the fortress at the center of Laniras, and then Pol collapsed, and the shield clattered to the ground next to him.

He glanced up to see his sister standing over him; her crystal blue eyes peered out from behind the dark hair blowing over her face. He shut his eyes, expecting her to strike him down, but instead felt her arms around him.

"I have to go," she said, holding him for as long as she could. "I love you, Pol. I love you so much. I am so sorry."

He opened his eyes to find that they were both sobbing great tears leaving trails down the blood and ash on their cheeks.

"Go," he whispered. "Go—Mara, I love you so much too. Please, go before it's too late!"

The last thing he saw before he lost consciousness was his sister taking flight and racing through the energy dome just as it closed off. Any Sangoran that did not flee from the white-hot sphere of light was obliterated, but a majority of Mara's forces had retreated just in time, leaving many of their fellow warriors behind to the mercy of King Verahim's will.

Far below, Shanthah raised a hand as Aleksander limped over and slumped next to him, his body covered in scrapes.

"Ah, good," Shanthah said. "You're alive too."

"Hanna's safe," Aleksander said, letting out a deep breath.

Shanthah nodded, his energy completely spent. "That's all I wanted. Thank you."

Aleksander returned the gesture, pressing his forehead against one knee as he pulled it close to his chest but looked up as a horn sounded over the city.

He and Shanthah limped to the other side of the tower to see a vast army clad in scarlet and gold armor washing over the Talohiran ground forces.

"Kurash," Aleksander said. "They came…"

"They didn't side with Talohira after all?" Shanthah asked as Hanna and Valis found them.

"Fortunate for us, huh?" Aleksander said, closing his eyes as he rested his head against the wall behind him.

Hanna slumped next to Shanthah and took his hand. They smiled at one another, and she stroked his hair.

"We made it," she said.

Valis looked out over the battle outside the dome. The fresh forces of Kurash laid waste to all that would not surrender, and soon, the battle was over, leaving the city burning.

"I don't understand," Valis said. "The Supreme One who is called Kadir never backs out of an agreement. Breaking one's promise is punishable by death in such a position…"

He trailed off.

"So, what do you think happened?" Aleksander asked. "Why would they turn on Talohira like that?"

"There's only one reason they ever would. They were ordered to by the one they signed the treaty with," Valis replied.

Hanna gasped. "That means—"

Valis nodded.

"My father is alive."

CHAPTER FORTY-ONE

THE FORGOTTEN ONE

The deposed king and his two hooded allies strode with purpose through the white stone tunnels of the labyrinthine facility under the mountain, never once taking a wrong turn. In time, the trio came to a solid metal door guarded by two soldiers with long spears.

"Thank you, but your services are no longer required," Valistaran said. The soldiers obeyed with a bow, disappearing around the corner.

"These men have been in the depths of this prison for a very long time. Surely, they have not heard news of Valistaran Talohir's death," said one of the men in a tone akin to a whisper. "Is this why they yet obey you?"

"Lord Jakoni, these men still follow me for the same reason that you and I have forged a new alliance. They share my vision, and they know what is at stake should we fail," Valistaran explained, gripping the wheel set in the heavy gate.

He groaned at the strain it took to turn the wheel, and for a moment, he wished he would have waited to dismiss the guards. His companions offered to help, but at that moment, the wheel budged, and metal screeched as the door revealed a dark chamber within. The mechanism groaned, as if it had not been used in many years.

"I think I'll wait outside," said the second companion.

"Do what you must, Elafris," said Valistaran. He didn't care what the others did. He knew Daniel would try to slip away given the chance, so he made sure Ronin was nearby to stop him.

Valistaran entered the chamber.

As if of their own accord, torches flickered to life on each wall. The opulence of the prison cell, if one could still call it that, was astounding; a garden of solid gold flowers adorned the posts of a bed with more pillows and blankets of fabrics finer than any in all of Talohira, and behind the bed was a bookshelf filled with thick tomes that each looked as if they had been read a thousand times.

"Valeniya?"

"Father!" cried the voice of a young woman, who wrapped her arms around Valistaran's shoulders. He held his daughter close, his hand brushing the bump where one of her wings had once been.

"Hello, Valeniya," said Valistaran. "Are you comfortable?"

Valeniya shrugged before saying, "I'm bored. They haven't let me out in—"

She stopped talking with an abruptness with which Valistaran had long since been acquainted.

"You know why that is," said Valistaran in the authoritative, yet loving voice of a stern father.

"Why can't I see mother?" asked Valeniya.

"She couldn't come today."

"That isn't what I mean," replied the young woman. Valistaran sighed and nodded. "Why can't I *see* her?"

"Your mother is dead."

"Oh, I thought so," was Valeniya's terse reply.

"I would like you to meet someone," said Valistaran in a tender voice as Ronin stepped into the chamber. "This is Lord Ronin Jakoni."

Ronin inched around the girl to peer into her face and stretched forth his clawed hand in introduction. Valeniya's sleek, black hair fell in simple curtains around her plain, yet striking visage.

"And what is he a lord of?" asked the girl.

"A lord of Sangora," said Valistaran.

"There are no lords of Sangora," Valeniya said. "Not anymore."

"He's from very far away, but that isn't important now. Valeniya, my daughter—we need you to find someone for us."

"Who?" asked Valeniya, the bright blue of her eyes clouding over with a white sheen which glowed in the dim torchlight of the marble room.

"Where is Thanatan?" Ronin asked.

Valeniya cocked her head in confusion at his question, and her eyes began to return to their former blue.

"You want me to find a *god?*" asked Valeniya. "I can't."

"Daniel," Valistaran ordered, and Daniel Elafris stepped forward. "Tell her what to look for."

Daniel nodded, describing Thanatan's physical features, his voice, and anything else she might need to know to find him, for in his long-gone life hundreds of years ago, he had known the one Thanatanos worshipped as a god.

Without warning, the white energy engulfed Valeniya Talohir's eyes.

Valistaran held his daughter against his shoulder to soothe her, but an inferno of black flame erupted from the air around her form like an aura of darkness, throwing both Valistaran and Ronin against the wall of her chamber. The fine linens and silks of her bed were reduced to ash.

"Valeniya!" shouted Valistaran, hurrying back to her side.

Such a thing had never happened before.

Daniel Elafris looked to the girl with an expression of concern on his weary face. With a wave of his hand, Valistaran willed the flames to cease, and his daughter wrapped her arms around his chest.

"What is it? Did you see him?"

"No, father—he saw *me!*"

CHAPTER FORTY-TWO
ONE MOMENT MORE

The comforting arms of Doftaan's grand library welcomed Mara home. While lying in the hospital for three days, all she wanted was to be surrounded by her books—the only friends she felt she deserved. She was happy to see that the books from Talohira's library had been transported here, and that they had already been sorted and placed in their rightful places.

Nearly tripping over her dress, she limped over to a luxurious looking corner lined with plush seating that enveloped her as she slumped into it, and yet, sleep did not accept her. A tear escaped the corner of her eye, and it trailed over the bridge of her nose as she lay on her side trying to get comfortable.

Or perhaps, the problem was that it was *too* comfortable.

With great effort, she dropped her legs off the sofa and limped toward a table of carved mahogany inlayed with gold and silver. She rested her backside on the edge of the table and groaned as she swung her legs up so that she could sit on its surface. She let out a deep breath as she managed to lower herself to lie flat on her back on top of the table. She raised her knees and covered her eyes with her hands as the sobs began.

She wished that someone—anyone, really—would find her there, but no one ever came. Who would? Her forces had rescued Lavinia and Vasilica and brought them back to Doftaan, but the only people alive that she had considered friends in the past nine years since her enslavement were miles away in Laniras.

But it wasn't the distance that caused her to weep. It was the terrible blade that life seemed to be driving deeper and deeper into her heart with every passing day—not only the fact that life had somehow made her hate the very people that once loved her closer than family, but the excruciating truth that they despised her even more. *That* was her true failure.

No, she didn't hate them—she never had, and she never could. Anger had made her do horrible things that led her down ever more terrible paths until—

Until what? It wasn't anyone's fault but her own, and she knew it. She knew that she had to stop blaming Drahomir. To forgive Shanthah and Hanna for leaving her behind against the Faceless. To let go of the hurt of Aleksander's betrayal—it had been an accident, after all. Why had she never realized that?

She wept, knowing that by following Valistaran's path for her, she had thrown away a beautiful future that could have been. Instead, she became a weapon for a tyrant—a blade held by a king to execute those that opposed him.

She dragged her hands down her face to wipe away the tears and let out a deep sigh before slipping off the uncomfortable shoes the well-intentioned healers had placed on her feet before she had left their care.

Mara kicked them off the table as she sat up and hurled her silver crown across the library; it struck a far-off shelf and bounced out of sight in the dark library, wobbling for a moment on the ground before coming to a stop.

She removed the pins keeping her hair in the elegant shape the royal hairdressers had insisted she wear to be 'presentable' to the people when she addressed them later that day. She dumped them on the ground and ruffled her hair to destroy their work, leaving it wild and messy.

Why had they insisted she leave the hospital looking like royalty rather than feeling like a person? She began to hyperventilate, and she frantically tore off and discarded the elegant prison of a dress. She used one of her razor-claws she had somehow managed to sneak past the healers to slice the tight laces of the corset stifling her breathing. Freedom.

She threw it into the air and blasted it with a bolt of lightning. Before the blackened scraps of the garment hit the ground, she had already destroyed the seemingly endless layers of frivolous clothes into which *they* had forced her and swept the remains off the table with one of her wings.

Finally free of the horrible dress, tears flowed down her face as she sat in her underwear, red-eyed and wild-haired amongst the chaos of shredded fabric. She folded one wing around herself like a blanket, the other bound tightly in a sling. She collapsed onto her side and pressed her forehead to her knees as she drew them to her chest, sobbing.

She had to bring everyone back together again; nothing was going to change if she didn't do something. Perhaps life wasn't driving a knife into her heart but spurring her on and giving her the opportunity to help the ones she loved—no, not only that, but also to help the Sangoran, Thannish, and Talohiran people she didn't even know so that they would never have to experience any of the horrors that she had. Maybe…

But even if she did, she was still alone.

She had gained everything most people could ever desire, but all she wanted was to be free; she would give it all up for one moment more filled with joyous laughter with Hanna, Aleksander, and the others.

Just one.

As she cursed herself and everything in her life, three little words flitted into her mind.

Spring always comes.

And there it was—one more moment with Rehor.

A spark of hope.

And then, in her mind's eye, she was hugging Hanna. Laughing at a stupid joke Shanthah had made. Marveling at Kamil's ingenuity and Josman's quiet kindness. Listening to Pol recount the forgotten legends from the Deadlands. And then her mind drifted to one of the last times she had *truly* felt joy: the time she had spent with Aleksander—*before* he was Aleksander.

She smiled.

And then she fell asleep on the table in the library surrounded with joyous memories and the hope of new spring.

CHAPTER FORTY-THREE
EMBERS

The entire city smoldered like the cinders of an extinguished campfire. The flames hissed as heaven's tears beat them back; the soothing sound of rain washed away the pain of the battle and clattered against King Verahim's armor as he stood beside a ruined statue of his father. He surveyed the desolation, and relief washed over his soul knowing the horrendous battle was over. His beloved people were safe, and that was all that mattered.

Verahim allowed a vast majority of Mara's forces to flee from the battle and follow their empress back to Sangora. The armies of Kurash had made quick work of Valistaran's men who refused to surrender, and thousands of corpses littered the battlefield beyond the city walls. Now his own army and generals, including Valakor, Manitrius, and Bovin, were hard at work helping the injured. The dead would have to wait their turn.

Verahim considered the great debt he now owed to the Kurashians, for without them, the city would have fallen even with Hokkod's energy shield.

He caught a glimpse of Aleksander, Shanthah, Josman, Pol, and the rest of their allies whom he did not know emerge from the castle's ruined front gates. They were each supporting one another as they limped from the palace. Together. A family.

Many survivors gathered in the empty space of the courtyard, and King Verahim looked over their anxious faces. They were battle worn and weary, and the overwhelming mood across his capital city was one of despair. He called out, but his words were lost on the wind; none heeded his words.

A king in title only.

He slumped against the ruined statue of his father and shut his eyes as if trying to absorb the dead king's wisdom.

"Help me, papa," he whispered. He took a deep breath and climbed onto the crumbling statue's back before raising his sword high into the air.

"My brothers, my sisters, hear me! Today a great evil has been inflicted on our people, one that has reduced us to the embers of a once great civilization. We are a people that has been knocked down far too many times, but one also that must now stand." Many of the survivors gathered while looking for friends and family lost in the conflict.

"I am a reluctant king forced into this position because my father and my brother were murdered. I am the sole ember of a family whose flame has been smothered, just like you among your fallen fathers, mothers, children, and friends—together, let us rebuild our home. Let us reignite the flame that is our people. Let us stand forever against this Empress of Blood who would have our light extinguished! But not in war—no, this cannot be the way. We have seen far too much bloodshed these past months. Not only in Thanatanos, but in Sangora and Talohira too. We must use our words to bring peace and love; please, my friends, do not hate those who live in Sangora or Talohira. We must all stand together if we wish to see the end of this war. Let us ignite the embers that remain of our people—let them burn! But until then, let that be enough words from a king who has yet to serve you." He paused for a moment and smiled then called, "Let us rebuild!"

He gestured toward a platoon of soldiers carrying relief supplies, and the crowd cheered; Verahim knew their enthusiasm was for food and not his own words, but he smiled, nonetheless, for his people would not starve. Not today. He hopped down from the statue before helping coordinate the distribution of supplies himself.

"Well, we made it," said Shanthah as the king departed. He grabbed a sack of grain to distribute to the masses.

"Are you sad about that?" asked Hanna with a laugh as she squeezed his hand; Pol caught sight of them holding hands and pointed with a wide smile on his face.

"Oh, yes! I've been waiting for this! We've all been waiting for this!" he exclaimed.

"*I knew it was coming for a while, but of course, I can read minds,*" said Kamil. The others laughed with one another; gone was the despair of the battle, replaced with the love of a new family, not one of blood, but bonded through the trials of life.

"It's about time," said Josman.

Drahomir faked a sound as if he were vomiting, but Alia smacked him on the back of the head, and he too expressed his congratulations.

The entire group sat next to one another as if in one big hug.

Aleksander smiled as they held one another, listening to them speak of happy things until sudden forgotten memories flittered into his mind.

These images were not ones implanted by the Secret Keepers of Kurash. No, these were his own memories.

Memories of his family filled his mind. He saw his father, his mother—not the family that had taken him in, however much they had loved him. No, he saw the faces of his true father, mother, and brother—he saw a storm, a village burning—and he saw Mara, her forehead pressed to his, before vile men tore them apart and took them to a massive ship—then, the most vivid memory of all: he remembered two words that haunted him more than any other.

He remembered his own name.

THE STORY CONTINUES IN:

ASHES

BOOK TWO OF THE
ASCENSION SAGA

Dear reader,

From the bottom of my heart, thank you for taking a chance on this world and these characters that I have come to love like very real friends and family. I hope you enjoyed the first entry into my world and that you will continue the adventure with Ashes, Spring Always Comes, and the upcoming prequel, Her Anthem for Ruin.

Anyone who knows me knows that I hate endings. I cry like a baby whenever a favorite TV show, book, or movie series ends, and so I never intend to stop writing or building this world that I love so much. I will never write the words 'the end' in any of my books.

I would also like to thank all of my writing Instagram friends who have supported me through this adventure.

My biggest thank you obviously goes to my biggest fan (and I'm her biggest fan, too) – my lovely wifey, Shay.

If you happen to work for a streaming service or in movie production, contact me **right this moment** because, well, duh.

Brock Mays

September 30, 2023

www.ingramcontent.com/pod-product-compliance
Lightning Source LLC
Chambersburg PA
CBHW050159110726
47898CB00008B/2870